Lady's Choice

OTHER BOOKS BY AMANDA SCOTT

PRINCE OF DANGER
LORD OF THE ISLES
HIGHLAND PRINCESS
THE SECRET CLAN: REIVER'S BRIDE
THE SECRET CLAN: HIGHLAND BRIDE
THE SECRET CLAN: HIDDEN HEIRESS
THE SECRET CLAN: ABDUCTED HEIRESS
BORDER FIRE
BORDER STORM
BORDER BRIDE
HIGHLAND FLING
HIGHLAND SECRETS
HIGHLAND TREASURE
HIGHLAND SPIRITS
THE BAWDY BRIDE
DANGEROUS ILLUSIONS
DANGEROUS ANGELS
DANGEROUS GAMES
DANGEROUS LADY
THE ROSE AT TWILIGHT

AMANDA SCOTT

Lady's Choice

WARNER
FOREVER

NEW YORK   BOSTON

Copyright © 2006 by Lynne Scott-Drennan
Excerpt from *Knight's Treasure* copyright © 2006 by Lynne Scott-Drennan.
All rights reserved. No part of this book may be reproduced in any form or by any electronic or mechanical means, including information storage and retrieval systems, without permission in writing from the publisher, except by a reviewer who may quote brief passages in a review.

Warner Forever and the Warner Forever logo are trademarks of Time Warner Inc. or an affiliated company. Used under license by Hachette Book Group, which is not affiliated with Time Warner Inc.

Cover design by Claire Brown
Cover art by Alan Ayers
Book design by Giorgetta Bell McRee

Warner Books
Hachette Book Group USA
1271 Avenue of the Americas
New York, NY 10020
Visit our Web site at www.HachetteBookGroupUSA.com

Printed in the United States of America

First Printing: August 2006

10 9 8 7 6 5 4 3 2 1

For Kevin,
Still and always, best of sisters!

Author's Note

Because "ch" is generally pronounced as an "h" in Gaelic, the Highland name Sorcha sounds like Sarah, rather than being phonetically pronounced. Sidony is Sidney. Kilchurn Castle is Kill-HERN. Dail Righ is Dal-REE.

SCOTTISH ISLES

1. Glenelg Village
2. Kildonan (Eigg)
3. Glenancross
4. Shielfoot
5. Lochbuie
6. Kinlocheil
7. Strontian
8. Oban
9. Dail Righ
10. Lochearnhead
11. Stirling
12. Glasgow
13. Linlithgow
14. Ratho
15. Edinburgh
16. Roslin Castle
17. Edgelaw

Prologue

~~

Roslin Castle, Scotland, August 1379

He couldn't believe that a mere female a foot shorter than he was had pushed him off the castle's wall-walk. He must have fallen a hundred feet and had hit the water with such stunning force that a lesser man would have died from the impact. But although he had gone headfirst over the parapet, he pushed himself away from the wall and twisted like a cat, managing to land feetfirst at an angle that put him face up in the water. He let the river Esk's swift current do the rest.

Even so, he soon hit one of the river's mighty boulders, which stunned him and spun him like a child's top. By using his great strength to avoid the next one, he managed to keep it from knocking him senseless. Then he was in the swiftest part of the flow, face up and feetfirst again, catapulting along at terrifying speed.

To be on his back, unable to see where he was going, gulping what seemed to be as much water as air, and otherwise letting the river control him went right against his nature. But knowing that the water would be deepest where it ran swiftest, he forced himself to let it carry him as it would until he could regain his wits.

The lass had taken him completely by surprise. But she would pay heavily for that, she and everyone she held dear. Whatever it took, he would survive to reclaim His treasure and seek his own vengeance.

Chapter 1

~

**Glenelg, the Scottish Highlands,
April 14, 1380**

Where *is* Sir Hugo?" nineteen-year-old Lady Sorcha Macleod demanded impatiently. She cradled a profusion of flowers in her arms as she gazed down the steep hill at the sparkling water of the Sound of Sleat, the deep sea-lane flowing between Glenelg, on the mainland, and the Isle of Skye.

Her younger sister, Lady Sidony, bending to pick some yellow celandine for their collection, said over her shoulder, "You cannot know that Sir Hugo even received your message. The messengers have not all returned. And, even if he did, you cannot know he will come for her or come in a boat if he does. He could easily ride from Lothian or come from somewhere else. He may even be in Caithness."

"Faith, Sidony, I don't care how the man arrives, just so he does," Sorcha said impatiently. "If he does not show his face soon, he will be too late."

...ad the Lord of the Isles had to die when he ...ny said as she arose and added her flowers to S... ...s. "Adela ought to be having as merry a wedding as everyone else has, but I fear that hers will be dreadfully dull. I still do not understand why Father agreed to hold the ceremony here instead of at Chalamine. The feast will take place at the castle, after all, and everyone else was married there."

"Not everyone," Sorcha reminded her. "Isobel married at Duart Castle."

"Yes, but Cristina, Maura, and Kate were all married at home. I hope you and I will be, too—*if* Father ever finds anyone who wants to marry us," she added.

"I don't want someone Father chooses," Sorcha said, grimacing. "At least Adela has a sunny day, and the wee kirk of Glenelg is a pretty site. Lord Pompous insisted that she marry him here on the kirk porch, since Father has no chaplain at Chalamine. And that settled the matter, of course, since Lord Pompous will be her husband unless Sir Hugo arrives in time to put a stop to this wedding."

"I do not know why you are so sure he'd want to," Sidony said, pushing a stray strand of her fair hair out of her face. As children, the two of them had looked enough alike to be twins with their fine, silky soft, white-blond curls and light-blue eyes. But although Sidony's waist-long hair retained its original color, silky fineness, and soft waves, Sorcha's had darkened to amber-gold and re-tained only its curls. To her chagrin, in the frequent High-land mist and rain, they tended to frizz.

Their eyes were still a matching light-blue color. But Sorcha's looked gray in certain light, and a black line rimmed each of her irises.

Semiconsciously mirroring her sister's gesture, she shifted her floral burden to one arm to tuck an errant curl under her coif.

Sidony went on, "You've made such a song about sending for him that nearly everyone expects him now. But Adela seems content enough with this wedding."

"Faugh," Sorcha retorted rudely, abandoning her hair. "Adela would marry anyone who'd have her. She wants to be quit of managing Father's household and us, especially now that he is to marry Lord Pompous's cousin, Lady Clendenen. But Sir Hugo holds Adela's heart, I'm sure. And I think he cares deeply for her, too."

"But they've met only twice," Sidony protested. "Once here in Glen Mòr last summer, and then shortly after that at Orkney."

"Aye, well, it only takes once," Sorcha said with more assurance than one might expect from a young woman who had never met a man she wanted to marry, or received an offer. "Adela talked of him for weeks after Prince Henry's installation."

"Do you think so?" Sidony asked doubtfully. "She said they quarreled the first time they met. The second time she emptied a basin of holy water over his head."

Still watching the Sound, Sorcha exclaimed, "Three boats are coming! Oh, but how vexing! If I don't mistake that banner, 'tis only Lord Pompous."

"You should not call him that," Sidony chided gently.

"Pooh," Sorcha said. "Ardelve is as pompous a man as walks and far too old for Adela. Why, he must be near Father's age, whilst she is but four-and-twenty."

"Nearly *five*-and-twenty," Sidony said.

"Even so, Sir Hugo is of a much more suitable age to

marry her. She is sacrificing herself, just to get away from Chalamine."

"Perhaps, but Father said he had despaired of *ever* seeing her marry," Sidony said. With a rueful smile, she added, "You and I are old for wedding, come to that. Not that I am sure I'd want to, even if anyone did want me."

"You are never sure of anything," Sorcha said, patting her shoulder. "Depend on it, if you do marry, 'twill be because Father commands it. If you had to make up your mind, the hopeful bridegroom would die of old age first."

"That *is* his lordship," Sidony said, too familiar with Sorcha's opinion of her indecisive nature to take offense. "And I see the wedding party coming. Do you not think we'd better go meet them if Adela is to carry the flowers we've gathered?"

"Aye, sure, especially since we already have enough for her chaplet, too," Sorcha said as they hurried to greet the riders.

As Lady Adela Macleod's wedding party forded the bubbling burn near the base of the hill and continued up toward the kirk, she felt almost wholly at peace. For the first time in too many years she was responsible for no one and nothing. She just had to be in a certain place at a certain time and say what the priest, a Macleod cousin of her father's from Lewis, told her to say.

The feeling was heady, and as she rode beside her father, Macleod of Glenelg, the silence that enveloped them was pleasant.

Except for the tiny tickle at the back of her mind, all was well.

The small cluster of smiling villagers and friends near the kirk steps stood quietly, waiting. Even her usually talkative aunt, Lady Euphemia Macleod, remained unnaturally silent. She rode just behind them in her boxy, sheepskin-lined sidesaddle between two gillies mounted on ponies as placid as her own. At fifty, the whip-slim Lady Euphemia disliked riding and focused all her energy on keeping the boat-on-waves motion of her cumbersome saddle from tossing her to the ground.

The rest of the party included Adela's older sister Maura, Maura's husband and three children, and a few of the castle servants. Others had remained behind to prepare the wedding feast. Guests were few only because MacDonald, Lord of the Isles, having died recently, nearly everyone else in the Highlands and Isles was preparing for the investiture in two days' time of his successor. Adela did not mind the small ceremony, though. She'd have been happy to marry by simple declaration, but women of her ilk rarely married in such a hasty, scrambling way.

She rode as her aunt did, sitting sideways, but with nothing between her and her favorite bay gelding except a dark-blue velvet caparison to protect her skirts. One of her younger sisters, Kate, had embroidered the caparison with branches of Macleod of Glenelg's green juniper and had sent it especially for the occasion.

Like all six of her sisters, Adela preferred to ride astride. But she had known better than to suggest doing so in the new sky-blue silk gown her father had given her for her wedding. Blue to keep her true, he had said, citing from an ancient rhyme. He had refused to allow her favorite color due to his strong belief that if she wore pink, her good fortune would sink.

She saw her two youngest sisters watching from the open, grassy hilltop near the kirk and realized how glad she was that she had sent them ahead to gather blooms for her bouquet and chaplet. She had done it not only because the hilltop produced myriad wildflowers in an otherwise heavily forested area, but also because she had wanted as little fuss as possible while she dressed for her wedding.

Her ever-superstitious father disliked the fact that she had not gathered her own flowers, a task he believed would bring her good luck. When he noted the day's sunshine, his strictures had ended, but no sooner did he clap eyes on Sorcha and Sidony than he sighed and said, "I hope ye mean to be a good wife to Ardelve, lass."

"I do, sir," Adela said. "I have always done my duty."

"Aye, 'tis true, but I'd feel better if ye'd done all ye could to bring good fortune on yourself today."

"The day is a perfectly splendid one," Adela said. Shooting a swift, oblique glance his way, she added gently, "Yesterday was not so beautiful, sir."

"'Tis true," he agreed. "Cursed wi' a gey thick mist, it were, from dawn's light till suppertime. So it be nobbut providential that when Ardelve and I arranged the settlements, I persuaded him to put off the ceremony for the one day."

"Why do you believe Friday is such a bad day to wed?" she asked. "Aunt Euphemia said many prefer it, because of its being dedicated to the Norse goddess of love. She said the notion that Friday is unlucky arose only during this past century."

"Aye, well, Euphemia doesna ken everything," Macleod said. "'Twas kind o' her to journey here from Lochbuie for your wedding, but everyone kens that when a Friday falls on the thirteenth o' the month, it does bring mortal bad luck. Bless me, lass," he added, "I'd no let any o' me daughters marry on such a bleak day!"

"But I don't think everyone does know," Adela persisted. "Ardelve did not. At least . . ." She fell silent, knowing he would not want to recall what Ardelve had said.

"Aye, I ken fine that the man thinks changing the day were nobbut a frippery notion o' mine," Macleod said, unabashed. "Still, he agreed, and as ye see, the Almighty ha' blessed the day I picked wi' sunshine."

Adela nodded, and when he fell silent, she made no attempt to continue the conversation. The only sounds until they reached the kirkyard were soft thuds of hooves on the dirt path, cries of seabirds soaring overhead, and scattered twitters and chatters from nearby woodland.

Her sense of peace had not returned, however, and when she realized she was peering intently at each guest, she knew why. Sorcha had made no secret of her hope that Sir Hugo Robison would arrive in time to stop the wedding, and although Adela was certain her younger sister was mistaken in thinking he would come, she could not help wondering if he would, or how she would feel if he did.

Seeing no sign of that large, energetic, not to mention handsome, gentleman, she drew a long breath and released it. If she felt disappointment, she told herself it was only that his dramatic arrival might have added excitement to what was so far, despite the sunshine, a rather dull day.

As a gillie helped her dismount, her two youngest sisters approached to arrange flowers in her chaplet and give her the bouquet they had gathered.

"These flowers are lovely," Adela said, smiling. "So bright and cheerful."

"Sorcha set a basket of rose petals yonder, too, for us to strew along the path before you," Sidony said, hugging her before they took their places and Macleod signed to his piper to begin playing.

Adela sighed, swept another nervous glance over the small group of onlookers, several of whom were looking around just as she was. Firmly dismissing Sir Hugo from her mind, she placed her hand on her father's forearm.

⁓

As pipes skirled and the wedding party made its way up the path to the shallow porch of the kirk, Sorcha scattered her petals and wondered if the piper had mistaken Adela's wedding for MacDonald's funeral procession. The tune he had selected seemed more appropriate for the latter rite.

Behind the makeshift altar, double doors stood shut and would not open to admit everyone for the nuptial Mass until the ceremony had ended. The priest, Wee Geordie Macleod of Lewis, stood sternly erect beside the altar with the bridegroom and his chief groomsman to welcome the bride and her maidens.

Calum Tolmie, Baron Ardelve, a close cousin of the widow Macleod intended to marry, held a vast tract of land on the north shore of Loch Alsh. He was both wealthy and amiable, and thus, according to Macleod, an excellent match for Adela.

Sorcha disagreed, thinking Sir Hugo more suitable, although admittedly, she had never laid eyes on him. She still cursed her bad luck in having missed the trip to Orkney to see its prince installed, because that had been when the more fortunate Adela and their sister Isobel, each having met Sir Hugo Robison briefly before, had met him again and come to know him better.

Isobel was now happily married to Sir Hugo's cousin, Michael St. Clair (or Sinclair, as the family had begun to spell their name), and they lived at Roslin Castle in Lothian. However, Sir Hugo had clearly made an impression on Adela, so Sorcha had made up her mind that Adela should marry him.

Reaching the porch steps, Sorcha turned and walked a few paces to the left, then watched as Sidony went right to make way for Adela and Macleod. He stopped on the lower of the two stone steps and let Adela go on alone to the porch, where Ardelve stepped forward to meet her in front of the altar.

Two low stools sat ready for them to kneel on, but before they did, the priest stepped forward and spread his arms wide.

The piper fell silent.

A gull screamed overhead.

Instead of the blessing that Sorcha expected to hear, Wee Geordie said in tones that carried to everyone, "Afore I pray to the Almighty, begging Him to ha' the goodness to shine His face upon this couple and bless the union into which they be entering, I'm bound to ask if there be any amongst ye who kens any just cause or impediment to prevent the aforesaid union's going forward. If ye do, speak now, mind ye, or forever keep silent about it."

As silence closed in around them, Sorcha turned her head to look at the crowd. Others, likewise, glanced at their neighbors.

A low rumble sounded in the distance, almost, Sorcha thought, as if God had grown impatient and were muttering to the priest to get on with it.

The thought made her smile, but when she saw heads still turning, all in the same direction, she collected her wits and looked that way, too. Joy stirred at the sight of four horsemen galloping toward them from woods to the south.

Neighbor looked at neighbor.

As delight surged through her, Sorcha glanced at Adela, expecting to see her own joy reflected in her sister, but although Adela clearly saw the riders, she showed no sign of delight. Doubtless she was stunned.

Hearing more than one gasp from the gathering, Sorcha grinned. Her neighbors and friends, she knew, would talk of this day for years.

But the riders were coming too fast for safety. Was their leader mad, or just drunk on the hope that he was not too late?

Villagers scattered as the riders bore down on the kirk steps.

Sorcha moved, but she saw that Adela stayed where she was, mouth agape.

Ardelve put his hands on his hips and glowered, but he did not move either. Sorcha decided that he thought no more of the interruption than that tardy wedding guests were making a scene.

Turning back, she saw that all four riders wore masks.

Prickling unease stirred.

Three of the men reined their horses in near villagers, making the animals rear and forcing folks back even farther.

As they did, the leader urged his horse right up the two steps.

Still smiling, Sorcha saw that he had eyes only for Adela, who moved toward him as if she expected him to speak to her.

Instead, he leaned near, stretched out an arm, and as if she weighed no more than a feather pillow, swept her up, and wheeled his mount away from the steps.

Astonished at such a show of strength, Sorcha let her mouth fall open.

One or two people in the crowd cheered, but most looked stupefied as the four horsemen rode off with their prize.

Kildonan, the Isle of Eigg, April 16, 1380

Sorcha had never set foot on the Isle of Eigg before, although she had passed it numerous times, because it lay only thirty miles from her home and just west of the route they followed from Glenelg to the Isle of Mull, where her sister Cristina lived. Moreover, their sister Isobel had lived with Cristina and her husband for years before Isobel's marriage the previous summer to Sir Michael Sinclair.

Sorcha had not seen Isobel or Cristina since. She had planned to visit both the previous fall, but winter had swept into the Highlands and Isles earlier than expected, making travel difficult by land to Isobel's new home at Roslin Castle south of Edinburgh, or by water to Cristina's on the Isle of Mull.

Therefore, she had not seen Isobel since the previous summer or Cristina for nearly two years. So she eagerly looked forward to seeing both at the upcoming ceremony, because much had happened in the meantime.

Not only had Isobel married Sir Michael, younger brother of the new Prince of Orkney, but John of Isla, the first man known as MacDonald, Lord of the Isles, had died two months before. His burial on the Holy Isle of Iona had come shortly afterward. And since his death, despite his own careful arrangements for the succession, the Kingdom of the Isles had lacked a ruler, because not everyone had agreed with MacDonald as to which of his sons should succeed him.

The judgment and necessary arrangements now made, his eldest son, Ranald of the Isles, had commanded this meeting at Kildonan on Eigg, once a base from which, according to her aunt Euphemia, aristocratic Norse settlers who had replaced the Viking raiders had traded with Iceland and points beyond. Today at high noon, Islesmen would inaugurate their new MacDonald at Kildonan.

Everyone who could manage to witness the grand event would attend, and Sorcha was looking forward to reuniting with many kinsmen besides her sisters. Most eagerly did she look forward to seeing Adela and learning whether she and Sir Hugo had married. If not, she hoped they had made arrangements to do so soon. To protect Adela's reputation, they must wed as quickly as possible.

As Macleod's oarsmen rowed his two longboats into the U-shaped harbor at the southeastern end of Eigg and approached the long pier, both helmsmen shouted as one, "Way enough," to stop their boats and allow three others to offload passengers and portions of their crews. Later arrivals would anchor a short distance offshore near the long, low islet known as Green Island. Other boats already crowded nearby beaches, and towboats scurried back and forth, carrying crews who had anchored their boats offshore to a landing at the head of the harbor.

As Sorcha's boat awaited its turn, she gazed at the high promontory to her right where the ceremony would take place near the ancient chapel of Kildonan. The chapel was all that remained of an important monastery founded by Donan, the Irish missionary who introduced Christianity to the island. According to seanachies' tales, Donan, having incurred the wrath of the local queen, was martyred there with his entire monastic community in the year 617. Today's occasion, Sorcha mused, would doubtless be more felicitous.

Already an increasing crowd of Islesmen with their families congregated on the hilltop, and lines of people hurried up from the harbor to join them, like an army of ants swarming an anthill. Colorful banners flew from a great tent near the chapel.

Beside her, Sidony said, "Everyone looks so splendid, Sorcha. 'Tis sure to be a grand day, but I thought events as important as this one all had to take place on the Isle of Isla, at Finlaggan."

"Were you not paying heed when our father explained that?" Sorcha demanded, giving her a stern look. "How do you expect to understand what goes on around you if you do not listen?"

"I do listen," Sidony said. "But I am not as interested in political matters as you and Isobel are." She nibbled her lower lip, making Sorcha sorry for scolding her.

"I know you do not care about such things," she said with a sigh. "But I do not know how you can manage to sit at the table whilst we discuss them and not come to understand at least matters as important as this is."

"I don't like bickering," Sidony said, clearly having given the matter some thought. "Such topics nearly always lead to discord, do they not? Why, when Isobel was home last summer, before she met Sir Michael—or do I call him something else now that his brother is a prince?"

"He is your brother now," Sorcha said. "You may call him Michael."

"Father would not agree, especially since his brother is Prince of Orkney and I do not know either of them," Sidony protested. "Indeed, I have never even met them yet. Neither have you, come to that."

"That will change today," Sorcha said. "I am sure Michael will be here, and I intend to call him Michael. I call Hector the Ferocious plain Hector, after all, and he, too, is only a brother by marriage. If he lets us treat him as we would our own brothers if we had any, who is Michael Sinclair to forbid it?"

"You did not answer my question," Sidony said quietly.

"Your question? Oh, yes, as to why we are not at Finlaggan. Well, you have only yourself to blame if I have not. You diverted me by speaking of Michael."

"I still want to know."

" 'Tis because the Kingdom of the Isles has grown so

much larger," Sorcha said. "And because most of the newer bits of it lie to the north."

"The Kingdom of the Isles has always seemed vast to me."

"Aye, well, the Lordship now extends more than two hundred miles, from the Butt of Lewis in the north to the Mull of Kintyre in the south. So, although Finlaggan was at the center of things to begin with, it no longer is. And by ancient Celtic law and custom, every subject of the Kingdom of the Isles must have an equal chance of personally witnessing the inauguration of any new sovereign, just as each one must be able to attend any Council of the Isles. Isla lies too far south of the kingdom's center now to allow such equality of opportunity to be practicable. Father said many folks complained of the difficulty when last year's Council met at Finlaggan, so Lord Ranald selected the Isle of Eigg for today's ceremony. Not only is it now at the center of the Lordship, but Eigg belongs to Ranald, so he can more easily control what happens here."

"I wish you would always explain such things so clearly," Sidony said. "Oh, good, we are moving again!"

Their boat followed their father's, and both young women fell silent as they approached the long pier, looking for familiar faces.

When the nearside oars flashed up and their boat eased gently into place behind Macleod's, men on the pier caught the ropes flung to them and made them fast, then hurried to help passengers from both boats alight onto the pier.

Sorcha and Sidony began meeting friends and kinsmen at once. As they made their way up the hill to

Kildonan, greeting, hugging, and chatting, Sorcha kept watch for her older sisters and their husbands, particularly for Isobel and her Michael. She had deduced one pertinent fact from Isobel's frequent messages, as well as from two single-page letters that she had written them, thanks to a gift from her husband of some fine writing paper from Italy. That fact was that wherever one found Sir Michael Sinclair of Roslin, one nearly always found his cousin, close friend, and boon companion, Sir Hugo Robison. And where one found Sir Hugo—today, at least—one was bound to find Adela.

Sorcha had much to say to both of them about courtesy and family duty. Disappearing into the woods two days before, depriving the village of any wedding, and afterward not letting everyone know that Adela was safe was outrageous behavior. She had every intention of telling them exactly what she thought of that behavior just as soon as she clapped eyes on them.

"There's Isobel!" Sidony exclaimed, adding on a note of astonishment, "Faith, I knew she was increasing, but she's enormous!"

"Aye, well, it happens," Sorcha said. "Her babe is due next month, I believe."

"I hope we are still with her when it comes," Sidony said.

Sorcha, too, was looking forward to welcoming a new child into the family, but she did not say so because she had seen two tall men walk up behind Isobel, and one of them rested both hands possessively on her shoulders.

"That must be Michael or he would not dare take such a liberty," she said. "I warrant the fellow with him must be Sir Hugo, but where is Adela?"

"I don't see her," Sidony said. "Where can she be?"

Aware of a sudden chill, Sorcha hurried forward, keeping her eyes on Sir Hugo—if the tall, handsome man by Michael Sinclair was in fact he.

He was even taller than Michael. His light-brown hair danced with red-gold highlights, and as she drew near, she saw that his eyes were the cerulean blue of a clear Scottish sky. Adela had said he was good-looking, but she had not mentioned his size, the breadth of his shoulders, or that he walked as if he ruled the world.

Isobel had seen her and was waving. Nearby Sorcha saw her eldest sister Cristina and Mairi of the Isles, Cristina's sister by marriage. The new Lord of the Isles was Mairi's younger brother, Donald of Isla.

With her shiny black hair and deep blue eyes, Mairi stood out in any gathering. Even approaching her thirtieth year, she retained her beauty. But the Macleod sisters could hold their own, and Sorcha thought the contrast between Mairi's raven tresses and Cristina's golden ones made a pleasing picture.

Rushing forward to hug all three women, she looked expectantly at Sir Michael and said, "You must be my new brother, sir. I am Sorcha Macleod."

"I had deduced as much, my lady," he said with a twinkle as he bent to kiss her cheek. "This must be the lady Sidony with you."

Sidony blushed but allowed him to kiss her cheek as well.

Impatiently, Sorcha looked at the other gentleman. Everyone else still chattered, and she heard Cristina ask a question but paid no heed. Still, as much as she wanted to know if the second man was Sir Hugo Robison, she knew better than to demand the name of any gentleman not yet properly presented to her.

He smiled at her then most impudently, and feeling fire surge to her cheeks, she glanced at Isobel.

Sir Michael, turning from his conversation with Sidony, said then with a gesture toward the man at his side, "But I must present to you both my cousin and closest friend, Sir Hugo Robison."

Still with that impudent grin, Sir Hugo made his bow. As he straightened, he said with amusement, "Don't stand too much on ceremony, Michael. Lady Sorcha has made it clear that she does not insist upon the finer points of courtesy."

Sorcha said instantly, "If you refer to *my* having sent you that message instead of my father, you will at least agree that the situation was urgent, sir. Faith, I should think you would be thanking me. But where is Adela? I want to see her."

He frowned, saying without a trace of humor, "Lady Adela married Baron Ardelve on Saturday, did she not? Where should she be, except with her husband?"

Chapter 2

~

At first, Adela had struggled fiercely, angrily, but she had quickly realized that at the speed they were moving, she would be wiser not to fight him, lest she fall and injure herself. At such a pace, a fall could cause serious injury, even death.

He held her clamped to his side, his arm like an iron bar around her, so tight that it dug into her ribs and brought tears to her eyes. She could scarcely breathe, let alone scream her fury. But did he care? Not he. He and his men rode like the wind, although no one had stirred a step to follow them.

They pounded away from the stunned gathering back to the woods, paying little heed to the terrain even when they neared a swiftly flowing burn. Their horses barely checked before plunging into the icy water and out the other side.

When they did slow at last, she tried to pry his arm

away enough to let her breathe freely, but he only gripped her tighter.

"You're hurting me!" She tried to scream the words at him, but the result was no more than a ragged croak.

He did not bother to respond or ease his hold. He did shift her so that she sat half on his thigh, half on his saddlebow, which was an improvement but scarcely a comfortable one. Nonetheless, she tried to force herself to relax, realizing that further exertion would only add more bruises to her sore ribs.

Despite her new position, their pace was still dangerous, even foolhardy. She doubted that anyone would follow them unless Ardelve wanted to reclaim his bride. He was a kind man, a gentle man, for all Sorcha thought him a pompous one. But he was of an age with Macleod, and lacked both Macleod's temperament and bluster.

She had thought all those qualities admirable when she had agreed to marry him. But she found it impossible to imagine Ardelve leaping into a saddle to pursue her abductors. Moreover, if he knew of Sorcha's attempts to inform Sir Hugo of her wedding, as so many others clearly did, and guessed that Hugo had taken her, perhaps Ardelve believed that she had wanted him to. If that were the case, then he, like Macleod, would be furious and do nothing.

She was angry herself, but if she had to be honest, she was also pleased that Sir Hugo had cared enough to come for her. Not that she would marry him, even so. Had he truly wanted her, he ought to have approached her father in the proper way, and then courted and wooed her. He had done none of that.

Indeed, Sir Hugo Robison had not struck her as a man

who would lift a finger to pursue any woman. He seemed more the sort who expected women to pursue him, and to swoon at his feet if he so much as glanced in their direction.

Adela would not swoon for any man, ever. Nor did she admire men who thought more of themselves than of others. Sir Hugo was in for a surprise if he thought this outrageous abduction would impress her.

The four men continued to ride without speaking, their pace picking up when they reached the top of a ridge she recognized as the south boundary of Glenelg. To the southwest lay the Sound of Sleat and the sea. To the southeast lay Loch Hourn.

They were well away from Chalamine and from Glen Shiel, through which ran the main track for travelers heading inland. So where on earth was he taking her? How much longer did he think he could carry her in such a way before she succumbed in his arms from lack of air?

They wended their way down through dense woodland almost aimlessly, and she had no idea how long they rode. Nor did she recognize the clearing where at long last they stopped. Feeling only relief that the wild ride was over, she looked forward to letting Sir Hugo Robison know what she thought of his impudence.

He dismounted without releasing her, apparently little the worse for carrying her so far in such rough-and-ready fashion. When he put her down, she stumbled and nearly fell, but he did nothing to steady her. Despite her weariness, her temper stirred again as he put a hand to his mask and pulled it off.

Having fully expected to see Sir Hugo's impudent grin, she beheld instead the grim face of a barely remembered stranger—if, indeed, it were even he. What little she had thought she knew of that man had no meaning, however, as evidenced by his very presence among mortals. She opened her mouth to demand to know what demon had possessed him to abduct her, but the look he gave her chilled her to her soul and froze the words in her throat.

"Well?" he said, planting his hands on his hips and glowering at her, his head at least a foot above her own. His hair, she saw, was darker than Hugo's, his eyes a grayer blue. He probably weighed twice the eight stone she weighed, and his powerful shoulders were easily twice as wide as hers. She trembled when she recalled the small heed he had paid to her struggles despite using only one arm to hold her.

Still glowering, he said, "You clearly have something to say to me. I am not always so generous, but I will allow you to speak your mind to me now."

"I . . . I thought you were dead."

"Nay, not yet," he replied. "God kept me alive to finish the task He's set for me. But I'm pleased to hear that you remember me. Our acquaintance was so brief, I doubted you'd recall it at all."

"In truth, sir, I do not remember your name."

"You've no need to remember it. You will call me 'master' or 'my lord.' "

She would call no man master, but he did not look as if he would respond well to a declaration of that fact, so she made none. Having endured a brief encounter with him at Orkney, she remembered only that he was somehow kin to the Sinclairs. He had been menacing even then, but surely, he was not implying that God had restored him to life after he had died. Only a madman could believe that.

"I did hear that you'd died last summer," she said. "In a tragic fall."

"I told you how it was. God spared me because He has further use for me."

"But He cannot have sent you to abduct me. Why did you?"

"I dislike ingratitude," he said, his eyes glittering so that she trembled again, beginning to think he *was* mad. "I was told that you sought rescue from an unwanted marriage," he added. "If my informant misled me, I'll hang him."

He made the threat so casually that she could not believe he meant it.

"If I say that he misinformed you, will you take me home?"

Instead of answering, he roared, "Fin Wylie, come hither to me!"

One of the three other men wheeled his horse and galloped it toward them. Reining in hard enough to make the animal rear, he faced his leader. "Aye, master?"

"Did you not tell me the lady Adela was unhappy with her father's choice of a husband for her and wanted the wedding stopped?"

"I did, my lord."

"She says you lie."

"Nay, master!" The man's face lost color, but he did not look at Adela.

Much as she would have liked to deny having called him a liar, she feared that to do so would further anger her captor. Still, the henchman's visible terror reinforced her earlier assessment of his master's mental state, and she feared he really would hang the poor fellow if she insisted he had lied.

The master said to the man, "I warrant her ladyship would like to hear how you came to know her thoughts, Fin Wylie."

"'Twas the messages, my lord, two o' them, both the same and meant for Sir Hugo Robison. But ye ken that, sir, since ye set us to watch for such messages. Ye ken, too, what we learned—*and* that the matter were gey urgent."

"So did those messages lie, lass?"

She wanted to tell him he should refer to her properly, not be so familiar. She was certain that, in the same situation, Sorcha or Isobel would have said he should, because neither had ever lacked courage. But Adela's courage had deserted her.

She would not call Sorcha a liar, though, even if her messages to Sir Hugo *had* caused the whole horrifying situation.

With forced calm, she said, "I did not send those messages."

He slapped her face so hard that she bit the inside of her lip and tasted blood. Equal amounts of shock and cold terror swept through her.

"When I ask you a question, you will answer it," he said harshly. "When I give you a command, you will obey it—instantly. In other words, you will do exactly as I say, when I say. Do you understand me?"

She nodded, licking blood from her lip.

"Do you understand me?" he repeated.

"Yes," she murmured.

"Yes, what?"

"Yes, sir." When his eyes narrowed, she remembered what he had told her to call him earlier and swiftly corrected herself. "Yes, my lord."

"Good lass," he said, patting her shoulder and sending cold tremors through her. "I'm sure we shall get on splendidly."

Tears pricked her eyes, but she told herself he could not get away with what he had done. The Highlands teemed with her father's allies, not to mention those of his even more powerful son-in-law, Hector Reaganach Maclean, and Hector's twin brother, Lachlan Lubanach, Lord High Admiral of the Isles.

Someone would come for her soon—surely.

As if he had heard her thoughts, he said in that same unnaturally casual tone, "Lest you hope for rescue, you should know that if anyone comes for you, I will kill you after I've killed them. And lest you think they can defeat me, I assure you they cannot. Whatever allies they may collect, my support will always be stronger."

His eyes gleamed, and she knew he wanted her to ask the question and knew just as surely that he would force her to ask it if she did not do so voluntarily.

"Who is stronger than the allies of the Lord of the Isles?" she asked quietly.

"God is. I told you, He snatched me from death. I am His warrior, so my cause is just. He will forgive all I do in His name, so I will prevail in all I do."

"Faith, then what is your cause?"

"I seek vengeance for a wrong done to His holy Kirk. So you see, lass, with God on my side, your very life depends on me. You would do well to remember that, because I'll severely punish any disobedience."

Adela fought to find words but could think of none.

He said quietly, "Highland women who boast of their independent natures could learn much from Frenchwomen, who are properly submissive to their men. But I mean to turn you into a good woman, so heed my lessons well, because if you put me to any trouble, I'll cut off your head and send it to your father in a sack."

Adela stared at him in horror, scarcely aware of a dizzying blackness until it overpowered her and she swooned at his feet.

The Isle of Eigg

Sorcha gaped at the frowning Sir Hugo in dismay. "But you said you'd received my message!" she exclaimed. "Surely, it was you who took h—"

Suddenly aware of their very large, very interested audience, she stopped, flushing hotly.

"I who took what?" Sir Hugo demanded, still frowning.

"Perhaps we should find a quieter place to talk," she said belatedly.

Sidony, who had been listening with visibly rising alarm, said in bewilderment, "Faith, sir, do you mean to say that Adela is not with you?"

"No, of course she is not. What could make you think such a thing?"

"Why, we thought you were the one who carried her off from the kirk, of course," Sidony said, wholly oblivious to the rapidly quieting crowd around them.

Sorcha groaned but fixed her fierce gaze on Sir Hugo. If Sidony had spoken unwisely, the fault was his.

"Carried her off?" His frown deepening, he said,

"Faith, my lady, do you think me such a villain that I would abduct a woman from her own wedding?"

"Do not snap at my sister," Sorcha said, angry enough now that she no longer cared a rap about their audience. "It is not her fault if she believes that, sir. It is no great leap to believe a villain capable of allowing an innocent young woman and her family to think he means to marry her, then of letting a lesser man lure her from him, might change his mind yet again and snatch her from the altar. In any event," she added, tossing her head, "if you know naught of the matter, we are wasting our time talking to you."

With that, she turned her back on him and would have left him standing with his mouth agape had he been content to allow it. However, the man dared to lay his great hands on her—one of them, anyway—and to spin her around with a snap to face him again.

"I do not understand your fury with me, Lady Sorcha," he said sternly. "Your sister and I had no formal understanding."

"Peace, Hugo," Sir Michael said. "Pray, tell us plainly what you mean, Lady Sorcha. Are we to understand that someone abducted your sister from her wedding?"

"Aye, sir, four men. And if their leader was not Sir Hugo—"

"It certainly was not," that gentleman declared.

"Well, it should have been," she retorted, turning on him again. Striving to keep her voice down, she said, "Adela talked of you for weeks after her return from Orkney last summer, making it plain that you had encouraged her to think you cared for her. Believing that, it was natural for me to assume you would want to know about the plan for her to marry so that you could do something!"

"So I could stop the ceremony, you mean. Of all the—"

"I thought you cared," Sorcha cried, oblivious of their audience again. "I did all I could do to help you and to keep poor Adela from marrying just to be marrying and moving away from Chalamine. I expected you to rush to her aid. Instead, you ignored my messages. She said you were mutton-headed and thought of no one but yourself, but I thought she was trying to keep us from teasing her. I never thought she meant it. But she did, because you are all she said you are, and now your selfish, arrogant indifference has ruined her!"

"Don't talk twaddle," he snapped. "There was no understanding between us, and since I was fully involved in preparations for today's ceremony—"

"A very important occasion, to be sure," Sorcha said, forcing her voice down again. "Nevertheless, I'm certain others could have arranged it all perfectly well without you, had you only told them you had pressing personal business to attend."

"But I didn't!" His eyes flashed blue fire. "Even if I'd had any, once it became clear that not every Islesman supported Ranald's decision to install Donald as Lord of the Isles, I gave them my word I'd support him. My word," he added grimly, "is as good as Ranald's own, my lady. I assure you that when my duty is clear, even important personal matters must await its performance."

"What of your duty to Adela?"

"Do you mean to tell me that Lady Adela herself expected me to rescue her?" he interjected, looking sternly into her eyes.

Sorcha flushed and would have looked away had she not feared he would dare to think less of her if she failed to meet that gimlet glare of his.

Stiffly, she said, "Adela would not have admitted such a thing, nor would she say it now, but since everyone at the kirk believed you and your men had abducted her and that she cared for you, no one followed them. Heaven knows where she is now and what may have happened to her! Surely, you must see that at the least you ought to have replied to my message if you could not come for her. Thanks to your failure to act, she is ruined now and no respectable man will want her."

"Don't be foolish. If her ruination is anyone's fault, it is your own, my lass, for meddling in a matter that was no concern of yours."

"How dare you!" Slapping him as hard as she could, she snapped, "I am *not* your lass, you conceited jackanapes! You should think shame to yourself for trying to cast your blame on someone else, but I doubt you have any shame in you. Indeed, I begin to understand at last why Adela, who is ever the soul of propriety, cast a basin of holy water in your face!"

Chapter 3

⁓

Amid a sea of gasps and chuckles, Sorcha heard a cry of dismay that sounded like Cristina and hastily stifled laughter that might have come from anyone. But she was too angry to care. The man was an insufferable lout and deserved to be smacked—often. She put her chin in the air and turned away with exaggerated dignity but not without catching a glimpse of Sir Hugo's face.

He was furious.

Accustomed to a father who was as likely as not to lash out in anger at an impertinent daughter, she thought perhaps Sir Hugo was even furious enough to strike back. But if he believed so strongly in honor, perhaps he also believed in chivalry. In any event, he could hardly strike her in front of such a vast crowd.

It occurred to her that she had been unfair to berate him so publicly, but he deserved that, as well. Her father looked angry, too, she noted as she took the first steps of her departure from the unexpected battlefield. But Macleod had been angry with her often before and would be angry again in the future. She had survived it before and would survive it now.

As she moved away, Sir Hugo said in a tone cold enough to freeze her blood in her veins, "It is to be hoped, Lady Sorcha, that before you are much older, your father will teach you better manners."

"You may be sure that I will, sir," Macleod said in a voice that promised dire consequences for her impulsive behavior. "We will talk, daughter, and more, when the ceremonies are over. I promise you we will."

Sorcha did not reply to either of them, assuring herself that she was not afraid of Sir Hugo and didn't care a whit what Macleod did to her.

But Sir Hugo wasn't finished.

Speaking loudly enough for his words to carry to everyone there, he said, "If you were my daughter, I'd take a stout switch to your backside until you howled your apologies. You'd take your meals standing for a sennight, lass, believe me."

Pretending she had not heard, Sorcha stalked away, so intent upon retaining her dignity that she paid no heed to where she was going or to any of a number of people who tried to speak to her.

"Sorcha, wait! Hold up, you gormless bairn. If I run after you, I'm likely to drop my babe right here!"

Recognizing Isobel's voice and realizing that, of all her sisters, she was the least likely to end her pursuit willingly, Sorcha stopped but did not turn.

"Noddy," Isobel said fondly when she joined her.

"You've been stalking about in a circle. Look ahead. In a minute, you'd have stormed right into his grace's procession. Do you want to explain your behavior to him or to Ranald of the Isles?"

Silently cursing her bad luck, Sorcha saw that Isobel was right. Doubtless, members of the royal procession had already seen her and wondered why she was leaving the chapel grounds just as the ceremony was to begin. Worse, as a Councilor of the Isles, her father was about to join them, and despite her earlier bravado, she did not want to anger him again.

"Dearling, I know you'd like to disappear," Isobel said. "But you'll have to wait until after the ceremony—aye, and the feasting that follows it. Then, unless you can persuade someone to give you space in another boat to Lochbuie, you'll have to travel with Father. So you'd better not anger him more today."

Sorcha stood still and listened, but when Isobel said no more, she drew a long breath and faced her. "I should not have struck him," she admitted. "But he made me so furious that I didn't even think before I did it. I hope I have not made trouble for you, Isobel. I know well that he is your husband's best friend."

"Faith, don't bother your head about that," Isobel said with a warm chuckle. "I've wanted to smack Hugo more times than I can count. He is the greatest tease I know, and he can behave so arrogantly that sometimes my palms just itch."

"Still . . ." Sorcha hesitated, not wanting to say more.

"Come, walk a little away from here with me," Isobel said. "We can say I was feeling indisposed."

"I shouldn't wonder at it if you were," Sorcha said,

worried that hurrying after her might have endangered Isobel or her bairn.

"I'm quite fit," Isobel assured her. "Moreover, I told Michael I was coming to rescue you and not to fly into a panic if someone told him I was unwell."

"He's probably angry with me, too," Sorcha said.

"Not a bit. He is married to me, remember. He is well acquainted with the Macleod temper, although he doesn't see much of it these days. His temperament is so mild that I find it easy just to tell him when aught displeases me. But Hugo is not Michael. Did you really think he wanted Adela?"

"Didn't you?"

"For a time, perhaps," Isobel admitted. "When we were all together at Orkney, he was certainly interested enough to flirt with her, and I suspect she had a tenderness for him, too. But I've seen enough of him now to know he flirts with any woman who is not a hag, an idiot, or in her dotage. I'm afraid he meant nothing by it."

Sorcha grimaced. "Then I'm glad I smacked him hard."

"Aye, sure, but you'd better keep out of his path for a while. He acts for Michael in much the same way that Hector acts for the Lord Admiral of the Isles, so he is accustomed to acting instinctively and decisively. He is not a man who counts cost, Sorcha. You test him further only at your peril."

"I'm not afraid of him," Sorcha said, ignoring the little shiver she had felt at Isobel's words. "Indeed, I doubt I shall see him again until I visit you someday at Roslin. Even then, surely, I'll have to suffer his presence only in company."

Isobel grinned. "You'll not get off that easily, dearling. He and Michael will stay at Lochbuie for nearly a sennight before they return to Roslin. Thus, they will be there whilst you and Sidony enjoy your visit with us."

"May the devil fly away with the man! How can I keep my temper if I must be in his company for so long a time?"

"Easily," Isobel said, still grinning. "Recall that your host will be Hector Reaganach. You would be wiser not to anger him, as I can well attest, having lived with him and Cristina as long as I did. You and Hugo would both do well to behave yourselves whilst you are Hector's guests."

"I forgot about Hector," Sorcha admitted, adding a moment later, "Mercy, I forgot about Cristina, too. She is bound to scold me as fiercely as Father will."

Isobel shook her head. "You should have thought of that earlier, but I know how it is when one loses one's temper. Just give thanks that Adela did not witness that scene with Hugo. She gives much fiercer scolds than Cristina does."

"Aye, but I wish she were here, though," Sorcha said.

"So do I," Isobel said, putting an arm around her.

"You'd better not do that unless you want me to burst into tears," Sorcha said. "Where can she be, Isobel? I cannot think of anyone but Sir Hugo who had reason to take her. Who could have done it, and where is she?"

Tears welled in her eyes, and she dashed them away with the back of her hand. "You'd better go on without me," she said. "I don't want anyone to see me like this, lest they think I'm wishing I had not smacked that dreadful man."

"Will you be all right?"

"Aye, and you should be with your husband to watch the ceremony. One Macleod sister stirring gossip is enough for one day."

"Very well, I'll go," Isobel said. "But don't miss the ceremony. There won't be another like it for years."

She went on ahead, but Sorcha soon followed, because the horns were sounding, calling everyone to assemble who wanted to witness the inauguration of the new Lord of the Isles. She joined Isobel, Sorcha, Hector, and Cristina, and Sir Michael soon found them all and stood beside his wife.

Sorcha feared for a moment that Sir Hugo would join them, too, but then saw him standing by Ranald of the Isles, apparently to help supervise the proceedings.

The processional was a grand affair in itself. It included not only Donald of Isla, his mother the princess Margaret Stewart, and the various bishops, abbots, and priests who would take part in the ceremony, but also every member of the Council of the Isles and a great many Brehons, the hereditary judges of the Isles.

The only important cleric Sorcha knew would not be there was the wicked Green Abbot of the Holy Isle. As a proven enemy of the Lord of the Isles, he was under close guard on the sacred isle. Lord Ranald had seen to it, according to Macleod, to ensure that the abbot could not prevent or disrupt Donald's installation.

Donald had dressed all in white, although other nobles in the procession wore the splendid velvet doublets, puffed hose, and black velvet robes of the royal court. Still others wore more traditional Highland garb, including kilted plaids and saffron shirts, and many carried swords. Hector Reaganach carried Lady Axe, Clan Gillean's legendary battle-axe, in her sling on his back. But no one appeared to be in a bellicose mood.

Pipes skirled and drums beat a tempo for the procession. Then all fell silent, and the prayers and blessings began. Sorcha began to fear that every cleric there meant to speak, but at last, Ranald stepped forward and spread his arms wide.

"To all who bear witness as Donald of Isla accepts his destiny today, I say this," he said. "All here know that his grace our lord father, John the Good of Isla, named Donald to be his lawful successor. And all know I have given my word that it shall be so. Therefore, let any who retain doubt or disloyalty step forward now to speak of it, or forsake it forever and swear fealty to Donald on this day of days."

Sorcha heard the same murmuring that she had heard when the priest had demanded that anyone who objected to Adela's marriage speak or forever keep silent. With a shiver, she realized she half expected to see masked riders bearing down on them again.

But the murmurs faded to silence when Ranald raised one arm high and cried, "Let *Lia Fail,* our sacred Footprint Stone of Destiny, be carried forth!"

Four men carried the sacred stone, said to be older even than the mainland Stone of Scone, on which Kings of Scots had been crowned until Edward of England had stolen it and carried it off to England nearly a century earlier. Before Ranald brought the Footprint Stone to Eigg, it had lived at Finlaggan.

They set the stone down reverently, and two priests stepped forward, bearing vials of holy petrel oil with which they lightly oiled it. Even from her rather distant vantage point, Sorcha could see that there were two prints, an outer, very large one, and an inner one the size of a normal man's foot.

When the priests moved away, Donald stepped forward and placed his bared left foot in the print, wriggling his toes to settle them in the hollows. His foot fit the inner print perfectly, stirring more murmurs, smiles, and nods from his audience.

The Bishop of Argyll handed him a white wand as an emblem of his solemn duty to maintain justice in his realms. Another bishop gave him the Great Sword, one of the two emblems of Clan Donald and the Lordship, to symbolize his position as Guardian of the Isles. After he had turned around three times to his right as a sign of the Trinity, and brandished the Great Sword three times on high, everyone there shouted, "MacDonald, MacDonald, MacDonald!"

Donald of Isla was now formally installed and accepted as Lord of the Isles.

～

On the day of her abduction, as Adela had come slowly to her senses after her swoon to find herself lying on something soft, hope stirred that her abduction had been only a nightmare. Then a nearby sound made her open her eyes.

Her captor stood a few feet away, watching her. They were in a tent large enough for him to stand upright, and she lay on a pile of furs and blankets that was doubtless his bed. Hope vanished, and a chill swept through her as she recalled what he had said to make her swoon at his feet. The shock she had felt when he pulled off his mask had been bad, but this felt much worse. She had remembered his name.

Something he'd said before her swoon awakened the memory, because at Orkney he had said that one of the things he liked most was teaching a woman her proper role in life. He had also declared himself without sin then, and he'd claimed God's favor. Although she had been in his presence only minutes then, she had seen his ruthlessness, so the memory provided nothing for her now but renewed terror. She pushed his name away lest she inadvertently anger him by speaking it aloud.

He did not speak, but his stern expression made her say hastily, "I . . . I was so dizzy. I cannot think what came over me."

"You've had nothing to eat since this morning, if then," he said. "I warrant you're just hungry. If you promise to behave, you may come now and eat with us."

"Oh, I do promise, thank you," she said, the intensity of the gratitude she felt nearly overwhelming her. If he meant to feed her, at least he did not mean to kill her, and perhaps she could soften his harshness if she did not anger him again.

After they had eaten, to her surprise, instead of retiring, they mounted horses again. She yearned for her own mount, but at least this time, he let her ride pillion.

The intense gratitude she had felt before increased with his decision to go on rather than camp where they had stopped for supper. But her fears increased, too.

Finding herself even so briefly on his bed, alone with him, had brought home to her how dire her situation was.

If he decided to rape her, he would, and no one would stop him. Faith, if he decided to kill her, he would, and no one would stop him. Doubtless, he just bided his time. To calm herself, she began to imagine her father and Hector at the head of an army, roaring down on them to rescue her. Then memory of what he had said he would do in such a case stirred a new fear, that any rescue attempt would merely endanger her and the rescuers, as well.

They soon emerged from the woods, and she was astonished to see that they had traveled no distance at all. Straight ahead lay the shore of Loch Hourn.

To her dismay, a galley waited there, and she soon found herself bundled aboard it. Although its oarsmen regarded her curiously, none spoke to her, and instinct warned her that she would displease his lordship if she spoke to them. Dusk turned to darkness as they headed into the Sound of Sleat and turned south.

She lost all sense of time and direction. Having no idea where they went, she held her tongue, remaining biddable and stoic, making no complaint about the weary hours of travel or the icy sea air. They reached landfall by the light of a half-moon.

Two men awaited them with horses, but she saw no sign of habitation and knew she need expect no rescue there. They made camp on the beach, and to her infinite relief, she slept alone in the great tent. When she awoke late Sunday morning, the galley was gone, but the men with the horses remained.

They made a late start and camped at dusk several miles east of a village one of them called Kinlocheil. Adela thought it sounded familiar but still had no idea where she was. She was exhausted, if not from riding pillion all day with his lordship then from the constant effort not to draw his ire, and from trying to deal with waves of unpredictable emotions that assaulted her.

If he offered food or water, she experienced the strange deep gratitude of the day before. Twice she was almost tempted to hug him for his kindness. And both times the impulse stirred, she felt repulsed, as if her own soul were betraying her. Was it her soul? Was he right in believing that God favored him? What if he was?

If he looked at her, she wondered how she had irritated him. If he did not, she feared he was vexed. The slightest change in his tone stirred worry, and the possibilities grew more terrifying with each mile they rode away from Glenelg.

On Monday, more riders joined their group, and it became apparent that her father's army would soon have to be a large one if he were to prevail. She knew that he and anyone else who might search for her would presently be on the Isle of Eigg at the installation of the second Lord of the Isles. As a Councilor of the Isles, Macleod could not absent himself from so important an occasion. One moment, she hoped he had sent someone after her, the next that he had not.

Too often her fearsome captor eyed her speculatively, making her skin crawl, reminding her of the threat he had made, and of other things he might do. And reminding her, too, that he expected her absolute obedience.

The installation ceremony had been impressive, but Sorcha was glad that it was over and that the crowd was moving with alacrity to the great tent for the feast. Hoping to keep out of her father's way, she let them sweep her along with them, taking care to avoid Sir Hugo Robison, too.

She trusted Isobel's judgment and wanted no further quarrel with the man.

Engrossed in her thoughts and hoping no one would try to engage her in conversation, she paid little heed to those around her except to be certain that neither Macleod nor anyone else who might think he had the authority to scold her was nearby. She paid no attention at all to what people were saying until she heard her father's name mentioned.

"One of Macleod's daughters, she is," declared a female voice.

"Shameless," said another. "Her father ought to put her across his knee, just as that handsome young man suggested."

"Aye, well, they're a wild lot, all seven of them," said a third voice.

"Surely, not all!" exclaimed the first.

"Well, until now, I'd have said Lady Adela was the exception, but you heard the scandal about her wedding. Sakes, I heard about that yesterday. But then to have her own sister—if that was she—shouting the details to all and sundry, well!"

"You know," said the first thoughtfully, "I wonder if those men meaning to camp near Kinlocheil yesterday might have been the lady Adela's abductors. A cousin we met on our way here told us about them and said a beautiful woman rode pillion with them. But I'm sure he said they numbered a dozen or more—accoutered as noblemen, too. Moreover, they were making for Edinburgh."

"If they were noblemen, mayhap it *was* she," her confidante said. "The Macleod sisters ken their worth as well as anyone, so if someone carried off Adela from her wedding, I'll wager she kens him fine."

Much as Sorcha would have liked to defend Adela or at least tell the three harridans what she thought of them for gossiping when they did not know anything about the matter, she held her tongue. Having recognized the one who'd mentioned the riders, she was tempted to go to her and demand more details but decided she might talk more freely to Macleod. Considering their opinion of her, she would be lucky if the woman would speak to her at all. So, much as she had hoped to delay the interview she had coming with her father, she could put it off no longer.

They had to find Adela.

⁓

Sir Hugo Robison had long since acquired the ability to set aside personal matters to devote his attention to duty. While engaged with Donald's installation ceremony, he had easily shut his mind to the scene that had preceded it.

However, as soon as Ranald and the new MacDonald of the Isles had retired to the great tent Ranald's men had erected and secured for the feast, Hugo looked around for the lass who had slapped him. When he did not see her, he indulged in a whimsical image of her father taking her off by an ear to give her a good skelping.

She certainly deserved one, he told himself, then realized he was smiling in thought of her fiery temper and the wee dimple that revealed itself below the left corner of her mouth as she berated him. Few girls would have the nerve to slap him, knowing who he was and the vast power his masters, the Sinclairs, wielded.

But if she had thought about that at all before striking him, she had believed the power they wielded would protect her as well as one of his closer kinsmen. She knew, after all, that her sister had married the younger brother of the Prince of Orkney—or Earl of Orkney, if one went by Henry's Scottish title and not his Norse one, which was next highest to that of the Norse King. She ought to have realized, though, that a family connection would hardly protect her if she deserved skelping.

In truth, he doubted that she cared a rap about who his connections were, or had spared a thought for her own, before she struck.

She was a beauty, too, more arresting in her own way than her sisters—the three he had met, anyway. And unlike most young women, who behaved coyly and affected shyness when meeting him, she had looked at him directly, albeit angrily.

Famished now, he strode toward the great tent, smiling again as he recalled how her dimple had peeped at him, the way her chin had come up, and how the curling amber-gold tendrils escaping her coif had gleamed in the sunlight. He even admired the way her wide-set, dark-lashed eyes had sparked flames at him and the whiteness of her teeth when she bared them at him. And, too, there was the tempting fullness of her rosy lips, lips clearly intended for kissing.

Knowing she was to stay at Lochbuie while he and Michael did, he thought it might be amusing to try to alter her opinion of him. He decided, though, that if she tried slapping him again, he would not leave it to Macleod to teach her manners.

"Hugo, I want a word with you."

Hearing in his cousin's voice the stern note rarely directed at himself, he stopped instantly and turned to wait for him.

Frowning, Sir Michael Sinclair glanced about at the crowd swarming to get its midday meal. He waited until a group of men passed them to enter the tent, then said quietly, "We'll delay our dinner a few minutes more. I would know more about that incident before the ceremony."

"You saw it," Hugo said. "You know as much as I do."

"You had nothing to do with that young woman's abduction."

Although Michael made it a statement and not a question, Hugo knew he would not have mentioned it had he not harbored at least small doubts. The knowledge stirred new irritation, but he kept his tone mild as he said, "You know I did not."

Michael held his gaze for a long moment before he said, "I hope so. Are you certain you gave Lady Adela no cause to think you wanted to marry her?"

"Don't be daft," Hugo said, but he felt heat in his cheeks as he said it.

Michael's gaze sharpened. "None at all?"

"Of course not." Hugo met that sharp gaze and gave his answer firmly, with no intention of sharing the niggling doubt that had just flitted through his mind—certainly not until he'd had time to give it more thought.

Accordingly, he was silent until Michael nodded and said, "That is all I wanted to know. If Macleod requests our help, we'll give it."

"Aye, sure," Hugo said as they continued toward the tent together.

When they had taken their places at the men's end of the high table, he saw that neither Lady Sorcha nor Isobel was present. He found then that his appetite was no longer as keen as it had been.

He bore his part in nearby conversation as needed, but his mind was no longer on the festivities. When Isobel entered the tent at last, with her sister Cristina and Hector Reaganach—the latter looking grim enough to remind Hugo that men had good reason to call him Hector the Ferocious—he hoped Hector's mood was due to annoyance with Lady Sorcha rather than with the man she had slapped.

Even more than he wanted to avoid Michael's displeasure did he want to avoid that of the powerful warrior who carried his family's legendary battle-axe with him everywhere he went. Unfortunately, though, he could think of only one way Lady Sorcha Macleod could have come to believe he had wanted to marry her sister. That was if Adela herself had led her to believe it.

Conversation ebbed and flowed around him as he tried to recall what he knew about Lady Adela. Besides her golden beauty, his strongest memory was the haughty way she had dismissed his casual flirting at Orkney. He recalled, too, that when he had responded to that dismissal as he always did to such setbacks, she had cast a basinful of holy water in his face.

Michael had witnessed that incident, too, but evidently did not recall what Hugo had said to her or what she spat at him as she doused him. In truth, the topic of marriage had raised its head, but only in that she'd said she would *never* marry him.

Clearly, she had told her sisters about the holy water, but he could recall nothing about her to suggest that she might lie to them. How else, though, could they have come to believe he would want to rescue her from an unwanted marriage?

He had continued to flirt with her when they made two of the party that had departed Orkney with Henry for Castle Sinclair in Caithness. But that had not altered her thinking, because she had stubbornly continued to spurn his advances. The thought that she might make him a suitable bride when and if he had time to marry had certainly entered his head. But until now he had not imagined for an instant that it had entered hers. Such thoughts were not supposed to enter gently bred young women's heads, although in truth, he supposed they occasionally did.

To his chagrin, he realized the only reason he had continued to assume she would accept him was that he had heard nothing to suggest she had developed an interest in anyone else. Nor, until Lady Sorcha's messenger found him, did he suspect that any other man had taken interest in Adela. He had simply assumed that when he wanted her, she would be available. He had assumed, as well, that her father would leap at the chance to welcome such a splendid bridegroom for her.

Hugo winced at such plain evidence of his own arrogance, deciding that the lass had been right to call him conceited. Still, he was sure that nothing he had said or done ought to have led her sisters to believe he intended anything beyond flirting. If Adela had declared anything else to them, she ought not to have done so. And even if she did think he meant marriage, her most unladylike sister Sorcha ought never to have sent messages to him as she had, let alone dared to slap him.

His thoughts were spinning in circles. If he was guiltless, then why, he asked himself, did he find it so hard to stop thinking about what the young vixen had said?

He saw her come into the tent at last, but to his surprise, she walked straight to her father. When she bent close to speak into his ear, Macleod looked no happier to see her than one might expect. Indeed, he began scolding her roundly, without regard for the interested men around him. Hugo told himself she deserved to hear whatever Macleod said, and ruthlessly suppressed an inexplicable urge to defend her.

⁓

"Please, sir, just talk to her," Sorcha said quietly. "It was Lady Clendenen's friend, Lady Gowrie. I'm sure those men her cousin saw must be the abductors. Heaven knows what they may be doing to Adela whilst we linger here!"

"Ye ken naught o' the matter," Macleod said, getting to his feet. "What's more, I ha' heard enough o' your prattle for one day. Ye'll come wi' me now or I'll make ye rue what ye did to Sir Hugo right here, afore everyone."

Taking her by an arm, he gave her no choice, for she dared not resist him. Her cheeks flamed when more than one chuckle accompanied their departure, but she told herself she did not care. She had to make him understand.

Outside, she tried again. "Please, sir, you cannot mean to abandon Adela. You cannot simply ignore what they did."

"Why not?" he demanded. "Ye made a fine fool o'

yourself, sending out the Lord kens how many messages to Sir Hugo, and ye've seen what came o' that. Every man for miles about learned o' them, and everyone believed 'twas Sir Hugo that scooped her up to his saddlebow. Now they'll ken that we all stood by and watched villains abduct me daughter. But Sir Hugo were right about one thing."

She wasn't going to ask him what that was, but he grabbed her by both arms and put his face close to hers. "He were right to say the fault be yours alone, Sorcha Macleod. Whatever Adela's fate be now, she can thank ye for it and no other."

"Then *I'll* find her," Sorcha said, stifling dismay. "If it is my fault, as you all say, then I'll put it right. You'll see, I will!"

"Ye'll do nae such daft thing," he said, giving her a shake. "I forbid it. Nor will ye be making mischief at Lochbuie, for I'm sending ye home. I'd meant to send one boat in any event, because I've a duty to get word to Ardelve o' what we learned today. I'll send both wi' ye, though, and go to Lochbuie wi' Hector Reaganach. Since I promised two boats for his grace's flotilla when he goes to swear fealty to the King, me lads can return to Lochbuie and collect me after they've seen ye home safe."

"You can't! Oh, Father, you mustn't. What will people think? Not just of me, for I don't care about that, but about poor Adela! You cannot abandon her when she did nothing to deserve what happened except have a sister who is a fool."

"Ye're a fool right enough, but how do I ken any such thing about Adela? If she encouraged one man, she might well ha' encouraged a dozen. She just stood there, did she know? I didna hear a single cry for help from the wicked lass."

"Because doubtless she, too, thought it was Sir Hugo."

"Then 'twas wickedness, and she's come by her just deserts. Ardelve went home a gey sorrowful man without her. Ye've yourself to thank for that, too."

"I doubt he was that sorrowful," she said. "He showed little joy in his marriage. And without joy, how could there be sorrow?"

"By heaven, almost d'ye persuade me to follow Robison's advice at once," Macleod snapped. "Get ye to yon boat, lass, afore I do take a strap to ye."

Sorcha knew she had pushed him as far as she dared. In general, his threats to his daughters were empty, but she had learned that if she pushed him too far, he would retaliate, and she had no wish to suffer what would amount to public punishment. Just the thought that Sir Hugo might make one of the audience was enough to make her beg her father's pardon and offer no further argument.

Chapter 4

$\sim$

Macleod walked away, and Sorcha made her way to the wharf. When she heard her name called again, she paused at the side of the path to wait for Sidony.

"You had no chance to eat, so I brought you a manchet loaf and some sliced mutton," her sister said, handing her a small linen-wrapped packet of food.

"Thank you," Sorcha said, realizing she was hungry.

"What did Father say to you? He looked so angry, but he did not speak a word to me when he passed me."

"He *is* angry," Sorcha said. "I heard two women talking about horsemen with a woman riding pillion near Kinlocheil. One was Lady Clendenen's friend, Lady Gowrie. I'm sure they are the ones who took Adela, and Lady Gowrie said they were making for Edinburgh. Imagine what could happen to her in such a great town!"

"What?"

"Many things," Sorcha said darkly. "None of them good."

"But I thought you wanted to attend the royal court there! When Father said he was going with his grace, did you not say you wished we could go, too?"

"Aye, but those men are not taking Adela to court. They must want her for some viler purpose, or they would not have whisked her off as they did. Evil begets evil, you know. No good ever comes of it."

"But I don't understand why Father is angry with you," Sidony said.

Sorcha just looked at her.

Sidony shrugged. "I know he is angry that you slapped Sir Hugo, because you were wrong to do that, and you know it. But he did provoke you, so if that is all it was, why did Father still look so black just now? Once he vents his anger, he usually becomes docile again. And if you told him that you discovered where they are taking Adela, he should be grateful to you."

"Aye, well, he's not," Sorcha said. "He said that whatever part of it is not my fault, Adela brought on herself. Ardelve is sorrowful, he said, but I wager Ardelve does not want her now. He is certainly not here, or if he is, I've not seen him."

"Nor I," Sidony admitted. "But mayhap he rode after Adela himself."

"Lord Pompous? I don't believe it. He wanted her only because she can run a large household. He won't bestir himself to fetch her any more than Father will. And like Father, I warrant Ardelve thinks folks are laughing at him."

"Well, some did cheer her abductors in the kirkyard,"

Sidony reminded her. "Ardelve cannot have enjoyed hearing that. Doubtless, he believed, as we did, that their leader was Sir Hugo and that Adela wanted to go with him."

Sorcha grimaced. "Siddy, no one is going to stir a step to help her, and I cannot stop hearing that horrid man bellow at me that it is all my fault."

"That was a wicked thing for him to say! You were only trying to help Adela—and him, too!"

"Even so, I begin to think he spoke the truth."

"I don't believe that!"

"What if whoever took her got the idea from hearing about my messages to Sir Hugo? What if it was someone who wants Adela for himself and knew he could not win her? Sakes, what if he just wanted one of the pretty Macleod sisters?"

"But could they have learned about the wedding so easily?" Sidony asked. "You did not set up a hue and cry, after all. You sent messengers only where one might expect to find Sir Hugo. They would not have spoken to just anyone."

"You know as well as I do that most of Glenelg and nearly every guest knew about it. We made no secret of it, after all, not after you told Adela what I'd done."

Sidony hung her head. "It just slipped out because she was looking sad. You promised you were not angry with me."

"I wasn't, and I'm not. I was going to tell her as soon as I'd had word from him, because I could scarcely *not* tell her. But I thought he would come or reply straightaway, and when he did not, I was afraid he might leave it to the last minute."

"Aye, many men seem to do that with everything."

"They do, and I did not want to fling it at her the day before her wedding. When it happened, I was glad we had warned her. And Father is right, you know," she added. "Adela did not cry out, Siddy, so I'm sure she was glad to believe Sir Hugo had come for her. How could she not have been?"

"She won't be glad to have found it was someone else, however."

"She must be terrified. That is why, if no one else will find her, I must."

"But how can you find her by yourself?"

"I don't know. But someone simply has to follow them to Edinburgh."

"Faith, you've never even been there! How would you know the way?"

"I'll ask people, or take someone with me who does know. Father has gillies who have traveled to the low-lands. I'll take one of them. And I've heard that one may stay at friaries or nunneries when traveling a great distance. I'll do that."

"But what if the riders Lady Gowrie mentioned were not the right ones?" Sidony said. "What if Adela's are not going to Edinburgh? Even if they are, you cannot go alone, Sorcha. Father would never allow it. Indeed, you could not do such a thing without hurling yourself to ruination right along with Adela."

"I don't care about that, but I shan't go alone," Sorcha said. "Did I not say I'd take a good stout gillie? Moreover, I was hoping . . ." She paused meaningfully.

"Oh, no!" Sidony looked aghast. "You cannot mean to make me go!"

"Will you not aid me in this, Siddy? I was sure that you would."

"You know I'll do anything you ask of me. But this is madness, surely. Whatever will Father say? And how do you think we can slip away from Lochbuie? We are to stay there for an entire month."

"No, we aren't," Sorcha said. "At least, I am not. Father is sending me straight home from here in disgrace. You may go to Lochbuie without me, of course, to visit with Cristina and Isobel. But since I cannot go, I mean to rescue Adela even if I do have to do it alone."

"I could not enjoy myself at Lochbuie without you," Sidony said, looking sad. "But I doubt I'd like going to Edinburgh in such a reckless way either. Indeed, I do not know what I should do."

"You never do know," Sorcha said with a fond smile. "But I won't try to talk you into something you do not want to do. You'll have to decide this for yourself."

"But I cannot ask Father or Cristina for advice, because I know what they will say. Oh, Sorcha, do you not think perhaps Hector Reaganach might rescue her? He is very powerful and commands hundreds of men."

"But his men serve the Lord of the Isles, as he does," Isobel said. "Not only will his grace require many of them to accompany him to Edinburgh, but such a force is too vast and important to send after one missing Macleod sister. Nor would Father seek their aid. He is so angry that he is behaving as if Adela arranged this all by herself to inconvenience him. Or, worse, to make him look foolish."

"Well, I do not know what to say, but I'll do as you ask me."

Sorcha shook her head. "When I know the course you

should take, I don't mind telling you, but don't you see, Siddy? If you make me decide, you lay all the burden for the consequences on my shoulders. I do have a conscience. I cannot press you to go when I have no way to know what the outcome may be."

Looking stricken, Sidony said, "If you go, I must go also."

"Then we must make a plan, and quickly, because Father will order his helmsmen to take us straight to Glenelg. If Adela's abductors are making for Edinburgh, every mile we travel north will take us farther from her."

"But do we not have to follow from where we last saw her?"

"To do that would be to have Father on our trail in a trice. For that matter, the abductors are already into their third day of travel, so we would be too far behind ever to catch up with them."

"Then we cannot do it," Sidony said, making no effort to hide her relief.

"When one must do a thing, one can always find a way," Sorcha said firmly. "The trick is to discover it."

⁓

True to his word, Macleod put Sorcha aboard one of the two longboats, and true to hers, Sidony insisted on going with her, as did the maidservant the two shared. When Macleod, as predicted, ordered both boats straight to Glenelg, the only salve to Sorcha's frustration was Cristina's pledge to try to persuade him to search for Adela.

"If Isobel and I cannot persuade him," Cristina said,

"then we will press Hector and Sir Michael to do it. If only we could know who took her!"

That was the rub, Sorcha thought with a sigh as she bade her elder sisters farewell and settled on the larboard-side seat near the high prow of the lead boat. Leaning her head back against the polished wood, she shut her eyes to think.

She could hear Sidony and Una MacIver, their maid-servant, talking as the helmsman shouted commands to their oarsmen, but soon all she heard were waves hushing alongside the boat, screams of gannets and gulls over-head, the creaking of the lines holding the mast, and the flapping of the lugsail as men hoisted it.

Their lack of speed seemed at first to be in her favor, because she needed time to plan and feared she would not have enough. The wind still came from the northeast, but now, instead of speeding them along as it had that morn-ing, it seemed determined to push them right back to the Isle of Eigg. Before long, the boat began pitching on larger waves, making it more difficult to think.

Una laughed after a contrary lurch of the boat. Her laugh was a high-pitched squeal, more akin to the screech of a gull than to feminine laughter. Sorcha opened her eyes. The laughter stopped instantly, and Una looked abashed.

"You laugh just like your mother," Sorcha shouted with a smile over the noise of the wind and the sail. She remembered buxom Bess MacIver fondly.

Una blushed. "Me da says I sound like a corncrake. I didna mean t' wake ye."

"I wasn't sleeping. I was trying to think how we—" She stopped short, scarcely able to breathe as she exam-ined the idea that had so abruptly come to her.

Fixing her gaze on Una, she said, "Your mother and Ranulf now live in North Morar, at Glenancross, do they not?"

"Ye ken fine that they do, m'lady. The mendicant friars bring word o' them whenever they pass through Glenelg on their way to Eilean Donan."

"Aye, sure," Sorcha said, moving to sit beside her so they need not shout.

Sidony, on Una's other side, eyed her sister warily. "You look as you always look when you are plotting mischief," she said. "You have a plan."

"I do," Sorcha said, leaning across Una to prevent her words from reaching any oarsman's ears. "Now, listen carefully. I know just what we must do."

Hugo stood staring into the distance at the weird volcanic mass the people of Eigg called the Sgurr. It was the most notable feature on the south half of Eigg.

Tall and narrow, not quite a column, and visible for miles, it provided a landmark for sailors and landsmen alike. He admired its strange beauty and could easily imagine ancient folk treating it with awed reverence. Staring at it was not helping him much at the moment, however.

He felt guilty, and the feeling was not a familiar one. Not that he never made mistakes, for he did. And when he did, Michael, Henry, or his own father would be quick to tell him so. But although it annoyed him to be called to account, his mistakes were rare, and he had long since come to realize that the men he respected most also respected him. They merely did their duty when they pointed out his errors. And since he was not careless or incompetent and his errors were honest ones, he rarely had cause to feel guilty.

But he felt guilty now, and he didn't like it. Nor did he like the fact that the lass had shown no respect for him, not one whit.

Damn her and all her relations! He decided to damn Michael, too, while he was about it, for nudging his thoughts in this uncomfortable direction.

Knowing only too well what his cousin would say if he were foolish enough to repeat his curses aloud, he smiled at the image that leaped to his mind.

"Something about that pile of rock amuses you?"

Hugo started and turned, instantly on guard when he saw that Hector Reaganach was addressing him.

"Stand easy, lad; I won't eat you," Hector said. "I would know more about this business with Lady Adela."

"Apparently, four men abducted her from her wedding, sir," Hugo said, knowing that he had better tread lightly.

"Macleod tells me that his next-to-youngest daughter, Lady Sorcha—" Breaking off, he added with a wry smile, "You've met the lass, I hear."

"I have," Hugo said dryly.

Hector's blue eyes twinkled. "You'll be relieved to know that her handprint is no longer visible on your cheek."

Hugo groaned. Doubtless, that handprint had been visible for at least an hour if not longer. He had thought the quickly hidden smiles he'd seen were merely hints of the amusement others had felt at seeing him smacked.

"I mean to improve my acquaintance with her at Lochbuie," he said.

"Then I'm sorry to tell you she won't be there," Hector said. "Macleod ordered her home, and the lady Sidony insisted on going with her. But he tells me that like their sister Isobel, whom you know well, our Sorcha is a spirited lass with a mind of her own. She is also, he said, deeply concerned about Adela."

"I did observe that," Hugo said, surprisingly disappointed to learn that he would be unable to cross verbal swords with her again at Lochbuie.

Hector nodded. "Then you'll understand Macleod's concern that, left to her own whims, she might impulsively set out to find her sister."

"Surely not!" For once in his life, Hugo was truly shocked.

Shaking his head at him, Hector said, "You have much to learn about women, lad. I've no doubt that Cristina and Isobel are even now urging Macleod to go in search of Adela, and that before any of us are much older they will be exerting themselves to send his grace's entire armed force to find her. To be sure, if we knew who had taken her, or where they were headed, I'd have men after them now."

"If only Macleod had set someone on their trail straightaway!"

"Aye, but recall that as he thought you were the abductor and she went willingly he had no good reason to follow. Moreover, he was furious with the pair of you for stirring scandal."

"He did have cause," Hugo admitted ruefully. "The lass was right to say I should have replied to her message.

At the time, I thought she had no business interfering in her sister's affairs, let alone mine, and did not deserve a reply. I never expected anything to come of it other than Adela's marrying Ardelve."

"An outcome, apparently, that caused you no distress."

In light of Hugo's recent recognition of his own arrogance, Hector's gentle tone did not deceive him. But he had no desire to share his new awareness with the older man, who would doubtless disapprove of it even more strongly than Hugo did himself. Neither, however, would he prevaricate with a man he greatly respected.

"What I thought at the time bears no repeating, sir," he said, meeting Hector's stern gaze and feeling guilt wash over him again. With a sigh, he added, "Meeting Lady Sorcha has had a salutary effect on me. I own, sir, I am not proud of my actions or their lack."

"Good lad," Hector said, clapping him hard on the back. "You must be sure to thank her for the lesson when next you meet."

"I'd rather wring her neck," Hugo said with feeling.

Hector laughed. "I've felt that inclination myself with more than one Macleod sister."

"I'll warrant you have," Hugo said, aware that Hector was not only married to Cristina but had fostered Isobel. "So what is to be done now?"

"We'll wait until we know more," Hector said. "As doubtless you are aware, my brother, the admiral, is the best-informed man in the Highlands and Isles, thanks to his vast network of informants. He has made it known that he seeks information about this business, so we should have news in a day or two."

"Can we do nothing straightaway?"

"As to that, Sorcha told Macleod she overheard Lady Gowrie of Glen Finnan mention well-equipped men riding through the clachan of Kinlocheil with a beautiful woman riding pillion. They apparently said they were riding to Edinburgh."

"Macleod got no more details?"

"As you may suspect, he is angry with Sorcha, and with Adela, too. He told Sorcha he did not want to hear more about the matter. I'm guessing he feels a fool for allowing them to ride off with Adela. Any man would. Moreover, he wants to avoid scandal, since he means to take a new wife soon."

"One, I surmise, who also dislikes scandal."

"No one likes it," Hector said. "But Gowrie and his lady had departed by the time Macleod shared that information with us, so if you are eager for action, you might seek her out to discover what more you can learn."

"I'm told that news flies quickly hereabouts," Hugo said. "Tracking a rumor to its source could eat up a great deal of time."

"A good point," Hector agreed. "I prefer to let Lachlan call the tune myself, because the more information one has the less likely one is to dash off in the wrong direction, and his men provide him a continuous flow of news from all over Scotland. Still, I understand your impatience, and if Lady Gowrie knows anything more, I warrant you'd get more information from her than even Lachlan's minions could."

"I'd certainly try, sir, but I must consult with Michael first, because my first duty is to him."

"He is on the wharf," Hector said. "I told him I'd find you, but as everyone is trying to leave at once, there can be no hurry. If you want to stand here staring at that rock for another half hour, I am sure he will not mind."

Hugo grinned. "If that is your belief, you don't know him at all."

They strode down to the harbor together, and as Hugo had expected, found Michael impatient to be off. Hugo soon cleared their way, and as their oarsmen rowed out of the harbor into the stiff wind, he looked northward, realizing that like themselves, Lady Sorcha was unlikely to reach her destination before nightfall, although Glenelg lay much closer than Lochbuie.

～

The pitching and rolling of Macleod's longboats on the windblown waves had increased so much that when Sorcha threw up nearly all the bread and mutton Sidony had provided her over the polished oak decking of the lead boat, she could be nearly certain that no one had seen her stick a finger down her throat.

Sidony shouted for the helmsman to put in to shore quickly.

That worthy signaled to his counterpart on the second boat, and at speed, both longboats made for the North Morar coast of the mainland.

While some men moved to help the stricken Sorcha, and others to clean up the mess, Sidony said anxiously, "What are we to do? She is very sick!"

Una, quick upon her cue, said, "My mam and da live nearby in Glenancross. Mam will know what to do for her ladyship can we but get her to their croft."

"Aye, sure, we must go there, Una," Sidony said, having learned her lines just as efficiently. To the helmsman, she said, "Bess and Ranulf MacIver will know what to do for her ladyship, but they cannot accommodate all your men."

"But, my lady, your lord father did command that we take ye straight to Glenelg. He'll be gey wroth that we've stopped at all."

"Nay then, he won't," Sidony said. "You ken well that Bess took care of us before she married Ranulf MacIver. Afterward, too, till one of our horses crippled him and she brought him here where her family can help her look after him. My father would trust Bess to know what to do, and you can see for yourself how sick the lady Sorcha is. Do you think my father will be pleased if, by following his instructions and dragging her all the way back to Chalamine, you let her die?"

"Nay, m'lady, I never said that," the helmsman said.

"Then what do you suggest?" Sidony asked.

"Please," Sorcha said weakly, "do whatever you must, but do it with haste. I think I am going to be sick again."

"Nay, then, you won't, my lady," Una said. "We'll have you in a warm bed with Mam looking after you in no time. We will, aye?" She glared at the helmsman.

Defeated, he said, "I'll ha' me lads carry her ladyship to yon croft o' the MacIvers then, but ye'll ha' to show 'em the way, Una MacIver."

"I'm going with her," Sidony said, her tone firmer than usual.

"Aye, m'lady, it wouldna be right for ye to travel alone wi' us men. But what'll I do about me lads? We didna plan to spend the night on the water, ye ken."

Sorcha felt obliged to take a hand again, sure that

making two decisions in a row would confound her sister. "Go on to Glenelg, of course. You cannot expect the folk here to feed and house you, and you can be home in a few hours. I warrant I'll be quite well again in a day or two. Then you must come back and collect us."

"Aye, sure, we can do that," he said. "But I'm thinking I'd best fetch ye tomorrow, since we'll ha' to take ye back to Glenelg afore we can collect the laird."

"You must do as you think best," Sorcha said, knowing if she insisted on two or three days to recover, he would suspect the worst, because she was never sick. "Do recall, though," she added, "that he means to stay at Lochbuie until his grace departs for the court at Edinburgh. You'll be left to kick your heels until then."

"Aye, 'tis true," he agreed. "But the laird will no be happy do we keep him waiting, and I'd as lief no ha' to answer for a longer delay."

"Indeed, m'lady," Una said, "ye'll surely be well again by morning."

"'Tis right, she is," the helmsman said. "I ha' never known ye to be sick for more than a few hours. We'll fetch ye in the morning then."

Knowing better than to argue, Sorcha leaned heavily against Sidony and said she was feeling worse. She was sorry and a little amused moments later when she realized the man carrying her feared she might be sick all over him at any moment.

At the MacIver croft, Una took charge, finding her mother and quickly explaining that Lady Sorcha had fallen ill on her return journey from Eigg.

That spurred Bess MacIver to inform the boatmen sternly that they could take themselves off to Glenelg at once and return for her ladyship when she was feeling better. If they chose to come back the following day, that was their business.

"But ye ken fine," she added, "that I'll no let her ladyship go anywhere till she be feeling gey hardy again."

After that, the helmsmen seemed happy enough to depart, leaving Sorcha and Sidony to Bess MacIver's capable ministrations.

"We've only the one bed, m'lady," Bess said. "But we'll ha' ye in it in a trice, tucked up wi' a hot brick to warm ye, for I warrant ye're chilled through after being out on the water in this oorlich wind."

Peeking through the tiny window in the main room of the croft to be sure the boatmen were gone, Sorcha said in her usual crisp way, "No one is going to take your bed, Bess. I am perfectly stout, I promise you."

"Bless me, then, what is this?" Bess demanded, looking at all three young women in much the same way as she had when Sorcha and Sidony were children in mischief. "I'm thinking now that despite your ages, all three o' ye want skelping, so ye'd best tell me what ye're up to. And be gey quick about it, too."

∽

The long hours of silent riding had given Adela time to think. Although she still took care not to think of his lordship by name even when that name floated near the surface of her mind, fearing still to anger him by speaking it aloud, she had recalled another detail about their meeting at Orkney. He had seemed then to ally himself with the Green Abbot of Iona, a fierce enemy of the Lord of the Isles.

For years, her sisters Cristina and Isobel had warned her that the abbot, once an ally of Macleod's, was evil and a sworn enemy of Clan Gillean and the Lord of the Isles. Her captor was certainly wicked to have abducted her, but even after more than two days in his company, she had persuaded herself that he was not truly evil.

To be sure, he had struck her the first day without real cause. But she had not known then how angry an oblique response to a question could make him. She knew now that he expected honest, direct answers, that equivocation infuriated him. She had seen that more than once.

For the most part, he had been kind enough yesterday, and so far today. He had even allowed her privacy to relieve herself, although he did surround the area with his men each time, and had said he would kill her if she tried to escape.

He had made that threat so often that she had come to hope he used the words without thought or true intent to do harm. Still, his men were afraid of him, and she wanted to survive. If she remained calm and submitted to his will whenever she could, surely she could hold out until an opportunity arose for escape or rescue.

Chapter 5

$\sim$

Hastily, Sorcha explained to Bess what had happened to Adela and their fear that no one was yet searching for her.

"We did hear about her wedding," Bess admitted. "But was the man who took her no the one she hoped would marry her?"

"We all thought he was," Sorcha said. "We did not learn that we were wrong until this morning, but my father says that is Adela's fault. And mine," she added conscientiously. "Sidony and I mean to find her, though, since no one else will, and you must help us, Bess. You simply must! It was you, after all, who told me that family counts more than anything else in this world."

"I did," Bess agreed. "Because it does."

"Aye, and when my mother died, you said we had you and Father, and our sisters, plus the rest of our clansmen to look after us. But we lost you when Ranulf was injured. Then Mariota died and Cristina, Kate, and

Isobel all married and moved away. Only Maura still lives nearby. I don't want to lose another sister."

"Sakes, m'lady, I ken fine that ye must be worried about Lady Adela, but ye havena lost the others—only your mam and the lady Mariota, poor dearling."

"Aye, but you know what I mean, Bess, and I mean to find Adela. You will help us, won't you?"

"Just what d'ye think I can do? The very notion o' three young lassies traveling about, thinking they can rescue another! That be plain daft."

"Three?"

"Ye dinna think I'll let the pair o' ye go without ye take Una. Ye've better sense than that, Sorcha Macleod."

"But we cannot travel as three young maidens," Sorcha said. "I do know that. And Una, as buxom as she is, could never fool anyone into thinking she is a man. I mean for just Sidony and me to go. We'll dress as lads. And we'll need a real one to travel with us if you know someone who would be suitable."

"And what do ye think ye'll do if ye find her?" Bess demanded. "Ye can scarcely wield a sword or beat off her abductors wi' your fists."

"I've thought about that," Sorcha assured her. "We'll just follow them to see where they take her. We've heard they are riding to Edinburgh, for they passed through Kinlocheil. I do not know where that is, but we'll find it, and when we do, discovering where they went next will be easy enough. Adela is pretty enough for people to notice her, and there cannot be many parties of four men and one woman."

"There may be more than four men by now," Sidony said thoughtfully.

"Aye, Lady Gowrie said there were twenty. Still, there will only be one Adela," Sorcha pointed out. "Unless you think they are riding about the Highlands, collecting brides."

"Faith, do you think they may be doing that?" Sidony demanded, blanching.

"No, goose, I do not." She turned to Bess. "Will you help us?"

"I expect that if I refuse, ye'll just go on your own," Bess said. "But I dinna think ye should go as lads, mistress. Can ye no go as common women instead?"

Before Sorcha could think how to reply, Una said, "Only look at them, Mam. Common or noble, they'd draw too much notice, dress them how ye would. Lady Sorcha be right. They'll travel safer as lads. But what'll ye do about your hair?"

"When Isobel dressed as a lad, she just stuffed hers in a cap," Sorcha said.

"Isobel wore lad's clothes only the one time," Sidony said. "And only long enough to cross the Kyle from Glenelg to Skye."

"She did it more than once," Sorcha said. "But you're right, Sidony. To do it longer would prove more difficult. We'll just have to cut our hair, that's all."

"Cut it?" Sidony stared at her. "How short?"

"Short enough to look like a lad's, of course. You can just keep your head covered afterward until it grows out again," she said. "You rarely let it hang loose, anyway, now that you are grown up."

"Not as often as you do, at all events," Sidony said. "Very well, I'll do it, but it is most improper, Sorcha."

"Abducting Adela was worse," Sorcha said with more sharpness than usual. "So is Father's refusal to go after her."

"You know," Sidony said, "I think he may have said that because he was angry with you. I don't think he will really abandon her."

"He already has," Sorcha said. "Think, Siddy. In less than a sennight now, nearly every member of the Council of the Isles will go with his grace to Edinburgh, to the King's court. Father won't have time to hunt for missing daughters."

Bess said quietly, "Ye've said ye mean to find where they've taken her ladyship, but ye didna say what ye think ye can do then."

Sorcha sighed. "In truth, I have not thought carefully about that yet, but I do know that Sidony and I cannot easily rescue her ourselves. Mayhap it is a sign from heaven that my father and the others will be in Edinburgh. If the villains really do take Adela there, or even somewhere in the vicinity, and if we can find out exactly where they take her, I'm sure we can get help quickly."

Bess shook her head. "'Tis plain daft, but I ken fine that ye mean to go, and ye'll ha' to keep safe. So ye'd best take along someone wi' a good head on his shoulders, who'll no let ye make fools o' yourselves or do summat crazy dangerous."

"We just need a stout lad who can look after our horses. Oh," Sorcha added with a start. "We'll also need horses!"

"Ye'll need more than horses," Bess said. "If the lady Adela's abductors left Glenelg Saturday and reached Kinlocheil yesterday, they're already more than two days ahead o' ye. Sithee, Kinlocheil lies well south o' here near Glen Finnan. To get so far, they must ha' taken a boat from Glenelg to Ardnish or Loch Ailort."

"Then, we'll need a boat, too, will we not?" Sorcha said. "Can we get one?"

"Aye, and I'm thinking now that whichever track they take afterward, they do ha' to go through the Great Glen," Bess said. "If they've ridden through Kinlocheil, they'll come to it a dozen miles or so north o' the Narrows and Loch Linnhe."

"But ye dinna go that way, Mam," Una said. "Ye always stay at Shielfoot."

"Aye," Bess agreed, falling thoughtfully silent.

Una laughed and said, "Ye did think o' many things, m'lady, but it be plain ye've no thought o' everything. Where will ye sleep nights, and what will ye eat?"

"Faith, there must be friaries or nunneries along the way, or even a monastery that will take in travelers," Sorcha said.

"Ye canna stay in a nunnery in men's clothes," Bess pointed out. "And most o' them other places put women in one great room and men in another. I saw as much whenever I traveled wi' your lady mother. So ye canna stay wi' them neither."

Sorcha muttered, "Then we'll sleep on the ground and eat roots and berries."

"We'll do no such thing!" Sidony exclaimed.

Dryly, Bess said, "It would be gey wiser to stay wi' kinsmen, as we do."

"But we don't know any kinsmen between here and the Great Glen who would not instantly restore us to Father," Sorcha protested.

"I were thinking o' Ranulf's kinsmen, and me own," Bess said. "If ye was to take our Rory as your gillie and boatman, he could see to all that for ye."

"Aye, that be a good notion," Una said. "Our Rory has a head, he does, and he's been to the Great Glen twice, m'lady. He'll keep ye safe."

Sorcha remembered Rory MacIver only as a lad who had teased her, with small respect for her rank, but she was not about to cast obstructions in her own path, so she said, "Very well, but we must leave today, Bess, as soon as possible. I want to get as far as Kinlocheil, so we can learn where they went from there."

"Well, ye can do that an ye will," Bess said. "But if ye go by way o' Loch Sunart and Glen Tarbert, ye can stay wi' me brother at Shielfoot and save more than a day's travel. The distance from here to Shielfoot be nearly the same as to Loch Ailort, but the distance to the Great Glen from Shielfoot be miles less."

"Then why did Adela's abductors not go that way?"

"Likely they didna ken the difference. Few who dinna live here do."

Sidony said, "But what about Lady Gowrie, Sorcha? Need we not follow the same route they did to find her and ask her to tell us everything she heard?"

"I'll wager I heard all she knows," Sorcha said. "She said a cousin told her. If he'd told her more, I'm sure she'd have repeated it to her friend. In any event, the way news flies around the Highlands, others are bound to know of them. We'll do as Bess suggests," she decided. "We'll need clothes, though, Bess, and quickly."

Bess agreed, and to Sorcha's surprise, Rory MacIver, now a strapping young man of twenty-two with dark curls, brawny shoulders, and a cheerful smile, seemed as eager as she was to find Adela. It was he who provided their clothing, taking note of their sizes and deciding exactly who might most likely both have and be willing to lend the required garments. The resulting clothing was tattered but clean, and Sidony regarded her share of it bleakly. But Sorcha received her brown leggings, long saffron shirt, quilted jerkin, stout boots, and hooded wool cloak with approval.

"I've thought of something else we need, though," she said. "My sister Isobel always carried a small dirk in a sheath under her skirt. Can you find us each some such thing to put in our boots?"

"Aye, mistress, I warrant I could," he said doubtfully.

Sidony said, "Oh, Sorcha, do you think we should? I doubt I could use a dirk. I do not even know how to wield one. Mightn't I injure someone with one?"

Sorcha regarded her sister speculatively before she said with a rueful smile, "It occurs to me that by the time you made up your mind to use it, it would be too late to do any good. Just one will do, Rory."

While Rory went to find her a weapon, Bess cut their hair, and while they donned their borrowed clothing, she packed a large supper to take and bundled their own clothing to carry with them in case they should need it. She tried to persuade them to stay at least overnight, but knowing that they had little time before Macleod learned what they had done, Sorcha insisted they leave as soon as possible.

To her amazement, when they were ready, Rory took them back to the beach, where a longboat waited, its bow on the shingle, with oarsmen ready to launch it.

"'Tis me brother's," Rory said. "He's a captain for Lord Ranald, but he's off wi' another o' his lordship's boats to Ardtornish to join the grand flotilla for his grace's journey to Edinburgh. His men here must keep fit themselves, though, and they've agreed that a fast trip to Shielfoot and back will do them good."

Thus, less than an hour after their arrival, Sorcha and Sidony departed. The oarsmen were powerful, the wind at their backs, and the boat relatively light. Three hours later, they landed. Before they sought Bess's brother, Sorcha asked Rory if they could not acquire horses at once and keep going for at least a few more miles.

"We'll no want horses yet, for tomorrow we'll walk across yon ridge south o' here to Loch Sunart," he said. "I ha' a cousin there wi' a boat, who'll take us to Strontian, at the head o' the loch. If the wind be as strong as today, we'll save more time by water and we can get horses from me cousin if the wind turns contrarisome."

Impatient though she was, Sorcha saw nothing to do but agree, especially since Sidony looked exhausted.

~

The party traveling to Lochbuie, on the south end of the Isle of Mull, arrived well after darkness had fallen, as Hugo had anticipated. But the castle servants had kept watch for them and had a hot supper waiting when they entered the great hall.

Everyone seemed tired, Macleod especially.

Hugo, sitting next to him at the high table, believed he was having second thoughts about his refusal to search for his missing daughter. To raise that subject might prove both tactless and unwise, but remembering his conversation with Hector, Hugo decided he had good reason to speak of something else.

He waited until Macleod had a goblet of Hector's excellent claret in hand. Then he said quietly, "I owe you an apology, sir."

"Do ye now, lad?"

"Aye, sir. The lady Sorcha was right to take me to task for my failure to reply to her message."

"Bless me, the baggage ought never to ha' sent ye any message."

Hugo agreed but said, "As she did, however, simple chivalry demanded a reply from any man claiming knighthood, and I failed to send one. Had I let her know—or you, sir—that I was fully engaged in his grace's installation preparations, mayhap the lady Adela would be safely wed now and at home with her husband."

"Ye're being gey courteous, lad, and I thank ye," Macleod said. "What others must think o' a Councilor o' the Isles who couldna protect his own daughter on her wedding day, I dinna want to think."

"Sakes, sir, you had no cause to expect trouble. The Highlands are at peace, as is all of Scotland—saving the Borders, of course, where peace is naught but a myth. No man could blame you for what happened."

"Aye, well, I canna even think where to look for the lass."

"What of Lady Gowrie?" Hector asked then. "Did she not perhaps see her?"

"Nay, for her ladyship had that tale from some cousin or other," Sorcha said. "Moreover, she's nobbut a foolish woman, so I doubt there be anything in it. We'd be days behind them now anyway, ye ken. They could ha' gone anywhere."

"They could," Hector agreed, for that was certainly true.

"'Tis plain to me now," Macleod added gloomily, "that a cautious man must beware for a sennight either side o' any Friday falling on the thirteenth. When I think that Ardelve wanted his wedding on that bleak day itself, I shudder to think what grief could ha' come of it."

Hugo's attention sharpened. "Do you believe that one should be wary of Fridays that fall on the thirteenth of any month?"

"Aye, sure, any man o' sense believes that," Macleod said firmly.

"Indeed," Hugo said. "And why is that, do you think? To most folks' minds, a Friday is just a Friday and as good as any other day."

Macleod shrugged. "There be good reason behind it, lad, and I'm no a man to go against superstition. For such to gain acceptance means it ha' proven itself many times over."

"Or perhaps that it relates to some event so significant that none can ever forget it, which leads men to fear anything having a connection to it."

"Aye, perhaps," Macleod agreed, looking narrowly at him.

"May I pour you more claret, sir?" Hugo asked quietly.

"Aye, ye may, lad, ye may indeed."

~

At dusk, his lordship had called a halt to make camp in a steep-sided, heavily wooded glen a half mile past four or five thatched huts and crofts in a loosely formed group that Highlanders called a clachan. Despite the steep, encroaching walls of the glen, he had avoided riding near or through their midst, as he had made it his habit to do with any habitation they could skirt. But Adela knew the alert ways of such folk and believed that someone must have seen them.

Darkness had fallen by the time the cook fires were ready, and after she had eaten a hasty meal, she approached his lordship and said quietly, "I would retire, my lord, but first I would beg leave for a few minutes of privacy, if I may."

As usual, her stomach clenched at having to ask his permission as much as at the fear that he might refuse it.

"Aye, lass, you may, although the moon will not rise for another hour. Can you see your way?"

Thinking only of getting away, she said she could, drew a deep breath, and hurried toward the area they had set aside for the purpose. As she neared it, one of the newer men stepped from behind a tree to bar her way.

"Dinna fear me, lass," he said quietly. "I hoped ye'd come by."

When she stepped back, he grasped her right arm and murmured near her ear, "Come now, give me a wee kiss, and mayhap I'll do summat useful for ye later."

As she jerked her arm away, astonished at such familiar treatment, a fist shot from nearby black shadows, knocking him flat.

Her captor stood over him and said to someone in the darkness behind him whom Adela could not see, "Throw a rope over a limb and hang this fool."

"Faith, sir," she exclaimed. "Is it not enough to have knocked him senseless? He was not going to harm me."

"I am not punishing him to protect you," he coldly. "I'm hanging him because I told eve that unless I command otherwise, they are to treat you with respect. He disobeyed me. See that you do not."

He walked away as silently as he had come, but Adela stood trembling in the darkness long afterward.

~

Roiling black clouds engulfed the sky, and lightning flashed through them in jagged spears. All else was black and formless, as if hell had engulfed the earth and heavens, and all that dwelt upon and within them.

Faint music sounded. Until that moment he had failed to realize that no thunder accompanied the lightning, but now he heard a harp or perhaps tinkling bells. Then, before his astonished gaze, the clouds parted, speared through by a narrow, circular beam of golden light. It began slowly to lengthen, then widen as if a single, solid ray of sunlight had broken through the clouds.

Doubtless only the sea existed below, for only the sea could look so black at such a time, but he thought it odd that the golden light seemed not to touch the water or reflect from it. The beam grew longer, the circle wider, and golden steps formed. At the top of them, a figure appeared, dark and menacing.

An icy chill made him shiver as he watched the figure descend the steps. Something familiar about its move- *its very shape—broad-shouldered and powerful-* *made him watch more intently.*

steps began to radiate light until at last he *where the water below touched tumul-* *bove. The steps appeared to end at* the water, although water and clouds seemed endless. He saw nothing that resembled dry land anywhere.

The eerie, tinkling music stopped when the figure reached the bottom of the steps, but the figure kept walking toward him as if it mattered not what the surface was that it walked upon. He had no sense of himself now other than as a pair of eyes, watching. Even the chill had gone.

He had no sense of standing on anything, no sense of touching or smelling, hearing or tasting, only of seeing. He could not move, did not seem to have limbs or a body. He could only watch as the figure drew near and the golden light spread out over the rippled sea.

Then light touched the figure's face, and he experienced mild shock, the sort of feeling one gets when one half expects something to be so, hopes that it isn't, and finds that it is. He knew that face as well as his own, but the body it belonged to had no business to be walking anywhere, let alone on the water as it appeared to do now. It had, after all, drowned in the river North Esk eight months ago.

The figure's eyes met his, and a familiar, challenging smile touched its lips. Then it stepped aside to reveal the smaller figure of Lady Adela Macleod. Abruptly, he could hear the sea, taste the salty dampness of the air, and feel the chill again.

The light passed, abandoning the figure's face to darkness as a still-familiar voice broke the silence. "My vengeance has begun," it boomed thunderously. "Your lady belongs to me and will serve me until my need for her ends."

He tried to speak, to rail against such vengeance and tell Adela to have courage. But he had no power to speak *or move, and as his mind struggled to overcome the lack, the golden light faded to impenetrable darkness.*

⌒

Hugo awoke sitting stiffly upright in bed, briefly disoriented not only from the dream but from a familiar need to recall exactly where he had gone to sleep. A crackling spark drew his attention to glowing embers on the hearth. Memory swept back, and he remembered he was at Lochbuie Castle, a guest of Hector Reaganach.

Within moments, he had scrambled into enough clothing to hurry to the next chamber, where Michael and Isobel lay sleeping.

He had no worry about waking his cousin, knowing that the soft click of the latch and the opening door would do so without disturbing Isobel.

"What is it?" Michael murmured as Hugo stuck his head in.

"Come," Hugo replied in the same soft tone. Then he eased the door to again and waited the few moments it took Michael to pull on breeks and join him.

When he did, Hugo gestured toward his own chamber and Michael followed him without a word. Inside, with the door shut, Hugo said bluntly, "It's Waldron."

"What is?"

"He has Adela."

"By heaven, Hugo, if I didn't know you better, I'd . . ."

When he hesitated, Hugo said, "I know it sounds daft. He's got to be dead, or we'd have heard from him long before now. But I'm nonetheless sure of it."

"*Have* we heard from him?" Michael demanded as he

grabbed the poker and bent to stir the embers, nudging the liveliest ones together as he reached for a log.

Hugo hesitated. Then, with a sigh, he said, "Nay, but I had a dream, and he spoke so plainly that when I awoke, I knew it must be true."

Michael laid his log on the embers and blew gently, waiting for flames to begin licking it. Then he straightened and said, "Perhaps you'd better tell me more about this dream."

Moving to warm his hands, Hugo said, "You'll recall that he told Isobel he would seek vengeance against all who had stood in the way of—"

"Careful," Michael warned. "There may be unfriendly ears, even here. I do remember what he told Isobel, and I'll admit I'd not have been surprised to learn that he survived that fall. He was always like a cat, landing on his feet when one least expected it. But I find it nearly impossible to believe he could be alive and yet have waited eight long months to seek his revenge."

"Mayhap he decided to lie low until opportunity presented itself. And mayhap, Adela's wedding provided that opportunity."

"But how could he have learned where and when she would marry?"

"The same way you or I would," Hugo said. "He gathered all the information he could. Lady Sorcha sent messages to me at a number of places. What is more likely than that Waldron intercepted one?"

"Then Adela may not have been his sole target," Michael said grimly. "Waldron would want vengeance against you and me more than he could possibly want to hurt Adela, and he is not a chivalrous man."

"True," Hugo said. "He'd not think twice about using a woman for bait to catch us off our guard."

Michael nodded. "Only think what a coup it would have been for him to lie in wait for you to appear at that wedding, or beforehand, and wreak whatever vengeance he had planned for you before the entire wedding party."

Another thought struck Hugo. "What if he sought more than that? Most folks would have expected you and Isobel to attend that wedding, would they not?"

"Aye, they would," Michael agreed. "Few outside the family know of her condition. No enemy could know that despite her insistence on how hearty she is, I persuaded her to consider the health and well-being of my heir. She travels nowhere without me. She yearned to attend that wedding, as you know well, but Henry had promised Ranald that the house of Sinclair would support Donald, so we could not."

"Aye, I do know that, to my own cost," Hugo said.

"Did you want the lass so badly then? You should have told me."

The blunt question made Hugo hesitate. "She would make any man a fine wife," he said at last. "But I don't have the feelings for her that you have for Isobel. Sakes, I've never felt that way about any woman, and I doubt I ever shall. I don't have time, because I'm married to my duty to you and to protecting the—"

He glanced around, remembering Michael's warning. ". . . to other obligations that must come before one's family and other personal business. I'll admit that her abduction has hit me harder than I'd have thought such a thing could, though."

"So your feelings for her are stronger than you knew," Michael said.

"Aye, perhaps," Hugo admitted. "Her wretched sister has brought it home to me that I do bear some responsibility for what happened to her. Moreover, if the poor lass fell into Waldron's clutches, she did so through no fault of her own and now faces more than unhappiness. Our cousin is capable of any evil, so if he does have her, I'm honor bound to do all I can to help her."

"Agreed," Michael said. "I've already told Macleod that we'll do all we can to help, but we've also decided that we'll do best to await news of their whereabouts from Lachlan Lubanach's sources before going in search of them."

"But we are constrained by matters of time, too," Hugo pointed out. "The King of Scots and his court move to Edinburgh in a sennight, and you've pledged us all to accompany Donald when he swears fealty as Lord of the Isles. And, too," he added quietly, "we have our own council at Roslin the following night."

"Aye, but if what the lady Sorcha told her father proves true, the villains will be in or near Edinburgh by then," Michael reminded him. "Indeed, if Waldron proves to be their leader, he may have the effrontery to take the lass to Edgelaw. For all we know, he has been living there these eight months past. It is his home, after all, and we do know he still has henchmen there. Without proof of his death, we did not order them off, and they have paid his rents. However, you have every authority to look around there when we return, and to ask if they've found his body yet."

"Aye, sure, but with your leave, I want to track down Lady Adela's abductors, whoever they are, and bring them to justice," Hugo said. "If Waldron and his men are guilty, I'll have served both you and her ladyship well."

"Do you remember any more details of this dream you had?"

"As clearly as I'd remember anything else that happened less than an hour ago," Hugo said. He recounted the dream as if he were reliving it.

"It struck you hard," Michael said when he had finished. "I know some think dreams can foretell events, but I'm guessing that one just put a few facts together to suggest a possibility that we cannot ignore. The vision you had of the sunbeam and stairs seems no more than a plaguey reminder that Waldron claims to be the hand of God, rather than the villain we know him to be. What do you want to do?"

"I'm not sure," Hugo admitted. "The lady Sorcha wanted Macleod to talk to Lady Gowrie to see if she knows more, but Macleod says she is a fool repeating information she had from a cousin. He says there's nothing in it."

"We cannot discount that opinion," Michael said. "She is friendly with the widow he means to marry, so he must know enough to form such a judgment."

"Aye, but he is also an exceedingly superstitious man who may just believe in letting well enough alone," Hugo said.

"Superstitious, eh? I've heard that, too. If I recall correctly, Hector Reaganach has the man's superstitious nature to thank for his own marriage to the lady Cristina. Do you think Macleod may be a fool?"

"Nay," Hugo said. Then, watching his cousin closely, he added, "Although he did object when Ardelve wanted to marry Adela on Friday last. Macleod insists that a Friday falling on the thirteenth of a month must always be unlucky."

Michael was silent for a long moment, frowning. Then his somber gaze met Hugo's as he said, "So Macleod will bear watching, too."

"Aye," Hugo said. "I'll leave that to you. I'm thinking now that even if Lady Gowrie might help, Lachlan Lubanach's minions will learn more in less time than it would take me to track her down. If the lady Adela's captors are making for Edinburgh or Edgelaw from the Highlands, I'd be wiser to take a score of our men and a boat to Oban, and take horses from there to intercept them."

"Aye, then we'll wait to hear from Lachlan," Michael agreed.

Chapter 6

Having spent the night on straw pallets in the cozy cottage belonging to Bess MacIver's brother, Sorcha and Sidony were up with the dawn's light. Wolfing a hasty repast of oatcakes, bramble jam, and mugs of warm milk provided by Bess's cheerful sister-in-law, they set out on foot with Rory for Loch Sunart.

"'Tis but a mile," he said. "Up yonder ridge and down again."

The ridge proved steep and wearing. As they approached the shore of the flat, calm loch an hour later, Sidony said, "'Tis easier walking in these clothes, but do you still think they make us safer? In truth, I don't think we can fool anyone for long."

"I don't mean to *try* to fool anyone up close," Sorcha said, well aware that it would be foolhardy to do so. "Rory must ask our questions for us. We'll keep our hoods up, our heads down, and our mouths shut, Siddy. If anyone asks why we behave so, he can say we are shy or stupid." Shooting a glance at the generally stoic gillie, she noted a twitching lip. "What's so funny?" she demanded.

"Nowt, m'lady," Rory said, his eyes twinkling.

"Tell me," she demanded.

"Well, I've no seen ye since we was bairns, mind ye, but I'm thinking that if I was daft enough t' call ye stupid, ye'd hand me me head in me lap and never spare a thought t' whether anyone did see ye do it."

Sorcha chuckled. "Aye, sure, you may be right. I've a bit of a temper."

"Ye'd a fierce one then, and ye still do. Or so I ha' heard."

"Faith, what else have you heard?"

"Nobbut that ye slapped a nobleman hard enough t' leave the mark o' your hand on his face most o' yester-morn," Rory replied. "Ye ken fine how quick gossip gets about, m'lady, and we did hear that ye had a sizeable audience then."

"And doubtless everyone who saw what happened feels obliged to chatter about it," Sorcha said. "But he deserved it."

"Aye, sure," Rory agreed amiably, adding, "There be me cousin's cottage yonder, so we'd best think on what ye want me to say to him. I ken fine we'll need horses, since we've nae wind and willna want to row me cousin's fishing coble all the way to Strontian. But will ye keep silent, or shall I tell him who ye be?"

In the event, he had only to ask for ponies, and the elderly cousin assured him he had three stout ones they could take. More to the point, in Sorcha's opinion, when Rory asked if he had heard of strangers in the glens, the man scratched his grizzled head and said, "Aye, then, our cousin Ian were by yestereve. He did say he'd seen some Sunday near Kinlocheil. Said they was a mean-looking bunch, too, for all they dressed fine and carried fine weapons. The lass wi' them were quiet enough, Ian said, but he'd nae trust the others." He glanced at Sorcha and Sidony, but when both remained mute, he politely refrained from addressing them directly.

"Did Ian chance to hear the men say aught o' their business?" Rory asked as they all headed to the byre to saddle the horses.

"Sakes, lad, they didna confide such stuff t' the likes o' Ian," the old man said. "Just said they was making for somewhere south o' Edinburgh—in Lothian, I think, but I canna say more than that. If ye're seeking them, I'd advise ye t' leave them be. Ian said they didna encourage conversation, but he says he can smell evil when he be in its presence. Said he thought the lass must be kin t' the leader, since she rode pillion wi' him. She didna open her mouth whilst they was there, he said."

Sorcha ground her teeth together to keep from saying what she thought of this Ian person, who could not tell an innocent victim of abduction from a villain's kinswoman. Surely, he must have seen that Adela was terrified out of her wits. What sort of man did nothing to help someone so obviously in need of help? But she could not ask such questions without revealing more about herself than she wanted to reveal, so she held her tongue, and they soon bade the old man good day.

Bess's sister-in-law in Shielfoot had packed food for them, but it occurred to Sorcha that it might be wise to get more if they could. Accordingly, she asked Rory if they might perhaps beg some from his kinsmen in Strontian when they got there.

"Aye, they'll spare a bit for us, I warrant," he said.

The cousin in Strontian proved generous but not without cost, as he had decided to take advantage of unseasonably dry weather to replace his roof. He and his wife had removed the old, soot-encrusted thatch, now piled beside the cottage, and they had new thatch nearly all in place. But they needed help carrying the old stuff to mix with the manure pile beside their byre to produce a nourishing mixture that they could spread on their fields.

"*If* the three o' ye lads dinna mind helping," he added with a minatory look.

Knowing no acceptable way to refuse, in view of the promised food and their own lack of means other than manual labor to repay his generosity any time soon, for the next hour and more, the three hauled thatch reeking of damp soot and mold and helped mix it with manure. Since the man and his wife worked beside them, Sorcha could not even express her feelings about the repellent task, but she was able to congratulate herself on her foresight later when the track they followed proved to be nearly barren of habitation. They rode until Sidony fell asleep on her horse.

It was midafternoon by then, so Sorcha called for a respite and sent Rory to fill a jug with water from a nearby burn. Sidony dismounted, still half asleep.

"My gloves are ruined, I reek of manure, my hands ache from carrying that horrid thatch, and we've not seen a soul since we left Strontian," she grumbled.

"Your hands will recover, we've plenty of food, and we washed as much off ourselves and our clothes as we could in the first burn we came to," Sorcha pointed out. "This part of the Highlands is just as rugged as Glenelg, so there are few farms or clachans, and thus few people to meet. But at least we can be sure that the men we follow have not taken another track."

"Nay, for there have been no other tracks," Sidony said with a long-suffering sigh. "The fact is that I did not know we would have to act as common laborers. Nor did I consider how much riding we would have to do in this pursuit of yours."

"Then you simply did not think," Sorcha retorted. "I did not bargain for the labor either, but how ever did you think we could follow them to Edinburgh without long hours of riding? It is days from home, Siddy, and although we got a good start by beginning at Glenancross instead of Glenelg, Edinburgh is still a very long way."

"I know," Sidony said. "But I did not know how tired I'd be. And what would we do if we caught up with them? You could hardly ride back to Strontian for help." She sighed. "I'm thinking that neither of us thought this through before we started."

"We are doing what we must," Sorcha said firmly. "When the time comes, we will know what we must do then, too. You'll see."

Sidony sighed again but made no further protest, and when Rory returned with the water, she ate the food Sorcha handed her, and afterward assured them both that she felt better. Even so, the day seemed to lengthen as they rode until even Sorcha began to wish something interesting would happen.

An hour later, not long after they entered the Great Glen, they met a man and his dog herding six shaggy brown-and-white Highland cows across the track. Sorcha made Rory ask him if he had seen a group of horsemen with a woman, but the man shook his head, said, "Nay, lad, nary a soul since I left home this morning."

That evening, finding no MacIver kinsmen in the area to which they had come, they sought shelter with a hospitable crofter and slept in clean straw in the byre that occupied one end of his croft. The family end was thick wattle and daub, flexible hazel rods woven together and daubed with a mixture of clay, heather, and straw. But the byre for the animals was no more than a woven hazel framework with no further insulation against the nighttime chill of early spring.

Rory, who had remained cheerfully uncritical, objected to the arrangement with more vigor than Sorcha had expected.

Clearly trying to keep his voice from carrying to the family end of the croft, he muttered, "'Tisna fittin' ye should sleep in straw wi' the beasts, m'lady, or that I should sleep in the same wee byre wi' ye. Me mam would throw up her hands and give us both the rough side o' her tongue for such doings."

"Hush now, for we can scarcely ask the crofter to let us sleep with his family," Sorcha said. "He thinks we are three lads."

"I ken that fine," Rory said. "But I ken, too, that I ha' nae business t' be sleeping wi' ye. Can ye tell me the laird your father would ha' nae objection to it?"

"I cannot say that," Sorcha said. "But I know that he would not look kindly upon your abandoning us here, either."

"I've nae intention o' doing such a cowardly thing," he

said with grave dignity. "I'll just stir up a pile o' that straw and sleep on the other side of it."

"Thank you, Rory," Sorcha said more graciously. "If anyone remarks upon the arrangement, be sure that I will accept all the blame. We are most grateful for your protection. I'll not let you suffer for having provided it."

When he said no more, merely arranging his nest to his own satisfaction while she helped Sidony settle in for the night, Sorcha began to think she was turning into an excellent manager. She would find Adela, rescue her, and show others—unspecified—just how such things ought to be done.

Once again, Adela had no idea where she was. They had been following much the same narrow track since disembarking from the longboat, but the territory was wholly unfamiliar to her. Whenever they neared a cottage, croft, or clachan, they rode well off the track and skirted it, taking care to keep out of sight, so the only people she had seen for the past three days had been at a considerable distance.

In some ways, her fears had increased. In others, they had eased, for her captor seemed more at ease with her now. Although he was still often brusque or uncivil, he had not spoken again of cutting off her head. Instead, he occasionally invited her to ask questions and then, half the time, refused to answer them. It was as if he teased her on purpose, so she would never know what to expect.

Since he allowed her to speak to no one else and had kept her separate from everyone else after hanging his henchman, she found herself eager to converse with him whenever he was willing. She told herself that talking could only put him more at ease with her and reduce the likelihood that he would kill her.

At least, she hoped so.

She still missed having her own horse, but at least riding pillion provided opportunities to talk to him. That very afternoon, when she had asked him to explain more clearly what he was doing for the Roman Kirk, he answered readily, "The Sinclairs, and others, have stolen something from the Kirk that must be returned. His Holiness, the Pope, expects me to find it and see it safely to the Vatican."

"Mercy, sir," she exclaimed softly. "What manner of thing is it?"

"That is not for you to know," he said. "You need know only that I'll not rest until I find it. I am a soldier of Christ—a hand of God, if you will. So I will do whatever I must to reclaim that which was lost through trickery and wicked deceit."

He seemed so confident, so certain of the rightness of what he did, that she was beginning to think he was not an evil man at all but merely a dedicated one. While she found it hard to imagine that Sir Michael Sinclair, Prince Henry, or even Sir Hugo would do anything so wicked as to steal from the Holy Kirk, she understood that his lordship sincerely believed that they had.

She knew he told her only what he wanted her to know, and that Sir Hugo and others would likely produce equally strong arguments in opposition. Since neither they nor any others who dared disagree with him were at hand, she could not know what those arguments were.

But if what he said was true, then perhaps his position was just, even if abducting her was not.

As the afternoon neared evening, they approached a clachan of four cottages but left the track as soon as the clachan came into sight. Riding well around it and deep into a nearby wood, they came to a clearing suitable for making camp.

His lordship's tent was soon up, and the cook fires lighted. Half an hour later, delicious smells of rabbit stew and roasting venison filled the air.

Adela realized she was famished. Even so, as had become her habit, she watched his lordship carefully, trying to judge his mood as he strode about the campsite, giving orders to his men. So far, he had made no move to have his way with her, but if he intended to teach her a woman's proper place, doubtless he would do so, and she still had not the slightest notion how she could prevent it.

He glanced at her from time to time and glanced, too, at the men as they tended their chores. Not one cast an eye in her direction. They had learned the lesson he'd meant to teach with the hanging, as had she. Just thinking about it knotted her stomach. Still, when he gestured to her, she went to sit beside him on a log, accepted the wooden trencher piled high with stew, and took the spoon he gave her. Although she dipped it into her stew, she did not think she could eat.

"We'll retire early, I think," he said casually as he settled himself and dug into his own food.

His words stopped the breath in her throat and the motion of her spoon halfway to her mouth.

Each of the past two nights he had hinted that he would sleep in his own bed, but each night he had sent her to the bed of furs alone and slept elsewhere. Once again she tried to think how she could stop him if he had decided the fateful night had come. Then a new, more frightening thought struck. What if her refusal was all that he sought as his excuse to lop off her head and send it home to Glenelg? Or worse, what if her body did not satisfy him and he killed her because of that?

Although she had wanted nothing more than to leave the onerous duties that had fallen to her at Chalamine since Cristina's marriage, and had been prepared to marry Ardelve because marriage to him would ease that load, she wished now with all her heart that she could magically whisk herself home again.

Since she could not, she forced herself to eat and went with him without objection when he had finished his supper. He showed her first to the privy area in the woods, and then escorted her to the burn from which they had taken their camp water, so she could wash her hands and face and clean her teeth. He did not speak as she tended her needs, but afterward he followed her into the tent, which he had not done since the first time she had found herself there.

Drawing breath, she faced him and said, "If you intend to ravish me, my lord, I wish you would say so and tell me what you want me to do."

"Nay, lass, for now I want only to talk with you. I find it helps me think, because you are the quietest woman I've ever met, and a good listener."

It was the first compliment he had paid her, and to her astonishment, she felt herself warming as if he had caressed her. Or, suggested a voice in the back of her mind sternly, as if she were a bitch that had been several times kicked and yet went running to lick its master's hand the moment it saw him.

Steeling herself, she said with forced calm, "If you do mean to ravish me, I wish you will get it over with. It is needlessly cruel to keep me guessing like this."

"Mayhap it pleases me to keep you guessing," he said, pulling up a small cushion for himself and gesturing for her to sit on the pallet of furs.

So lightly had he spoken, and so nearly did the words match her thoughts about his behavior, that she almost made a spirited retort. But something in his expression stopped her. Reminding herself that her emotions and instincts had become sadly untrustworthy, she seated herself on the bed instead, tucking the skirt of her once-new wedding dress neatly around her.

He regarded her for a moment, then said, "I have no intention of forcing you to couple with me. Indeed, I feel no lust for you, nor should I."

"You don't?" Realizing how that must have sounded, she added hastily, "I mean, you don't intend to compel me?"

"Nay, for God has made it plain that I must not."

"I thought you said He would forgive you anything you do in His name."

"Aye, well, I expect that means anything I believe is necessary to accomplish the task He has set me," he said. "He made it clear, however, that 'ravishing,' as you call it, is neither necessary nor acceptable to Him."

"Mercy, how did He do that?"

"He let your sister Isobel push me off the ramparts of Roslin Castle."

"Isobel!"

"Aye, did she not tell you?"

Adela shook her head. "Such a thing seems most unlike her. I cannot imagine how someone so much smaller could have done that to you."

He grimaced. "For once, you did not listen. I admit I provoked her, but she could not have done it had God not lent her the strength."

"You attempted to ravish her?"

"I threatened to, to force her to tell me about things I thought she knew."

His expression warned her not to ask about those things.

"I did want her, though," he said. "I'll not deny it, since God kens the truth, and that wanting was my error. Fear is an excellent weapon, as He kens fine, and a wench as seductive as Lady Isobel would tempt the strongest will. But sithee, I vowed to sacrifice all worldly pleasure to serve His needs, and thus swore chastity. So whilst the threat might have proven useful, I risked breaking my vow."

"But if Isobel did that to you, why abduct me? I'd expect you to seek your vengeance against her. Not that I want you to do that, of course. Vengeance should be left to God."

"I am His arm," he said. "As to why I took you, you are dear to her, and in truth, your wedding afforded me an opportunity to set my plans into motion."

"And you learned of it through my sister Sorcha's messages to Sir Hugo."

"Aye, your younger sister is an impulsive, headstrong lass. I'm glad you show better sense."

"I still do not understand why you took me."

"To draw the others in, of course. Michael and Henry Sinclair, and your Hugo, have all annoyed me, and they must all suffer the consequences. And do not think that I have forgotten Isobel."

"She is eight months with child!" Adela exclaimed.

He shrugged. "You will know what to do," he said.

"What do you mean?"

"When the child comes, of course."

"Then you do mean to let me go," she said with nearly overwhelming relief.

"Nay, why would I? I'll bring Isobel to you."

Hugo, feeling no less impatience after making his decision, had left for Duart Castle soon after dawn Tuesday morning to do his waiting for news of the abductors with Lachlan himself. Discovering upon his arrival that the High Admiral already had received pertinent information, the bulk of which indicated that the abductors were indeed making for Edinburgh, Hugo revealed his intent to intercept them.

"I'll want to take at least a score of our men and leave from Oban," he said. "Will we find enough horses there to accommodate us?"

"Hector keeps his own in Oban, as do I," Lachlan said. "His grace's flotilla will sail to Glasgow, so what horses we have in Oban are yours if you need them."

Thanking him, Hugo took his leave, intending to depart from Lochbuie by dawn's light the next morning.

Although from one cause or another, he did not manage to get away so early Wednesday, he was on the point of leaving after enjoying a solitary breakfast, when a guard from the ramparts reported that one of Macleod's boats had returned.

"Should we rouse the master, sir?"

"Nay, for the Laird of Glenelg is expecting his boats, although I do not think he expected them until tonight. I'm going down to the wharf anyway. If they have need of Hector Reaganach or Macleod, I'll see to it."

To his astonishment, Macleod's chief helmsman met him halfway and insisted on waking Macleod, who was, as far as Hugo knew, still abed. The man's distress was so great that he walked back with him to hear what news he had brought.

"It is not about Lady Adela, is it?" he demanded of the man as they went.

"Nay, sir," the man replied. "I only wish it were good news I bring."

"Then what?" Hugo demanded as they entered the hall to see Macleod striding into the chamber from the other side.

Clearly, he had been awake and had learned for himself that his boats had come early, for he greeted his man with a blustery demand to know what was amiss.

"It be the lady Sorcha, laird," the unhappy helmsman told him. "She took sick on the way to Glenelg Monday afternoon, so we put ashore at Glenancross, meaning for Bess MacIver to look after her."

"Indeed," Macleod said, apparently reserving judgment about such an arrangement. "Bess would ken fine what to do for her—if the lass really was sick."

"Aye, and so I thought," the helmsman said, looking miserable. "The lady Sorcha did say we ought to go on to

Glenelg without her, there being nae good place nearby to provide for so many men. I didna like it, so I said I'd come right back wi' one boat to be sure all were well wi' her. Which I did, laird, only to learn that she and the lady Sidony had left Glenancross soon after they got there."

"A pox on the wicked lass! Gone where?"

"I dinna ken, laird. I came straight on here to tell ye they'd gone. The winds failed us, or I'd ha' been here yestereve." He hesitated, then added bravely, "Bess MacIver did say they was wearing lads' clothing, and they took Colin MacIver's boat, laird, to Shielfoot. Bess said that when she saw her ladyship had got her mind made up in her old way, she knew there'd be nae stopping her."

"Bless me, she should ha' tied her to a bedpost," Macleod declared angrily.

"Likely, they dinna ha' bedposts in yon cottage, laird, nor do I think Bess could hold her ladyship long enough to tie her to anything. She's a temper on her, her ladyship does. Bess did say, though, that she'd persuaded them to take her Rory wi' them, and he's a lad wi' a good head, that one. He'll look after them."

Hugo grimaced and exchanged a look with Michael.

Macleod said, "If they went by way o' Shielfoot, 'tis because the wicked lass believes the men who took Adela be making for the Great Glen and Edinburgh." He looked bleakly at Hugo. "I'm told ye mean to look for Adela yourself."

"I'm leaving straightaway for Oban, sir, with a score of men. I'll find them."

"I'd be that grateful to ye," Macleod said. "Take a good stout strap wi' ye."

Hugo nearly said he would not need a strap but instead

just assured the older man that he would find his daughters and do his best to bring them all back safely.

Taking leave of the others and walking with Michael to the harbor, Hugo said irritably, "That lass needs a firmer hand. Just what do you suppose she thinks she can accomplish, riding about like a heathen, not to mention subjecting her younger sister to such a dangerous enterprise. I'd wager all I own that it would never have entered the lady Sidony's head to do such a thing."

"Nay," Michael said. "Isobel told me it is always Sorcha who leads and Sidony who follows. But she said, too, that although Sorcha often landed them in the suds, she always got them out again." He grinned. "I doubt the lass is as intrepid as my lady, but at this point I'm just hoping she isn't as curious. I swear, in the same situation, Isobel would follow Waldron to his lair just to see what it looks like."

"And I wager that you'd just tell her to mind her head," Hugo said dryly. "I've yet to see you shorten rein when she takes the bit between her teeth."

Michael smiled. "You won't see it, either. I don't do so when others are about, nor do I need to do so often. She's a sensible woman, my Isobel."

"Well, her wretched sister is not," Hugo said grimly. "When I find her, I'll send her right back to her father, most likely with a sore backside—at least, I will if she hasn't run into Waldron before I can catch her. If he has her, I'll have three to rescue instead of one. And, believe me, if I have to do that, I'll make her even sorrier for putting me to the trouble."

Laughing, Michael said, "Aye, well, I wish you joy, cousin. But my experience with Macleod sisters is that they are not as predictable as one might hope. Take care that she does not end up having to rescue you."

"She won't," Hugo said. "Nor should I have to rescue her, come to that. Just tracking her down will considerably delay my efforts to rescue Adela, though."

"Aye, but pray recall that you're tracking Sidony, too, not just Sorcha," Michael said, still grinning. "I doubt you'll have any trouble finding them, either, because by now, if everyone in the area is not talking about the abductors and Adela, they will certainly be gossiping about the two pretty lads who are following them."

Hugo groaned.

When Sorcha saw darkening clouds in the west late Wednesday afternoon, she cast a measuring glance at Sidony, knowing well that her sister had bargained even less for bad weather than for carrying thatch or long hours of riding.

Sorcha was certain they still followed Adela and her abductors, because they had passed only local tracks that seemed to lead to farms and tiny clachans. She thought the riders must still be two days ahead, perhaps more if they had means to change horses and could thus ride faster than she and her companions could.

Therefore, it was with mixed feelings of surprise, relief, and dismay that she discovered when they came to a clachan of four cottages an hour later that a group of some twenty riders had made camp the night before in a nearby forest clearing.

The elderly, rather deaf man who relayed that information admitted in answer to Rory's shouted questions that he had not seen any of them himself, but assured them that one of the lads had caught a glimpse of a large tent and well-accoutered men striding about the site. No mention was made of a woman, he said, but Sorcha was sure by then that no other men of such description were in the area.

That the group really had enlarged so much was daunting, but she could not be surprised that someone daring enough to steal a bride from her wedding might have a large force at his command. The surprise was that she, Sidony, and Rory were catching up despite traveling at a speed dictated by having only the three horses Rory's cousin had provided and no means to hire more.

They could no longer ignore the piling black clouds, some of which started spitting at them as Sorcha was saying in a voice low enough that she hoped the old man would not hear that they must lose no time in pursuing the riders.

Sidony instantly protested. "You cannot mean to ride into the teeth of a storm without having the least notion where we can find shelter ahead. Where will we sleep? How will we build a fire to keep warm?"

"Don't fret," Sorcha said, casting a warning look in the old man's direction. "We'll build our own shelter, and I'm sure Rory knows how to make a fire in the woods even in the rain. Men do it all the time when they hunt or fish or go to war."

"But—"

"We'll be fine, Siddy. We don't want them to get too far ahead of us. Had I known they were so close, I'd have urged a faster pace."

Sidony cast a pleading look at Rory.

He was already shaking his head. "It won't answer, m'lady," he said to Sorcha. "A spring storm wi' clouds like them black ones yonder could fair drown all three o' us *and* the ponies. We'd do better to take shelter here."

The spitting turned to drizzle, and lightning crackled in the distance as Sorcha opened her mouth to protest. She shut it again, knowing that although Sidony was the most biddable of sisters, she was afraid of thunderstorms.

Highland rules of hospitality being what they were, the clachan's residents welcomed them as guests for the night. Indeed, so welcome were they that, despite thunder, lightning, and pelting rain, two large families who did not live there showed up at suppertime with baskets of food, resulting in an impromptu ceilidh.

With people crowded into the largest of the four cottages to sing, eat, drink, and tell bard's tales around its small central cook fire, Sorcha found it impossible to sustain her masculine guise. She was sure Sidony fooled no one, and a sudden silent hope leaped to her mind that word of what they were doing would never get back to her father or to any other unspecified person before they had rescued Adela.

No one was so impolite as to question them, however, and when the visiting families departed during a lull in the storm, and the rest of the company dispersed among the four cottages, she reassured herself that no one thought them anything but what they appeared to be. She was able to enjoy a good night's sleep on her pallet in a snug byre and to waken to a bright morning, the air smelling crisply clean and fresh after the rain. However, the sun was higher than she had expected.

Startled to realize that they had slept hours longer than she had intended, she hastily woke the other two, straightened her clothing, and went with Rory to collect their horses from the clachan's enclosure, leaving Sidony to see to her own needs and make sure that they left nothing behind.

After helping Rory saddle their mounts outside the byre, she went to find the housewife to request food to break their fast, only to stop short when she saw what looked to be at least twenty riders approaching the clachan, the last leading a string of six or seven extra horses and at least four sumpter ponies.

Even at that distance and with the bright morning sun glaring at her, she had no difficulty recognizing their leader as Sir Hugo Robison.

Chapter 7

Hugo saw Sorcha standing near the byre end of the largest of four crofts that made up the clachan. To his outrage, she wore a tattered cap, dusty brown leggings, a mid-thigh-length saffron shirt, a dirty padded-cloth jerkin, and common hide boots with the hair still on them. When he saw that she had not ended her perfidy there but had hacked off her lovely amber-golden hair to no more than chin length, a strong desire possessed him to swoop down on her in the same fashion that the villains had swooped down on the wedding party, and beat some sense into her.

At the same time, seeing her safe, he experienced profound relief.

Whether in reaction to the former feeling or the latter, he held up a hand in command to his men to draw rein, then rode on to confront her alone.

Noting the grim look on Sir Hugo's face as he approached her on the big black horse he rode, and realizing that he had recognized her despite her disguise, Sorcha felt sudden, unexpected alarm. At the same time, knowing she was close on the heels of the villains who had taken Adela, she was glad to see him and annoyed that he had brought so few men with him. Surely, he ought to have brought twice as many to be sure of defeating the villains and rescuing Adela.

She greeted him, glowering and arms akimbo. "Where are the rest of your men?" she demanded. "For that matter, where are my father and Hector?"

In response, he reined in and dismounted.

She had forgotten how tall he was, how broad his shoulders were, and how powerful he looked. He dropped the reins to the ground, evidently expecting the huge beast to stand quietly. Irritatingly, it did. And since she was as certain as she could be that it was not his horse but one he had hired in Oban or borrowed from Hector or the Admiral of the Isles, the sight stirred her temper again.

Then he put his hands on his hips, blatantly imitating her posture and making her feel smaller, which only increased her fury.

"Well?" she demanded. "Art mute, sir?"

His voice surprisingly quiet, since his expression warned her that an explosion must be imminent, he said, "I think you will prefer to have this conversation privately . . . my lady."

The last words being clearly an afterthought, his tone just short of taunting, she felt her temper straining to rip free. "I see no cause for privacy," she said.

"I think you will shortly change your mind about that."

She raised her chin. "Will I? Why should I?"

"Because you will not like being soundly thrashed in front of my men and the inhabitants of this clachan. By now, all of them are watching us."

A thrill of fear swept through her, because she believed he would do it, but that belief just fueled her temper. Still glowering, hoping he would believe that his threat did not intimidate her, she said with forced lightness, "Is that how you deal with adversity? You beat it into submission?"

"I do when the 'adversity' in question deserves beating," he replied.

"Well, you have no right to correct me or to beat me, so if you lay a hand on me, it will be naught but assault. That is still a crime in Scotland, I believe."

"Aye, it is, but only if your father agrees to call it a crime. Do you doubt that he gave me leave to punish you for what you have done?"

Unfortunately, she had no doubt that Macleod had told him to make her smart. But she held her head high, daring him to do it.

He met her angry gaze, and suddenly, to her even greater vexation, she thought she detected a twinkle in his eyes. Then, when they continued to twinkle, she felt her fury ease. She had forgotten what an unusual color his eyes were, that extraordinary cerulean blue that no mere male should possess. His lashes, too, were longer and darker than any man's had a right to be.

The twinkle faded, but his gaze continued to hold hers so intensely that when he spoke, the harsh sound of his voice startled her. "If you prefer, we can walk in yon woods to have our talk," he said. "I'd suggest, though, that you restrain your inclination to defy me, because I rarely react tolerantly to defiance."

Thinking it best to ignore that suggestion, since she had no intention of obeying it, she said, "My sister will return soon."

"When she does, my men will tell her that we'll be back shortly."

"I'd prefer to wait for her."

"Nay then, we're going to talk."

"She'll be frightened if she does not—"

Her words ended in a screech when he scooped her up, tossed her over his right shoulder, and began striding toward the woods with her. Raising her head, she saw his men watching, their expressions carefully blank. The villagers were not so tactful. She saw grins and realized ruefully that had not everyone already guessed she was female, her screeching had made them a gift of that fact.

Being so abruptly plopped facedown over Sir Hugo's shoulder had knocked most of the wind out of her, so it was a minute before she recovered wits and voice enough to order him to put her down.

When he ignored her, she pounded his back with both fists.

His answer was a hard smack on her backside that made her yelp again.

"Put me down, you beast," she cried. "By heaven, if you don't I'll—"

She broke off, grinding her teeth, unable to think of anything terrible enough that she could do to him. No one, man or woman, had ever treated her so—not since childhood, at all events—and she had no intention of allowing him to continue to think he could. On the other hand, she had no idea how to stop him.

Deciding she could not gain the upper hand or regain her breath as long as he loped along with her bouncing painfully on his shoulder, she held her tongue, hoping he would put her down when they were out of sight of the others.

When he did, setting her on her feet in the middle of the path, she drew a deep breath and said hastily, "Before you read me a lecture or do whatever you mean to do, you should know that those villains are just a day ahead of us. They camped near here night before last. Moreover, there are more than a score of them now. You'll need more men to defeat them."

"So now you are going to command me, are you?" His voice had acquired an edge that she had not heard before, one that raised the hair on her neck and made her want to put distance between them.

Before she could, his hands clamped tight to her shoulders, hands powerful enough to do with her as he would.

"I didn't mean to give orders," she said curtly to his chest. "I just meant . . ."

Again, words failed her. Feeling at a distinct disadvantage with her nose almost touching that broad chest, she looked up and discovered that, that close, to look him in the eye, she had to look up a good distance.

"What did you mean?" he asked, those blue eyes locking with hers again, their expression intense. Her emotions shifted suddenly from anger and undeniable trepidation to something else, something she had never felt before.

Giving himself a mental shake, Hugo silently cursed himself. To be standing thus with a lass—nay, with a lady born, despite the disreputable outfit—was as mad as her own behavior in dashing off to pursue her sister's abductors. If she deserved skelping for that, then by heaven, so did he for what he was feeling now.

She looked so small in her boy's clothing. Worse, the clothing did nothing to disguise her shapely legs and slender but well-rounded figure.

Nevertheless, he could not let her think she had bested him. Her misbehavior had been dangerous, his own merely thoughtless. He had a duty to see her safe, and that duty demanded that he show her the error of her ways at once.

When she tried again to step away from him, he allowed it but kept his expression stern. "I should put you over my knee," he told her. "But you need to ride a considerable distance yet, and for that, you must be able to sit."

"Aye, and we must go straightaway if we are to catch them."

"You are going back to your father," he said.

"If he wanted me, why did he not come after me himself?"

"Because he promised to join his grace's flotilla, and he must keep his word. Moreover, I told him I would come. I warrant he'll be pleased to see you, though, if only to punish you as you should be punished for what you have done."

"Well, you cannot send me anywhere," she snapped.

"Not only do you bear no authority to order my coming and going, but I have no intention of leaving Adela's safety in the hands of a man whose *duty* may demand that he abandon the search before he can rescue her. Moreover," she added, stepping back hastily when he reached for her again, "you need me and Sidony *both* if you are to preserve any appearance of decorum whilst we travel together."

"Decorum!" He burst into laughter. "*You* dare preach decorum to me? I should think the word would turn to ashes in your mouth. You should be soundly punished, my lass, not only for disobeying your father— Oh, aye, he told me he forbade you to follow your sister. Did you think he would not?"

"I paid that no heed," she declared rashly. "When no one else would go after her, I had to go. And if you are here because my father discovered I had gone, then I'm glad I did it. At least, now someone besides me is trying to find her."

"By heaven," he said, seizing her shoulders again and giving her a shake, "I don't care if you do have to ride all the way to Oban with a sore backside. I'm going to teach you respect for those with authority over you."

"But, you have no knowledge of Adela's condition!" she cried. "Even if those men have not harmed her—which I doubt—she will be terrified and hysterical after such an ordeal. You will need me and Sidony both to look after her!"

He hesitated, appalled at the image she had forced into his mind.

"Indeed, sir," she went on quickly, "if you and your men rescue her without us, and take her all the way home, you will just exacerbate the position that her abductors have put her in. She will certainly have to travel with you for more than a day. Sakes, your own honor, if you have any, would bind you to marry her."

"Don't impugn my honor," he said curtly. "I'd not be here had you not made me realize that I bear nearly as much responsibility for this mess as you do."

"I don't!"

"Aye, sure, you do. You know you had no right to involve yourself in your sister's affairs, let alone mine. And if her abductors did not learn of her wedding by intercepting one of your messages to me, I shall be very much surprised."

"Oh." Her eyes widened, so either she had not considered that possibility or had hoped it would not occur to him.

"Moreover," he went on relentlessly, "you bear sole responsibility for the fact that no one pursued them. Had you not told all of Glenelg that you expected me to stop the wedding, and that Adela hoped I would, every man who was there would have begged, borrowed, or stolen a horse to ride to her rescue."

She was silent before she said with a sigh, "You are right, sir. That was my fault. Do you really think my message is how they learned of the wedding?"

"Aye, and what's more, I think it suggested the plan they used."

After another thoughtful silence, she said, "If you accept responsibility for what happened, does that mean you will marry Adela when she is safe again?"

"My intention is to rescue her if she requires rescuing and return her to Chalamine, if necessary, or to your father at Edinburgh—where he should be by Monday next—if that course proves more practical, as I expect it will."

"But Ardelve's failure to search for her proves he has no intention now of marrying her. And after she has spent such a long time with so many men, one cannot blame him. If you will not marry her either, what is to become of her?"

"I have not said I will not," he said more gently. "I know that by having assumed any responsibility for the lady Adela, honor will demand that I offer her the protection of my name unless she refuses it. But she does retain that right, and I will not force myself upon her or allow your father, or you, to force her to accept me. That decision must be hers alone."

Clearly relieved, she said, "Adela is not a fool."

Hugo agreed. No sensible woman would be foolish enough to spurn such an offer, and the lady Adela was a sensible woman.

After another silence, which Sorcha showed no inclination to break, he said, "Since we are agreed that I am honor bound to offer her my protection, you must also agree now that it would be better and safer for you to return home."

She stiffened. "I will agree to no such thing, and I do not know how you think you can make me go. I slipped away from two boatloads of my father's men, after all. Do you imagine I cannot outwit the few you would spare to go with us? And how foolish is it to deplete your force to provide us an escort? Not to mention that whether honor binds you to Adela or not, you have said it must be for her to decide if she will accept you. Until she does, to be alone with you and your men will just add to the destruction of her reputation, will it not?"

He realized that further argument would be a waste of breath. Not only had she made several persuasive arguments, but he knew that if Waldron was collecting men as he went, he would need to acquire more himself before they met.

Another point occurred to him. Since following the abductors had proven easy enough for the two young ladies to manage it, he suspected their leader of using Adela to bait a trap. If that was the case, he did not want to ride into it, especially if Sorcha and Sidony insisted on going along, as Sorcha clearly would.

His mind leaped to another possibility. If the villain was Waldron and he was laying a trap, might he not seize any opportunity to snatch two more Macleod sisters to supplement his bait? Hugo knew the likelihood was strong.

He knew, too, that his cousin wanted to catch Michael and himself more than he wanted to hold the Macleods. He might seek revenge against Isobel for pushing him off the wall-walk, of course, but she was beyond his reach.

Perhaps he also sought revenge against Henry, but that was less likely. Henry's power was too great. As Prince of Orkney, he could draw on the Norse King to support him, as well as on the King of Scots. But perhaps Waldron was confident enough to believe that with enough bait he could entice even Henry.

It required but a moment's further thought for Hugo to decide that he could not send Sorcha and Sidony home with an escort of only two or three men. He would therefore have to keep them, but he needed a way to divest himself of them as quickly as possible. He also needed reinforcements and sound advice. He could think of only one place where he could fulfill all three necessities.

If Waldron *was* heading for Edgelaw, he would not risk a confrontation on unknown terrain if he could avoid it. Although the temptation to attack Hugo's small force with his greater one might be strong, Waldron—or whatever villain had taken Adela—would wisely assume that Hugo had an alternative plan of defense. If the leader of the abductors had studied his opponents, he would also assume that Lachlan Lubanach's spies were at work and that Hector Reaganach was raising an army to rescue Adela. The one thing Waldron himself was unlikely to imagine was that Hugo and Michael already suspected that he had abducted Adela.

Therefore—or so Hugo hoped—Waldron would continue to lead them toward the battleground of his choosing, a battleground much nearer to Edgelaw than to the Highlands. They were only fifteen miles or so from Lochearnhead and could make Edinburgh in two days' time. From there it was less than ten miles south to Roslin Castle, where Hugo would find not only his aunt, the formidable Isabella, Countess of Strathearn and Caithness, but his father, as well. Sir Edward Robison would be at Roslin now, making preparations for the important gathering that they and the Sinclairs had arranged to coincide with the spring removal of the King of Scots' court from Stirling to Edinburgh.

Both Isabella and Sir Edward would provide him with

advice, Roslin would provide at least some of the reinforcements he needed, and Isabella would know exactly how to deal with the irrepressible Lady Sorcha.

Accordingly, he said, "In truth, lass, what damage your sister's reputation has suffered cannot be undone or worsened by traveling with me and my men. But we have other things to consider, for although we were able to travel at speed, thanks to Hector Reaganach's horses, we'll be slower now unless we can find fresh mounts for you three. I'm thinking we're more likely to find horses ahead than behind, though. And I agree that dividing my men would be to our disadvantage."

"Aye, sure," she said, nodding.

He went on, "I had not expected to find you so close to the abductors, but they still outdistance us by at least a day and will doubtless continue to do so. I think our best course is to continue following them without trying to engage them yet. We are but two days from Edinburgh, so the sensible course is to press on."

He sounded too glib, he knew, but she lacked his experience and, he hoped, the ability to understand an enemy's tactics or strategy. In any event, he was not going to share his thoughts with her about Waldron and the treasure he sought.

Sorcha felt only relief. Something in Hugo's expression told her that her arguments alone had not persuaded him, but at least he had listened to her when many men would not have. Certainly, her father would not.

Feeling more in charity with him than she had since meeting him, she said, "I'll fetch Sidony so we can be on our way."

As she moved to pass him, however, he stopped her with a firm hand on her shoulder, stirring a prickling of unease that his next words did nothing to dispel.

"One moment, my lady, we have not finished our talk."

She looked at him. "I cannot think what more we have to say."

"Only this, lass. Do not press me too far. I am not your father, nor do I always follow the rules of civil behavior. Too often, in a crisis, such rules get in the way, and if we are to travel together, you will be wise to understand that. If you defy me, I will have no more compassion or consideration for you or your sensibilities than I would for any disobedient lad under my command."

"What would you do?"

"What do you think I would do?" His startling blue gaze met hers again, rekindling that odd, unfamiliar sensation inside. For a brief, crazy moment, she felt a compelling urge to defy him, to discover exactly what he would do. Then, in a blink, she decided she would be wiser to leave well enough alone, at least as long as she was still dressed as the lad to which he had just compared her.

She knew what her father did to disobedient lads. He ordered them flogged.

So instead of provoking him further, she said, "If I knew what you would do, I would not have asked. Still, I know I would not like it, so I will strive to remember all you have said to me."

"See that you do," he said with a look that seemed to

pierce through her. Glancing over his shoulder, he added, "Your sister is coming."

She peered past him to see Sidony some distance down the path, hurrying toward them. She looked frightened.

"Pray, sir, do not terrify her. She fears you, and none of this was her doing. She accompanied me only because she could not bear to let me come alone."

"Something you doubtless counted on," he retorted. "If you feel no shame for anything else you have done, you should feel some for endangering her."

"She has not been in danger," Sorcha said. "Nor would I do that."

"Would you have me believe you witless?" he demanded, frowning heavily enough to stir the hairs on the back of her neck again. "Despite your recklessness, I have given you credit for integrity. But either you are deluded or you have not given a moment's thought to all that you have done."

"Helping Adela is all that counts," she said stiffly. "Nothing else matters."

"I recommend that you consider the nature of the men you follow."

"I know naught of them but that they captured her."

"Exactly, so you know they believe they had reason to abduct at least one Macleod sister," he said. "You also know that they are even more daring and reckless than you are."

"Don't call me reckless," she snapped. "I have taken great care."

"Aye, sure, and how did you know when you stopped here that they were not camped in these very woods?"

"But they weren't here anymore!" she said as Sidony silently joined them.

"You didn't know that, and they could have been," he replied, paying Sidony no heed. "Had they been here, what was to prevent them from adding two more Macleod sisters to their string, like fishermen taking fish from the sea?"

She glowered at him. "You won't frighten me with fairy tales, sir, but you are frightening Sidony, and I want you to stop."

Sidony said in a tremulous tone, "But, Sorcha, what if they had been here?"

"Don't let him scare you, love," Sorcha said, forcing calm into her voice despite wanting to shriek like an alewife at Hugo for his thoughtlessness. "If they had still been camped here, the good folk of the clachan would have warned us when we arrived. Only recall how quickly the old man told us they had been here."

"That's true, sir," Sidony said, looking at Hugo. "He told us straightaway that strangers had camped here, and he told us how many there were. I assure you, had they still been here, we would have left at once."

Sorcha could see that he had to fight to retain his calm, but his tone revealed little of his annoyance when he said quietly to Sidony, "My lady, we are all going to leave shortly, so I would count it a favor if you would go and ask your lad to show my men where they can water their horses."

"Is Sorcha not coming, too?"

"Aye, we will all go, but I have something more to say to her before we do, so if you would be so kind . . ." He smiled at her, gently lifting his eyebrows.

Without hesitation, she smiled back and said, "Aye, sir, I'll tell Rory."

"Whilst you're about it," he added, "see if the women in the clachan have more appropriate clothing they would be willing to lend you and your sister. These garments are none too clean."

"Yes, sir," she said, smiling more widely yet. "That would be that dreadful manure. We tried to clean it off, but the smell just clings, so I'll be *glad* to do that."

"Tell me about the dreadful manure," he said as they watched her hurry off.

Sorcha shrugged. "We helped a man and his wife carry away the old thatch from their roof and mix it with the pile near their byre."

"I see," he said. "And you did this because of your generous hearts?"

"We did it because we had asked them for food. Not that we could have objected, of course, not without revealing that we were females."

When he chuckled, she muttered a few choice words.

"What was that you said?" he asked.

"Nothing," she said, promising herself that she would explain to Sidony that artless prattle and blind obedience were not what would serve them best with this man. "I am sure your men could find water for their horses without Rory's aid, and the women here probably have no more clothes than those on their backs. In any event, Bess bundled our other clothes, so we could wear those if we had to."

"If you mean the dresses you wore to his grace's installation, they won't do. I don't want you looking like noblewomen."

"She'll do as you bade her," Sorcha said. "She always does. But you sent her off so you could speak to me," she added. "What more can you have to say?"

He grew stern again as he said, "I warned you about challenging me. I have restrained myself, but do not think in future that your sister's presence will protect you if you speak to me as you did just before she joined us. I did not suggest that the villains might want more than one Macleod sister just to scare you."

"I don't believe that."

"Have a care," he warned. "I will not lie to you. I may not always tell you all I know, but I won't lie. I cannot deny that I'd hoped my words would frighten you, and I readily admit I'd not have spoken as I did had I remembered the lady Sidony was likely close enough by then to hear me, but—"

"But she did hear you," she interjected.

"Aye, she did, but the brutal truth is that if the man we follow is who I think he is, he seeks revenge against several people. He believes he can do as he wants with impunity and will not care how many Macleod sisters he hurts in the process."

"Who is he?"

Ignoring her, he said, "If you had stumbled on this clachan before he and his men had left it, no old man's warning would have protected you. Moreover, he probably knows exactly who is following him and how close you are. Had he chosen to stay here longer, he would have been waiting for you, and you would have had no way to defend yourself."

She shivered but said staunchly, "How can you know that? Indeed, how can you know anything about him?"

"He is my cousin," Hugo said. "He was born out of wedlock in France, but I have known him since he was fourteen, when he came here. I was eleven."

"Faith, are you in league with him?" she demanded.

～

Hugo was beginning to read her better, and he knew he had succeeded in frightening her a little, even shocking her, but despite the fact that such emotions might make her more tractable and thus suit his purpose better than the truth, he could not let her think he might be an ally of Waldron's.

"Nay, lass," he said. "In truth, I cannot even say for certain that he is leading that band of ruffians."

"Then, how dare you—?"

Her hand flashed up, but he caught it easily and held it tight.

"Nay, you wee skelpie," he said. "You'll not strike me again."

"You said you'd never lie to me," she said through her teeth.

"Nor have I." When her jaw remained tense, he realized he was hurting her and eased his grip without releasing her hand.

"You said you know him, that he is your cousin."

"I said *if* he is the man I believe him to be, he is my cousin."

"But you don't know!"

"I have no proof," he said. "I'm as sure as I can be, though."

"Why?"

"I had a dream," he said reluctantly, knowing he could not adequately explain his certainty that the dream's message was true.

He expected another burst of temper, but she only frowned and said, "What sort of dream?"

He found it surprisingly easy to describe it for her, much easier than describing it to Michael. She listened with an intensity he had rarely noted in anyone, male or female, and when he described the moment Waldron had stepped aside to reveal Adela, she nodded with a satisfied air.

"A truly striking dream, sir. I warrant Adela was trying to reach out to you, and somehow you connected with her thoughts in the dream world."

"My cousin Michael said it was more likely the result of too much brogac after supper, or mayhap, at best, merely ordinary logic," he said.

"But why would it be logical to suspect that another of your cousins had taken Adela?" she asked.

"In truth, it would not be, since we both thought he was dead."

"Dead! But when did he die?"

"Last summer," Hugo said, anticipating both her next question and her likely reaction to the answer.

"How did he die?"

"Your sister Isobel pushed him off the ramparts of Roslin Castle into the river North Esk," he said, watching her.

"Isobel! But why?"

"She had good reason," Hugo said. "I'll tell you about it another time, but I think we had better go now. I warrant the lady Sidony will have found suitable clothing for you both by now. I don't want anyone thinking I've encouraged you to ride about the countryside in those disreputable garments."

"Very well," she said. "But you need not think we have finished this conversation, sir, because I mean to have the whole tale out of you. In truth, I think you have much more explaining to do than I have."

Knowing he could not tell her the whole tale and wondering how he could tell her enough to satisfy her without telling her too much, Hugo cursed himself for a fool and hoped she was not a prattler.

Chapter 8

Sidony, thanks to Rory's help and the ordinary Highlanders' strong sense of hospitality, had indeed collected clothes for herself and Sorcha by the time Sorcha and Sir Hugo returned to the clachan. But she eyed her sister warily as they approached.

Sir Hugo said, "Lady Sidony looks as if she expects you to eat her, lass."

"I wish you would address me properly."

"Do you want me to announce to all and sundry that you are the lady Sorcha Macleod, traveling in borrowed clothing—or your own, for that matter—with a man she scarcely knows as her sole protector?"

"No, of course I don't want that. But you could manage to show some respect for my rank if for nothing else."

"Respect? My dear child, you have upended your own world and mine, not to mention Sidony's and Adela's. In view of all that, I believe I've shown you exceptional respect by not following my first and strongest inclination when I found you this morning."

She bit her lip, wishing she had held her tongue. Oddly, the fact that he had called her his dear child rankled more than his general refusal to address her properly. To be sure, they might have reason to avoid that when they met strangers, but such reason did not pertain when they spoke privately. She was tempted to tell him so but decided not to provoke him again, especially since she could not deny a certain truth in his accusation about turning worlds upside down.

He was right about Sidony, too. She did look wary.

"Don't fret, goose," Sorcha said lightly when they met. "I don't care how awful the garments are. Sir Hugo has explained that we cannot wear the things we wore for his grace's installation, since they proclaim our rank rather loudly. But I'm as tired as you must be of pretending to be male when anyone of sense can see in seconds that we're no such thing. It was a stupid idea."

"Not as stupid as all that," Hugo said. "Unless I miss my guess, that clothing may have kept Waldron from suspecting that you have been following him."

"But you told me just minutes ago that he knows exactly who is following him and how close we are," she protested.

"I wanted to make it clear how dangerous he is," he said. "And before you accuse me of lying to you, which I said I'd never do, let me explain. I may have equivocated by not explaining thoroughly, but I did not lie. My guess is his men have been riding about, watching his trail. If they have, they may know that three lads are on the track behind them now, but I doubt they can have learned much about those lads by asking pointed questions of anyone they met along the way."

"That's true, Sorcha," Sidony said. "They are all strangers, so unless they claimed to be Lord Ranald's men or his grace's, folks would tell them precious little. The likelihood that anyone would have voiced suspicion about our sex to a total stranger must be remote."

Sorcha had to agree. Then she thought of something else. "What about you, sir? If they're keeping watch, won't they know you are hard on their heels now?"

"Very likely," he admitted. "I reached Oban yesterday and Kilchurn Castle last night, so I have been traveling an entirely different route. However, although they cannot possibly be watching every glen betwixt here and the sea, I warrant they'd expect Hector Reaganach to be searching for his wife's sister, so Waldron may well have the track from Oban under watch as a precaution."

"We did not follow them from Glenelg," Sidony said, brightening. "We did not meet their trail until the Great Glen. They may not know about us at all."

"You came from Glenancross, near Mallaig," he said.

Sidony looked surprised. "How do you know that?"

"Your father's chief helmsman brought word to Lochbuie when he learned that you'd fled," he said. "He told us you'd even managed to get to Loch Sunart."

"We'll go and change now," Sorcha said, grabbing Sidony's arm. "We want to get started just as soon as possible. Are our horses ready, Rory?"

"Aye, mistress. Sir Hugo's lads gave me a hand wi' them, and we've our dinner and supper packed, thanks to folks o' the clachan. We'll eat well today."

"Why did we rush away?" Sidony asked as they changed in the largest croft.

"Because he looked ready to lecture us again," Sorcha said, slipping a shabby russet skirt on over her head. "I did not want to hear it."

If she thought the skirt, matching bodice, and gray cloak provided for her were not what she liked, at least the skirt was full enough to let her ride astride, and she told the crofter's wife sincerely that she was grateful for them. She thanked the other donors, too. Highlanders rarely expected or requested recompense of any sort for their generous hospitality, but Sorcha vowed privately to send gifts to everyone in the clachan as soon as she and her sisters were safely home again.

Twenty minutes after they had left him, they rejoined Sir Hugo and his men, and were soon on their way. They traveled at a steady pace that seemed slower than what Sorcha had urged before. But she soon realized they had to stop less often to rest the horses and decided it was a more practical pace for their purpose.

For the first quarter hour or so, they rode in pairs without talking. But as they passed through a busy village, Sir Hugo guided his mount up beside Sorcha and Sidony and said amiably that the name of the village was Dail Righ.

"Robert the Bruce suffered defeat here years before Bannockburn," he said.

"Did he?" Sorcha said. "I hope you do not mean to preach history to us everywhere we go."

"I thought you would prefer history to scolding," he said. "However . . ."

He let the word hang in the air between them.

She glanced at him, saw that his eyes were twinkling,

and said, "If I must choose, I suppose I would prefer history. But if you can talk sensibly, I'd rather talk of other things."

"Then tell me about your family. I have met the ladies Adela and Isobel, of course, but I thought I'd heard that your father had eight daughters."

"We're only seven now," Sorcha said. "Our sister Mariota died years ago."

"I'm sorry," he said. "I didn't know."

"It happened a long time ago," Sorcha said. "Sidony and I were but wee lassocks then, and she never paid any attention to us, so we scarcely knew her."

"Your mother died when you were young, too, did she not?"

"Aye. Siddy was still a bairn and I not much older. We don't remember her. And I hope you won't say as most people do that we must recall something," she added, giving him a minatory look.

"I wasn't going to," he assured her. "Do people really say that?"

"They do," she said. "They'll say, 'But you *must* remember her tucking you into your cot at night or singing you lullabies.' "

"When they say that," Sidony said, "you often say you *do* remember."

"Because I get tired of them looking at me as if I were a bit off. The fact is that I don't remember her. I remember Aunt Euphemia telling us stories about Roman gods and goddesses and Father telling her she would make us as daft as she is. And I remember Cristina sitting by my cot when I was sick. One time she told me she had *wished* me well, and I believed her. Cristina was more of a mother to us than anyone else, because she was the eldest and managed our father's household until she married Hector and moved to Lochbuie."

"I have met Lady Euphemia," Sir Hugo said with a smile.

"She is sometimes a bit eccentric but always very kind," Sidony said.

"Aye, she is," Sorcha agreed. "I like her stories. She lived with us after our mother died, but when Cristina married Hector, she went to live with them. Isobel did, too," she added. "We visit them once a year or so, but it is not the same as when they lived at home. We've missed them dreadfully."

"You had others to look after you, did you not? And your father," Hugo said.

"Adela looked after us, because it was her duty. She did not like it, though, and one can scarcely blame her."

"No," Sidony agreed.

"Maura and Kate did not attempt any mothering, because they married soon after Cristina did. And then Isobel married Sir Michael. As for Father"—Sorcha chuckled—"his notion of looking after us is to issue orders when it suits him, and warn us against breaking any of his silly superstitions. As if it would have been worse for Adela to marry Ardelve on Friday! If she had, she would be safe now."

"If she had," Hugo said gently, "Waldron would have taken her on Friday instead. That's all."

She sighed. "I suppose you are right. And, pray, sir, I know it was my fault. You need not say so again."

"I won't. I know how much you care about Lady Adela. And whatever else I may think about what happened, I know you meant it for the best."

"Well, it did not turn out for the best," she said. "But we *will* find her, and you will marry her. Then all will be well again."

"Won't you miss her when she marries?" he asked. "Even if she did not enjoy managing your father's household, she must be the one who stands most in the place of a mother to you now. Perhaps she will not want to leave."

"Oh, she wants to leave," Sorcha said. "Father intends to marry again."

"Aye, sure, Lady Clendenen. I forgot about her," he said.

"She refuses to live in a household long managed by another female still living there. Nor does she wish to take our mother's place. So he wants us to find husbands, and quickly. That is why Adela accepted Ardelve, but I do not mean to oblige him so easily. I want a man of sense, not one so puffed up in his own mind that he thinks God created Himself in *his* image rather than the other way round."

She shot him an oblique look and saw him wince.

"I suppose I number amongst their ilk, do I not?" he said.

She grinned. "I'll say this of you, sir. You are not stupid."

"Nor am I fond of flippant females who delight in impertinent behavior," he said mildly. "I tend to think of them as impudent skelpies."

"You called me that before," she said. "What's a skelpie?"

"'Tis a lowland term for a naughty child who badly wants smacking," he said. "Have you more criticism that you would like to offer me?"

"Not just now," she said airily. "But I warrant I'll think of more later."

He smiled then, and she grinned back, deciding he was perhaps more likeable than she had thought. She would not tell him so, though. Since he was clearly unaccustomed to criticism, more could only benefit him.

They continued talking desultorily until they stopped to eat their midday meal. Sorcha had no idea where they were, and Rory confessed that he had no more idea than she did, so she applied to Sir Hugo.

"We've entered Glen Dochart," he said. "We should make some miles beyond Lochearnhead by nightfall unless we encounter another thunderstorm."

Clouds had gathered overhead, to be sure, but they seemed high and unthreatening. "What comes after Lochearnhead?" Sorcha asked.

"Strathyre Forest, a road through rolling green braes to Loch Lubnaig, the towns of Doune and Dunblane, then Stirling, Linlithgow, and Edinburgh," he said.

"How long before we reach Edinburgh?" Sidony asked him.

"If we reach Loch Lubnaig tonight, we'll make Stirling by midday tomorrow and mayhap Linlithgow by suppertime. Edinburgh lies fifteen miles beyond it."

"Then we must press on," Sorcha said. "They are but a day ahead now, and since they may not know we are so close, we should take advantage of that. The closer we can get to them before Edinburgh, the more likely we are to discover exactly where they go. All roads lead to Edinburgh, so clearly many roads must lead out of it. We would be foolish to risk losing them there."

He did not comment. But he did order his men to

increase the pace until the time came to stop for their midday meal, so Sorcha assumed he agreed with her.

Hugo did not think it was a propitious moment to inform her that he did not mean to take her to Edinburgh. For one thing, he was certain Waldron was heading for his own easily defended lair at Edgelaw. For another, he wanted reinforcements.

He had increased their pace because it would prevent further discussion of Edinburgh. She was right in saying that nearly all roads led there, but he knew of at least one track from Linlithgow that skirted the royal burgh and would take them south. He was certain Waldron also knew it. In any event, he meant to see his two charges safe at Roslin before he went after Adela and her abductors.

He felt guilty about not sharing those intentions with her, but he was tired of fratching with the lass, and he was certain she would fly into a fury again when he told her where he was taking her. He enjoyed crossing swords with her, but he realized that he wanted even more to win her good opinion. That he was unlikely to do so stirred an unfamiliar shadow in his mind that he found hard to identify.

He glanced at her, admiring the proud tilt of her head. She had pulled off the tattered headscarf the crofter's wife had given her, and her hair gleamed like polished gold whenever the sun's rays danced out from behind the fluffy but ominously graying clouds to shine on it. She looked as calmly confident in the croft woman's clothing as she had in the more elegant garments she wore at Kildonan.

She caught him watching, raised her tip-tilted little nose into the air, and pushed a strand of raggedly cut hair from her cheek. A lustful jolt stirred his loins. He had never known his emotions to be so unpredictable, making him yearn to kiss her one moment and beat her the next. God knew, she deserved skelping for nearly all she had done in the past sennight, but most of all for cutting her beautiful hair.

He remembered how he had responded when she had said he was not stupid, chastising her as if she had been six years old. But he remembered, too, the impudent way she had made him laugh afterward. She was certainly different from other women he had met. He wondered briefly if he could tame her but shoved the tantalizing thought out of his mind, recalling that he had no business to be thinking such thoughts of anyone, let alone the sister of the woman he would most likely have to marry as soon as he rescued her.

A shower of rain caught them a few minutes later and lasted until just before he called the halt for their meal. They ate quickly, conversing desultorily until his men began readying the horses again. Neither Sorcha nor her sister seemed to mind the rain, although he had thought Sidony seemed tired before they stopped. Now, having eaten, she seemed as eager to go on as Sorcha was.

The clouds began to thin, and glancing at them, Hugo reflected with little satisfaction that unless blacker ones began gathering and spat thunder, lightning, and rain at them during the late afternoon, they would easily make Loch Lubnaig by sundown. The end of their journey together was fast approaching.

Tuesday night, learning of his lordship's vow not to rape her had acted on Adela like a mug of heady brogac, but the sensation lasted only until he spoke of Isobel and her babe. With that new fear added to her old ones, she had all she could do to maintain her air of false calm through Wednesday's journey.

They had risen before dawn and expected to put a great distance behind them until a thunderstorm in the late afternoon forced them to seek shelter in the woods again and make camp. By then they had come to a more heavily populated part of the countryside, but his lordship evidently knew the area well. Despite the bad weather he easily found an isolated place for their encampment.

Another storm struck just before they stopped for their midday meal on Thursday. Ahead of them, Adela saw Stirling Castle on its high, craggy perch. As they remounted half an hour later, one of the men said casually that they were likely to make Linlithgow by sunset.

Adela had never been to the royal burghs of Stirling or Linlithgow, but as shabby as she was, she felt no disappointment when they skirted Stirling. She was tired of riding, tired of being terrified one minute and flushed with gratitude or dizzy with relief the next. And she was especially tired of the clothes she had worn for five days. She had hoped the rain would wash away some of their odor but feared it had only made things worse. She knew she must smell as bad as most of the men around her, and some of them were disgustingly rank.

From the moment his lordship had mentioned bringing Isobel to her, she had desperately wanted to ask just what he had meant. But she knew she would not like the answer and might make him angry simply by asking. Nor could she prevent his behaving as he chose. Furthermore, having noted that men departed the camp as often as new ones arrived, she had deduced that he must have arranged some form of communication similar to the one she had heard Cristina say Lachlan Lubanach used to keep himself informed of news throughout the Highlands and Isles.

That thought stirred her to wonder if Lachlan knew where she was. Surely, although they had rarely stopped in villages or clachans, folks would talk of these men and the direction they rode. Despite her persistent dreams of magical rescue, the possibility of a real attempt stirred not hope but fear.

What if Lachlan and Hector were following, just waiting for an opportunity to strike? What if they struck and his lordship's men were ready for them, as he had promised they would be? If that happened and they killed everyone, including herself and Isobel, she decided grimly that it would be Sorcha's fault just like all the rest—and Hugo's, too.

What manner of man was Hugo that he had not replied to at least one of Sorcha's messages? Had he been present at the wedding, if only to smile that crooked smile of his and say he was sorry he had led anyone to believe he held a tenderness for her and had come only to wish her well, it would have been enough to prevent her abduction. Of that she was certain.

Was he not an accomplished warrior? Did not Sir Michael depend on him to keep safe from harm all that the Sinclairs held dear? Had he been there, instead of only a few villagers and a minimal wedding party, his lordship would have seen the deterring sight of Sir Hugo and at least twenty men-at-arms. She was certain Hugo never went anywhere without such a tail. He was too important, and if any man knew his own worth, Hugo did.

So, it was entirely his fault and Sorcha's that she was where she was, and if his lordship succeeded in capturing Isobel, it would serve Hugo right, because he would see then that the world did not turn just to suit his notions and needs alone.

That last thought stirred prickling tears and a choking sensation that warned her she was about to cry. She could only be grateful that his lordship's men rarely paid her any heed and that she was facing his back, clinging to his waist with her cheek against his cloak. Struggling to compose herself, she wondered how she could even think such wicked thoughts.

What had happened to make her feelings and reactions so unpredictable, so apparently unmanageable? She had always been able to control herself, and to manage those around her, for that matter. Unlike Sorcha, for example, who never even tried to manage anyone, including herself, Adela had exerted herself to deal with her blustery, temperamental father, and her equally unpredictable sisters. But even more, she had worked to control herself, never to reveal her most private feelings to anyone else, lest they somehow use the knowledge to plague her.

But no matter what Sorcha had done, blaming her for his lordship's wicked actions was unfair, so why could she not dismiss the notion from her mind? Sorcha had certainly done nothing to make him go after the very pregnant Isobel.

If his lordship did capture Isobel, surely, Adela told herself, the babe would be in no jeopardy. Only a truly evil man could believe God would approve of killing an innocent bairn. And she herself ought to be safe enough if she did not anger him again. He had ruined her reputation. That should be enough punishment to satisfy any man.

Suddenly doubting her logic, she wondered if it might help if she offered to persuade Hugo and Michael to meet with him, and to help him explain his position so they would understand why they should help him fulfill his holy mission. Whatever it was, she believed more strongly each day that he believed it was right. If the Pope believed in it, too, who was she or anyone else to say they were wrong?

In any event, she hoped she was learning to read him, to see things more clearly through his eyes. He was not really a bad man, just a normal one with determination to do what was right no matter who got hurt in the process. Surely, knowing all that, she should soon stop feeling so much on edge with him. And then, if she could just help him fix everything, all would be well.

When they stopped at dusk for the night, well off the main road and some miles short of Linlithgow, she thanked him quietly for helping her dismount, and then, when the men had the tent up and his gear unpacked, she went to tidy things and arrange her fur pallet. She would have bartered her soul for clean clothes and a comb. Although she had long since lost the flowers Sorcha and Sidony had gathered for her, she still had her veil and chaplet and could manage to plait her hair with her fingers. But oh, how she longed to be truly clean and tidy again!

He entered the tent without ceremony just as she heaved a deep sigh.

"Art tired, lass?" he asked brusquely, handing her a jug when she turned.

"Aye, sir. Oh, thank you," she added, smiling as she took the jug and saw that it was full. "I was longing for a wash. After we eat, with your permission, I mean to go right to bed. I believe I'll sleep well."

"Good, because you'll need your rest. I'm going to want your help soon."

"Oh, yes, my lord. I'm sure I can help you. Thank you again for being so kind as to bring me this water yourself."

"I need your chaplet," he said.

"My chaplet?"

His frown reminded her that he did not like her to question him, so she reached at once to pull it off, saying, "Of course, you may have it, although I cannot imagine what you can want with it."

He took it from her and left without another word.

Adela heaved another sigh of mixed relief and bewilderment, soaked a cloth with water from the jug, and began to scrub her face and hands for supper.

Chapter 9

Sir Hugo called a halt at sundown near the southern end of Loch Lubnaig, and as dusk washed over the rolling green hills and wide patches of forestland that flanked the narrow, mile-long loch, they made camp near its eastern shore on a grassy slope that led into a forest about twenty yards above them.

While Rory and some of the other men built the cook fire, laid out sleeping rolls, collected water, and erected the small tent that was to serve as Sorcha and Sidony's bedchamber, other men cast lines into the loch for fish. Still others skinned and gutted rabbits they had killed that afternoon for roasting. One man pulled a cloth sack from the small kist each carried strapped to his saddle, and produced bannocks for toasting over the fire and a pot of jam to share until it ran out. Others produced similar treats.

Sorcha enjoyed the hum of activity. The men had clearly traveled together often and enjoyed one another's company. When the rabbits were spitted and beginning to sizzle, several men adjourned to the edge of the camp nearest the track and began to polish weapons and tend other gear.

In the glow of the firelight as dusk faded to darkness, she watched Hugo drift from one small group to another. At one he talked quietly, at another he shared a joke, and at yet another, two men demanded that he settle a disagreement, which he did with laughter and a clap on the back for one of them.

"He moves like a cat," Sorcha said quietly to Sidony.

"That is what Isobel says about Sir Michael," her sister replied. "She says he moves so silently that he can be beside her before she knows he is nearby. I don't think Sir Hugo is like that."

"Nay, that he is not," Sorcha said, thinking of the powerful sense of energy the man radiated. "I think one would be aware of him even if he were silent and the place pitch black."

"He is a most attractive man, don't you agree?" Sidony said.

Sorcha did not answer, but watching him as he put back his head and laughed at something one of his men said, his strong, white teeth gleaming in the firelight, she was thinking the same thing. Why on earth, she wondered, had Adela not made a stronger push to attract the man, to encourage him to ask for her hand? She knew Isobel had invited Adela to visit Roslin, because she had invited them all, saying they might come together or perhaps one or all of her three unwed sisters might travel south with another family if Macleod did not wish to make the journey. And Adela had known that Sir Hugo would likely be at Roslin much of that time. Yet she had put off going until the early winter had made it impossible. Had it been Sorcha instead who had met him at Orkney . . .

She set that thought aside, unfinished. It would not do to be thinking that way, not when Sir Hugo was the only hope Adela had of restoring her reputation.

Realizing that Sidony had repeated her question, she said, "He is handsome enough, but in my opinion, he is like most attractive men, insufferably fond of himself."

That was so, she told herself, but he was far more amusing than most of his ilk, and she enjoyed talking with him. At least, she did when he was not flinging orders at her, or scolding her, or telling her to straighten her veil. But in truth he had not done much of that after they had left the clachan that morning.

Soon after she finished her excellent supper of roasted rabbit and bannocks, she detected a halo of light edging the hilltops east of them and realized the moon was rising.

Yawning, Sidony said, "I'm ready for bed. Shall we go?"

"You go ahead," Sorcha said. "I want to watch the moonrise."

"It is not even a full moon yet," Sidony protested.

Sorcha shrugged. "I like to watch it, even so. It will be full in a few days, so it is round enough to suit me."

Hugging her, Sidony bade her goodnight and walked toward their tent.

Sorcha got up from the boulder on which she had sat to eat her supper and began to wander along the loch shore, away from the firelight. She wanted to savor the moonrise without distractions. She had strolled for only a few minutes, however, before the hair on the back of her neck lifted. Even so, the light hand touching her shoulder gave her a severe start.

With a shriek, she whirled, ready to strike.

As he had before, Sir Hugo caught her hand easily, saying, "Nay, Skelpie, I told you, you'll not strike me again."

"I wasn't hitting *you*, exactly. You just startled me."

"Where are you going?"

She lifted her chin, wanting to jerk her hand away but not certain he would allow it and not wanting to give him the satisfaction of disallowing it. "Could you not simply suppose that I was seeking the privy pits, and leave me to find my way?"

"You are going the wrong way," he said. "We would never dig the pits this close to the water, as you should know. They lie yonder in the woods."

"Well, I wasn't going there, anyway," she said. Then, recalling what Sidony had said about Michael's silent movement, she said, "Do all men from Lothian walk like ghosts in the dark?"

He chuckled, and the sound warmed her. The hand still lightly holding her wrist warmed her, too. She swallowed, not sure what more to say when he did not answer her.

At last, in a voice that sounded strangely uneven, he said, "I just wanted to be sure you did not wander far. It would not be safe to go beyond sight of our encampment except at the pits. I have men posted around that area to guard against strangers. But I'm sorry if I gave you a fright, lass. I did not mean to."

"You didn't frighten me," she said. "You just startled me, and I don't like being startled. Do you mean to hold my hand all night?"

"Mayhap I should," he said, lightly stroking the inside of her wrist with his thumb as he looked into her eyes, holding her gaze with his. "I've come to fear that you may fall into trouble if I don't watch you closely."

Although she knew the stroking was probably just an idle gesture of which he was unaware, added to the way he was looking at her, it produced an odd feeling deep inside that made it hard to think or to breathe properly.

"Why did you wander away from the rest of us?" he asked.

"I wanted to watch the moonrise," she said, wrenching her gaze from his. "See, there it comes now. It's peeking at us over that hilltop."

"Aye," he said quietly. "I see."

Silvery light began to spill down the hillside to the loch, touching its still water and turning it into a long, silver, serpentine ribbon between the dark hills.

"Isn't it beautiful?" she said.

"Aye," he agreed.

She glanced up. "You're not looking at it!"

"Nay," he said, capturing her gaze again. "I'm looking at a wee golden witch, and one I should not be alone with, staring at the moon." He hesitated, still looking into her eyes. A moment later, he said gruffly, "Where's your sister?"

"She's gone to bed," Sorcha said, tugging gently to free her hand from his. To her disappointment, he did not try to hold on to it. "But I don't want to go back yet," she said. "I want to watch the moon for a while, but you can go back if you like. I promise you, I'll go no farther."

"Nay, lassie, I'll stay."

In the silence that followed, she found it hard to concentrate on the moon. Although he did not say another word, his presence loomed beside her, making her more aware of him than she had been only moments before.

He did not touch her, but she could sense his strength and feel warmth radiating from his body. His clothing smelled of wood smoke, and she could hear him breathing. When he had looked into her eyes her heart had begun beating harder than the slight exertion of walking alongside the loch warranted, but she could feel its pounding easing. Her body began to relax.

When the rounding moon had risen free of the crest of the hill, knowing he would soon insist they return, Sorcha said into the stillness, "What does he want?"

"Who?"

She did not bother to reply, and after a long moment, he said, "I told you, he seeks vengeance."

"I know that is what you said, but I have been thinking, and if revenge is all he wants, why take Adela? And if he wants to punish her, why not send her back now that he has ruined her, to reap the horrors of her ruination? Why take her all the way to Edinburgh? What does he really want, and why does he think that holding her prisoner will get it for him?"

Again, silence followed before he said, "I cannot tell you the whole tale, because it is not mine to tell. But I will tell you this much. He believes the Sinclairs have something that belongs to the Roman Kirk, something he says he means to return to the Pope when he finds it. And he is certain he will find it."

"Sakes," she said, astonished. "What is it?"

"That is the part I cannot tell you. I have sworn an oath, lass, and I cannot break it, certainly not without greater cause than a woman's curiosity."

"Duty and your sacred honor again, I suppose."

"Aye, and you need not say it like that. Trust is always a matter of honor, and a vow can never be more than a matter of trust. That is why Michael and I, and so many others, support Ranald of the Isles. He is a true Celt. He could easily have raised an army and taken the Lordship into his own hands, and many would have supported him. But he did not do it, because he had given his word to his father that he would see his grace's wishes fulfilled and would see Donald of Isla installed as the new MacDonald. Ranald's word is as good as any legal document, and better than many. Because of that, all men who know him trust him completely."

"Are you as trustworthy as Ranald of the Isles?" she asked.

He hesitated, making her wonder what consideration she had stirred to delay his response. But then he said firmly, "If I give you my word, you may trust it."

"Then give me your word that you will marry Adela when we find her."

"Nay, I'll not do that," he said. "We've already gnawed that bone, and you should know that I meant what I said. It must be her ladyship's choice, not mine or yours. Now, though, I must return you to your sister."

He put a hand on her shoulder and turned her toward the firelight, and she did not resist. Indeed, she enjoyed the warm feeling of him touching her and wondered again at Adela's stupidity. It occurred to her that he had not answered the part of her question about why Waldron had abducted Adela. But looking up at his strong profile as they walked, she decided she did not want to press the point. Likely, he would just tell her it was a part of the story he could not reveal. In any event, she did not want to break the easy mood between them.

For one flickering moment, earlier, when he had been looking into her eyes, she had thought he might kiss her and had felt a surge of disappointment when he had not. But thinking of it now, she scolded herself again for a fool, because common sense warned her that if he had kissed her, it would have stirred a whole new set of problems that she did not even want to contemplate.

Still, she was glad he had refused to promise he would marry Adela. If only she could think that Adela would be stupid enough to refuse his offer.

But Adela was not stupid. If she had accepted Ardelve, she would simply leap at the chance to marry Hugo.

Any woman would.

Walking back to the fire with him in companionable silence, she saw that Sidony had not gone to bed after all. Instead she sat near the fire, watching Rory toast a remaining bannock, talking earnestly with him. He glanced at her and nodded from time to time, clearly trying to keep one eye on the bannock dangling precariously from his slender toasting stick, and the other on Sidony as she talked.

As Sorcha and Sir Hugo neared the pair, Rory slipped the bannock from the stick, broke it in half, and gave half to Sidony. When she broke off a piece and put it gingerly to her lips, Rory said something, and she smiled, making Sorcha wonder what on earth they had been talking about.

Sir Hugo muttered abruptly, "How well do you two know that lad?"

Sorcha shrugged. "We've known him since we were all children at Chalamine together. His mother, Bess MacIver, was our mother's waiting woman. She stayed as our housekeeper for several years after Mother died, until her husband, Ranulf, was badly kicked by one of Father's horses. Father helped them buy the cottage in Glenancross, near her family, and they have lived there since."

"In other words, you don't know that lad well at all," he said. "I'm thinking he has designs on your sister."

"Rory? You must be daft," Sorcha said. "He would not think of such a thing. He has been very good to us, very protective, and he kens fine that his mother would have the hide off him if he were to hurt either one of us or seek aught from us that was unsuitable. He is an honorable man, too, Sir Hugo, and his honor means as much to him as yours does to you."

"Pax, lass. I meant no offense. I do not know him, which is why I asked."

Sorcha sighed. Once again, he had put her in the wrong without even raising his voice. She wanted to apologize, and at the same time, she wanted to smack him. She did neither, resorting to silence instead.

Sidony saw them and stood, bidding Rory goodnight before she hurried to meet them, saying, "I decided to wait for you, after all. They had a few bannocks left over, and Rory toasted one for me. I know I did not need more to eat, but it was delicious. Are you going to bed now, Sorcha?"

Wondering what demon possessed her usually bashful sister to babble on so, Sorcha agreed that she was indeed ready to sleep and bade Sir Hugo a dignified goodnight. The moment she and Sidony were alone in their tent, however, she said, "What were you talking to Rory about so intently?"

Sidony sighed as she turned to let Sorcha undo the lacing at the back of her borrowed bodice. "I was telling him how worried I am about Adela, that's all," she said. "She has been missing for days, Sorcha, days that she has had to spend with those horrid men. I don't mean to complain when I know we are doing all we can, but I keep wondering what they may be doing to her, and it frightens me."

"Then don't think about it," Sorcha advised bluntly. "It won't help Adela for you to torture yourself so on her behalf. Nor should you complain to Rory, dearling," she added in a gentler tone. "He can do nothing to help her either, you know—none of us can until we find her."

"No, I suppose not," Sidony said, sighing. "Still, it did make me feel better to talk to him. I just wish we could know she is safe."

"She will be soon. But no more burdening Rory with your worries."

Chastened, Sidony promised she would not do so again.

They went to bed, and curled up beside Sidony in bedding that Sir Hugo and his men had provided for them, Sorcha slept deeply and well.

But the next morning, when they emerged from their tent a short time after dawn broke over the hills, the first thing they learned was that Rory had disappeared from the camp and had taken his pony with him.

One of Sir Hugo's men approached them before they had walked more than a few yards from their tent. Explaining what had happened, he said that his master wanted to speak to them.

"We are going to break our fast now," Sorcha said. "Tell him we'll be glad to discuss it with him as we eat, though."

The man glanced over his shoulder, then leaned nearer to say in a brusque undertone, "I wouldna advise that course, m'lady. The master be in a rare temper, because he thinks ye kent fine that the lad were a-going, so unless ye want everyone to hear all he says to ye, I'd advise ye to go to him now."

"I'll go, then," Sorcha said firmly. "Siddy, you go on over by the fire and fetch us both something to eat. I warrant this will not take me long."

"Beg pardon, m'lady, but he said ye both should come," the man said.

Sorcha opened her mouth to tell him what she thought of that but shut it again without saying a word. She would not allow Hugo to bully Sidony, but neither would she allow his dictatorial ways to stir her to the even more inappropriate behavior of voicing her opinions about him to his minions. So, instead, she nodded her head regally and gestured for Sidony to follow her.

"Faith, he'll murder us both," Sidony murmured in a tremulous voice.

"No, he won't," Sorcha said. "I shan't let him. He may think he can bellow at us. Indeed, we cannot stop him if he does. But he will not do more than that, for all he may threaten. Just keep silent, dearling. I'll manage him."

One look at his face, however, was enough to shake her confidence. To say that he was in a black rage would not, she thought, be stretching the truth an inch.

Three of his men were with him, but to her relief he dismissed them all when she and Sidony approached. He did not, however, wait until the men were beyond earshot before he snapped, "Where the devil is he?"

"If you mean Rory, sir, we've no more idea than you do where he has gone," Sorcha replied. "We did not know he had left until your man told us, but I'm sure he'll return soon, so if that is all you wanted to ask us, we will go and eat now. Come, Siddy," she added, touching her sister's arm.

"Not so fast, lass," he said harshly enough to stop her in her tracks.

Sidony had not moved.

"Lady Sidony, do you know aught of that lad's whereabouts?"

Sorcha felt Sidony's arm tremble, but her sister just shook her head.

"Look at me," Hugo commanded.

Obediently, Sidony did so, but the sight of tears welling in her eyes fired Sorcha's temper.

"You're frightening my sister, and to no purpose," she snapped. "She knows no more than I do."

"Are you so certain of that?" he demanded. "I thought you told me Rory MacIver had a sense of honor. Honorable men do not disobey orders, nor do they abandon women they have sworn to protect."

Sorcha realized what he was doing and turned quickly to soothe her sister's predictable distress, but she was too late.

"Rory *is* honorable," Sidony said through her tears. "This is all my fault. I'm sure of it! Oh, Sorcha, you were right to scold me last night!"

"So, you did ask him to do something for you," Hugo said, moving to confront Sidony directly. "What was it?"

Sidony sobbed, and Sorcha stepped between them. "Leave her alone!"

In response, Sir Hugo moved her bodily out of his way and said curtly, "Don't interfere again. The lad's life may depend on how quickly I can get to the bottom of this." Turning back to Sidony, he said, "Tell me at once, lassie. I must know."

With another sob, Sidony wailed, "But I don't know where he is! I just know it's my fault that he left."

"Why is it your fault?" he asked, and this time, Sorcha noted, his tone was a more coaxing one. Reluctantly realizing that he was more likely to get the answers he wanted without her help, she kept silent.

Sidony glanced at her, but Hugo did not. When Sorcha said nothing, tears began to spill down Sidony's cheeks. She turned back to Hugo with another sob.

He said gently, "Come now, tell me."

She drew a long breath, then said, "I was so worried about Adela, sir. I told him that. But . . . but I also told him I would give anything just to know she was safe, to know for certain that those horrid men had not already killed her."

"Sakes, did you offer him a reward if he could produce such information?"

"No!" she cried. "My stupidity was in not realizing he might want to please me, might even take it upon himself to set out in search of her. I cannot imagine any other reason for him to have left us, Sir Hugo. But surely, he must realize that you and your men are much better suited to find her than he is."

Sorcha saw him grimace, but he said only, "If he has set out to look for her, he must be somewhere on the road ahead. Eat quickly, and we'll be on our way."

"Go on without me, Siddy," Sorcha said, giving her arm a gentle squeeze. "Find me something I can eat as we ride. I want to speak with Sir Hugo."

Sidony nodded and, looking much calmer, walked away.

Sorcha had intended to wait until she was beyond hearing, but Hugo said abruptly, "If you mean to take me to task for that, you can save your breath."

"I don't," she said, glancing back at Sidony to see how far she had gone. "You managed her better than I would have, sir, but I want to know why you looked as you did when she said your men are better able to find Adela than he is."

He grimaced again, but his stern posture relaxed, and she detected a rueful glint in his eyes. "You are determined to find fault with me, are you not?"

"No," she said honestly. "I just want to know if Rory is truly in danger."

"Aye, sure, he is. No sensible man would go in search of Waldron without greater skill and more weapons than that lad has."

"But if he only wants to see if she is safe, he will hardly walk into their encampment. Moreover, I cannot see why that would make you look as if you'd been caught doing something you should not have done."

"Is that how I looked?" he asked.

She nodded, wishing he would not gaze at her so directly. It made her feel as if he was trying to see into her mind and read her thoughts.

"I did feel guilty," he admitted. "In truth, you've had that effect on me since the day we met. But in this case, it is not anything I've said or done. I just realized that the only way that lad could have ridden away without my sentries stopping him is if he rode with or after the three men I'd sent on ahead."

"You sent men to look for Adela?"

"Nay, although I did tell them that if they learned aught of her whereabouts, one of them should ride back and tell me. Otherwise they will go to Roslin to bring reinforcements, so if we should meet Waldron before we get there oursel—"

"Sakes, sir, you should have sent for reinforcements straightaway!"

"I had only twenty men with me, lass. Waldron has twice that many by now. Moreover, I sent two of mine back to Oban when I found you, to let Hector Reaganach's men know where you were and that we were going to Edinburgh."

Sorcha stared at him. "Do you mean to say Hector is following us?"

He chuckled. "That gives you pause, does it? Well, I cannot blame you for that. The man terrifies me, too. But nay, lass, Hector is committed to accompanying Donald—or MacDonald, as we should call him now—just as your father and Michael are. I merely wanted to let his men know, because he asked me to do so."

"Do you think we'll have enough men if they don't send some to help us?"

"I hope we have enough for our present needs, at least. I've sent lads ahead and behind from the first day to watch for trouble, but I dared not send them any farther than they could ride back each night. Now that we are nearing Stirling and Edinburgh, I decided it would be safe enough to send those three on ahead."

"And you think Rory went with them?"

"I don't know," he said. "I'm guessing, but I'm afraid their going may have given your young protector sufficient cover to slip away."

"Perhaps he persuaded them to take him with them," Sorcha said.

"Unlikely, since they know they'd face my wrath. He may have said that he had my permission, of course. I'll question the lads when they return, but I'm thinking he just slipped by my guards. Their duty is to watch for intruders, so they may not have paid any heed to an extra man leaving."

"Would your cousin really harm him?"

"Waldron is capable of anything," he said. "Remember that. And, lass," he added, giving her one of those straight looks that seemed to see right through her.

"Aye, sir," she said with a sigh.

To her surprise, he reached out and casually brushed a strand of hair from her cheek as he said, "Truly, I am not an ogre. Stop trying to paint me as one."

⁓

Hugo's fingertips still retained warmth from touching her cheek. In fact, they fairly tingled, and he knew that every time he touched her, he was venturing into treacherous territory. Just thinking of other places he might touch her wakened parts of his body that had no business waking in her presence, making him grateful for the shadowy darkness where they stood and for her maidenly innocence.

She smiled ruefully and said, "I do not think you an ogre, sir, merely a normal man who thinks he must order the lives of everyone he comes near. If you learn more about where Rory has gone, I would like you to tell me."

He agreed, because it seemed a small thing to ask, and he wanted to please her when he could, if only to avoid more fratching. He still had not told her that he intended to bypass Edinburgh and make straight for Roslin, although he had nearly let it slip when he said his lads had gone for reinforcements. Since he was certain Waldron would likewise skirt the royal burgh and head southeast to Edgelaw, he had no qualms about waiting until they reached Linlithgow to tell her.

Therefore, agreeing to share information he acquired about Rory MacIver seemed only fair. But in the event, he had no need to tell her about him, because three hours later, shortly after they passed through the town of Dunblane with its beautiful century-and-a-half-old, red-sandstone cathedral, they found the poor lad bound to one of several chestnut trees at the side of the road.

His body slumped lifelessly forward, and someone had put a woman's silver chaplet on his head.

Chapter 10

Sorcha flung herself from her horse and rushed to Rory's side, but Hugo caught her as she reached him and pulled her back.

"Wait, lass, let me," he said. "He's breathing, but he's been hurt, and sometimes when a man regains consciousness after such an experience, he can be violent without realizing he strikes one who is trying to aid him."

Relieved to know that Rory was breathing, she was willing to let Hugo attend him, but she hovered over them until she heard Rory groan.

"Thank heaven," she exclaimed as she knelt swiftly beside him, appalled to see deep purple-black bruises on his face. "I thought you were dead! Speak to me, Rory. Why did you leave? What happened to you?"

"Easy," Hugo said. "He's barely conscious." As he began to untie Rory from the tree, he shouted to his men,

"Einar Logan, fetch some water, and you others keep watch lest the lad be bait for a trap!"

"You don't really think they would attack us here on the highroad," Sorcha said, looking about for any sign of villains. "We've only come a few miles past Dunblane, but I see a great castle in the distance, on that massive outcropping."

"Aye, that's Stirling," Hugo said, holding Rory by the shoulders as another of his men knelt by them to help untie the bindings. "I don't think we need fear attack here," he went on. "But I don't want to be too confident where Waldron is concerned. My guess is the lad got too close to some of his men, but where they could have come by that pretty bauble on his head, I have no notion."

"That's Adela's chaplet," she said quietly. "I'm sure of it."

"It is just a simple one," he said, taking it off Rory's head and handing it to her. While she examined it, he helped Rory, untied at last, to lie more comfortably on the ground. "Are you sure it is hers?"

"Aye, because it was our mother's, and her initials are engraved here on the band," Sorcha said, moving to make room for another of his men, a wiry-looking one with a dark, neatly-trimmed beard, who brought him a jug of water.

"Get something to slip under his head, Einar," Hugo said as he took the jug, poured water in one hand, and sprinkled it on Rory's face.

"He can ha' me jerkin, sir," Einar said, shrugging it off.

As she watched him ease the bunched jerkin gently under Rory's head, Sorcha said, "Rory cannot have caught up with those villains unless they are traveling much slower than we thought they were."

"True," Hugo agreed, but he said no more because, as he tried to give Rory a sip of water from the jug, the lad stirred convulsively and tried to sit up.

"I think he's going to be sick," Sorcha warned, stepping back.

Hugo did not pause to question her judgment but shoved the jug at Einar Logan, seized Rory again, and turned him just in time to prevent him from spewing the contents of his stomach all over Hugo and himself.

Einar, just as quick, snatched his jerkin from harm's way in time to spare nearly all of it. Without comment, he sluiced the small portion that did not escape with water from the jug, then rubbed it clean against the bark of the chestnut tree.

Rory's face was whiter than ever around the horrible bruises as he fixed his gaze on Sorcha and muttered, "Sorry, m'lady."

"Sakes, I'm just glad you aren't dead!" she exclaimed. "When I first saw you, I was as sure as I could be that you were. Whatever happened to you?"

"Not here, lass, and not now," Hugo said. "We'll get him on his feet first and see if he's fit to go on with us."

"I'm fit, sir, though 'tis likely ye'll be ripe t' flog me," Rory said miserably.

"What did they give you?" Hugo asked.

"A rare beating first of all, then summat bitter to drink. I dinna ken aught about what happened after that. Next thing, I were here and ye were a-holding me."

"Were they ordinary brigands or otherwise?"

"They'd ha' been the ones we be following," Rory said. "Leastwise, they said I were one o' the men following *them,* so they must ha' been."

"All right, let's see if you can stand up," Hugo said.

Sorcha wanted to insist that they let him recover before they made him move about, because she was afraid Hugo did mean to punish him for leaving the camp. That he had not reassured him suggested that Rory was right to be fearful.

She knew better than to question Hugo in front of his men, but she could not let him hurt Rory more than Waldron's men already had. He was clearly in pain, because he could hardly stand, even with Hugo propping him up.

To stall for time, she held out the silver chaplet so Rory could see it, and said, "How came you by this?"

Hugo frowned, but he did not say Rory should not answer.

Rory looked bewildered. "I didna come by it, m'lady. I never saw it afore."

"'Tis likely they put it on his head after they'd tied him, and after whatever they gave him had already rendered him unconscious," Hugo said.

"Sakes, sir," she said, "what manner of men are they that they could have such a potion with them?"

"I've told you, lass, we must assume they are capable of anything."

Sorcha shivered but said nothing more, bending to pick up the jug as Einar moved to Rory's other side. Between them, he and Hugo helped him walk back to where the others waited with the horses. Rory's pony was nowhere in sight, so she was glad Hugo's men had brought extra mounts.

Hugo scanned the nearby area. "We'll make for that thicket yonder," he said, pointing to a grove of trees a quarter of a mile from the road. "We can rest for an hour and have our midday meal. The lad should be able to ride by then. I'll put him up with one of you other men for now and perhaps later, too, unless he feels stronger after he eats."

"He can ride wi' me, sir," Einar said. "The pair o' us willna tax a horse as much as it would did the lad ride wi' one o' them other great louts."

The man who had helped unbind Rory had been following them, and Hugo turned the lad over to both of them.

Then, to Sorcha, he said, "Come, lass, I'll help you mount."

She hesitated, glancing about to be sure the other men and Sidony were not close enough to hear. Then she said quietly, "You won't flog him, will you?"

"He disobeyed me," Hugo replied just as quietly. "I'll have some things to say to him that he will not like hearing, because I want to make certain he won't do such a thing again, but I won't do more."

"Thank you," she said with relief as she turned toward her horse.

He stopped her with a hand on her arm. "Don't mistake me," he said when she looked back at him. "I am not sparing him to please you. I may need him, and he won't be of any use if he cannot recover quickly from his injuries. My men know me well, and they will understand that. I mean to make sure that Rory does, too."

Sorcha was silent, knowing he meant to make sure she understood as well. Then, realizing he was waiting for some sort of response, she nodded.

Satisfied, he released her and, putting a hand to her shoulder instead, kept it there as they walked to her horse.

Still silent, he lifted her to its back, steadied the animal while she gathered the reins and settled herself, and then strode to his own mount and swung himself onto the saddle.

The ride to the thicket took only minutes, and once there, the men prepared a hasty repast. By the time they had eaten, Sorcha thought Rory looked more alert and moved with greater ease. She kept a close watch on Hugo, though, and saw that he watched the lad nearly as closely as she did. She hoped Rory's quick recovery would not lead him to change his mind about punishing him.

When Hugo finished his meal and stood, then walked toward Rory, Sorcha quickly followed, determined to be near enough to intervene if necessary.

Hugo cast her a quick, measuring glance but made no objection. Squatting to his heels beside Rory, he said, "We'll talk some now before we ride on."

"Aye, sir," the lad replied, eyeing him warily.

Sorcha opened her mouth, but before she could speak, Hugo held up a hand and said, "If you want to stay, you may, but only if you do not speak."

Shutting her mouth, she nodded.

"Now," he said to Rory, "I want you to tell me everything that happened to you. Begin with how and why you slipped away."

Rory swallowed hard, visibly frightened about making such a confession. But after a brief silence, he said, "I heard ye tell them three they might come upon signs o' her ladyship's abductors, so when they went to get horses, I followed, 'cause Lady Sidony be worrying so about the lady Adela, and I thought I could learn summat.

One man guarding the horses did ask what I were about, but them three had mounted, so I . . . I told him ye'd said I were to go wi' them."

"I see," Hugo said in a tone that neither Sorcha nor Rory could mistake for anything but strong disapproval, but all he added was, "What then?"

Swallowing again, not taking his eyes off Hugo, Rory said, "I followed them easy, sir, on account o' the moon being so bright. Whilst the road wound amongst them hills beyond the loch, I didna fear them seeing me, but when it straightened, I feared one might look back, so I lagged back more. I dinna ken how long we rode, but I were passing one o' them patches o' forest and . . . and the woods closed in to the road on both sides o' me till the place seemed fair haunted, so I'd kicked me pony to catch them up a bit when five horsemen rode out and surrounded me."

"Five?"

"Aye, sir, and they seemed t' ken who I were, too. One o' them told their leader I were your man."

"He named me?"

"Aye, sir."

"What manner of man was their leader?"

Rory looked thoughtful, then said, "About the size o' Einar Logan, mayhap not quite so tall but lanky and tough-talking—younger than what Einar be wi' light hair and a big nose as sticks out like a hawk's beak."

"You use your eyes well," Hugo said. "What else did you see?"

"Nobbut them, sir," Rory said. "They pulled me off me horse into the woods, where the hawk's-beak one said t' tell them all I could o' your men and your plan. When I said I kent naught o' such things, being I'd only just met ye all yestermorn, he said he'd ha' to teach me a lesson. He ordered his men t' beat me wi' their fists. Then they asked me again, but I had nowt to say but what I'd said afore, so they forced me to drink some nasty stuff that the hawk's-beak one carried in a wee vial in his pouch. After that, I were as I were till ye woke me. Me cousin's going to be gey wroth wi' me for losing his pony," he added with a grimace.

"Did they say anything else that you recall?"

"Nobbut what I said, sir, just wanting t' ken what I could say o' plans and such." He frowned in a puzzled way, then added, "Wait, though. One o' them did say Lord Waldron wouldna be pleased that I kent so little."

Hearing Hugo release a quick breath, Sorcha glanced at him, but he still watched Rory intently. When the lad made no further comment, he murmured, "Anything else? Anything at all? What is the last thing that you recall?"

Rory squinted as if by doing so he could squeeze more out of his memory.

Sorcha wanted to tell Hugo it was enough that he could name Waldron. But she was afraid he'd send her away, and she wanted to hear everything they said.

At last, Rory said, "There do be one wee thing, sir. I dinna ken when I heard it, or even if I did, but the word Ratho came to me. I ken naught o' what it means. Sakes, I canna even say I didna dream it."

"You've done well to recall as much as you have," Hugo said.

Sorcha had looked at Hugo the moment Rory said the odd word, and had seen that it meant something to him.

So when he turned casually to her and said, "You may leave us now, lass," she shot him a mutinous look.

"I would know more of this Ratho, sir," she said.

"I doubt that it means much," he said.

"Nevertheless—"

"That will do," he said curtly. "I have some things to say to this lad now, and he will not thank you for staying to hear them."

Rory looked miserable again, but Sorcha knew she could not help him. She could only trust Hugo to keep his word. Accordingly, she turned without another word and went to join the others.

Hugo and Rory soon joined them, and at a gesture from Hugo, Rory limped to Einar Logan, who helped him mount. Whatever Hugo had said to the lad had left him looking wretched, so when Sidony suggested that she and Sorcha might ride beside him and Einar, Sorcha shook her head.

"He would not thank us for our sympathy," she said. "Nor would he want us to fuss over him like anxious nursemaids. However, I do want to have a word with Sir Hugo, dearling, so if you want to ride beside Rory for a short time, you should do so now, but only if you can promise not to talk of his injuries or his ordeal."

Sidony agreed, and Sorcha watched to be sure that neither Rory nor Einar would object to her riding alongside them before she kicked her own pony and urged it on to where Sir Hugo rode in the lead.

"You should hang back amidst the others, lass," he said when she guided her mount up beside his. "You are too much exposed here for my liking."

"You have already said that no one will attack us so

close to Stirling, sir," she said. "We'll be there shortly. And in any event, I want to talk to you."

"Ratho," he said, smiling at her and thus giving her a more encouraging reaction than she had expected.

"Just so," she said, returning the smile. "I know you recognized the word. What is it? Some sort of password or secret place?"

"You have a vivid imagination," he said. "Ratho is just a village."

"Between here and Edinburgh?"

"Nay, it lies southeast of Linlithgow near the Glasgow road."

"Then we must go straight on there from Linlithgow," she said. "Indeed, if it is not too far, we should strive to reach Ratho tonight. They must be going there if Rory heard them mention it."

"More likely, they mentioned it to put us off their track," he said. "Edgelaw, which is Waldron's seat, lies likewise to the southeast. But he will more likely ride cross-country through the hills than pass through Ratho. As you have doubtless noted, he avoids most places of habitation."

"I thought he was going to Edinburgh."

"He'll go where he pleases," he said. "I'm guessing the reason his men mentioned Ratho in the lad's hearing was to put us off the track so we don't catch up with him until he is ready for us. We've followed them with surprising ease, you know. If he had not wanted us to know where he was taking your sister, we'd not have heard a whisper about him or his men after they'd abducted her."

"Faith, sir, I do not think it is surprising that we were able to follow them. You know as well as I do how quickly news flies around the Highlands. Someone would have heard or seen enough to tell us their direction."

"Not if Waldron had not wished it," Hugo said.

"But they had to follow beaten tracks to avoid getting lost," she insisted.

"Waldron has no need of tracks to find his way. Had he desired secrecy, no Highlander would have seen him and lived to tell anyone else."

"Sakes, would he kill a man just for catching sight of him?"

"He would if he wanted to preserve secrecy."

"But you cannot be certain he does *not* mean to go to Ratho."

"I am certain he can have only one reason to have let Rory hear the name Ratho," Hugo said. "And that is because he wants us to go there. So we will not."

Instinct told her he was holding something back.

"You promised you would share any information you acquired about my sister's whereabouts, sir. And since she is with Waldron . . ."

"In fact, lass, my promise was to share information I acquired about the lad's whereabouts," he said, calmly meeting her challenging gaze.

"Aye, well, there is something you are not telling me about this village. I want to know what it is."

He shook his head. "Ratho is just a village."

"There *is* something," she insisted.

⁓

Hugo grimaced. He had hoped this moment would delay itself until they had made camp for the evening.

However, he already knew her well enough to be sure she would not let the subject drop merely because he asked her to.

His thoughts leaped to the two most likely reasons Waldron had let slip the name Ratho. Either he was laying a trap or he meant to misdirect them. From that thought followed Hugo's instant awareness that he could waste no more time before getting Sorcha and Sidony out of harm's way.

With a glance back at the others to reassure himself that no one was near enough to overhear unless she shrieked at him, he said, "First, I am certain Waldron has no intention of riding through the streets of Edinburgh with your sister. I think his men told folks that just so we would know what direction to follow them."

"Then where is he going?"

"Most likely, to Edgelaw," Hugo said. "It lies three miles south of Roslin. Its walls are strong and his men well trained, so he can hold out there for some time."

"But if Ratho lies south of Edinburgh, and we go to Ratho, then we'll still be following him, will we not? Even if he continues past Ratho to Edgelaw?"

The time had come. He could see no acceptable way to avoid it any longer.

"*We* are not going to follow him after today," he said with gentle emphasis. "Now that we are closing in on him, I mean to take you and Sidony to Roslin and leave you in the care of my aunt, the countess Isabella. Tomorrow, at Torfinn's Crossing, a mile this side of the royal burgh, we'll turn southeast toward Roslin. Recall that I've sent ahead for reinforcements. They should meet us in—"

"I *won't* go to Roslin without Adela," she interjected fiercely.

He gave her a look, and although she met it bravely, her cheeks drained of color. He knew he need say no more. She understood him, and she understood, too, that she could do nothing to avoid obeying him.

Hoping to ease the sudden tension between them, he said quietly, "Try to understand, lass. My men and I cannot attend to rescuing your sister if we must also protect you and the lady Sidony. You do want us to set Adela free, do you not?"

"Aye, sure, I do," she said. "But she's going to need us! Why cannot we—?"

"As I told you, Edgelaw is only three miles south of Roslin. Whether we find him there or at Ratho, we can get her safely to you in a trice."

"If you are not killed, and if she is not harmed!"

"I shan't be killed," he said. "As to any harm that may have befallen her, I cannot speak to that yet. But Waldron does have his own sense of honor."

"Aye, he's so honorable that Isobel pushed him off the ramparts of Roslin Castle to teach him manners," she retorted scornfully.

There being nothing to say to that that she would accept, he kept silent.

A moment later, she said, "What made him as he is, if he is your cousin?"

Welcoming a change of subject, he said, "As I told you, he is the baseborn son of a deceased French Sinclair cousin. Michael's father did not learn of his existence until he was five, and saw no reason then to remove him from France. But he had my father collect him when he took Henry, Michael, and me to study in France years later. That is when we learned the kinsmen who'd provided his early training had passed on some regrettable notions from forebears who took part in the Crusades."

"What sort of notions?"

"They believed that a soldier of God answers only to God and that God will forgive anything that man does in His name. Many factions at the time believed as much," he added. "But Waldron's instructors taught him that God not only forgives but rewards each of His soldiers when the man enters heaven."

"Sakes, do you mean to say that your cousin believes he will receive his reward no matter what horrors he perpetrates in the meantime?"

"That is just what I mean," he said. "That is what makes him so dangerous."

"But if he believes he can do anything he likes to Adela with impunity, how can you say that he has *any* notion of honor?"

"Because he can claim an even greater reward if he does *not* touch her," he explained. "He once told us the reward in heaven for a soldier of God who stayed celibate would be all the pleasure he'd sacrificed in holy service, and more."

She gaped at him. "So such a man would forever have women to pleasure him? What of those women, though? That does not sound like heaven for them!"

With a wry smile, he said, "He would assure you that they'd enjoy it. Indeed, when Michael asked the same question, Waldron said that the maidens—for so he promised that all of them would be—would know what an honor such a position was for them and would glory in serving such brave and noble men."

Wrinkling her nose, she said scornfully, "Those maidens would none of them be Scotswomen then. That's certain!"

As he stifled a nearly overwhelming urge to laugh, it occurred to Hugo that the discussion was a highly improper one. But he had never known a woman he could talk with as easily and openly as he talked with her. She was so forthright that even when she annoyed, nay, infuriated him, he felt as if he had known her and discussed such forbidden subjects with her all his life.

His three sisters had rarely had a real conversation with him, certainly never on any topic such as this one. His sister Eliza was three years older than he, Kate and Meg seven and eight years younger, and all had fostered with kinsmen after his mother died. If he thought of them at all, he thought them all rather silly.

But Lady Sorcha, as maddening as she could be, was never silly. Nor did she put on airs to be interesting, and if she realized now that their conversation was unseemly, she did not care a whit. Nevertheless, he decided he'd be wiser not to reply to her comment about Scottish women.

They rode in thoughtful silence until she said abruptly, "How on earth does a man come by such a notion even in such odd places as Crusaders must have seen?"

So easy did he feel with her that he nearly told her, but knowing that further explanation would lead only to more questions, including some that he could not in good conscience answer, he said only, "There are many places in the world where people believe things we do not believe, lass. My father did what he could to put such outrageous notions out of Waldron's head, but I'm afraid he failed."

Wanting to divert her, he added ruefully, "I can tell you that we all smarted after he overheard one member of Waldron's fascinated audience exclaim that a bevy of maidens at one's command sounded like a prime reward for any man."

"Which one of you said it?"

"I'd prefer not to answer that."

"I see. Well, I hope you had to take your meals standing for a fortnight."

Chuckling, he said, "I don't think it was quite as long as that."

The chuckle had a warming effect on Sorcha and stirred an urge to see if she could make him laugh again. He had a most attractive smile, too. And so, as much as she would have liked to argue further with him about his absurd decision to send her and her sister to the countess at Roslin, she did not.

It had become clear in the short time she had known him that once he made up his mind to a course of action, persuading him to do otherwise was difficult. However, delighted as she was to have stirred his sense of humor, she had no intention of sitting helplessly at Roslin while Adela remained in danger.

Accordingly, when he asked her to tell him what she liked to do to entertain herself at home, she said she loved riding about, exploring the countryside.

"Do you make a habit of riding alone?"

Rolling her eyes, she said, "Pray, do not be so tiresome as to say I should not. 'Tis exactly why men lead more interesting lives than women. If a man wants to go somewhere, he goes. He does not have to beg permission or have escorts. He simply orders someone to prepare a horse or a boat for him and he goes."

"It is not always as easy as that," he said.

"Bah," she said scornfully. "You know it is. Moreover, if one asks a man a question, he is more likely to say the topic is not suitable for a lady to discuss than he is to answer the question. I detest that! If I ask a question, I want to know the answer. Adela says curiosity is unbecoming to females, but Isobel is the most curious person I know, so I do not think it can be odd that I should want to know about things. Do you think it is odd?"

"I do not," he said, smiling almost as if he understood. "But it is a fact that one cannot discuss some topics as openly as others."

Making a rude noise, she said, "Secrets! I loathe them."

He laughed. But he said, "I've told you there are things I cannot discuss because they are not my tales to tell. But I will answer any question you ask that I'm free to answer if you ask me privately. What would you like to know?"

A host of things, she thought, but settled for asking him about Roslin and his own home at Dunclathy in Strathearn. He described them for her, apparently having forgotten that it was unsafe for her to be riding in the lead with him.

"Is Dunclathy near Roslin?" she asked. "I own, I do not know Strathearn."

" 'Tis a day's ride to the north," he said. "Dunclathy is

my father's seat, but for many years, I've generally spent more time at Roslin and Hawthornden."

"Hawthornden?"

"'Tis another Sinclair castle about a mile down the glen from Roslin. It is little more than a stone keep on a high crag rising from the east bank of the river North Esk, but I liked to ride there often when I was a lad, so years ago Henry named me its constable. He did so in jest, but 'tis a picturesque spot, and I like it. For one thing, when Roslin becomes overcrowded with visitors, as it frequently does, Hawthornden affords me an occasional peaceful retreat."

If Sorcha recalled that Sidony still rode beside Einar Logan and Rory, she did not dwell on that. Instead she encouraged Hugo to continue and listened carefully to all he could tell her about the roads leading to and from Roslin. And if her thoughts drifted at all from their conversation, they drifted only to Ratho and her nagging frustration that he would not take her with him.

But it was not until that evening, as the setting sun painted distant puffy clouds to the west pink, gold, and orange, that it came to her what she must do.

∼

By the time the sun slipped below the horizon, Adela could hardly keep her eyes open. They had got a late start again that morning, waiting for five stragglers, so his lordship pressed them hard all day. And since the road they followed passed through one town or village after another, they spent more time than usual riding around and about, rather than straight through them.

They traveled east for much of the day, then changed direction before stopping for the night. She knew they had turned south, because the setting sun was on her right, rather than behind them. So sleepy that she had all she could do to cling to his lordship and not fall off, she paid no attention to their surroundings until he drew rein at last and said, "Look yonder, lass. See the surprise I've brought you."

A chill of fear stirred, but she leaned obediently forward and peered into the shadows ahead. To her shock, her sister Isobel, great with her expected child, stood in the ambient glow of a cook fire between two men Adela had not seen before.

Isobel clearly had not seen her. She stared at his lordship, her expression reflecting Adela's own horror.

"Waldron," Isobel exclaimed, "I thought you were dead!"

"Greet your sister, Lady Adela," he said sardonically. "Then go to your own tent and stay there. I'll see to her comfort."

Sir Hugo's party had pressed hard all afternoon, too, even through crowded streets in the royal burghs of Stirling and Linlithgow. But Sorcha did not suggest slowing their pace. She wanted as badly as he did to shorten the distance between them and their quarry.

The road was good, and they made excellent speed, riding on after the sun had set and darkness shadowed the landscape. The moon, nearly full, was high even then, and lit their way almost as brightly as the sun had. The few puffy clouds that had lingered to create the splendid sunset had disappeared by the time they stopped near a small loch and Hugo ordered his men to make camp.

"Where are we?" Sorcha asked as he helped her dismount.

"About two miles short of Torfinn's Crossing," he said. "That is Loch Gogar."

She yawned widely. "I'm almost too tired to eat."

"It has been a long day, lass," he said with a smile. "You'll sleep well."

"Aye," she said, although she had no intention of sleeping.

Chapter 11

~

Not until Sidony was fast asleep did Sorcha stir from the makeshift bed they shared in the little tent. Having taken advantage of a few moments when duties on the other side of the encampment occupied Hugo as they prepared for the night, she had complained to one of the men who erected the tent that moonlight shining through its opening would keep them awake. He had obligingly shifted it nearer the woods and had turned the open end toward the trees so their height and a few long branches would continue to block the moon's light as the night progressed.

Congratulating herself on her cleverness, Sorcha crept cautiously out on her hands and knees, then eased into the dark shadows of the nearest large tree and around it into the shelter of the woodland before she looked back.

The camp was quiet, but embers still glowed in the stone circle where the cook fire had burned, and she knew that sentries stood watch somewhere. She had bundled her brown leggings and saffron shirt under an arm, and had put on her dark-gray hooded cloak over the shift and bodice she'd worn to bed. She had also tugged on the hide boots Rory had given her, to protect her bare feet.

In the deepest shadow behind the big tree, moving with extreme caution and watching for sentries, she donned the rest of her lad's clothing, then shoved her shift and bodice into a space between two boulders. As she finished the latter task, a footstep nearby startled her nearly out of her skin.

Hunching low, hoping her dark cloak would blend into nearby undergrowth, she held her breath and waited.

The man passed within a few feet of her, clearly walking his area while keeping inside the tree line. That way, she knew, he could see anyone entering the camp and could also surprise anyone trying to sneak up on them.

Silently thanking whichever of the Fates had allowed her to avoid discovery, and listening carefully to the slight sounds of his retreat, she inched away from the route he had followed, hoping he would not be able to see into her tent easily enough to realize that only one person now slept there.

She also hoped Hugo was a heavy sleeper.

Having taken careful note of several landmarks before going to bed, and having learned as a child to find the North Star, she had expected to maintain a westward course without difficulty long enough to find the crossing they had passed shortly before stopping to make camp.

Having heard one of the men refer to that crossing as

the Glasgow road, she hoped that by going back to it, she could elude Sir Hugo's inevitable search for her and still find the village of Ratho.

Unfortunately, first she had to find her way out of the woods, which proved more difficult than expected. She could see starlight and moonlight through the trees, but she could not see the North Star, and the dense canopy blocked all but an occasional clear view of the moon. Her sense of direction was generally excellent. However, having to wend her way among the trees, she was horrified ten minutes later to see that the moon had somehow shifted from her left to her right.

She stopped and listened, aware that she was heading back toward the camp and in dire peril of walking right into one of Hugo's sentries, if not Hugo himself. She wanting to shriek in frustration, but she could not stay where she was. Staying lost in the stupid woods all night would do neither Adela nor herself any good.

She could not hope to persuade Hugo that she had lost herself looking for the privy pits, since he would certainly wonder why she had changed into leggings and a shirt to look for them. And what he would do to her when he deduced that her destination had been the village of Ratho did not bear thinking about.

Her strongest impulse was to sneak back into the tent and lie down beside Sidony, but she could not do that either.

Since they had seen no sign of reinforcements from Roslin or Lochbuie by the time darkness fell, Sorcha doubted that they would arrive before the next morning at the earliest. Hugo had clearly expected to meet the ones from Roslin on the road, after all. But she had a dreadful feeling that if anything delayed them, Adela might forfeit her last chance to survive. In any event, she meant to do all she could to force Hugo into action as soon as possible.

He was being cautious, she knew, in wanting to send them to Roslin, but too much caution with Adela's safety in the balance was naught but foolishness.

She knew he would follow her as soon as he discovered she was missing, and she doubted that this time she would escape his retribution. But he could do as he liked to her if she could assure Adela's rescue.

The woods were eerily silent. Deciding that since she had seen no further sign of any sentry she could risk keeping a closer eye on the moon's position long enough to find her way out of them, she began to do so. She also increased her pace.

The eerie silence reminded her of Rory's haunted wood, but when a rustle of leaves nearby made her turn her head sharply, she scolded herself for a surfeit of imagination and hurried on, certain she was going the right way at last.

When brighter moonlight ahead assured her that she was near the edge of the wood, she slowed again and took particular care not to make any noise. It occurred to her that if she just stayed hidden, Hugo might still assume she had gone to Ratho and go after her with his men. But she quickly dismissed the notion.

Not only would hiding from him be cowardly, but she had no idea how large the wood was, and he might well find her easily by daylight. Worse, she would not be at hand to comfort Adela. And, too, she told herself ruefully, she had already sealed her fate where Hugo was concerned. Her punishment would likely be as harsh whether she hid in the wood or faced the villains alone.

One might as well be skelped for the whole deed as for its mere intent.

As her mind presented the image of what Hugo would look like and what he would probably do to her, the night darkened, an odiferous cloth engulfed her, a heavy hand clapped over it hard against her face and mouth, and a muscular arm wrapped tight round her waist.

She struggled fiercely against the strength of that arm as it lifted her from the ground. Kicking and squirming, she tried to bite the hand over her mouth through the thick cloth as whoever held her began to run. Alarm shot through her. If he tripped over a root, he might easily fall on her and squash her flat.

She told herself that if the man who held her was Hugo, as she both hoped and feared, he would take care not to harm her. Not that that would help her much in the end, she knew. That thought made her kick harder, and one foot connected solidly enough to elicit a loud grunt of pain from her captor.

The sound stopped the breath in her throat, for by no stretch of imagination could she believe any longer that Hugo had caught her. No grunt from him would sound like that. She realized then that he would not have run as this man was running, either. He would have tossed her over his shoulder as he had done before and, also as he had done before, would likely have smacked her for her furious struggles long before she could have kicked him hard enough to hurt him.

She tried to believe that an ordinary ruffian had caught her, but plain logic insisted that it was one of the men who had hurt Rory. If that was true, she could only hope he did not discover her sex before she could escape.

That hope died when the man carrying her slowed in response to another voice calling softly, "Here, Fin. Did ye get the lass?"

"I got one o' them," the man holding her muttered back. "I dinna ken which, but she's got a fine, lovely body, this one. I watched her change clothes, and I'm telling ye now that if the master says we can enjoy her a bit before he's nae more use for her, I'm for it. The wee vixen kicked me, and I dinna doubt but what she'd bite me hand right off did I give her the chance, so she owes me summat nice!"

Sorcha was certain the lout had not seen much of her, because she had been crouched in heavy shadows at the time. He still held his hand and the heavy cloth tightly across her mouth, and she was beginning to feel faint from lack of air.

The thought that she might lose consciousness made her think of Rory again and the awful stuff they had given him that had made him sick. Perhaps it would be better, she decided, if she did faint from lack of air.

Accordingly, she slumped as limply as she could in the villain's arms.

"Sakes," he exclaimed, "I think I've suffocated her."

"Ye'd best hope ye havena done any such thing, Fin Wylie," the other speaker said. "Carry her into the light here and let's ha' a look at her."

When they pulled the cloth off, she had all she could do to remain still. She was frightened of them but more frightened that they might try to tilt some of their awful potion down her throat.

"She's just gone off into a swoon," the second man said. "We'd best find the other lads and get back afore the master sends someone t' find us."

The impulse to draw a deep breath of fresh air into her lungs was nearly more than Sorcha could control, but she managed to breathe evenly until the two found their companions and mounted horses.

When they lifted her to a saddlebow to lean against the one they called Fin Wylie, she nearly lost control again, because the idea of riding any distance with such a man holding her around the waist was abhorrent.

Only when the one who had done most of the talking warned him that he'd best keep his hands to himself unless he wanted to explain himself to the master was she able to relax and hope that Waldron had imposed his extraordinary beliefs about the hereafter on his men.

Finally able to fill her lungs with fresh air, albeit carefully so as not to alert Fin Wylie to the fact that she was conscious, she soon began to feel more herself again and to wonder how long it would be before Hugo discovered her absence.

Although the possibility had occurred to her that she might fall into the hands of the villains, she had assumed it could not happen before she found their camp, at least several hours after she had slipped away from her own.

She had *hoped* Hugo would not learn what she had done until dawn, but then even her best-laid plans rarely came off as expected. One had only to remember Adela's wedding to realize that. And dawn certainly seemed a long way off now.

Their journey was shorter than she had thought it would be, because surely less than an hour passed before they rode into the enemy camp. She had kept her eyes shut nearly the whole way in fear that one or another of the men would notice if she opened them. From time to time, though, she had opened them to narrow slits and peered through her lashes, but she had seen little to tell her where she was.

When Fin Wylie drew rein, the temptation stirred again to open them, but she resisted and was glad she had when two strong hands gripped her waist and lifted her from the saddle. She found it impossible, however, to maintain her limp posture. When her feet touched the ground and the man holding her let go, she automatically opened her eyes and caught herself.

"Well, well," the man said. "What have we here?" He was as tall as Hugo, with a similar look about him, making her certain she faced Waldron of Edgelaw.

"She's a wee vixen, master," Fin Wylie said. "Kicked me, and tried to bite me."

"Did she?" Waldron said. "Are these your customary clothes, lass?"

Sorcha gave him a blank stare but did not reply, seeing nothing to gain by it.

"I will ask you one more time," he said with enough menace in his voice to make her shiver. "Do you customarily dress in male clothing?"

"No."

"No, what?"

"No, I do not customarily dress like this."

Peripheral awareness of the four men who had captured her looking at one another told her she had answered incorrectly, but she continued to gaze at their master, straightening her shoulders as she did.

He was silent for a long moment before he said, "You want manners, my lady, and I think I shall enjoy teaching them to you. But for the moment you will come with me. There is someone who will be eager to see you."

Gripping her upper arm, he urged her to a nearby tent and shoved her inside. Expecting to see Adela, she stopped short at the sight of Isobel, wide awake, lying awkwardly on a pile of furs with her wrists bound to a tent post.

"Sorcha!" she exclaimed. "What are you doing here?"

"Searching for Adela, of course. But how did you get here?"

"They captured me when I walked a short distance from the castle after Michael and the others left with the flotilla," Isobel said. "I thought I heard a child crying, so I went farther than usual, but it was a trap. They were waiting for me."

"But if his grace and the others left before you, why are they not here yet?"

"Because they went around the Mull of Kintyre so others from the south could join them, whilst we came across the isthmus from West Loch Tarbert." Isobel tried to sit up, then said in frustration, "Can you untie me?"

Sorcha took a step toward her, but the hand that had so recently released her caught her arm again.

"You will ask my permission first," Waldron said.

Sorcha looked up at him. "Why should I when you will simply refuse it?"

"Because you do not know I will," he replied calmly. "Until you know me better, lass, you would do well to tread lightly. I hold two of your sisters, after all. 'Tis they who will pay the price for your insolence if you try me further."

"Sakes, would you hurt a woman big with child? Only a mons—"

"Sorcha, be silent," Isobel said sharply. "You do not know him."

"Wise advice, Lady Isobel. Let us hope your insolent little sister accepts it."

Gritting her teeth, Sorcha inhaled deeply and exhaled before she said, "Very well then, may I untie her hands?"

"Certainly," he said. "I doubt she will try to escape whilst you and Adela are here, or that she can get far if she does."

Isobel said, "I would like to have a few minutes of privacy outside, if I may."

"You just went an hour ago," he said.

"Aye, but women in my condition require frequent relief," she said.

"I'll have one of my men take you then."

"That's barbaric," Sorcha said. "I'll take her. If you like, I'll give you my word that we won't try to escape. We are not going anywhere without Adela."

To her surprise, he smiled, but it was not a pleasant smile, and she had no wish to ask him what he thought was funny. Expecting him to refuse permission, she was surprised again when he nodded. "Take her then, but do not stay long."

Outside, he directed them to the area they wanted, and when they had found a suitable place, Isobel moved to brace herself against a tree, murmuring so that her words barely reached Sorcha's ears, "Is anyone with you or close behind?"

"I don't think so," Sorcha said quietly. "When Hugo finds out that—"

"So Hugo found you?"

"Aye, yestermorn, but I doubt he knows yet that I've left camp. He is expecting some of Hector's men, and likewise some from Roslin, but I do not know when they will arrive. He'll come, though, as soon as he learns that I've gone. He'll know I meant to come here. That is, he will, if we are near the village of Ratho."

"Sakes, I haven't a notion where we are," Isobel said.

"I don't, either, but Rory MacIver heard them say the name, and Hugo said it lay somewhere hereabouts."

Isobel made a sound then that sounded like a groan.

"Are you ill?" Sorcha demanded. "It cannot have been good for you to travel so far, as big with child as you are. You must have made all speed, too, if you left after Michael and his grace left. That was likewise yestermorn, was it not?"

"Aye," Isobel said, straightening again with the support of the tree. "The men had a galley, doubtless the one Michael thinks they used to take Adela south from Glenelg to Loch Ailort. He believes they had it from the wicked Green Abbot of the Holy Isle, who has helped Waldron before. You do know that Waldron is a cousin to the Sinclairs, and thus also cousin to Sir Hugo."

"Aye, Hugo told me."

"Another galley waited for us in East Loch Tarbert, so we walked across the isthmus, made Dumbarton by morning, and reached this place late this afternoon."

"If he managed to summon up two galleys, even from the Green Abbot, he must have planned this venture carefully beforehand," Sorcha murmured.

"Aye, sure, but what else did Hugo tell you? Nay, never mind," Isobel added hastily, looking around as if she expected the very trees to have ears. "But do take care not to infuriate Waldron, Sorcha. He is a demon, believe me."

"Did you really push him off the ramparts at Roslin? Hugo said you did."

"I did, and by rights he should be dead, but demons don't die easily."

She spoke more loudly than before, so Sorcha was not surprised to hear Waldron say, "Come, ladies, it is time to go back to your wee tent."

Exchanging a look with Isobel, Sorcha wondered, just as her sister clearly did, how much he had heard them say.

He gave no indication that he had heard any of it as he guided them back to the tent, saying only, "You will sleep here with your sister, Lady Sorcha."

"I want to see Adela first," Sorcha said.

"Not tonight," he said. "She is asleep."

Sorcha would have protested, but Isobel pinched her arm, silencing her.

When they were alone in the tent, Isobel said, "Adela will not thank you for being here, Sorcha. She was absolutely furious to see me."

"Well, she should have been furious," Sorcha said. "The very idea that Waldron and his louts would force a woman in your condition to travel all the way from Lochbuie to this horrid place should infuriate any civilized person."

"Aye, sure, but she seemed angry with me, not him. And I suspect that she will be just as unhappy to see you."

Adela was too angry to sleep. She had lain awake, mentally flaying everyone she could think of, especially Isobel. What, she wondered, had Isobel been thinking to let herself be captured? And where was Michael, that he'd allowed such a thing?

Although she tried, she could not seem to ease her fury. Since no one could have abducted Isobel from inside the walls of Lochbuie, she must have done something stupid to get herself captured. Not only had she thus put herself and her baby in danger, but she had also spoken the name Waldron aloud. Since that moment, Adela had been unable to think of him any longer as simply his lordship, a man with sincere beliefs whom she might eventually persuade to be more civil. That image had evaporated in the horror-stricken moment when Isobel's very presence had reminded her of how evil he could be and the threats he had made. What would he do now?

Between them, Isobel and Sorcha had always been her two most troublesome sisters, with Isobel's unending curiosity and Sorcha's headstrong defiance often leading each into mischief. Had it not been enough that Sorcha had interfered in a matter that was none of her business? Adela was still angry with her, too, so angry that at one point in her reflections she thought that she heard Sorcha's voice.

Then, realizing that her thoughts had taken her full circle, she tried to bring herself up short, to remind herself again that Waldron was the one at fault. But she dared not rail at him, for by no means could she persuade herself that he would not react brutally if she did. And who would he use then to teach her a lesson?

She believed he had come to like her a little. Had he not said she was a good listener? Did he not speak civilly to her? He had not even lost his temper when she'd said he should take her at once if he meant to take her at all. In fact, he had not done anything brutal since the hanging Monday night, four whole nights ago—a lifetime.

But capturing the pregnant Isobel had hardly been civil. Adela tried to push the nagging reminder away, but she could not, because something inside told her that only a thoroughly evil man could do such a thing. Still, she tried to persuade herself that Waldron could not be thoroughly evil. Although evil men or evil thoughts must have influenced him to act as he had, only the devil himself was evil clear through.

Waldron served God, and God was not evil. God had a purpose in all He did.

On that thought, Waldron entered the tent without warning.

"Good, you're awake," he said.

She gazed blankly at him, wondering why he had come to her at such an hour. Could he mean at last to break the vow that he had made to God and to her?

"I couldn't sleep," she said warily.

"You'll have to get up. I'm having them move this tent into the woods. We'll leave the other where it is for now, but from any distance, I want this area to look as if no one else is here."

"Then you mean to use Isobel as bait to catch Michael and Hugo," she said, forcing herself to speak matter-of-factly as she thrust off the blanket. "She ought never to have come here."

He shrugged. "She did not come by choice. I needed her."

Without thinking, she snapped, "But how could you? To have endangered her baby—" She broke off, furious with herself and terrified that she had stirred his anger again, anger that could now endanger Isobel and her baby even more. "I beg your pardon, my lord," she said hastily, wondering what demon had taken possession of her tongue. "I know I should not speak so to you."

To her astonishment, she thought she heard a trace of defensiveness as he said, "Until you told me, I did not know her time was so near. By then it was too late to do anything about it, but no harm has come to her, and I needed her."

"To set a trap so you can kill her husband and Sir Hugo."

"I won't kill them," he said. "Not straightaway. First, I must learn all they can tell me about the treasure."

"Treasure?" She barely said the word aloud, but although he had tolerated her earlier plain speaking, his eyes narrowed ominously now.

"Surely, you know that anything stolen from the Kirk must be thought of as treasure," he said. "Heretics held it, and when the Pope ordered its return and disbanded their unholy organization, they fled with it. The Kirk has been searching for it since the early years of this century, and as I have kinsmen amongst the family chiefly suspected of concealing it, I became one of the chosen."

Drawing breath to steady her voice, she said, "I agree that if the Sinclairs have taken something that does not belong to them they must return it, but you must not use Isobel to bait your trap. If a fight breaks out, she could easily be hurt."

"Aye, well, I'll think about that," he said. "I've no wish to harm any babe unless it becomes necessary. Mayhap the lady Sorcha will suffice as my bait."

"Sorcha!" She remembered the voice she had heard.

"Aye, she came to pay us a visit just before the moon went down, and I've no doubt that Hugo must be close on her heels. So pick up all you can carry and bring it with you. I want to get everyone out of sight straightaway."

⁓

Two hours before dawn, Hugo awoke to darkness, fully alert and aware that someone stood silently nearby, just beyond his view. The moon had set, the black sky above was full of stars, and the air felt cold and damp. He lay perfectly still, relying on his senses for further information before he reacted.

Whoever it was was neither large nor heavy, for although he detected faster than normal breathing, it was soft, not labored or stertorous. With that awareness, a slight scent of lavender wafted to him. His first deduction was that it might be Sorcha, but the knowledge that she would not hesitate to wake him brought him swiftly to the obvious but less welcome conclusion.

Slowly, as though he still slept, he turned his head.

Discerning the slender shape huddled in a cloak in shadows nearby, he saw that it definitely was not Sorcha, and despite having already reached that conclusion, the disappointment he felt startled him with its sharpness.

Then he saw that Sidony was wringing her hands.

Knowing he could easily frighten her, he forced calm into his voice as he said, "What's amiss, my lady?"

"Oh, thank heaven you are awake, sir!" she said without coming a step nearer. "I could not decide if I should disturb you, but I am dreadfully afraid."

With every instinct now warning him to bring her quickly to the point, he said, "What has frightened you?"

"I . . . I truly do not know if I should tell you," she said.

"Why not?"

"I fear it will make you angry," she said. "Or perhaps it will . . ."

When she hesitated again, he sat up, fighting to keep his patience. "Or perhaps you believe it will anger your sister. Come now, where is she?"

"I . . . I do not know," Sidony admitted, and he heard tears in her voice.

Shoving back the blanket, he stood up, and although he kept his distance from her, he said more sternly, "Are you sure you do not know where she is?"

"I swear it, sir. The cold woke me, and I saw at once that she was gone."

"Mayhap she merely sought to—"

"No, sir. I waited long enough to be sure of that before I came to find you."

"Did you ask the men if anyone had seen her?"

She shook her head, looking horrified at the thought.

"By heaven," he said, "if she has—"

"Oh, please, Sir Hugo, I'm so afraid that she went to find Adela just as Rory tried to do. I know she was unhappy with your decision to send us to Roslin instead of taking us with you. But if they have caught her, as they caught Rory, they may do something horrible to her. Can we not go at once and find her?"

"Lady Sidony, your sister deserves whatever they do to her," Hugo said wrathfully. "And whatever they may have done by the time I find her, I promise you, I'll do more. But you are not going with me. I'm sending you to Roslin, where you will be safe. Then I'll collect your sisters, both of them. You have my word."

His promises did not seem to have relieved her mind. She readily expressed confidence that he would find them, however, so he knew she was only worried about what he would do to Sorcha.

And, indeed, he muttered to himself, she had every reason to be worried about that.

Chapter 12

~

Hugo wasted no time. Shouting to waken his men, he ordered a party out to search the nearby woods while others prepared for a hasty departure. A member of the search party returned minutes later with Sorcha's bodice and shift.

"That is what she was sleeping in!" Sidony exclaimed. "You don't think they can have stripped—"

"What I think is that she put on the clothing she was wearing when I found you," he interjected harshly. "If you look, I'll wager you'll find it's missing."

She ran to the tent as men were about to dismantle it, plunged inside, and emerged again with a bundle that proved to be her male clothing and Sorcha's russet skirt and jerkin. Sorcha's shirt, leggings, and cloak were all missing.

Hugo lingered only long enough after that for his men to finish their search and find evidence of standing horses, boot prints, and some sort of a struggle near a track leading toward a glacial ridge to the south. Aware that the village of Ratho lay beyond that ridge, he gathered his men and gave them their orders as they hastily wolfed cold food to sustain them through the next few hours.

Selecting the best warriors to go with him, he sent two men back toward Linlithgow to guide Hector's men to Ratho if they met them, then sent a third with Rory to escort Sidony. "Take the extra horses with you and follow the road to Torfinn's Crossing," he said. "Turn south there toward Roslin, and when you meet our reinforcements from the castle, speed them on their way to Ratho."

They agreed, and watching them go, he realized that he had only thirteen men left to him and wondered what Macleod would say to the number. He also wondered how many men Waldron had amassed.

Nearly an hour had passed since Sidony had wakened him.

He spent the twenty-minute ride up the ridge pondering what strategy would serve him best. His men, though few, were highly trained, seasoned warriors. Most had learned as he had to fight in the open if possible but to employ skillful stealth if openness would not serve. A frontal attack would be out of the question. Not only did Waldron very likely now hold two defenseless women as hostages, but he doubtless also knew how many men Hugo had, and expected him to ride straight into his trap.

It occurred to Hugo then that if his cousin had set up an ambush, he might have moved the women out of harm's way. Waldron would not hesitate to threaten them or even to hurt them if he thought doing either would force Hugo to lead him to the treasure, but Hugo doubted that he would harm either woman unless he believed such action would serve his primary purpose.

He tried to imagine a way that he and his men might skirt Waldron's camp and come on it from behind but realized such a tactic would prove futile. His cousin would not be waiting for him anyplace where they could so easily surprise him.

It had grown light enough by then to reveal that the glacial ridge was mostly granite with scattered, windblown shrubs and scrawny trees, which Hugo knew would provide scant cover as they rode up the slope, or when they reached the top. By the same token, there was scant cover for watchers above. That they had seen none seemed to indicate that Waldron was confident enough of their coming that he felt no need to set a watch at any distance from his trap.

When they neared the crest, Hugo signaled a halt and dismounted. Leaving his men, he strode ahead to the crest on foot. Once there, despite the still-shadowy twilight, he kept low and took advantage of any black shadow he found. Scanning the area below, he tried to think as Waldron would.

He saw no sign of anyone moving down the southern slope, but below and to his right lay patches of woodland and the village of Ratho, consisting of a steepled stone kirk, a dozen or so thatched cottages, a few shops, and a smithy, all arranged around a small market square.

To the east, a thick stretch of woodland gave way to a long oval clearing, then more woodland extending into low hills. Beyond those hills lay Roslin and Edgelaw. He could discern the track Waldron's men had followed from the ridge to the woods. He also saw a small tent centered near the south edge of the clearing.

Slipping back down the north slope to his waiting men, he said crisply, "Einar Logan, Tam Swanson, and Wat MacComas, you'll stay with me. Fergus Mann, you take the others and ride into the village, where you'll ask if anyone has seen riders or women, and anything else it may occur to you to ask."

Fergus Mann, whose thick torso belied the fact that he was one of Hugo's finest swordsmen, raised an eyebrow and said, "Ye're no coming with us, sir?"

"You are going to provide a diversion," Hugo said. "The village lies a half mile to the west of us. A half mile east of us lies a clearing with a single small tent in it. If you see any activity there as you descend from the crest, ignore it and continue toward the village. If, as I anticipate, his watchers decide I have split my forces even more than I have, they'll believe I'm with you and will be too far away to see otherwise. My intent is to divert their attention, perhaps delay things a little, and hope reinforcements arrive. So let it be known in the village that you'll ride to the clearing from there, so that anyone coming from the north to help can find us."

Fergus said lightly, "And what will ye be doing, sir, if a man may ask?"

Hugo grinned. "We four will be afoot, scrambling downhill into the stretch of woods on this side of the clearing. We'll try not to draw attention, but it is quickly growing light and that slope has no more cover than this one does. Still, if they are watching you, we can hope they'll not see us. I'll wager that if we can slip into those woods and make it around to the south side, we can

handle any trouble we meet there and might manage to
even things up a bit for our side."

"How long d'ye need?" Fergus asked.

"As long as you can manage," Hugo said. "When you
leave the village, ride slowly and take care to search any
woodland you pass through on your way to the clearing,
but keep your eyes open for trouble."

"Aye, we'll do that, right enough."

"I'll wager that at some point, an incident will occur
to direct your attention wherever Waldron wants it directed," Hugo added. "When that happens, use your own
judgment."

"I warrant ye mean that if Waldron captures Wat, Einar,
Tam, and yerself, and looks about to hang ye all, ye'd like
us to interfere," Fergus said, shooting a grin at Einar.

Einar just shook his head, but Hugo said, "Aye, Fergus,
that's it exactly."

He and the three men he had chosen to stay with him
tethered their horses and hurried eastward, keeping out of
sight near the top of the ridge until the others had made
their way halfway down the south slope. Then, putting
distance between themselves to be less noticeable from
below, they made their way swiftly but cautiously down
the slope toward the long patch of woods.

Minutes later, Hugo saw movement in the clearing. A
man stepped out of the woods on the south edge of the
clearing, walked to the tent, and ducked his head inside.
Then he straightened, pulling two figures from the tent.
One wore skirts, the other a man's shirt and leggings, and
Hugo's heart clenched at the sight of the latter. Although
her hair looked pale and colorless in the lingering twilight, it was unmistakably Sorcha. Then the other one

turned, and he saw clearly that it was a woman big with child. The shock of recognizing Isobel shook him to his core.

Hastily signaling to Wat MacComas, some yards to his right, Hugo met him behind a clump of shrubbery. "Do you see them?" he asked.

"Aye, sir, a man, a lad, and a woman."

"I cannot say for sure that the man is Waldron, but the other two are the lady Sorcha and Sir Michael's lady."

"Lady Isobel?" Wat looked again, but the women had disappeared.

"Aye," Hugo said. "They are the bait to draw us in. He showed them so we would see them, but the lads will ride on to the village as I bade them. Still, Lady Isobel's presence alters things. I want you to go back to the horses, Wat, and wait for our reinforcements. Warn any that come that Lady Isobel is one of his hostages. We must take the greatest care to see that neither she nor the babe suffers any hurt."

"Aye, sir, I'll go straightaway."

Hugo stayed where he was until Wat had got well away, then made his way quickly down to the wood.

~

Sorcha was furious. "The nerve of that horrid man," she muttered angrily.

"Hush, dearling," Isobel said. "He will hear you."

"I don't care if he does," Sorcha declared. "Did you hear him? He has archers in the woods, he said, with their arrows aimed right at this tent! They will let fly, he says, if we make any attempt to leave it."

"I heard him," Isobel said, gently rubbing her belly.

"Did the baby move?"

"I think he wants out," she said. "I just hope he can be patient until we are all safe again." She paused, then added, "They won't shoot us, you know."

"Not until Hugo comes, or Michael," Sorcha said sourly.

"Not then, either," Isobel said confidently.

"Then we should just leave."

"Nay, he'd put us back and tie us as he tied me before. He'll want us at hand so he can threaten us, to force them to tell him all he wants to know."

"Do you know what that is?"

"I know what he wants," Isobel admitted. "I don't know where it is."

"What is it?"

"What did Hugo tell you?"

"Just that Waldron thinks the Sinclairs have something belonging to the Roman Kirk." She paused, hoping Isobel would tell her more. When she did not, Sorcha said with a sigh, "He said he cannot tell me what it is because he has sworn an oath not to. But you cannot have sworn any such oath, so tell me what you know."

"I promised, too, Sorcha. I must not."

Fairly groaning with frustration, Sorcha said, "Men play the game of life with stupid rules, and you are doing the same thing. Here we are, our lives at risk because of such a game, and you will not tell me even the little you know."

"Would you, if you had sworn not to talk about something important?"

"Aye, sure . . . nay, perhaps not," Sorcha said, realizing that if she had made such a promise to Hugo, or to

Michael or Hector Reaganach, she would feel obliged to keep her word. With another sigh, she said, "No, I wouldn't in such a case, but this is different, because we are sisters. You should know you can trust me."

"I do know that. I can even trust you not to press me further now that I have explained why I cannot speak."

Recognizing defeat, for the moment, Sorcha gave up.

By the time Hugo reached the woods to the south, the sky had lightened considerably and a golden halo over the hills to the east announced the sun's imminent appearance. On his way, he had spied at least one man in the woods watching Fergus and the other horsemen, but the fellow had paused only long enough to get a good look at them before turning away. He showed no sign of having seen Hugo, Einar, or Tam Swanson making their way downhill on foot.

To his right, Hugo saw Tam flit like a wraith among the trees. To his left, barely visible in the shadows, Einar stood against the wide trunk of a tall beech. Even as Hugo watched him, the smaller man seemed to blend into the bark of the tree and disappear, and he reflected that Einar was almost as skilled as Michael was at moving silently on unfamiliar terrain.

Hearing a sound to his right, he looked back at Tam to see him stretch overhead and pull himself hand over hand into the spreading branches of an ancient oak. It was not Tam who had made the sound, though. Another man crept through nearby foliage, a long dirk in one hand, peering about as if he hunted game.

Slipping behind the nearest tree, Hugo caught Einar's eye and gestured.

When Einar nodded and disappeared, Hugo turned back to see the hunter pass beneath Tam's tree.

Tam dropped lightly behind him from the branches, caught him by the jaw with one hand, and slit his throat in a swift move with the dagger he held in the other before the man could lift his own weapon.

Hugo went to help Tam drag the body under a bush, and as they turned from that task, Einar appeared from the shadows, holding up a finger and pointing west with his other hand. When they joined him, he murmured, "I dealt wi' one yonder, creeping about wi' his pig sticker like that one, but others be set nearby to ambush our lads—near a score o' them. Some ha' bows already fixed with arrows."

"And likely another score lining every side but the one from which they expect our approach," Hugo muttered in reply.

"Aye, and they'd close that side behind our lads were they so foolish as to ride into such a trap," Tam said.

"Did you catch sight of Waldron?" Hugo asked Einar.

"Nay, I did not. Likely, he'll be conferring somewhere wi' his captains."

"Then let's dispatch a few more strays before they miss these two," Hugo said. He had no need to tell them to remember where they had stowed the bodies of any men they killed. They knew his ways and knew they'd not leave before giving each dead man a proper burial.

With any luck, they'd have more than two villains to put underground and could let whatever prisoners they took dig the graves.

No sooner did Adela step outside after restoring Waldron's things to their proper places after his men had repositioned the tent a short distance inside the woods than he gestured sharply for her to go back. But with only her turbulent thoughts for company, she could not wait patiently in the tent.

She wanted to vent her feelings, to scream her fury, but she could not. And although the tent was larger than the one in which he had put Isobel, it was not large enough for pacing. Thoughts of his evil ways soon returned to haunt her.

If only Isobel were not pregnant! If only Waldron's men had not found her! But Adela had long since learned the futility of "if only," and found no comfort there.

As for Sorcha, what was that impetuous, disobedient child doing in such a place on her own? And how had she managed it? Waldron had made no attempt to conceal the fact that he had somehow induced Sir Hugo to follow them, but by no stretch of Adela's imagination could she imagine Hugo saddling himself with Sorcha. Nor could she imagine Macleod or anyone else allowing her to set off on her own.

But she could easily imagine Sorcha defying them all and setting out to look for her without anyone's permission. Such behavior would be just like her, so doubtless she deserved whatever happened to her now.

Adela said the same things to herself over and over, but no matter how many times she did, she could not feel anything but sorrow for what would doubtless happen to both Sorcha and Isobel. What Waldron was doing was evil! No matter what his reasons or how thoroughly he believed in the rightness of his cause, to kill innocent women to further that cause could be naught *but* evil. She could not think straight from one minute to the next, could not predict her own behavior, and could not imagine how a holy mission could be evil, but she knew evil when she saw it.

But she could do nothing to prevent it. She was still standing there, staring bleakly at the fur pallet that served as her bed, when she heard a distant shout.

Thought ceased, and she darted to the entrance to peer outside.

The men near the tent had vanished, as had Waldron. But she saw movement at the clearing's edge and knew that some of them must be there. Moving as warily as she knew how from one tree to the next, she sought a hiding place from which she could see the little tent where he had put Isobel and doubtless Sorcha, as well.

Adela had noted that he had not promised to move Isobel to safety but had said only that he would think about using Sorcha for bait. And doubtless he had forgotten those words as soon as he had left her. Even so, she kept glancing over her shoulder lest he return with Isobel and find her missing.

Under the circumstances, she knew that if he discovered her absence, no excuse would shield her from his anger. He would kill her without a second thought. After all, he would have Isobel, her baby, and Sorcha as his hostages. Moreover, he would believe killing her would teach them a lesson in how they must behave.

The increasing confidence she had developed in her ability to manage him vanished at the thought, but as it did, her fear for herself seemed to ease as well. She soon found a place that would conceal her from the few men she could see, yet provide a view of the tent. As she cautiously took her position, she saw Waldron stride to the little tent and peer inside. Perhaps he did mean to protect Isobel.

He seemed to be speaking to someone inside, and hope leaped that he was telling Isobel she could come out. Poised to run to her own tent, even if it meant casting caution to the wind, Adela waited to see what he would do next.

To her disappointment and frustration, he straightened and walked back amid the trees. When she lost sight of him, she stopped breathing, fearing he might walk straight to her. Then she saw him again, moving away along the perimeter, murmuring to men who waited there for their quarry to appear.

Nothing had explained the shout she'd heard, but when she looked toward the tent again, she saw horsemen approaching from the west, perhaps a dozen, riding slowly. They paused where the clearing widened before them, and she saw that they carried no banner. The few of Waldron's men that she could see grew more alert, drawing swords and fitting arrows to bowstrings.

The little tent sat right in the line of fire, and the big-sister part of Adela, the part that had taken care of her family for years, wanted to run and snatch Isobel and Sorcha to safety. The rest of her, the small, still-terrified part, wanted to run to her own tent and curl up tight with her hands over her ears.

As she stood hesitating, a large hand clamped over her mouth and an arm snapped around her waist. Terrified to her bones that Waldron had sneaked up behind her and meant to throttle her for her disobedience, or cut off her head and fling it into the path of the approaching horsemen, she fainted dead away.

⁓

When Waldron had walked away from the tent, Sorcha watched him go, then went back inside, where she knelt at the rear and lifted the tent's edge to look out.

"He's right, Isobel," she said. "Horsemen are coming, but barely half of Hugo's force. Although Waldron said he's leading them, I don't see him."

"Well, they wouldn't be here without him," Isobel said.

She lay awkwardly on the fur pallet that had served them as a bed. Her face was too pale for Sorcha's liking, and she was clearly in great discomfort, although she steadfastly insisted that she was fine, that the babe was merely restless, as it had been all through the night.

Sorcha squinted, trying to see more clearly. "They are still a good distance away," she said. "But I'm sure Hugo is not with them. For one thing, he nearly always rides Hector's Black Thunder, and I don't see a single black horse."

A muffled groan was the only answer.

Turning her head, she saw that Isobel had curled onto her side and was clearly trying to find a more comfortable position.

"Can I help?" she asked, moving swiftly to her side.

Isobel managed a smile. "Nay, I'm just—" Breaking off, she gasped to choke off another cry of pain, then closed her eyes for a long moment before she said, "Mercy, that was the strongest yet, and they're coming closer and closer together."

A jolt of fear surged through Sorcha. "It's too soon!"

"Aye, it is, but I think this babe wants to be born."

Taking a deep breath to calm herself, Sorcha said, "Then, pray, tell me quickly what I must do if it does come, for I haven't a notion."

"Sakes, do you think I know?" Isobel demanded. "I was two when you were born, three for Sidony. I thought Cristina would be at hand when he came, and Mairi. Between them they have borne eight children, but I hadn't even been at Lochbuie long enough to discuss it with them before those men caught m—"

Again her words ended in a cry of pain. This time the episode lasted longer.

"Isobel, what's happening? Tell me! Tell me what to do!"

"Don't do anything," Isobel gasped. "You might do something wrong. If this babe is coming, he's coming, and we'll just have to figure out what to do when he does." She gasped again, then seemed to find it easier to breathe normally. She eased herself back to her earlier, supine position on the pallet of furs.

"Maybe Adela knows," Sorcha said. "I'll ask someone to send for her."

"Has she ever attended a birthing?"

"I don't think so, but she is older. She must know more than we do."

She stood and turned toward the tent entrance, but before she got there, Isobel cried out, "Wait, something's wrong! Something horrible is happening!"

She tugged her skirt up, and even before she pulled it past her knees, Sorcha saw blood mixed with other fluids and did the only thing she could think to do.

She screamed as loudly as she could.

~

Hugo heard Sorcha scream as he was trying to cope with Adela's dead weight in his arms. He had stolen up behind her and taken the precaution of silencing her, because he could not count on her to keep quiet if she saw him or he startled her. But the wretched lass had swooned in his arms.

Lowering her to the ground and signing to Einar to watch her, he ran toward the tent from which the scream had come. In the distance, he saw his men urging their ponies to a faster pace and wondered if Waldron had somehow forced the scream to draw them into his trap.

Experience warned him that he should move cautiously, but his feet wouldn't listen. She was screaming for help, and now he could hear Isobel's cries as well. He was running as fast as he could, so when Waldron leaped from the woods in front of him, sword drawn, Hugo nearly impaled himself before he managed to leap back and snatch out his own sword.

As Waldron's men rushed from the woods toward the oncoming horsemen and Hugo set himself to meet Waldron, Sorcha appeared in the opening of the tent and screamed, "Isobel's having her baby, and something's wrong. She needs help! Please, she may die unless you can fetch someone who knows about birthing."

Hugo did not take his eyes from Waldron. "Do you want that babe's death, or Isobel's, on your conscience when you meet your Maker, cousin?"

Waldron's gaze flicked toward the tent, where Sorcha stood, arms akimbo, glowering at them both equally.

"Don't just stand there like posts," she snapped. "Get help!"

Waldron looked at Hugo. "How many other men have you in these woods?"

"Two," Hugo said.

Waldron smiled. "Then go and help her if you must. We'll have our contest afterward. My men will have defeated yours by the time the child comes, so I am willing to wait, if only to spare us both distraction. I would not want you or anyone else to think I'd bested you because of a woman's screams."

Hugo thought of Adela, still in the woods, but he did not mention her, hoping she had got safely away. He had left Einar to watch her, but since that left only Tam to deal with the other archers they had seen, Einar might not have stayed there.

Glancing toward his horsemen and Waldron's men racing to meet them, he saw that his lads were still beyond reach of any but the most skilled marksmen, but unless Einar and Tam could prevent it, arrows soon would be flying.

When Sorcha screamed, "Hurry!" he ran to the tent but kept his sword in hand, knowing he could not trust his cousin to keep his word.

"What are you doing?" Sorcha demanded, blocking the entrance. "Get help!"

"I'll help her, lass," he said gently. "You can help, too."

"But what can you know of birthing? She wants a woman!"

"She wants someone who can help her," Hugo said. "Now, either come outside and leave her to me, or stay and help us. But get out of my way."

"Sorcha, don't leave," he heard Isobel say, gasping. "If Hugo says he knows what to do, we can trust that he does."

"In troth, my lady," he said, pushing past Sorcha and ducking into the tent, "I have birthed many newborn animals, but only two babes. Still, you are healthy and strong. I warrant we shall do the thing easily together."

"She's bleeding, Hugo," Sorcha said behind him, clearly striving for calm despite her evident fear. "And our . . . our mother died in childbirth."

He turned his head to smile reassuringly at her as he said, "Lass, birthing is a messy, noisy, and sometimes scary process, but 'tis a natural one for all that. All manner of women have given birth since time began with little or no help. Now, I'm going to need room, so see if you can get behind her and help support her. She'll not want to lie flat, and I need to see if the babe is visible yet."

Sorcha looked as if she would protest that need, but Isobel winced and cried out louder than before, impelling her to move quickly to her side and try to prop her up. The result was that when the next pain came, Isobel nearly knocked her flat.

"Would it not be better for her just to lie down?" Sorcha asked him as she helped Isobel sit up again.

" 'Tis said to be easier if she can sit up a bit to push the babe out," Hugo said. "If we had a birthing stool, it would be easier yet. Try sitting behind her, back to back, and letting her push against you. This may take a good while."

"I don't think it will," Isobel said, still gasping from the last pains. "This laddie wants to be born. He has *not* inherited his father's patience."

Hugo did not argue, but he knew a first child could take a long time to be born even if all went well. And if it didn't go well, tragedy could lie ahead. He wished that his abilities matched the confidence he was trying to display. Sending up a prayer that he would be able to pay attention to what he had to do and would not let the noise of the battle raging outside distract him, he set to work.

The baby's head was well in view, which was good. It was not coming feetfirst and might come quickly. He looked at Isobel, whose face was bright red with the contraction she was suffering as she gave a mighty effort to push the babe out.

"Breathe, my lady," he said. "Try to think of something other than the pain. Think of Michael and—"

"A pox on Michael," she snapped. "He did this. He should share the pain!"

"Then just concentrate on breathing as you decide how to punish him," Hugo said, repressing an urge to laugh. "The child needs the air as much as you do."

He glanced at Sorcha, who sat as he had recommended, bracing Isobel as she strained to push. Sorcha looked over her shoulder at him, and he saw that despite her worry, the tantalizing dimple showed and her eyes were twinkling.

Sorcha had to exert every muscle to support Isobel. A tent with nothing for furnishing but a few furs piled together to make a bed was no place to birth a baby. They needed pillows to support her properly and blankets and water for washing.

Hugo had been right to say the process was a messy one. It made her queasy to look at the blood, so except for glancing back at Hugo now and again, she kept her eyes fixed straight ahead and tried to ignore all the noise outside.

She had always known Isobel was strong, but as she tried to support her in a half-sitting, half-lying position, she had all she could do not to be flattened again when the pains struck and her sister fought to push against them. And where, she wondered, was Adela? Surely, she had heard them screaming. Why had she not come to help? Her presence would be of greater use than her absence was even if she didn't know more than they did.

She was glad Hugo was there and glad she had stopped the fight between him and Waldron, but she knew that others might be shocked to learn he had delivered Isobel's babe. For that matter, despite Isobel's insistence, to have a man who was not her husband doing such a thing must be most trying for her.

She glanced at him again and saw that he was concentrating on his task, his hands between Isobel's legs. Moments later, Hugo held a tiny, moist baby in those hands. As he turned him and gently wiped a huge hand across his tiny lips and nose, the baby began to cry, and then to squall lustily.

"You have a fine wee laddie, Isobel," Hugo said. "He's

clearly got a fine, strong pair of lungs, too, which augurs well for the rest of him."

His sparkling gaze met Sorcha's as she shifted position to see better. When she saw that his delight equaled her own, her heart turned over.

⟶

Adela returned to consciousness to find herself lying on the ground under a large bush. She had a dim, disorienting memory of a voice shouting at her to wake up, then hands pulling her, but she decided it must have been a dream. Gazing up at the thicket of branches just over her head, she lay still for a long moment, staring at dust-mote-strewn rays of sunlight that pierced through here and there, before the shouting, clashing of swords, and other noises of battle reached her ears.

Memory swept back, and she scrambled to her feet. She saw no sign of who had grabbed her and dragged her under the bush. The woods seemed empty.

Hurrying toward the noise, she saw that the battle was fierce between the horsemen she had seen and Waldron's men. Then the tent came into view, and she saw to her shock that he stood outside it, pacing back and forth as if there were no battle. Beyond, the two forces seemed more nearly matched than she had expected.

Waldron still had more men than Hugo, but a number of men lay wounded or dead on the field, and some of the archers she had seen earlier were lying quite still under trees at the edge of the clearing. But if the outcome of the battle remained in question, why was Waldron not with his men?

She saw him stiffen and take a step toward the tent, sword in hand.

Then she heard a baby squalling.

Chills swept over her, and terror.

He stopped. He was staring at the tent. Had he just been awaiting the birth of Isobel's child so he could kill it? Would he kill Isobel and Sorcha, too? And if that was his intent, whatever could they do to stop him?

Looking toward heaven, as if God Himself might write a message to her on the sky, she saw riders swarming over the ridge to the north, dozens of them. Without thought for her own safety, she dashed out of the woods and ran as fast as she could toward Waldron.

Chapter 13

⁓

Inside the tent, Sorcha watched as Hugo carefully cut the cord with his dagger and tied it off with a strip he had cut from Isobel's underskirt. Then he handed the babe to Isobel and sought something to wipe his hands.

"Use my skirt, Hugo," Isobel said. "I'll have to throw these clothes away, anyway, as soon as I can get some to replace them."

He was about to do as she asked when he paused. "We'll need something to wrap the laddie in, my lady."

"Take all you need. I feel no more modesty where you are concerned, sir."

He grinned at her. "We'll hope Michael understands that lack."

"He will care for naught but the safety of his son," she said.

"He'll care for more than that," he said, slicing away a large piece of the cleanest part of her skirt for the babe.

He handed it to Sorcha, then went to wipe his hands on the tent flap instead.

"Help me unfasten my bodice," Isobel said to her. "He wants to suckle and the sooner he can do that, the better, I think."

But Sorcha was watching Hugo, who still stood at the entrance to the tent, looking out, his body tense.

"Lass," he murmured without turning. "Fetch my sword, and quickly."

Without questioning him, she moved swiftly to obey, dragging the heavy weapon to him and shoving its hilt into his outstretched hand. He had not turned his attention from whatever was outside, nor did he do so now.

"What is it?" she demanded, keeping her voice low.

"Waldron," he said. "He said the battle would be swift, but they are still fighting. Yet he is right outside with sword in hand. I must deal with him before we can think about what to do next."

It occurred to her that if Waldron's men won the battle, she and the others would have no say in their fate. She reached out silently to squeeze Hugo's arm.

"Go help your sister with the babe," he commanded. "Do not come outside for any reason." Without looking back, he stepped out of the tent.

Sorcha moved to the entrance in time to see Adela race toward the two men from the woods.

Hugo saw Adela, too, his astonishment visible in the way his body stiffened as he glanced briefly toward her—for just one tiny second.

It was a second too long.

Waldron swung his heavy sword, and as Sorcha screamed, "Watch out!" Hugo flung up his own weapon to parry the thrust. Although his sword caught the tip of Waldron's, it only deflected it, so that the flat of Waldron's blade slid up and off it to strike Hugo's head a heavy blow.

Stunned, he stumbled and fell.

Waldron leaped to finish him, but Adela flung herself at Waldron, tugging his sword arm with both hands, crying, "My lord, look to the north! We must flee if you are to get safely away. You can achieve no victory if they catch you here."

"Adela," Sorcha shouted as she ran to the fallen Hugo. "Help me!"

"Help yourself," Adela cried. "This is all your fault, Sorcha. If Hugo dies, you will be responsible. And wearing those dreadful clothes, too! Come, sir," she added, catching Waldron's arm. "I'll go with you. Together, we can still achieve your most vital goal, but we must hurry or they'll be upon us. Many of your men are already laying down their weapons."

He looked north, saw the army spilling down the slope, and said calmly, "Go ahead of me, lass. You know where the horses are. I'll be behind you with my sword. We'll finish this another time," he shouted to the fallen Hugo as he followed her.

Sorcha rose to run after Adela, but a strong hand clamped onto her right ankle and jerked her back.

"We can't let her go with him," she cried, trying to pull her leg free of Hugo's grip. "She does not know what she is doing!"

"You cannot stop either of them, lass," he said. "He still has his sword, and he would not hesitate to use it."

"Then you go! Pick up your sword and run after him!" But even as she said the words, she saw the heavy bruise forming on his temple and wished she could take them back.

He looked ruefully at her as he released her and sat up with a grimace, putting a hand to the swiftly swelling lump on his head.

Silence fell around them with surprising abruptness.

Adela and Waldron had vanished into the woods, and on the battlefield the men had stopped fighting. Looking north, Sorcha saw the army of horsemen ride into the clearing under a familiar golden banner with a little-black-ship device.

"Mercy, that is his grace's banner!"

"Aye, and Hector's beside it," Hugo said. "Although he and the High Admiral promised men to follow me if I needed them, I did not expect so many."

"I wish they had come sooner," she said.

"You should be happy they came at all," he said, and a note in his voice reminded her that he might still believe he had cause to be displeased with her.

The thought that he might be angry with her after all that had happened brought a tightness to her throat that warned her she might cry any minute. She was certain the feeling was only a natural reaction to exhaustion and the many emotions that had assailed her over the past hours, but she did not want Hugo to see her cry.

She said gruffly, "I am glad I could be here, sir, and even gladder that you were. If you are going to lop my head off for that, go ahead."

"Look at me," he said.

Reluctantly, she did so, and saw a softer expression on his face than she had ever seen there before.

"I'm glad we were here, too," he said, getting to his feet with unusual awkwardness. "What Michael will say about it all, I don't want to imagine, but I'd not have wanted the lady Isobel to have to birth her child alone. And I'm thinking that's exactly what would have happened had you not been here."

"You thought he was going to kill them both, didn't you?"

"I don't know what he intended," he said. "He had his sword in his hand and was walking toward the tent with a look of purpose on his face. He may only have wanted to see what was keeping me, or mayhap to kill me before I could lay hand to my sword. But who is to say now what he would have done? If I had to guess, I'd say he would not have killed the bairn. He would think it the best hostage he could hold, and if Adela is now in league with him—"

"How dare you! She is not! She *could* not!" Sorcha said, automatically raising her hand. When he only looked at her and made no attempt to stop her, she lowered it again. She could not strike him. She was too afraid he might be right.

She bit her lip hard to stem the tears that welled into her eyes, but one trickled down her cheek. When she brushed it angrily away and turned back toward the tent, he stopped her with a hand on her shoulder.

"Come here," he said gently, and when she shook her head, he cupped her other shoulder and pulled her closer. "Think of what we did today," he said in that same gentle, un-Hugo-like voice. "As men died here, a new one was born, lassie. Think of your nephew, fighting his way into this world. With battle raging around him, he squalled in its face."

She smiled at the image he painted, but her tears flowed freely nonetheless, and when he pulled her close she did not resist, leaning into his strength and letting the flood come, sobbing away the hours of tension. For just one moment, she would put Adela out of her head, let Hugo hold her, and try to imagine a world of peace where two people might meet properly, get to know each other in a normal fashion, and love each other in a more acceptable way. Then one of them would not have to marry a mad woman and restore her to respectability.

When she had no more tears to cry, she straightened reluctantly, then began at once to feel guilty about weeping all over him.

"If you ever tell anyone I did that," she growled, staring at his chest, "I'll poison your claret and dance on your grave."

"I'll not tell a soul," he promised.

She heard laughter in his voice, and when she looked up and saw that his eyes were twinkling, she wished she had not looked. Although the emotional storm had passed, her emotions did not seem to know it.

"It is *not* funny," she said. "And Adela did *not* run away with that villain. I warrant she was afraid, as you were, that he was going to kill the bairn."

"Perhaps," he said. Then in a more positive tone of voice, he added, "Do you know what they mean to call him?"

"Faith, sir, even if I did, I'd not say the name aloud until he has been properly baptized! Even for that, his father will write the name for the priest to say."

"Sakes, lass, I thought your father was the only superstitious Macleod."

"That's not superstition; it's Celtic tradition," she said. "A most important one, too, that goes back to a time long before Christianity came to the Isles. The naming ceremony is what legitimizes a child and guarantees its inheritance. We equate its name with its soul. We protect the soul in the meantime, though, so that if the worst happens the babe can still lie in hallowed ground. But we've left Isobel alone all this time without so much as a basin of water to cleanse the poor laddie!"

"You attend to her, and I'll find someone to fetch the water," he said.

She watched him go to be sure he was steady on his feet. Reassured by his grin and the jaunty way he slipped the sword back into its scabbard, she hurried into the tent to find Isobel contentedly nursing her son.

Isobel looked up from the contented baby and smiled. "Is he not perfect?"

"Aye, he is," Sorcha agreed. "But we must sanctify him before we leave this tent. Hugo is finding someone to fetch water. The battle is over," she added, "but Waldron fled with Adela."

Isobel frowned. "How did he get away from Hugo?"

"Adela distracted him, and Waldron tried to kill him. I would have run after them, but Hugo stopped me."

"I should hope so!" Isobel exclaimed. "I wonder how Waldron forced Adela to go with him. She must have seen that the battle was nearly over."

"I don't know," Sorcha said. "I think she heard the baby cry and saw Waldron with his sword out. She must have feared for your life and the baby's."

"If that is so, she ought to have left matters to Hugo," Isobel said. "I learned long ago to trust both him and Michael whenever they have a weapon in hand."

"Aye, perhaps, but Waldron knocked Hugo down."

"You said Adela distracted him."

"Not intentionally, and he should not have taken his eyes off Waldron," Sorcha said. "He will surely say that much himself."

"Aye, and so will Michael," Isobel said with a sigh. "Are you sure Hugo went to fetch water? I'm all sticky and so is my son."

Sorcha went to look and met Hugo at the entrance.

"They've brought our horses and supplies from where we left them on the ridge," he said, handing her a bundle of clothing. "So, you can put on a skirt again. I brought blankets and some clothing for you, too, my lady," he said to Isobel.

"Sakes, Hugo, do you carry a store of women's clothing with you?"

"Nay," he said with a chuckle. "But I did collect a couple of long shirts that will keep you decent along the way, since you'll be in a litter with the bairn, and otherwise modestly covered."

"You can have my skirt and bodice, Isobel," Sorcha said. "I shan't need them, for I see no reason to change just to ride from here to Roslin." She looked at Hugo and added airily, "It is not so far now, is it?"

"About ten miles," he said. "And it would serve you right if I let you wear those things. Recall that you will be meeting my aunt when we arrive, and consider whether you want to have to explain your idea of suitable dress to her."

"I cannot see how it concerns her," Sorcha said.

As if she had not spoken, he added gently, "Recall, too, that your father and the others will arrive on Monday, and that when the countess sees them, she will likely regale them all with a description of your attire, even if she approves of it."

Isobel said diplomatically, "A skirt or bodice that fits you will be too tight on me, Sorcha. I'm larger than usual, you know. Is that water you have there, Hugo? I hope there is enough for us to tidy ourselves, but Sorcha wants to sanctify my son first. Since you served as our midwife, you are the most proper person to do it."

"'Twould be a great honor," he said. "What must I do?"

"First we'll clean him up," Sorcha said, pleased to see that Hugo had brought cloths for the purpose. "Then you sprinkle water on his forehead in the name of the Father, Son, and Holy Ghost. We could have used spittle rather than fresh water. According to the common folk, it has more magical qualities than plain water and is guaranteed to protect newborn babies from mischievous fairies and evil creatures."

"We'll use water," he said, smiling at Isobel.

Sorcha cleaned the baby as thoroughly as she could under the circumstances, and he yelled lustily throughout the process. Although she was sure Hugo would have preferred to go to his men, he showed no sign of impatience as he watched her tend the bairn. Isobel, too, watched with a tender smile.

But at last the baby was tidy enough to suit them all, and she wrapped him in a blanket that Hugo had managed to find. Then, coaching him through the ritual of birth sanctification, she handed the bairn back to Isobel.

"I'll leave you now," Hugo said. "My lads and the others are seeing to the dead and injured, so they'll be a while yet. But as soon as you are ready, I mean for us to be on our way. The others can catch up with us easily enough."

Isobel said, "Have you someone you can send to meet his grace's cavalcade, Hugo? Michael will want to know of his son's arrival as soon as possible."

"Aye, sure," Hugo said. "I sent two men straightaway with the message."

"What if Waldron is lying in wait for us somewhere betwixt here and Roslin?" Sorcha asked. "Should we not wait until everyone is ready to go?"

"Waldron's forces are sadly depleted," Hugo said. "If he sent for men from Edgelaw, I'm sure our lads from Roslin have intercepted them. We'll take thirty men with us, which will be enough. Now, help your sister, lass, and don't forget to change your clothes. I don't want to see those leggings or that shirt ever again."

She did not reply, and when he had gone, Isobel said, "He is right, Sorcha. I don't know why you challenge him so, or why he allows it. I'd not have expected Hugo to suffer such impertinence lightly."

"He wields no authority over me," Sorcha said.

Isobel chuckled. "That would not weigh with him in the least, as I should think you must have learned before traveling a mile in his company."

Sorcha lifted her chin in response, but she would change her clothes, because she knew as well as Isobel apparently did that Hugo would not hesitate to change

them for her if she continued to defy him. The thought
made her smile.

They were ready when he returned for them, and he
nodded approvingly when he saw Sorcha in her borrowed
skirt and bodice. By then she had remembered that she
had left her shift and the bodice under a rock, and hoped
he would not recall that, but when he had seen Isobel and
the bairn settled in the makeshift litter his men had created for them, he said casually that Sorcha was to ride
with him.

"I'd rather ride beside Isobel," she said.

"She will sleep now, and the bairn likewise, so you'd
only be bored," he said. "Besides, I want to talk with
you."

"What if I don't want to talk to you?"

He gave her a look, and she decided silence would
serve better than speech.

The men had prepared food they could all eat as they
rode, and Sorcha realized she was hungry. She saw that
Isobel had accepted a manchet loaf, some cheese, and an
apple, and that she ate at least some of it before she fell
asleep.

Her litter consisted of a blanket slung between two
poles. One end of it was harnessed to one of the horses,
and a man led the horse while two other men on foot carried the back of the litter, trading places every hour or so
with two of the riders. In this way, they were able to travel
almost as fast as they would have had Isobel been able to
ride, and she and the baby were able to rest.

Reassured that her sister was as comfortable as they
could make her, Sorcha found that she was looking forward to another conversation with Hugo.

To take the wind out of his sails, she spoke first, saying, "If you mean to scold me for leaving our camp as I did, I wish you would get it over with."

"I warrant you do," he replied equably. He said nothing further, and that not having been the reply she had wanted to hear, she scoured her imagination for something to say that might produce a more satisfactory one.

The best she could come up with was "Well, then?"

He gazed expressionlessly into the distance.

Looking behind them, she saw that his men had fallen back and guessed that he had told them to do so, doubtless expecting her to be fractious. But his silence was beginning to annoy her. If the man had something to say, he ought to say it and be done. A less welcome thought struck her. Mayhap she had annoyed him so much that he no longer cared enough about what she did to scold her for it.

Affecting a casual tone, she said, "As you have already agreed that it was a good thing I was there for Isobel, I expect you are no longer even angry, so we can talk about something else."

"Aye, sure, if you like."

"Is that all you're going to say?" she demanded indignantly.

He looked at her then, and his piercing gaze seemed to strike a chord deep inside, one that vibrated through her as if her blood had begun to hum. That look was discomfiting, to say the least, but even as she squirmed on her saddle, she assured herself that she would, under no circumstances, look away.

"Do you really want to know what I'm thinking?" he asked.

He held her gaze, and her voice seemed to have stuck somewhere in her throat, so she just nodded.

"I'm thinking it's a good thing you decided to put on that skirt before all these men and the others we left behind us saw you in those damnable leggings."

She swallowed, trying to think of a reply, and decided to see what he would say to the truth. "I thought, most likely, you would put it on for me if I defied you."

"I'm glad to hear that you were thinking clearly, for once," he said.

Nettled, she said, "You would have, would you not?"

"Aye, sure, I would," he agreed. "Moreover, I'd have had to do it in full view of everyone, lest someone accuse me of improper behavior toward you."

"And what, pray, could be more improper than forcing me to change my clothing in front of all your men?"

"A number of things," he said.

"Name one."

"Stripping off those damnable leggings and giving you the skelping you so richly deserve before that same audience," he answered promptly.

"That would be worse," she agreed, feeling her cheeks burn at the image his words brought to mind.

"Pax, lassie?"

"Aye," she said with welcome relief.

"In truth, you frightened me witless," he said quietly.

"You made me angry when you threatened to send me to your aunt whilst you went to find Adela. I was afraid you would get to her too late, and I knew you would follow me. But if we are to speak the truth, mayhap you should know that I had nearly changed my mind when they caught me. They must have been watching for someone to stray far enough for them to snatch." Truth or not, she would not tell him that Waldron's greeting to his men indicated that he had sent them to find her.

"I hope we can always speak the truth to each other, lass."

She forced a weak smile as she said, "There is no 'we,' sir. Adela still needs you, so if you still believe in honor . . ." She let the word speak for itself.

"She is your sister," he said. "So we will see much of each other, even if she does agree that she and I should marry. But I do not believe she will. You heard her yourself. She urged him to flee. You want to think she feared he was going to harm the bairn, but I cannot agree. He is most persuasive, lass. I warrant he has persuaded her to his way of thinking about things."

"She wouldn't!" Sorcha exclaimed. "You do not know her as I do."

"No," he said. "That's true, and you are right to remind me of my duty."

For once, she did not want to hear that she was right. She felt a clenching sensation near where she suspected her heart lay, not to mention a sudden prickling of tears in her eyes. And she could think of nothing to say.

~

As the silence between them lengthened, Hugo glanced at her and saw that she had taken her lower lip firmly between her teeth. Her eyes swam with tears, making him want to kick himself for reminding her of what Adela had done.

He had not intended to take her to task at all, but it

seemed as if the lass had only to open her mouth to stir some demon in him to correct her.

He could not count the times since she had walked into his life that he had wanted to throttle her or shake her or kiss her. And he certainly had had no intention of falling in love with her, but that was exactly what he had done.

The knowledge had struck him hard as he had watched her tending Isobel's baby. But he realized straightaway that he had suffered pangs of it long before that, and now he did not have the slightest idea what he was going to do about it.

Instinct had warned him from the first that the little skelpie stirred his senses as no other woman had ever done, although the first day she had stirred only a strong desire to put her across his knee. After all, for a significant part of his grace's installation day he had sported her handprint on his face for all to see. No one could blame him afterward for believing that the only reason she stirred his blood was that she could so easily ignite his fury.

To be sure, she was as beautiful as any of her sisters if not more so, and when she was angry, the way her eyes sparked flames one moment and turned stony gray the next fascinated him. Her temper was another matter, though. It had not escaped his notice that she had stood up to Waldron just as she did to him, so doubtless she lacked common sense or even a simple sense of self-preservation. But he could not deny that he had been proud of the way she had ignored the tension between them, and their weapons, and had demanded their help for Isobel.

In short, although he condemned her impulsive, defiant behavior and would continue to do so, he recognized in her not only a generous spirit but also a sense of honor and duty that he found wholly admirable. She was untrained and impetuous, but her belief in her duty to her family seemed instinctive and natural, rather than a product of any training, and so far she had managed to come through her adventures unscathed and undaunted. At least, she had until Adela had run away with Waldron, betraying all that Sorcha had tried to do for her.

Afterward, though, Sorcha had set Adela's treachery aside to devote her attention to Isobel's needs and those of her bairn. And Hugo had no doubt that had he not been there, had she and Isobel been all alone, Sorcha would have delivered the wee laddie by herself, calmly and with complete success.

Thinking of Isobel reminded him of yet another thing he liked about Sorcha. His cousin's lady, despite her airy charm and delicate femininity, had a habit of shading the truth when the whole seemed unpalatable to her. From all he had seen, Sorcha lacked that habit altogether. She said what she thought, and her tongue was even sharper than Isobel's could be, but Hugo preferred straight talk himself, and would not have had Michael's tolerance for Isobel's prevarications.

Glancing at Sorcha again, he saw that she had recovered her composure and decided he would do better not to apologize for reminding her of Adela's perfidy. Although she had defended her sister, she had not persuaded him that Adela had acted only to protect Isobel and the bairn, let alone Sorcha and himself as well. Adela had sounded too fervent, too concerned for Waldron's safety to have spared thought for anyone else's, including her own.

She had to know how dangerous his cousin was. Waldron was incapable of hiding that part of himself from others, especially from any woman he held under his control. With an army in view, as it had been, Adela had to have known that she need only hide long enough and her ordeal would end. The only possible conclusion was that she had gone with Waldron willingly.

Sorcha would recognize the truth soon enough, though. He had no need to convince her, and it would be kinder to let her come to it in her own good time.

Noting that she had herself in hand again, he casually mentioned Michael's undoubted delight when he learned that he had an heir, and his own intention to purchase Black Thunder from Hector if the man would allow it. Their conversation thus progressed until they were fully in charity with each other again.

She rode astride easily and liked a man's flat leather saddle, as her sisters did. Isobel had once told him that all eight of Macleod's daughters had ridden astride since childhood, with or without saddles.

He liked watching her but soon found himself imagining away the skirt and seeing her again in the damnable leggings. The way they outlined her smooth thighs and rounded calves, not to mention other rounded parts, stirred his imagination until he realized she was regarding him quizzically, and reined himself up short.

"What is it, lass?" he said. Hearing the gruffness of his tone, he cleared his throat, trying to banish the vision that still warmed his imagination and other things.

"I asked you how much farther it is to Roslin," she said, but the dimple below the left corner of her mouth winked at him, and her beautiful eyes danced.

The bubble of laughter in Sorcha's throat lingered even after Hugo had collected his wits. He looked around as if to orient himself and said they ought to reach the castle within the hour.

He had been gazing at her as if he had never seen her before, and the look in his eyes had warmed her through and through. Really, she thought, when he was being civil, he was a most amusing, informative companion.

That he admired the Sinclair brothers, afforded tremendous respect to the aunt he described unabashedly as terrifying, and loved Roslin Castle almost as much as his own home at Dunclathy was clear in every word he uttered in describing them.

He spoke of his sisters, showing respect for the eldest, Eliza, and warmth for the younger ones, Kate and Meg. He seemed scarcely to know them, though, and she felt sorry for that. Family was important. A man should know his sisters.

She envied him his travels though, for not only had he seen much more of Scotland than she had, but he had traveled to Paris, France, and to Spain and exotic countries that her aunt Euphemia and Ian Dubh, who was Cristina's father-by-marriage, had described to her in tales from their extensive studies. She suspected at one point that Hugo might have traveled even farther, but when he had seemed to misspeak, he deftly changed the subject, and she decided she must have imagined it.

When the baby wakened and squalled, they paused to rest while Isobel settled him to nurse, but when he had taken his fill, they rode on again.

Soon afterward, they entered dense woodland and followed a cart track until they came to an arched stone bridge across a tumbling river. On a high promontory beyond it, outlined against the blue sky and a few floating, puffy white clouds, stood the rounded towers and square southwest-corner keep of Roslin Castle.

The trail led back and forth up the hill until it came to a narrow land bridge, where the earth on both sides fell steeply away to the river thirty feet below. As their party made its way single file across to the entrance gates, Sorcha realized that the river North Esk flowed nearly all the way around the castle's steep promontory.

"Henry has begun to extend the wall and parts of the keep," Hugo said. "The work can be noisy, but with the bairn and Isobel needing rest, and Michael coming home, I'll have good reason to order a period of peace whilst we're all here."

The gates stood open, and when they rode into the flagstone-paved courtyard, a tall woman in a long sable-trimmed red kirtle, with gold lacing and a bejeweled, linked belt set low on her hips, swept gracefully down the stairs from the main entrance of the keep to meet them. The white veil she wore ruched back from her face flowed softly to her shoulders, over which she had flung a dark-green mantle against the late afternoon chill. Intricately plaited dark hair showed beneath the veil as it fluttered gently with her movements.

"You are about to meet my aunt," Hugo murmured. "Mind your manners."

Sorcha, more aware than she had thought she could be of her shabby attire, gave thanks to God that she was not wearing her leggings and saffron shirt.

She straightened on her saddle and held her head high.

Chapter 14

Isabella, Countess of Strathearn and Caithness, rushed past Sorcha and Hugo to Isobel's litter, demanding to see her grandson.

"Sidony cannot have told her, since she does not know the wee laddie exists," Sorcha said to Hugo. "You must have sent a message here, as well."

"I'm no fool, lass," he said. "I sent it when I sent men to meet Michael. I had to let her know about the birth of her grandson and that Isobel was with me. She'd have handed me my head in my lap had I done aught else."

"Aye, sure," Sorcha agreed, eyeing the countess warily.

But Isabella had eyes only for her grandson. She took the baby gently from Isobel's arms and gestured to several menservants who had followed her outside.

Ordering them to carry Isobel on her litter to her bedchamber, she said to her affectionately, "I ordered a fire to warm your room as soon as I received Hugo's message, and my Martha will see that you both have a wash and fresh clothing. Then you can enjoy your supper in quiet comfort, for you will want to rest well before Michael comes."

"Thank you, madam," Isobel said with a smile. "He'll come soon, I think."

"Aye, he'll waste no time," the countess said. Then, turning to Hugo, she said, "Do you mean to sit there on that horse until he does, sir?"

"No, madam, certainly not," he said as he swiftly dismounted and made his bow to her. "I did not want to interrupt your reunion."

Returning the baby to Isobel's arms as four men picked up the litter to carry her into the keep, Isabella turned back to Hugo, acknowledging Sorcha's presence with a flickering glance. As he moved to lift her down from her horse, Isabella said dryly, "I warrant you have news for me."

"Aye, madam, but first allow me to present to you Isobel's sister, the lady Sorcha Macleod. Make your curtsy, lass," he added.

As if, Sorcha thought with annoyance, she were twelve and backward in her manners. Determined to show that, shabby clothing or not, her manners were excellent, she obeyed him with her head high. Smiling politely, she said, "I am honored to make your acquaintance, madam."

"I own, your presence here stirs my curiosity," Isabella said as Sorcha arose from her curtsy. With a twinkle, she added, "Where came you by that awful dress?"

"Hugo made me wear it," Sorcha said, casting that gentleman a black look.

"I could hardly allow the two of them to ride here in the garments they wore to his grace's installation," Hugo said. "Or in the disreputable rags they wore when I found them trying to masquerade as lads near Dail Righ village."

"I see," Isabella said, gazing thoughtfully at him for a moment before she added decisively, "I look forward to hearing the whole tale. Sidony has not been entirely forthcoming, you see. She seems worried that you would not want her to tell me about it, Sorcha, but nearly certain that Hugo would. An indecisive child but otherwise quite unexceptionable. You were right to send her to me, Hugo."

"You relieve my mind, madam," he replied with a teasing smile. "I was afraid you would be furious."

"Impertinence is never becoming, sir, but I do see that you have had your hands full. Let us go inside. I'll wager that you are starving for your supper and that Sorcha will welcome a wash and change of clothing as much as Isobel will. She can attend to that before we eat—no disreputable leggings, though," she added firmly.

"No, madam, certainly not," Sorcha replied, deciding that the countess was not nearly as formidable as Hugo had described her.

An hour later, she was not so sure.

In the meantime, Isabella had provided her with a comfortable bedchamber all to herself, clothing from Isobel's wardrobe, and warm, scented water to wash the worst of the dirt away. She had also sent up her seamstress at once to begin altering a few of Isobel's garments to fit Sorcha's slimmer body.

Accompanying the seamstress, Sidony flung herself

into Sorcha's arms, burst into tears, and sobbed, "I was terrified! Sir Hugo was so furious! I feared if the horrid men who hurt Rory did not murder you, *he* would. Oh, I do hope you are not angry that I told him. But whatever were you thinking to do such a frightful thing?"

"Hush now," Sorcha said, gently extricating herself, all too aware of the fascinated seamstress. "I'm safe now, and we'll tell you all about it presently. Have you seen the bairn?" she added as she moved to make use of the ewer and basin.

"Aye," Sidony said. "I went to see Isobel first, because I could not otherwise have believed she was here. He is beautiful. But she would tell me only that men she thinks must have been in league with Waldron had— What?" she added in bewildered tones when Sorcha turned with a finger over her lips.

"We'll talk about it later," Sorcha said firmly. "Countess Isabella said they will serve supper soon. Are you ready to go downstairs?"

"Aye, sure, and my room is across the way if I need anything. Is this not pretty?" she added, showing off the pale-blue kirtle and the sideless, embroidered yellow surcoat she wore over it. "It is Isobel's," she added. "The countess told me to choose anything of hers to wear. I thought perhaps Isobel would not quite like it, but she said of course I should borrow whatever I need. Was that not kind of her?"

"Very kind, but you should have known she would not mind," Sorcha said. "You would be just as generous if she were the one in need."

"Aye, but all the same, one dislikes taking things without asking."

Sorcha knew she was tired but thought her sister's conversation even more tedious than usual. Taking herself sternly to task for the uncharitable thought, she nonetheless looked forward to seeing Hugo and the countess again at supper. His conversation would always be stimulating, and Isabella intrigued her as well.

With Sidony's help and that of the seamstress, Sorcha was soon ready. With her raggedly cut curls confined in a gold net under a simple veil, she could feel confident that she looked well in the crimson-and-black-striped silk kirtle that Isobel had lent her. Fastening matching crimson silk slippers on her feet and a narrow girdle of gold links low on her hips, she pronounced herself ready for supper.

Not seeing Hugo among those gathering in the great hall when they entered, she felt a pang of disappointment. But Isabella stood warming her hands by the upper hall's stone fireplace in the east wall near the dais.

"Hugo will return shortly," she said as Sorcha and Sidony joined her. Without pause, she added, "I thought at first, and despite your dreadful clothes, that you must have traveled with Isobel. I feared, you see, that she had defied Michael and somehow managed to leave Lochbuie on her own. But since that is not what happened, how ever did the two of you contrive to meet Hugo at Dail Righ?"

Sidony nibbled her lower lip. Sorcha hesitated, too, trying to think what to say, but she abandoned the effort at the sound of Hugo's voice behind her, and turned with mixed relief and trepidation to greet him.

"Quizzing our guests already, madam?" he said with a smile. "Shall we take our seats first and tell the lads to put up the privy screens?"

"Aye, it might be better so," Isabella agreed. Striding onto the dais, she summoned a gillie and relayed the command.

Then, taking her seat in one of two armchairs near the fireplace end of the high table, and directing Sorcha and Sidony to a pair of back-stools opposite her on the long side facing the end wall, she said, "Take Michael's chair, Hugo. I doubt that he can get here before tomorrow evening."

"Aye," Hugo agreed as he obeyed. "The intent is for his grace's flotilla to land at Dumbarton tonight, put up at the castle, and form a mounted cavalcade in the morning after kirk. The lads should meet them with my message around midday near Glasgow. But even if Michael leaves the others behind and presses hard, he's unlikely to get here before Vespers."

"Or later," Isabella said. Nodding to the gillie poised to fill her goblet, she said to Sorcha, "Now, tell me all about your adventures and how you met Hugo."

Hugo said dampingly, "Pray, madam, do not encourage her to think that what she did was aught but foolhardy."

"Nonsense, 'twas a daring feat!" the countess retorted, smiling at Sorcha.

Thus encouraged but avoiding Hugo's gaze, Sorcha said with a confiding smile to the countess, "You see, I had reason to believe that my sister Adela would be unhappy in the marriage our father had arranged for her, and so—"

"Why?" Isabella interjected. "Is the proposed bridegroom so dreadful?"

"He is much older and very dull," Sorcha said, but the

interruption had given her time to realize where her explanation must lead. She could not be confident that Isabella would understand about her messages to Hugo, nor did she want to bring up his responsibility, or anyone else's, for what had happened.

Therefore, when Isabella agreed that marriage to a very old, very dull man should be avoided, Sorcha said glibly, "That is what we thought, so when someone snatched Adela from the kirk steps and rode away with her, everyone thought it was someone she wanted to marry who had come for her."

Isabella peered shrewdly at her but said only, "Indeed?"

"Aye," Sorcha said, her confidence abruptly ebbing. "Only . . . only then we learned that was not what had happened."

"And how did you learn that?" Isabella asked.

Sorcha glanced at Hugo.

"Aye, lass," he said. "Explain that. But first you might take some meat from that platter Ivor is holding for you. The rest of us would like some, too."

Startled to think she had been unaware of the gillie beside her, she used her eating knife to serve herself two pieces of roast lamb from the platter. A bowl of chopped cabbage with small roasted onions came next, and since vegetables other than nettle soup in springtime were a rare luxury at Chalamine due to the poor Highland soil, she took a generous spoonful of cabbage, too.

Isabella waited patiently, but when Sorcha still hesitated, Hugo said, "You disappoint me, lass. Where is your customary candor? You've made no secret before now of where you lay the blame for your sister's abduction."

Sidony made a small squeak of protest, but although Isabella glanced at her, no one else did, and she did not speak.

Collecting her wits, Sorcha said, "Sir Hugo is right, madam. I did blame him, and he bears some responsibility for what happened. But I'm the one who behaved badly when we met." To Hugo, she said, "For that, I do apologize to you, sir."

"Do you, Skelpie?"

A smile touched his lips, but why the unusual warmth in his voice or that smile should stir a prickling in her eyes, she could not have said. To counter what felt ominously like welling tears, she turned back to the countess and said quickly and with her customary frankness, "I slapped his face as hard as I could, madam."

"Doubtless a salutary lesson for him," Isabella said, regarding Hugo now rather enigmatically. "This incident occurred at Dail Righ, did it?"

"It occurred at Kildonan in view of the whole throng at his grace's installation," Hugo said. "I wore the wee skelpie's handprint on my cheek for some time afterward. In truth, though," he added, looking at Sorcha, "I deserved it."

"Salutary indeed, then," Isabella said. "But I'd like to know how you came to think Hugo could so far forget himself as to abduct a bride from her wedding."

When Sorcha glanced at him again, he chuckled. "She believed it because she had sent messages to me herself to suggest that I should."

"Nay, then," Sidony said indignantly. "She did not say that."

"As near as made no difference," he insisted.

"*She* sent a message to you?"

The emphatic surprise in Isabella's voice made Sorcha wince, but Hugo said, "She did, and fool that I was, I did not bother to reply to such impertinence."

"That was not well done of you, Hugo," Isabella said severely. "Moreover, sir, if she believed so strongly that you cared about her sister, you must have given someone the notion that you did. As I recall, last summer you flirted shamefully with Lady Adela at Orkney."

Isabella's tone, added to Hugo's instantly sober expression, reminded Sorcha of his description of his aunt, and her wariness returned in full measure.

Sidony, clearly abashed by her own impulsive comment, fixed her attention on her trencher as Hugo and the countess continued to gaze intently at each other.

He, just as clearly, seemed reluctant to defend himself, and Sorcha could think of nothing to say that would not make matters worse.

Breaking the silence at last, Isabella said, "Hugo?"

The quiet way she said it raised hairs on Sorcha's neck, but Hugo nodded.

"I don't deny that I behaved badly, Aunt Isabella," he said, "or that I richly deserved Lady Sorcha's anger, although I did not think so at the time. But she—"

When he broke off, cocking his head to listen, Sorcha realized that the general din had increased significantly in the lower hall, where servants of the household and Hugo's men were taking their supper at long trestle tables.

Exchanging a look with the countess, who smiled ruefully at him, Hugo rose and strode to the end of the privy screen as an older man stepped onto the dais there.

Seeing the two together, Sorcha had no doubt who the newcomer must be.

Hugo exclaimed, "Sir! Where did you spring from?"

"Dunclathy, of course," the other said, clapping him hard on the shoulder and pulling him into a rough hug. "I reached Hawthornden yestereve, and your aunt sent word to me there as soon as she learned of your anticipated arrival."

"I'm glad to see you," Hugo said. "I expected you to stay at Henry's house in Edinburgh at least until Mac-Donald, Michael, and the others arrived in town."

With a twinkle that reminded Sorcha of the one she often saw in Hugo's eyes, the older man said, "I'll wager that Michael will come directly here, too."

"He will if he wants to see his heir," Hugo agreed. "But, come, sir, I must make known to you the ladies Sorcha and Sidony Macleod, Isobel's two youngest sisters. This is my father, Sir Edward Robison," he added.

The amenities soon over, the countess having ordered food for Sir Edward and told the henchmen who had accompanied him to find seats in the lower hall, he sat at his son's side and soon had a full trencher and goblet before him.

Having drunk deeply from the goblet and gestured for a refill, he said, "But I interrupted your conversation, madam. I trust you were discussing naught that you cannot easily continue to discuss in my presence."

"Lady Sorcha and Hugo were merely relating their recent adventures to me," Isabella said lightly. "'Tis all rather astonishing, because heartless villains carried off her sister Adela from her own wedding. Sorcha and Sidony set off to find her and met Hugo in the village of Dail Righ. We had got nearly that far when you arrived, so you must be sure to make Hugo repeat all the details of the first part of the tale to you later. Sorcha, my dear, do tell us what happened after Dail Righ."

Sorcha had seen Hugo wince at his aunt's proposal that he should tell Sir Edward the whole later, and she was not too comfortable with that idea herself.

But Hugo said only, "Before she continues, madam, I am afraid we should reveal one important detail without waiting until we reach the part of our journey when we came to be certain of it ourselves. I regret to tell you that the man who abducted Lady Adela was Waldron."

Isabella gasped. "But he's dead!"

"Evidently not," Sir Edward said dryly, shooting a speculative look at Hugo.

In the gatehouse on the uppermost level of the round gate tower at Edgelaw, Adela stood at the window gazing down at the road that passed below her into the square forecourt. She felt numb.

She and Waldron had ridden that way only half an hour before. She recalled the echoing *click-clack* of the horses' hooves on the cobblestones, because the sound had seemed to echo the speeding seconds of what little time she had left.

He had brought her to the little chamber, told her she would be comfortable, and left her there. She had heard the key turn in the lock. How long, she wondered, would it take him to realize he had no more use for her now that the others had seen her run off willingly with him? Perhaps he realized as much already.

That thought sat in her mind like a heavy stone that she could not dislodge. Its weight seemed to affect every muscle in her body, because she had no energy, nor sufficient will to think clearly or to act.

The light had nearly gone. She had watched the sunset before the castle came into view, but dusk lasted longer each night, and so they had been able to see well enough when they arrived. Some of his men had escaped, too. A few had reached Edgelaw before them, and four more had passed beneath her prison since.

Apparently no one had pursued them, which told her she need expect no further interference from Sorcha or Sir Hugo. And certainly Isobel would not urge anyone to come looking for her, not after the horrid things Adela had said to her. But Isobel had not understood the danger her presence had created. Sorcha had not understood that either, but then Sorcha never did recognize her own foolhardiness.

Adela wondered how the babe fared. It had come early, which often meant trouble. Remembering her mother's death, she forcibly put the bairn out of her mind. She could not afford such distraction now, for she could not trust herself to think properly as it was. Moreover, every time she thought she was coming to understand Waldron, he did something to prove she did not know him at all.

Still, he did seem to listen to her from time to time, so perhaps she could think of some way yet to influence him.

When he had first threatened to kill her, she had instinctively sought to distract him, to win his favor. Learning that she could not escape him, that he held her very life in his hands and would not hesitate to snuff it out, she had come to fear rescue, to fear that any such attempt would endanger her rescuers as well as herself. He had even persuaded her that he sincerely believed in his holy mission as a just cause, and indeed, perhaps he truly did believe that. In any event, she knew now that she had focused on his faith in God, on even his smallest kindness to her, to persuade herself that he was a normal man, even one who was coming to like her.

However, no normal man who liked her would have used her or her sisters, especially one big with child, to bait a trap for his enemies. But knowing all that—even recognizing that the deep gratitude she felt every time he did something normal stemmed from no more than a false hope that he was growing less brutal, less evil—did not seem to do anything but frighten her more. The earlier easing of her fear had vanished as soon as she had found herself alone with him again, and she wondered if the time she had spent with him had driven her mad. Warning him, then running with him had been impulsive and purely instinctive, but it had been pure madness, too.

She knew she ought to lie down and rest while she could. But the knowledge of what she ought to do and the doing seemed unrelated.

Dread surged through her at the sound of the key in the lock, but when he entered, he just nodded at her and said, "I know you must be as hungry as I am, but I had some things to see to. Supper is ready now if you'd like to come to the hall."

"Yes, please," she said, surprised that her voice sounded steady and natural.

When he stepped aside, she passed close to him and

went down the narrow stairway to the cobbled courtyard. The air had grown chillier since their arrival, but they crossed the yard quickly and went inside.

A fire blazed on the hearth in the hall, but she felt little warmth from it as he guided her to the high table, past standing, silent men on each side of three trestle tables. Indicating a place for her at the end of the nearer bench, he then took his seat on a plain back-stool at one end of the table.

When the men in the lower hall behind her sat and began talking quietly, the resulting low, steady murmur made her feel as if she were alone with him again, but she could not read his mood. He signed for a gillie to serve them, and she ate silently, waiting for him to speak.

At last, he pushed the trencher away and leaned back with his wine goblet in hand. "I've been thinking," he said. "It has occurred to me that you may want a bath and some clean clothes."

Adela nearly burst into tears at the thought of being clean again, but with a ruthlessness she had not known she possessed, she suppressed the impulse. Even so, she had to wait a moment to be sure she could speak calmly before she said, "I'd like that, sir. How kind of you to think of it."

"I'm never kind, lass. But I want you to do something for me, and it won't do for you to be reeking when you do it."

The flood of relief at learning he still needed her overcame her determination not to cry. Tears spilled down her cheeks, but she smiled through them, hoping he would think that her delight in at last being able to take a bath had stirred them.

Sorcha had never before known any conversation to possess so many pitfalls, but in the course of describing their journey to the countess and Sir Edward, she and Hugo seemed to fall into one after another. The countess had only to hear a glib remark to pounce on it and demand elucidation. And Sir Edward, displaying an uncanny knack for recognizing a partial truth, did the same thing.

He also showed Sorcha where his son had acquired the piercingly stern gaze that had often disconcerted her in their brief association when a question directed to Hugo inadvertently revealed that certain details Sir Edward had missed in the earlier discussion might be of greater interest than Isabella had led him to believe.

When he demanded the whole tale, Sorcha was astonished to note the same resigned guilt on Hugo's face that she had often felt on her own. But when they had revealed everything up to the previous night, Sir Edward was not as severe as the countess had been, saying no more to his son than, "We will talk more of this."

"Yes, sir," Hugo replied calmly.

"But do go on now, both of you, and tell us the rest," Isabella said.

The rest of the tale seemed to flow more easily, particularly the part about the baby's birth in the midst of battle. And if Isabella gasped and scolded when she learned of Sorcha's decision to leave Hugo's camp, and if Sir Edward shook his head more than once, the worst was over. The gratitude that both of them expressed at having Isobel and her baby safe at Roslin was sincere and profound.

"But I am grievously vexed with Waldron," Isabella added with a heavy frown. "'Twas wickedness, first to abduct a bride from her wedding and then to order the same done to a woman great with child. His behavior has been quite unforgivable, and I want him to understand that. Do you know where he is now?"

Hesitating, Hugo looked at his father. But when Sir Edward gazed serenely back, he said, "Aye, madam, I do. He is at Edgelaw, but—"

"I shall send for him tomorrow," she declared.

"I doubt he will come," Hugo said.

"He will if he wants to continue calling himself Waldron of Edgelaw," Isabella said. "He merely serves as our constable there. He does not own the place."

"Then doubtless when Henry learns what he has done, he will—"

"Henry has nothing to say about it," Isabella snapped. "'Tis at *my* pleasure, not his, that Waldron inhabits Edgelaw."

"I did not know that," Hugo said. "I knew he did not own Edgelaw, any more than I own Hawthornden, but I assumed that my uncle had gifted him the tenancy there for the term of his life as Henry did for me."

"Edgelaw is *my* property, settled on me when I married William," she said. "I offered it to Waldron as a residence because he had little to show for his training with you and Michael, and much to overcome in the circumstance of his birth. And, too, he always behaved charmingly to me. I liked him. However, had I not thought him dead, I'd have turned him out after that dreadful business last year with Isobel and Michael. The only reason I did not order his people to leave is that those who were not already loyal swore fealty to me. And they take excellent care of the land."

"Did Waldron keep the rents?" Hugo asked.

"A generous portion of them," Isabella said. "The rest he paid to me or my bailiff. Since last summer, his people have paid the entire sum each quarter day, except what they required for upkeep of the castle."

Noting that Sidony was scarcely able to keep her eyes open, Sorcha took advantage of the silence that followed to say, "I know you must want to discuss these matters further, madam, but I trust you will forgive Sidony and me if we beg to be excused now. This has been a very long day for us."

Isabella nodded, and they stood to take their leave.

Hugo and Sir Edward likewise stood, and Hugo said, "Don't go to bed yet, lass. I want a word with you before you do."

Hearing the note of determination in his voice, she was about to suggest that they could as easily talk in the morning, when he caught her gaze and held it.

Easily deducing that he meant to have his way, she said, "I will take Sidony upstairs first and see her settled, sir, but I can return here afterward."

"No need for that," he said. "I'll just go up with you."

Expecting the countess or Sir Edward to protest that intention, since their earlier reactions suggested that they would disapprove of any private chat between a maiden and a single gentleman, Sorcha glanced from one to the other. Neither spoke, however, so she and Sidony made their curtsies and went with Hugo.

Passing through an archway in the west wall and turning to their right, they entered a short corridor, at the northwest corner of which was the spiral stairway they had come down earlier.

"This wall to our right is the west end of the ladies' solar Henry built for his mother and Isobel last fall," Hugo said. "You may have noticed its entrance at the back of the dais. It all used to be part of the upper hall, so that wall is new, too."

"Isobel wrote us a letter about the solar," Sidony said. "She sent two of them with mendicant friars, written on the smoothest paper we had ever seen."

"Aye, it was very fine," Sorcha agreed. "She said Michael had given it to her." She remembered something else Isobel had written, about the solar, and although she did not think she ought to tell Hugo that her sister had mentioned Roslin's laird's peek, she did note the narrow doorway on the half-landing.

On the next level, they found a chambermaid waiting to assist Sidony, so at Hugo's suggestion, Sorcha left her sleepy sister to the young woman's ministrations.

When Sidony's chamber door had shut behind the two, Sorcha said, "I'm tired, sir, so pray say what you want to say to me and let me go to bed."

"Such pretty manners," he said in a teasing voice as he put his arm around her shoulders and urged her back toward the stairway. "We cannot talk here or in your chamber, so come upstairs with me. I want to show you the ramparts."

Fetching her cloak from her chamber first, she went up the stairs ahead of him. Halfway, recalling what he had told her about Waldron, she said over her shoulder, "I hope you are not so vexed with me that you mean to toss me into the river."

"Nay, Skelpie, I'd never do that."

At the top, he leaned past her to open the door. A light, icy breeze stirred the air as she stepped onto the moonlit walkway and nearly bumped into a guardsman.

The young man nodded politely, then stiffened to attention, saying, "Good evening, Sir Hugo."

"Good evening, Jeb Elliot," Hugo replied. "Are you alone up here?"

"Nay, sir, me brother Tam be a-watching from the east wall. All seems quiet enough, though. We havena seen a soul since Sir Edward arrived."

"Excellent," Hugo said. "I would have a few moments alone with the lady Sorcha, however, so you may do your watching from the north hoarding for a time. I'll keep watch for you to the west."

"Aye, sir. Just give a shout when ye want me to watch both bits again."

When he had disappeared around the corner, Hugo guided her nearer the southwest corner of the keep, which also proved to be the southwest corner of the curtain wall. Standing at the parapet, Sorcha looked down to see moonlight glinting on the river as it tumbled noisily from right to left around the promontory's base.

"'Tis a long way down," she said.

"Aye," he agreed, moving so close that she could feel his body's warmth. "It flows north from here and empties into the Firth of Forth."

Without looking at him, she said, "I hope your intention is not to scold me for aught that I said to your father and the countess."

"Sakes, lass," he said with a chuckle, "I'm not daft. I know too well what it is like to suffer interrogation by that pair. Indeed, I doubt my part of it is over yet."

"They seemed displeased more often with me than with you."

"Perhaps, but you'll recall that my father wants to speak further with me."

"I doubt you fear him much."

"Do you? I promise you, he has a fearsome temper."

"But words cannot hurt you. I doubt he would try to put you over his knee," she added, glancing up with a sudden grin at the image her words brought to mind. Meeting a sudden intensity in his gaze, she looked quickly back at the river.

"'Tis true I'm a mite large for skelping," he agreed. "But I do not want to talk about that." He turned her so she faced him and put his hands on her shoulders.

She could feel their warmth even through her wool cloak and gown. He stood so for a long, silent moment while she stared at his broad chest. Moonlight gleamed on the silver aglets of his doublet lacing.

"Look at me," he said softly.

His tone stirred sensual warmth in her that had nothing to do with the touch of his hands or with the likelihood that, despite his promise not to scold, he meant to say something that she would not want to hear.

Dampening suddenly dry lips, she obeyed him, and her lips parted in response to the unmistakable look of hunger in his eyes.

Chapter 15

Hugo had not had any intention of kissing her until she grinned at him, impishly showing her dimple. Even then he had hesitated, calling himself several kinds of fool, but he had wanted to see her face again, to see if the dimple still showed. He wanted to see, too, if moonlight would ignite silvery fire in her eyes.

So he'd asked her to look at him, never realizing what a mistake it would be.

She did look, warily, almost shyly, her moist lips parted as if in expectation of kissing, and his body if not his good sense leaped in response. His hands gripped her shoulders, pulling her close, and his head lowered so his lips could claim hers.

He could not say he'd made the decision to kiss her. He did not stop to think or consider consequences. He simply did as instinct compelled him to do.

To his delight, she responded in kind, her full, tender

lips softening under his, her body meeting his as naturally as if they had made a long practice of such behavior. He moved a hand to cradle the back of her head and felt the silky soft veil she wore over her beautiful amber-golden hair. Pulling the veil off, he let it float to the river below. The gold netting followed, and as soft curls entwined his fingers, her lips moved under his. He savored their slightly salty taste.

As he moved his free hand to the center of her back and delighted in the taut suppleness of her slim body, his imagination stirred pictures that he knew would shock her if she could see them. Lust stirred again, and feeling her body tense, he knew she had felt its stirring.

She did not pull away, and with a low groan, he slid his tongue gently across her lower lip, then to the opening of her mouth. Her lips parted, but when his tongue slid inside to explore its velvet softness, she tensed again, and when he stroked her and pulled her tighter against him, she moved her hands to his chest and pushed.

"What are you doing?" she asked huskily as she shot a glance northward, evidently remembering that Jeb stood guard round the corner.

"You know what I'm doing," Hugo murmured. "You were doing it, too."

"I was not!"

He raised his eyebrows and felt his lips twitch.

She grimaced. "Aye, well, for a moment, perhaps I was. But I certainly did not instigate it, and 'twas gey wicked of you to."

"Why?"

"You know perfectly well why," she said. "Sakes, but I am here under your aunt's protection if not your own, and you are promised to Adela. Well, mayhap not promised exactly," she amended swiftly. "But—"

"I have no obligation to her now that she has gone willingly with Waldron," he interjected. "I won't say I'm sorry, either, because much as I have struggled against the inclination, I am growing daily more attracted to her younger sister."

Her mouth dropped open before she said indignantly, "Hugo, you are daft, and I'd be daft to believe you. Well, I do believe the struggling part," she said. "Nevertheless, you are still Adela's only hope to recover her reputation, and you know it. What's more, you don't know that she went willingly rather than to save Isobel and the child. Indeed, we do not even know where she is."

"Waldron is at Edgelaw, and we know that she is with him."

"We do not," she retorted, "because if he even suspects that you or I think she went with him willingly, he is likely to decide he has no further use for her. Indeed, he may already have abandoned her or given her to his men, or . . . or he may even have . . ." She clapped a hand over her mouth to stop the words before she could finish the thought, and he saw tears sparkle in her eyes.

He reached for her to draw her back into the comfort of his arms, but she pulled away, saying, "I'm going to bed, sir. Goodnight."

As she turned to go, he caught her arm. "One moment, lass," he said. "I have something else I want to say to you."

"You have said enough for one night," she snapped, jerking her arm free.

"Wait," he said as she strode to the stairway door. "I

want to apologize. I was a fool to stir your anger, especially when you are so tired. Also, you are right. I should not have taken advantage of my position here, or of yours."

She had stopped moving at the word "apologize," but she did not turn.

Gently he added, "I do know that Waldron did not abandon Adela or harm her. They are both at Edgelaw now, and she was certainly alive when they got there."

~

Sorcha turned, brushing a tear from her cheek with the back of her hand as she eyed him narrowly. He had never given her reason to doubt his word, but when the topic shifted to Adela's safety, unexpected emotion had jarred her into realizing how worried she was about her.

She knew she was not thinking straight. The last thing she had expected was for him to kiss her, right up to the half second before he did. And even when she had seen that he meant to do it, she had felt no urge to stop him.

That thought floated in her mind for a moment before honesty intervened. She might pretend to him that his kiss outraged her. She might even persuade him. But she could not expect to persuade herself—not when just the thought of his marrying Adela made her want to sink down to the stones of the walkway and squall like her new nephew had squalled at his first glimpse of the noisy, battle-filled world he'd popped into.

But she could not curl up and cry. She had to maintain her dignity and her resolution. Adela loved Hugo. How could she not, when anyone would? And, too, sacrifice was noble. Everyone said so.

Everyone was mad.

Sacrifice was horrid when you were the one who had to do the sacrificing.

Hugo was still watching her, waiting for her to speak, and she knew he had seen the tear and could easily guess how close she was to a collapse of one sort or another—simple exhaustion if nothing else. She had slept some in the tent with Isobel the previous night, but not nearly enough.

Drawing a deep breath, she let it out, then asked the questions that she knew she ought to have asked straightaway. "How can you know that Adela is at Edgelaw? For that matter, how did you learn that Waldron is there?"

"Einar followed them."

"But how could he? Was he not one of the men who crept up on Waldron's encampment with you? Did you not tell the countess and Sir Edward that all of you left your horses behind?"

"He took one of the enemy horses," he said. "If Waldron left men to guard them, either Einar dealt with them first or they had already died or joined the fight. I did not ask him which it was. He is one of the best men I have for such tasks, so they'll not have seen him, but he followed the two of them closely enough to see them ride through the gateway into Edgelaw's forecourt."

"But—"

"Moreover," he went on firmly, "I can assure you that if Waldron did not abandon or kill your sister straightaway so that she could not hinder his escape, he will not do so at Edgelaw whilst he still has any use for her."

"Thank you, that does make sense," Sorcha said, gathering her dignity tightly around her. "I will sleep better, knowing she is safe. Now, goodnight, sir."

"Not yet," he said, stepping closer to the door to stop her. "I have more to say, and because I have told you where they are, you *will* listen to me."

She sighed. "Very well, but I warn you, if you do not say it quickly, I am likely to fall asleep just standing here."

"I would suggest that you pay close attention," he said. "I have told you where your sister is because I agreed to tell you as much as I could about that. And I have told you how I know because you asked me. Now I will tell you one more thing. You are not to try to find your way to Edgelaw to visit her, to try to rescue her, or for any other purpose that might occur to you. Do you understand me?"

"Aye, but if you think I'll abandon Adela to that horrible man, you are much mistaken. She is *not* there willingly, and we are her only hope for rescue. To abandon her now would be a betrayal of the highest order. I won't do it."

He caught her by the shoulders again before she realized his intent, and gave her a shake, saying, "You will obey me this time, lass. I say that as your protector, guardian, or whatever you have made me with your persistence in following Waldron and your sister. If you will not promise, I'll see that you have no choice but to obey. *Now* do you understand?"

"How would you do that?" she asked, curious to know how far he would go.

His grip tightened until she feared she would wear

bracelets of bruises on each arm. But although she continued to gaze steadily at him, he seemed to realize he must be hurting her, because with a growl of exasperation, he released her before he snapped, "Don't be a fool. Who do you think commands Roslin's guards? Do you really want me to issue orders that would make you a virtual prisoner here?"

Heat surged into her cheeks at the thought. Then she wondered if, even without such orders, any guard at Roslin would let a lone female leave the castle, particularly one he knew had never been there before. She decided she would be wiser not to test Hugo's irritation further by asking him.

Instead, she said with careful dignity, "I am not such a fool as to go riding over strange countryside by myself."

She could not be sure what the sound was that came from him then, but it sounded somewhere between laughter and a snort of derision. He glanced upward as if seeking guidance—or patience—before he said, "Nay, Skelpie, you walk there instead. The last time you did so, you walked straight into Waldron's arms."

Much as she would have liked to explain that had resulted from unique circumstances, ones that she had believed, and still believed, to be quite desperate, she did not want to stir the coals of that particular venture again either. Retaining her dignity with considerable effort, she said, "I meant only that I will engage not to ride away from Roslin without an escort, sir. But since it pleases you to throw that other incident in my face, I will likewise engage not to *walk* away from here alone."

"That won't serve," he said. "I want your solemn promise that you will make no attempt whatsoever, without first gaining my permission, to visit your sister at Edgelaw or anywhere else whilst you are here at Roslin. You are not going to leave this walkway until I have that promise."

"What if my father comes here? He is likely to do so, you know."

She was not at all certain Macleod would come, as he seemed to have washed his hands of both Adela and her. But she doubted that Hugo would think of that.

Nor did he, for he smiled sardonically and said, "If you can persuade your father to let you ride to Edgelaw or to take you there himself, I'll be astonished. But if you think he would do either of those things without consulting me first, you are not thinking at all, my lass."

She sighed, knowing he was right and knowing, too, as she had from the start, that she had no choice but to obey him. "I'll give you my promise," she said. "But I also promise that I'll give you no rest until you make Adela safe again. You say you care for me, Hugo. If you do, you will *not* abandon her."

With that, she thrust him aside, opened the door, and did not look back.

～

After she had gone, Hugo turned back to gaze down at the river and the deeply shadowed woods to the west, wondering if she would keep her word. He knew he had not handled the discussion well, that he had angered her. But after he had told her where Adela was, he had feared with all his being that she might slip away again to find her. And heaven only knew what might come of that.

He dared not take such a risk, but neither had he wanted to infuriate her, and he certainly would do that if he gave orders to his men to keep her inside the castle walls. As for whether he cared for her . . .

He smiled, wondering what demon had possessed him to fall in love with her. She bore not the least resemblance to the eventual wife of his imagination. That woman was perfectly familiar to him. She would be a calm, honest, competent female of pleasing looks and figure, who would manage his household and bear him numerous sons and a few well-behaved daughters without any fuss or distress.

In return, he would exert himself to be an excellent husband and father, and they would all enjoy an affection that placed no strain on the emotions and thus would likewise share a happy home, free of fractious strife. If he'd expected to wait a few more years before acquiring that paragon, it was only because, for a long while, more important matters had filled his time and demanded his attention.

Lady Adela had certainly seemed to be such a woman if one could dismiss the holy-water incident. That, admittedly, had cast a damper on his intentions in more ways than one. But he had realized at the time that Adela was under great tension and had been willing to forgive the incident if no others of its nature occurred.

Remembering that image of the perfect wife now caused him to shake his head at himself and send up a prayer of thanksgiving that Sorcha would never know about it. He realized, thinking about Sorcha, that his perfect family might have turned out to be a trifle boring. Certainly that perfect wife seemed boring the instant he compared her to the temperamental skelpie he had fallen for instead.

Trying to imagine Sorcha giving him well-behaved daughters made him grin. It was far more likely that she would give him a dozen just like herself. That is, she would if he could first figure out what the devil to do about Adela.

"Beg pardon, Sir Hugo. It were so quiet here, I thought ye'd gone."

Hugo straightened and smiled ruefully. "Sorry, Jeb, I should have called you. I got lost in my own thoughts, but I'm leaving now. Goodnight to you."

As he shut the door behind him and went down the stairs, he grimaced at what lay ahead. Doubtless his father was either sitting with the countess in her new solar or they both still lingered with their claret at the high table. One thing was certain, though. Having said he wanted to talk more with his son, Sir Edward would not go to bed until he had.

Sorcha's mood had not improved by the time she reached her bedchamber, and she nearly slammed the door behind her before realizing she was not alone. The room had been dark when she'd left it after fetching her cloak. Now, candles glowed, and the sleepy-looking chambermaid who had assisted Sidony stood up rather too quickly to bob an awkward curtsy.

"The housekeeper said Countess Isabella wanted me to wait up for ye, me lady," she said with a wary look. "But if ye dinna want me . . ."

Sorcha's ready sense of humor stirred. The whole place provided pitfalls at every turn, and Hugo was one of them. Trust him to inflame her temper to such a pitch that she could terrify innocent maidservants!

Sternly taking herself in hand, she said, "What is your name?"

"I be Kenna, me lady, Kenna Elliot."

"Are you kin to the guardsman Jeb Elliot?"

"Aye, he's me brother," Kenna said, looking surprised. "Tam's another."

"Sir Hugo was kind enough to show me the view from the ramparts, and we met Jeb up there," she said. "He mentioned Tam, too. I did not know you'd be waiting," she added. "But I am glad you are. Would it be possible for me to order a bath? I have been traveling for nigh onto a sennight, you see, and although I washed the worst off before supper . . ."

She stopped, because Kenna was already nodding.

"Aye, sure, ye can ha' what ye like," she said. "I'll just run and tell them to fetch a tub and hot water up here, and I'll ask the countess's Martha if ye can use some o' her mistress's scented soap. Will ye be wanting to wash your hair, too?"

Sorcha frowned. "I'd like that, but it takes hours to dry."

Kenna's smile crinkled up her hazel eyes until they almost disappeared. "As short as it be, it willna take so long, me lady," she said. "But there be nae fire in this room. Ye'd ha' to go down to the hall fire or to the kitchen one to dry it proper. Or I could ha' them fill a tub right in the kitchen if ye like. There'll be nae one save the baker's wife there and mayhap a lad to tend the fire. She kneads her dough for the manchets, and leaves it to rise after they bank the fire for the night. We've a screen and all, if ye dinna mind. Or we can wait till tomorrow," she added cheerfully.

Since Sorcha and her sisters all bathed in the kitchen at Chalamine, she did not mind in the least doing so at Roslin and said so.

"Then I'll see to it straightaway, me lady. I've set out a robe and one o' Lady Isobel's clean shifts for ye. Will ye come wi' me now, or shall I return to fetch ye?"

"Now," Sorcha decided, and the two went together down to the kitchen level.

The fireplace there lay in the east wall, doubtless directly below one of the two hall fires, and in less time than she had thought possible, Sorcha was stepping naked into her bath. The screen Kenna had produced was solid enough both to provide privacy and to prevent much of the fire's heat from escaping. The baker's plump wife had banished the lad tending the fire, and the rhythmic thumping of her dough on a table at the far side of the chamber provided a soothing background.

As Sorcha slid down in the hot water and let Kenna wash her hair, she began to relax, but her sleepy thoughts still resisted order. No matter how hard she tried to concentrate on helping Adela, she could think only of Hugo's kisses and what he had said to her. Angry as she had been when she left him, she had harbored a small hope that he would follow her, if only to say something to indicate that he really meant to do all he could to protect both Adela and Adela's good name.

"He doesn't want to, though," she muttered. "So I hope his father flays him."

"What's that ye say, me lady?"

"Nothing, Kenna, nothing at all."

⁓

Hugo had entered the upper hall to find Sir Edward sitting alone before the fire, wine goblet in hand, evidently in rapt contemplation of the leaping flames.

Although the trestles in the lower hall were gone, the privacy screen stood as it had earlier, because a number of the men had lingered and many would sleep there. Two of them, Hugo noted, were casting dice near the lower hall fire. Others had begun laying out pallets for the night.

Sir Edward turned his head at the hollow sound of Hugo's footsteps on the dais. "I was beginning to think you had got lost," he said.

"No, sir," Hugo said. "I had something important to say to Lady Sorcha."

"I warrant she's been a handful," Sir Edward said. "This problem with Waldron has developed into quite a tangle, has it not?"

"Aye," Hugo agreed.

"And not entirely by fault of the lady Sorcha."

"No, sir."

Two more guardsmen strode into the lower hall on a burst of laughter. When one offered to share the jest with the others, they roundly cheered him.

Sir Edward stood up and set his goblet on the high table. "I trust you can provide a place with greater privacy to continue our talk."

Hugo nodded and led the way to his own chamber.

Since it was above the hall and boasted a small hearth, a fire already burned there, and the manservant who looked after his things at Roslin sat on a low stool before it, brushing a dark-blue velvet doublet. The room was small but comfortable, with a high curtained bed, a pair of back-stools by a small table nearby, and a washstand in one corner.

The manservant got up, bowed to Sir Edward, then said to Hugo, "I'll just take this gear away wi' me, sir. Will ye be wanting anything more?"

Hugo glanced at his father, who shook his head. "Not tonight," he said. "But wake me at dawn."

When the man had gone, Hugo drew both back-stools nearer the fire and said, "Take a seat, sir. I don't doubt you have much to say to me."

Sir Edward arranged the back-stool to his liking and sat down. Stretching his long legs to the fire, he said, "I did have much I wanted to say before you went upstairs. But it occurred to me, as I sat staring at the fire, that you have been your own master for a long while now, lad. I believe I can trust you to manage your affairs without bringing dishonor to our name. And you'll likely do a better job of it without my sticking an oar into such murky waters as these have become."

"Thank you for your faith in me, sir," Hugo said as he turned his own stool with its back to his father and straddled it. "In truth, though, I had almost looked forward to your reproaches, hoping you would tell me what to do next."

"Sakes, lad, you know without my saying it that you bear some responsibility for what happened to Lady Adela, and for the ladies Sorcha and Sidony, too. I shall be interested to learn, after you settle it all, just how you managed to do it."

"I'd rather like to know how I'll do it, too," Hugo said, folding his arms across the top of the stool's back. "At risk of displeasing you more, I must confess that I've taken a strong interest in Sorcha. Unfortunately, she is determined to make me save Adela from Waldron and then restore Adela's reputation by marrying her."

"So you've fallen for the lass, have you," his father said. "Isabella told me you had, but I did not believe it. Do you not recall once describing for me, in considerable detail, just what sort of wife you meant to have?"

That his shrewd aunt had seen through him was no great surprise, but Hugo had hoped no one would remember his perfect wife. "I was thinking about that earlier," he admitted. "Do you know, now that Sorcha has brought me face-to-face with my own arrogance, I am appalled at how colossal it was."

"Then she has taught you much, my son, and my confidence increases that you will do whatever is both right and honorable. But now, tell me what remains to do in preparation for the council? Do you require aught of me?"

Instead of answering immediately, Hugo moved to the door and opened it, peering out at the small landing and the spiral stairway up which they had come. The chamber on the opposite side of the landing was empty and securely locked.

Shutting his door again, he said, "This room affords me considerable privacy, but I try never to take it for granted."

"'Tis wise to be certain. But now, the council."

"Doubtless Michael will arrive tomorrow evening," Hugo said. "Then, on Tuesday, as you know, everyone will attend the court in Edinburgh to show support for MacDonald of the Isles when he pledges his fealty to the King."

"It can surprise no one that young Donald means to ally himself with his grandfather," Sir Edward said. "But when he does, there will be a smile or two from those who recall how stubbornly his father resisted doing the same."

"He did it, though," Hugo said. "Moreover, Donald means to continue his father's habit of refusing to wear a hat in the King's presence."

"So that he need never take it off," Sir Edward said with a chuckle. "Does Ranald expect any trouble at court?"

"Nay, but he wants to make a good show of strength nonetheless, so no one will believe the Isles are still unsettled over Donald's ascension to the Lordship instead of his own. 'Tis why Ranald wants so many of us to attend."

"It also affords us cover," Sir Edward said. "How many do you expect?"

Hugo knew he no longer spoke of the royal court. "I don't know exactly," he admitted. "So much secrecy has attended the Order, and for so many years now, that we know of only small groups here and there. The list of names we found in the chest with Henry's much-beloved maps gave us a turn, as you know, but . . ."

". . . but that list is at least seventy-three years old," Sir Edward said, finishing his sentence. "So we must take great care."

"We made contact only with members known to other

members," Hugo said. "Even so, we've relied heavily on secret signs and symbols, and only commanders will attend this council. None of them will learn its exact location."

"I'd expected that by now you'd know just how many will come."

"I might have, had Henry not decided to spend a month in Stirling with the court and travel from there to Edinburgh with the King. Or if I had not been in the Isles, busy with preparations for Donald's installation. I know only of six men, mayhap seven from the west, but I wager Henry will know of more. We could not risk exchanging that information through ordinary messengers."

"But how is it you do not at least know the exact number from the Isles?"

"Because Michael intended to look into one or two more possibilities."

"Such as?"

" 'Tis possible that Macleod of Glenelg may be one of us," Hugo said quietly.

"Indeed?"

"Aye, sir. Michael was going to do what he could to look into it before they both joined his grace's flotilla or try to create an opportunity to do so on the way."

"What stirred this intention?"

"It seems Macleod is a notoriously superstitious gentleman," Hugo said. "So superstitious, in fact, that he refused to allow Adela to marry on Friday last, although her intended bridegroom originally chose that date."

"I see. If I am not mistaken, that Friday fell on the thirteenth."

"It did."

"Aye, well, be sure that you and Michael keep me

apprised of any progress there, and anything else that may affect the council. But now, tell me about Donald's installation. Is Ranald satisfied that all will be well?"

Perfectly willing to accept the change of subject, Hugo complied. But as he prepared for bed two hours later, he could not help wishing his father had proven more helpful in the matter chiefly occupying his own thoughts.

He had enjoyed their conversation far more than he had anticipated, and was encouraged that Sir Edward had revealed no disapproval at learning of his interest in Sorcha. But Hugo knew he would happily have endured the severest reprimand if it had produced some of Sir Edward's generally excellent advice.

Chapter 16

~

Sorcha had not closed her bed curtains, so waking to gray light, despite feeling refreshed by a deep, dreamless sleep, she decided it must be nearing sunrise. Getting out of bed, she wrapped her cloak around her to ward off the room's icy chill, then went to the window and looked outside.

A thick Scottish mist cast a desolate pall over everything, including the river. The time might have been any hour between dawn and dusk.

Finding a dark-green kirtle and a striped rose-pink-and-white silk surcoat folded neatly on a stool, she realized that Kenna must have come in and decided not to wake her. Pleased that she had managed to bathe and wash her hair before retiring the night before, she poured cold water from the ewer into the basin on its stand and washed her face and hands. Then, discovering that the kirtle laced up the front, she quickly dressed herself and went to waken Sidony.

Finding her sister's room empty, she went downstairs, where she found Sidony at the high table with the countess, Sir Edward, and Hugo. Only then did she realize that it must be later than she had thought.

Stepping onto the dais, she bade them all a good morning.

"'Tis a gey dreary one, but come sit by me," Sidony said cheerfully as the countess nodded and the men stood politely and echoed Sorcha's greeting. "I was just about to go up and pull you out of bed."

"You and Kenna should not have let me sleep so long," Sorcha said.

"They knew you needed sleep, my dear," the countess said. "Moreover, Roslin has its own chapel and my chaplain to say Mass this morning. As we can therefore linger whilst you break your fast, sit now and tell Ivor what you would like."

"Thank you, madam," Sorcha said, doing so at once and agreeing with the gillie that a loaf, a boiled egg, and a small grilled trout would suit her well. He produced the trout and loaf from a hob near the fireplace, where he had kept them warm, then moved a jam pot that sat near Hugo closer to her.

Sidony had fallen silent, as usual, and the others returned to their discussion, apparently continuing from where they had stopped at Sorcha's entrance.

When Hugo mentioned the King, she inferred that they were discussing their likely activities for the next day or so. Having small interest except insofar as they might pertain to Adela or herself, she listened with only half an ear as she contentedly applied herself to her breakfast.

Not until Sir Edward mentioned Macleod did she take particular notice of what they were saying.

Glancing at Hugo, her gaze locked with his as he said, "I expect he will come here, sir. Whether he will ride with Michael or wait until after he attends the royal court I cannot say. But he will know shortly, if he does not already, that three of his daughters are here at Roslin and that we have knowledge of Adela. He would be a most unusual father if he did not want to see all of them."

"There is his grandson to meet, too, don't forget," the countess said.

"Aye," Hugo said, grinning. "I'm not likely to forget the bairn."

"Nor am I likely to forget how he came into this world," Isabella said with tightening lips and a frown. "I said last night that I would send for Waldron, and so I shall this very day. I know you do not believe he will come, Hugo, but I want to ask him just what he hoped to accomplish by abducting Adela and our Isobel."

Sorcha saw Hugo exchange a glance with Sir Edward. She thought he was silently asking a question, but if that was the case, Sir Edward gave no sign of replying before shifting his gaze back to Isabella.

"Furthermore," she went on, "if Macleod of Glenelg should express a desire to lodge a grievance against him, I mean to allow it. Indeed, I don't doubt that Henry will agree to hold court right here, since he intends to stay for several weeks before he returns to Caithness and Orkney for the summer. I should think Isobel's involvement means that he and I share equal jurisdiction over this matter."

Hugo's jaw tightened, and again he glanced at his father.

But Sir Edward's gaze remained fixed on the countess.

Isabella said, "What is it, Hugo? If you have something to say, please say it."

"Forgive me, madam," he said, flushing. "I do have information that I would like to impart to you, but I should do so more privately."

Sir Edward did look at him then but still said nothing.

Sorcha decided that she and Sidony might as well not have existed for all the heed the others paid them, and her curiosity burned fiercely.

Isabella stood, smoothing her skirt as she said, "I would not have my chaplain think us heathens, so we will proceed to the chapel now. Afterward, Hugo, you may join me in the solar and say what you will. I cannot imagine what you think may sway me from my course, but I will listen to you. Are you ready, my dears?" she added, speaking to Sorcha and Sidony for the first time since Sorcha had joined them.

Ivor appeared at Sorcha's side with a damp cloth and fingerbowl, so she quickly washed her hands and rose to follow the others.

Sidony fell into step beside her, saying quietly, "One cannot help but wonder what that was all about. I do not like secrets, do you?"

Sorcha nearly said something rude but satisfied herself with a firm, "No."

"Secrets make me feel uncomfortable," her sister confided.

It was not the first time that Sorcha had wished she could share her thoughts more freely with Sidony, but it was too easy to distress her younger sister. She was certain that, even now, Sidony had little notion of what dangers Adela faced.

In fairness, Sorcha told herself as they hurried along in the countess's wake, she had not truly comprehended Adela's situation herself until Waldron's men had captured Rory MacIver and beaten him. She had at least understood then why Hugo had been so angry with her when he'd first caught up with them.

She occupied the next few minutes wondering what secrets he meant to share with the countess, and how she herself might possibly discover them.

To her surprise, when they reached the little chapel and she moved to follow Isabella inside, Hugo gently stopped her and gestured for Sidony to go ahead. Then, nodding to Sorcha to precede him, he followed her in.

A number of the servants had taken places on the left, leaving a narrow central aisle, and to the right of it, Sorcha saw that low padded, needlework-covered kneeling stools were already in place for each of the family. A definite benefit to having one's own chapel was that one need not carry one's own stool in each time.

Sir Edward stepped around the countess to take his place beside her, with Sidony on her other side. Hugo and Sorcha knelt behind them, and as soon as the countess had had time to offer a private prayer, her chaplain began to say the Mass.

Sorcha's mind tended to wander at such times, and with Hugo beside her, she could not seem to think of anything but how close he was and how pleasant his deep voice was as he gave the responses and murmured the prayers.

Moments later, her thoughts shifted abruptly to Waldron, and she wondered if Isabella knew that Isobel had pushed the horrid man off the ramparts the previous summer, or that Waldron harbored a desire for vengeance against everyone involved in that incident.

Lost in thought, she murmured her responses automatically, and before she knew so much time had passed, the chaplain invited them to partake of communion. Shortly afterward, he said the benediction and everyone stood again to depart.

Hugo stepped back to let her precede him from the chapel. As she moved past him, she glanced up and saw a twinkle in his eyes.

Tempted for no reason that she could fathom to grin at him, she resisted the impulse as sacrilegious and looked quickly away. Outside, though, as everyone strolled back to the keep, she fell back a bit with him and looked up at him again.

"Pray, sir, what was so amusing back there?"

He chuckled. "I was just wondering how many prayers you had offered. You looked as if you were plotting more sins rather than begging forgiveness for those you've already committed."

She grinned impishly at him. "Since the good Lord sees into my mind and into my heart, sir, He knows how contrite I am."

"And when you are not contrite at all. Don't forget that, Skelpie."

Thankful that he could not see into her mind and heart, and not wanting to quarrel with him—at least, not until she learned what he and the countess would decide to do about Adela—she changed the subject.

They chatted amiably until he excused himself to accompany Isabella to the ladies' solar and Sorcha went with Sidony to visit their wee nephew and Isobel.

"Very well, Hugo," his aunt said as they entered the comfortable new solar from the dais in the great hall. "Say what you will to me."

He moved to shut the door first, but pressure from the other side stopped it as his father followed them inside.

Isabella arched her eyebrows. "You, too, Edward?"

"Aye, madam," he said easily. "I hope you will not forbid it."

Hugo looked from one to the other and felt energy between them that he had not noted before. His aunt had stiffened, but as her gaze met his father's and Sir Edward said nothing more, her tension eased.

"Very well," she said. "But if the pair of you expect to form a league against me, you will find that it will not serve. What Waldron has done is most serious."

"I agree," Sir Edward said. "Will you not take a seat, madam?"

"Aye, but the two of you must do likewise," she said. "I won't have Hugo looming over me like a Colossus whilst he tries to persuade me that I ought not to confront Waldron. That *is* what you mean to do, is it not, sir?"

"Perhaps," he admitted, taking a pair of stools from near one of two narrow, arched windows overlooking the courtyard and moving them nearer her chair. His father sat on one and Hugo took the other, saying, "You recall that in our discussion last night, you mentioned the incident here last summer."

"Of course I remember," she replied testily. "I am not senile, Hugo. Had I not believed that Waldron must have died when he fell from the ramparts, I should have called him to account for his actions straightaway."

"He believes those actions and his recent ones were righteous, aunt."

"Nonsense, how could he?"

"You asked few questions about that at the time."

"Aye, well, I had learned to ask little about men's affairs except when they affected Strathearn or Caithness," she said. "Your uncle was rarely forthcoming about anything having to do with Sinclair affairs. And, during the time that Sir Edward acted as Henry's guardian, he also generally neglected to discuss matters of Sinclair business with me."

She shot Sir Edward a look of irritation, if not resentment, that Hugo realized was similar to one he had several times seen on Sorcha's face. Clearly, tension existed between his father and the countess that he had failed to recognize, and it occurred to him that a countess in her own right might well resent being denied guardianship of her heir. For as much as Henry was heir to Roslin and other Sinclair holdings, so was he heir to the even more valuable lands of Strathearn and Caithness. Moreover, his Orkney princedom had come to him because of his mother's kinship with the Norse King. Despite those details, Sir William Sinclair had awarded guardianship of his sons to his friend and fellow knight, Sir Edward Robison. And doubtless he had done so without explaining his reasons to their mother.

These thoughts flashed through Hugo's mind as he said, "So you do not know what Waldron sought here at Roslin."

"I did not know he sought anything. I know only that

you and Michael were quite oppressively secretive about the whole business. Then Henry, when he came here shortly afterward, behaved in a similar manner. Something excited him at the time, though. I do remember that. Do you mean to tell me what it was?"

Hugo glanced at Sir Edward, whose lips tightened slightly.

The look was sufficient to strengthen Hugo's instinctive reaction. "That is Henry's tale to tell, madam. I do sincerely believe that if you ask him, he will tell you, but the matter is delicate. I dare not reveal it without first having his leave."

"I see."

"Pray believe that I do not mean to offend you, Aunt Isabella," Hugo said. "I have faith in your discretion, and I know Henry does, too. That we have not shared it with you before is due to our concern for your safety, and that of many others."

Isabella looked thoughtfully at him before she said, "I will do you the courtesy of believing that you mean what you say, Hugo, as you have always been truthful to me. But surely you do not mean to say that honor precludes your telling me why I should not demand that Waldron account to me for his sins."

"I won't say that," Hugo said. "Indeed, I would not presume to tell you what to do or not to do, because I do not have that right. But I would like to know how soon you'd expect him to come here."

"Why, straightaway, of course, although as I have not yet sent the summons, I expect he will choose to come tomorrow."

"Michael will arrive tonight," Hugo reminded her.

"The rest of his grace's cavalcade will be in Edinburgh tomorrow by midday. Did you not mean to attend the King's court with us all on Tuesday?"

"I should go, I expect. But the court will remain in Edinburgh for some time. As Isobel and my new grandson are here now, I have decided to stay with them."

"And if Waldron does not come here tomorrow? What then?"

Now it was she who looked at Sir Edward—ruefully—and the expression with which he met that look was another with which Hugo was familiar.

It was the same stern look that his father was apt to acquire whenever he learned of something that Hugo had hoped to accomplish without his knowledge.

Thus, he easily deciphered the unspoken exchange between them and said with a sigh to his aunt, "You would ride over to Edgelaw to confront him."

"Indeed, she would," Sir Edward said.

Stiffening indignantly, Isabella said, "Waldron has sworn fealty to me as his liege. He would not dare to harm me."

Sir Edward continued to regard her solemnly, but Hugo said, "He does not count cost when he believes he is right, madam. He has also sworn fealty to Henry and to the King of Scots, yet he not only invaded Henry's home here at Roslin last summer but abducted two wholly innocent subjects of the King's a sennight ago. Waldron believes that God will forgive him anything he does in His service, and you may be sure that in this matter he believes he serves both the Almighty and the Roman Kirk."

"Mercy, I had no idea. In what manner does he serve them?"

"I can tell you only that he believes the Sinclairs took something long ago that belongs to the Kirk. That belief is false, of course, but I cannot explain more about that now. Still, I do want you to understand that you cannot depend on Waldron to behave in a chivalrous manner, even toward you."

"Then you do not want me to send for him."

"On the contrary," Hugo said, allowing himself a wry smile, knowing that what he wanted was immaterial unless he could persuade her. "I would like you to send for him, because his reaction will reveal something about his situation and how many men he has left to serve him. He still holds the lady Adela, after all, and her sisters maintain, despite evidence to the contrary, that she stays with him against her will. I mean to set extra guards on the ramparts here, and throughout the glen, after you send your message. But I do ask for your promise that you'll not leave the castle until we return from Edinburgh and can confer about what to do next."

She was silent for some time. Then she said, "You seem certain he will not come. What if he does?"

"If he comes tomorrow morning, we will be here to meet him. If he does not, my men will have orders to stop him before he ever reaches Roslin."

"If he comes alone, I want them to let him through."

Hugo hesitated. He could not be sure Waldron would not agree to come alone if he thought it was the only way he could gain access to Isabella. And although they could pack the castle with men and weapons, they could not thereby guarantee her safety or that of Isobel and her baby if Waldron, alone or not, were inside its walls.

The last thought decided it, and he said, "Even if I

were to agree to that, madam, you know that Michael will not, because even alone, Waldron is too dangerous. He seeks vengeance against all of us for his mishap last summer. And if he should manage to get to Isobel or to the bairn . . ."

When he stopped to let the rest speak for itself, she nodded and said, "You are right, and I am a fool not to have considered their safety. Waldron has ever sought revenge for perceived slights against himself, and what Isobel did to him goes far beyond that, especially if he believes his own actions were justified." Pausing briefly to reflect, she said, "Very well, Hugo, I accept your judgment."

Profoundly relieved, he thanked her.

After a quarter hour of exchanging news and amenities with Isobel, when Sidony picked up the baby and retired to cuddle him quietly on the deep, pillowed bench in the window embrasure, Sorcha leaned closer to her older sister and said quietly, "I am glad you feel rested. I have something I want to ask you."

Isobel smiled. "About Waldron?"

"Aye, because any number of secrets seem to be associated with him. At least, Hugo resists discussing him despite his holding Adela."

"You should not call him Hugo, dearling."

"Sakes, we delivered your bairn together! I don't stand on any ceremony with the man. Nor do you!"

"Only when no others are about," Isobel pointed out. "He is Michael's best friend, and he has come to mean as much to me as one imagines a brother should."

"Well, I don't want him for *my* brother," Sorcha said roundly. "He is too quick to scold and to issue commands to people over whom he has no authority."

"None? Did you not rather thrust yourselves upon him?"

"Rather it was he who thrust himself upon us," Sorcha said. "We were doing very well by ourselves. We had nearly caught up with Adela and her abductors when he came upon us. But from that moment, he took it upon himself—"

Noting her older sister's amusement, she broke off, then said with dignity, "But you will not want to be hearing about all that. And I am more interested in what Waldron wants. What pressed him to abduct Adela in the first place?"

"I have already told you that I've given my promise," Isobel said. "You cannot expect me to tell you if Hugo will not. What exactly did he say, anyway?"

"Only that Waldron believes they took something belonging to the Holy Kirk. Won't you even tell me *why* he thinks they took it?"

"Sakes, Sorcha, you have passed a sennight in Hugo's company. Does he strike you as a man who would steal from the Kirk? Does Michael?"

"I scarcely know Michael, and I do not know Prince Henry at all."

When Isobel's eyes flashed with anger, Sorcha added hastily, "I am sure that Sir Michael is all that is honorable, for I know you love him. But how can you know that Prince Henry had naught to do with such a misdeed?"

"But I do know that, and so would you after ten

minutes in Henry's company. Moreover, it all happened long before any of them were born."

"Then you do know about it! Oh, Isobel, pray tell me. I swear it will go no farther," she added, lowering her voice and casting a look toward the window embrasure where Sidony remained reassuringly attentive to their nephew.

But Isobel was shaking her head. "I can tell you nothing more," she said firmly. "Indeed, I ought not to have said that much."

"But why should you know if I cannot?"

"Because I'm married to Michael. He and Ian Dubh, Hector Reaganach's father by marriage, told me everything the night before my wedding. I had already learned certain things due to my insatiable curiosity, you see, and they feared that it might lead me into danger if they did not persuade me to take greater care."

"But I am curious, too," Sorcha said. "Moreover, if I must outwit Waldron to rescue Adela, it would help to know exactly what he believes."

"A very sound argument," Isobel said, adding sweetly, "Try it on Hugo."

Emitting a near growl of exasperation, Sorcha rolled her eyes.

"Or mayhap you should marry him," Isobel suggested. "I warrant he may tell you then, if only in hopes of keeping you from flinging yourself into the suds again."

"Marry him! Don't be such a noddy. Not only must he marry Adela to restore her reputation, but he would not suit me at all as a husband. Indeed, Isobel, I am surprised you would suggest it. Did you not often say you would never marry, because *all* men are too quick to scold and command?"

"I was wrong," Isobel said with a softer smile. "Michael is not like that."

"Mercy, why ever not?"

"I think 'tis because Isabella is a countess in her own right," Isobel said. "And if a lad does not see his father giving his mother orders at every turn, perhaps he grows up to be different from other men. Can you imagine any man commanding Isabella? Henry will inherit Strathearn and Caithness, but she rules both regions now."

Sorcha frowned. "Hugo means to tell her she must not send for Waldron."

"To come here? Sakes, why would she do that?"

"Because he has committed dreadful crimes, Isobel. It cannot be lawful to go about abducting young women."

"I'm sure it is not, but since I'd thought him dead until I saw him with my own eyes, I did not consider any consequences he might face. I doubt he'll come here simply because she summons him, though. In any event, Michael will be here tonight or early tomorrow morning. I warrant he will side with Hugo."

"But if Countess Isabella always goes her own road . . ."

The baby began to cry, and Sidony said, "I think he's hungry again, Isobel."

"Then bring him to me, dearling, and I'll tend him. Perhaps, then, you could send someone to fetch his nurse."

"How often does he suckle?" Sorcha asked curiously.

"Every two hours," Isobel replied with a laugh. "I warrant he is trying to see how quickly he can grow to be as big as his father."

Watching her take the baby into her arms, Sorcha

found herself idly wondering what Hugo's sons would be like.

Realizing with a jolt just where her thoughts had taken her, she told Sidony abruptly that they should leave mother and child to enjoy each other's company and find someone to fetch the nurse.

~

Adela, having wakened to the same gray morning, had neither kirk nor child to occupy her time. She had much enjoyed her bath the previous night, however. Afterward, to her relief, his lordship had given her a thick wool robe and had taken her to a larger chamber than the gate-tower room. Nevertheless, when he left her, she heard a key turn in the lock again and knew she was as much his prisoner as ever, and more vulnerable than ever without her dress.

She had no needlework or other means of occupying herself, and for several hours after she awoke, she feared she would have nothing to eat. Bored, hungry, and inexplicably sleepy, considering that she had done nothing to weary herself, she lay down on the chamber's narrow cot again and dozed.

When the key rattled in the lock again, she wakened, sat up, and swept hair out of her eyes, expecting to see Waldron. But the door opened to reveal two strange men, one with a wooden tray, the other clearly having unlocked the door for him. The man with the tray entered silently and set it on a stool near the bed. Then the two left and locked her in again.

The tray contained an apple, a mug of ale, and some bread. She picked up the apple and ate it slowly. Fearing they might bring her nothing else, she saved the bread and lay down again, falling quickly asleep.

When she awoke again to the sound of the key, she assumed the same two had returned, and did not sit up. But although there were two, the one who entered with the tray was Waldron. He shut the door and set the tray on the stool.

"What hour is it?" she asked sleepily as she sat up, rubbing her eyes and pulling the robe closer around her.

He shrugged. "Nearly Vespers, I expect. I brought your dress and some good sliced beef," he added brusquely.

"I'm not very hungry."

"Well, you should be, so eat something. I want to talk to you."

A shiver of fear darted through her until she recalled that he had said he needed her to do something for him.

Relaxing slightly, she broke off a small piece of bread and nibbled it.

"I've received a summons from Isabella of Strathearn," he said.

"She is my sister Isobel's mother by marriage," she said, trying to decide if she ought to eat some beef.

"She has demanded my presence at Roslin," he said. "Are you sick?"

"Nay, just tired," she said. "I cannot think why I should be. I've scarcely stirred a step today."

A look flitted across his face that in any other man she might have mistaken for concern, but he said only, "Well, pay attention. I'm no dog to run to Isabella's whistling, or any woman's, come to that."

"Do you want to make her angry?"

"I don't care if I do. Everyone at Roslin did mean to

attend the King's court in Edinburgh on Tuesday, but if I know Isabella, she may come here to confront me instead if I ignore her summons. If she does, I'll have another hostage, but in case she doesn't, I want you to send a message to Roslin."

"Me? What could I have to say to Countess Isabella or she to me?"

"Don't be foolish. Your message is for your sister Sorcha, of course, but I want no one else to know what you say. I'm told all the Macleod sisters can read and write."

"Aye, sir. My aunt Euphemia taught us until she moved to Lochbuie. Then, I taught my younger sisters. Father gives me calves' vellum to record recipes for things he likes to eat, and for ointments, scents, and such that we make at Chalamine. That way, we do not have to remember them all."

"You won't have to write on vellum," he said. "I have something smoother."

"But what am I to say?"

"I'm going to send you to Roslin," he said casually. "I want you to bid Lady Sorcha to come and fetch you."

Stunned, Adela stared at him. She did not believe for a moment that he meant to release her, let alone allow her to go to Roslin. He just wanted to use her to bait another of his traps. But if she refused to do as he bade her, he would kill her.

"Don't worry," he said. "I'll tell you exactly what to say. I could even write it for you if you like."

"I must write it," Adela said, collecting her wits with effort. "Sorcha knows my hand. But you may have to tell me how to spell some of the words."

He nodded, his satisfaction a relief to see.

It occurred to her after he had gone, as she was changing back into her somewhat cleaner blue dress, that he might simply intend to kill her later and replace her with Sorcha. But she pushed that unbearable notion right out of her head.

Chapter 17

❧

Sir Michael Sinclair arrived at Roslin an hour after darkness, while everyone still lingered at the supper table. At Hugo's suggestion, they had not set up the privacy screens, so they were able to see Michael as he strode into the hall and thrust whip, gloves, and cloak at a gillie who hurried to assist him.

"Where is she?" Michael demanded as soon as he saw Hugo.

It was Isabella, however, who said, "Where else should she be but in her bedchamber with my new grandson, Michael? Have you forgotten your courtesy in your great rush?"

He smiled, made a perfunctory bow, kissed her, and greeted Sir Edward. Nodding to Sorcha and Sidony, he added, "Good evening to you, too, but I hope you will all forgive me if I do not linger. I want to see Isobel and our wee son."

"Shall I order a tray for you there, or will you join us after you have admired him and tucked up your lady for the night?" Isabella asked.

"I suppose I ought to come down," he said with reluctance, looking at Hugo. "I warrant we have much to discuss."

"Aye," Hugo agreed.

"Then order more food," Michael said, casting an eye over the table, which by then was nearly empty of platters and bowls. "And fetch out the best claret, too."

Grinning, Hugo sent a gillie to the kitchen and another to fetch the wine.

As Michael strode to the stairway corridor, Sorcha said casually to Hugo, "I'd like more of the wine in that jug by your elbow, sir, if any remains."

Since he had sent the gillies away, he rose to pour it for her himself, catching her eye as he did. "Don't expect to gain much by lingering, Skelpie," he said with a teasing smile. "We'll not invite you to take part in our conversation."

"I did not expect that, sir," she said with airy dignity. "That my safety and Sidony's may be at risk because we do not know what is going on or what your cousin can hope to accomplish is of no account to me whatsoever."

She saw him hesitate and knew a brief hope that he would see the danger to her and to Sidony as sufficient reason to explain everything, just as Michael had done for Isobel.

But Hugo only gave a slight shake of his head as if to clear it before he said, "You will be at no risk, lass, if you stay inside the castle walls as I bade you. Do you mean to join us for our talk, sir?" he asked Sir Edward.

"I doubt you need me," Sir Edward said. "Moreover, I have promised to give the countess a game of chess. Shall we adjourn to your solar, madam, or play here?"

Resisting a strong temptation to get up and pour her wine over Hugo's head, Sorcha followed Sir Edward's gaze to Isabella and met a shrewd look from the countess. Feeling heat in her cheeks, she raised her chin and told herself not to be a noddy, that most likely the countess knew no more than she did about any of it.

Isabella shifted her attention to Sir Edward again, saying with a slight smile, "I am thinking Michael and Hugo should talk in the solar, whilst you and I stay here, sir. They will not want to talk out here, but they may want to confer with you. If so, it will prove more convenient for all of us if they need only step out here rather than return here from Hugo's chamber or some other. Moreover, when Michael returns, if they serve him in the solar, he and Hugo can begin their talk straightaway, thereby allowing him to return to his wife and child the sooner."

Hugo nodded. "As always, madam, your suggestion is an excellent one."

Thus, when Michael returned, his supper awaited him in the solar, and he and Hugo adjourned there. As they left the dais, Sir Edward asked Isabella with a laugh if the chessboard and pieces were not stored in the solar, and when she agreed that they were, he followed the other two inside.

He returned moments later with the board and a wooden box. Removing the pieces from it, he began arranging them on the board's inlaid-leather squares.

Sidony cast a pleading look at Sorcha, who said at

once, "Pray, excuse us, madam. We'll leave you to your game, and visit Isobel and our nephew now."

"Don't stay long," Isabella said, her attention already on the board. "New mothers and their bairns need their sleep."

Hurrying up the stairway, Sorcha stopped at the half-landing and told Sidony to go ahead without her. "I'll join you in a few moments, but I've just thought of something I want to do first."

Sidony nodded and, as usual, displayed no curiosity. As soon as she had disappeared around the next curve, Sorcha peered down the stairway to be sure she was alone, then turned to the door in its tiny recess. Half expecting to find it locked, she was delighted when the latch lifted easily and silently. The door swung inward.

When she shut the door, the tiny chamber was dark inside except for a dim, rectangular glow revealing the laird's peek. It was about six inches wide, perhaps two in height, and a good inch or more above her head when she stood on tiptoe.

Cursing herself for not finding time before to examine it, especially since she could hear only the murmur of their voices and not make out one word they said, she groped for one wall of the chamber and bent to feel about on the floor. When her hands met rough-covered padding, then the wooden frame and legs of a footstool or prayer stool, she gave mental thanks to Isobel, certain her older sister's insatiable curiosity was responsible for the stool's presence.

Taking care to move silently, she set the stool below the peek and stood on it to find that it provided an excellent view of the solar. The gillies had set a table for

Michael's supper near the small fireplace, and Hugo sat opposite him. She could see them both clearly. Even better, she could make out what Hugo was saying.

～

Knowing Michael would not want to discuss anything until he had heard whatever Hugo could tell him that Isobel had not about how he had found her and delivered her baby, Hugo tried to explain it briefly.

Michael listened with his usual patience, although his interest in Sorcha was clearly as nothing to his interest in his wife and child. And Hugo found it hard to omit his frequent irritation with Sorcha. Noting distinct signs of amusement in his cousin, he strove to limit his complaints and did so easily when he began to describe the events in the clearing near Ratho.

"Sorcha was most helpful to us both," he admitted at the end. "But to have set out alone, knowing she risked the same fate as the lad she had persuaded to go with them, was both dangerous and foolhardy. She can be glad her father did not accompany you tonight, for if I were he—"

"I know that feeling," Michael interjected. "'Tis why I was glad to leave Isobel at Lochbuie, where I thought she would be safe. If I were to learn that she—"

"She did naught to deserve censure," Hugo said quickly. "She believes it was the wicked abbot's men who captured her as she returned to the castle after bidding you farewell." He sighed, adding ruefully, "To be fair, I should also say that had Sorcha not been so impulsive, I would not have reached Isobel in time."

Michael nodded, but Hugo had reminded himself with his own words that Michael's own father had married a woman also prone to impulse.

"Your mother, as you might surmise, is wroth with Waldron," he said. "She has commanded him to present himself here and explain himself. I think I have persuaded her not to confront him if he fails to obey her."

"Faith, she summoned him here?"

"She sent a message this afternoon and was prepared to confront him at Edgelaw if he ignored it. I think my father's presence may have helped persuade her to listen to reason."

"Aye, well, she has great respect for him, as we all do."

"Did you know that Waldron holds Edgelaw only at her pleasure?"

"I never thought about it," Michael said. "But I do seem to recall now that it is mentioned amongst my parents' marriage settlements."

Hugo grimaced. "I ought to have realized how it is. But she and Henry hold joint baron's courts, both here and in the north, and I tend to forget that she wields the same powers in Strathearn and Caithness that he wields in Orkney, except for the power to coin her own money. I suppose I just assumed that he controlled all the estates and gave her free rein over Strathearn and Caithness when both he and you are absent. In any event, she means to evict him if he does not come here."

"I trust you mean Waldron and not Henry," Michael said with a grin that faded as he added, "This could complicate matters for us here Tuesday night if Waldron decides to slip men into the glen to keep a watch on her."

"Aye, it could," Hugo said. "I've set extra guards, and

I've also let it be known that I mean to be away only the one night. That in itself may present a problem since the moon will rise early Tuesday. I'd as lief that no watcher see me leave again so soon after my return from Edinburgh."

"Use the tunnel," Michael recommended.

"I'm thinking I'll have to, although I don't like to do so at such an hour, when anyone guarding the entrance is more likely to draw attention to it. Also, we had hoped the moonlight would make matters easier for those who come here, but if Waldron sets watchers, it may—" Breaking off, he fought a sudden, compelling urge to look up at the west wall of the solar and added hastily, "—not do that."

He knew Michael had caught the slight hesitation, and as their eyes met, Hugo reached for the wine jug and poured wine into his own still-half-full goblet.

Michael said, "Do you think you might bestir yourself to find someone to refill that jug? I want to finish this excellent mutton before it gets cold."

"Aye, sure," Hugo replied, standing. "I'll return shortly," he added as he strode quickly to the door.

～

Sorcha, too, had discerned Hugo's hesitation and knew with a sudden, panic-stricken certainty that he had felt her watching them. Swiftly, she bent to replace the stool, then straightened to feel for the door latch. Lifting it as quietly as she could, knowing he would not pause to shout for wine or anything else, she slipped out of the chamber, shut the door, snatched up her skirts, and fled upstairs to Isobel's room.

Stopping just outside it, she drew a breath to steady her pulse, listening hard for the slightest sound of his approach. Hearing none, she opened the door and stepped inside, smiling at the tender scene before her.

Both Sidony and Isobel sat on Isobel's bed, gazing at the sleeping baby in Isobel's arms. He held his tiny hands clasped beneath his rounded chin.

Sidony put a finger to her lips, murmuring, "We wondered where you'd disappeared to. But come and look at this precious wee laddie, won't you? Isobel says they mean to name him tomorrow before Michael has to leave again."

Sorcha pulled a stool near the bed and sat down, smiling at the baby and hoping both of her sisters would believe he held her full attention, although her ears strained for the first hint of Hugo's footsteps. She had no doubt that he would come.

They were discussing the naming ceremony when the light rap on the door interrupted Isobel. "Who can that be?" she said. "Michael would not knock."

"Sidony, go and see," Sorcha said.

She did so, opening the door to Hugo. "Good evening, sir," she said. "Our wee lad is sleeping, but if you've come to see him, I know that you are welcome."

"Aye, sure," Isobel said, smiling at him. "Come in, Hugo."

Hugo was looking at Sorcha with an intensity that sent heat to her cheeks. But it stirred heat in other places, too, allowing her to hope he would think her merely discomposed by his entrance into her sister's bedchamber.

Realizing he was unlikely to believe such discomposure could last long with her, she lifted her chin defiantly and said in what she hoped would pass for a sweet voice, "I wager Michael will be here soon if your conversation has ended, sir. 'Tis fortunate for you that you can claim two such fine chaperones, is it not?"

His eyes narrowed, but he shifted his gaze to Isobel and said, "He won't come straightaway, my lady, for we have more yet to discuss. I came up for another purpose and thought I should let you know that he may be longer than you'd expected. I'm glad to see that your sisters are still here with you."

Isobel thanked him, but when he left the room and shut the door, she shifted her gaze to Sorcha and said sternly, "I saw that look he gave you. So I'm guessing you're lucky he does not know you just came in here. Just what mischief have you been up to now?"

Sorcha shrugged. "I cannot think why you should believe I have been up to anything. Will the babe's naming ceremony be directly after breakfast?"

Isobel held her gaze a moment longer, then agreed that it would be and added that Michael had declared they would hold the ceremony in the bedchamber as tradition demanded. "Thus, Father will have naught to complain about," she added with a smile. "His new grandson will not leave this room before he is properly baptized, to tempt any wicked fairy to make off with him."

If she retained her suspicions of Sorcha, she said no more about them, and Sorcha escaped with Sidony before Michael came upstairs.

Bidding Sidony goodnight at her bedchamber, Sorcha could not resist slipping back down to the chamber on the half-landing again. Making certain no one was nearby on the stairs, she opened the door again and slipped inside, shutting it behind her. The intense blackness of the room threatened to swallow her, and she quickly opened the door again. Someone had pushed cloth of some sort into the laird's peek, and she had no doubt who had done it or that he was at that very moment watching from below to see if it moved by so much as a hair's breadth.

That she had learned so little was frustrating. That he undoubtedly suspected her might prove unfortunate, but she doubted that he would ask her if she had been watching them. For one thing, he could not be sure unless it occurred to him to ask her sister Isobel that she even knew the laird's peek existed. And he certainly would not want to be the one to inform her of it.

Shutting the door, she went to her bedchamber, where she idled away the few minutes before Kenna came to help her prepare for bed by wondering where the tunnel that Hugo had mentioned might lie. She wondered, too, what mischief he and Michael had planned for Tuesday night that a full moon could reveal to someone from whom they had expected to stay hidden.

⌒

"Who was at the peek?" Michael asked when Hugo returned. "Please tell me it was not Isobel."

"I cannot say for certain that anyone was there," Hugo said. "Instinct tells me someone was, *and* that it was that skelpie Sorcha. But instinct is not evidence, and I found none. I found all three of them together with the bairn."

"I see that you did take the precaution of stuffing the hole with a white cloth," Michael said, grinning. "We ought to have thought of that when we realized that closing off this part of the hall put the laird's peek over the solar, but since no one uses the peek now, I expect everyone forgot. I did until you reacted as you did."

"Aye, well, one does not expect to find spies in the walls here," Hugo said. "Also, we have not used this room for private talks before. I did think about the peek when my aunt invited me here to discuss confronting Waldron, but I felt no such threat then. I certainly did tonight."

"I, too, had a brief sense of being watched but dismissed it. As you say, one does not expect spies to hover about here the way they might elsewhere."

"If we have spies here, I do not know them," Hugo said. "And since our indoor servants are all local folk with strong loyalty to Roslin, the Sinclairs, and to me, I think we can eliminate that possibility. Our men-at-arms have all been tested often. If I trust some more than others, 'tis because of a greater level of skill rather than matters of integrity or loyalty."

"Aye," Michael agreed. After a pause, he added with a reflective look, "A point has occurred to me that you may find interesting."

"What?"

"Lady Adela's would-be bridegroom accompanies his grace's cavalcade. Ardelve arrived at Lochbuie with Macleod's second boat when it returned. He's announced that he, too, means to support his grace in Edinburgh."

"And why, pray tell, did you think I should find that interesting?"

"I just thought it might. Another matter that I hope will interest you is that we're going to name the lad in the morning. I'd like you to stand *gosti* for him."

"Aye, sure," Hugo said, truly pleased. "You honor me.

As to Tuesday night, you'll be with the others, and my father as well, so I think I will sup here and use the tunnel. That will draw less curiosity at this end than if I were to ride out again after dark. I'm guessing your mother will have heard from Waldron by then, too, and if he defies her, as I warrant he will, she is going to press for action."

"Aye, sure, she will, and 'tis a wonder you were able to persuade her to delay it until then. Are you sure you succeeded?"

"She gave me her word," Hugo said. "Sorcha did, too. Both promised not to leave the castle without first consulting me."

Michael nodded. "Mother won't break her word."

"I hope Sorcha won't, either," Hugo said. The instinct that rarely failed him when it came to reading people had so far remained utterly mute on that point.

The following morning emerged from darkness in new curtains of mist above a milky fog that hovered close to the river, muffling its sound. Drifting wisps of gray and white settled like veils over treetops or nested amid the shrubbery.

Wanting exercise after a day spent almost entirely withindoors, Sorcha dressed herself before Kenna came to her chamber. Then she threw on her cloak, hurried downstairs, and came face-to-face with Hugo as she entered the hall.

He greeted her with a look that was half smile, half frown.

Thinking he would demand to know where she was

going, she forestalled him by saying, "I want to walk outside. I've been lying awake this past hour, and I want fresh air and exercise. I am not accustomed to being caged."

"I'll go with you," he said promptly. "We must not stay out long, though. The countess rises early, and as soon as we all break our fast, Michael and Isobel want to hold the bairn's naming ceremony."

She nearly told him she would prefer to walk by herself but resisted, knowing perfectly well that she wanted nothing of the sort. If all went as she hoped, he was unlikely to invite her to walk with him again, because Adela would be free as soon as the countess dealt with the horrid Waldron.

Outside, the mist spilled around corners and over the walls of the courtyard. It was the clinging sort, made up of droplets so tiny they lacked weight enough to fall, so they stuck to one's eyelashes and kissed one's cheeks.

In the northeast corner, the tall lantern tower seemed to disappear in a dense cloud of the stuff, and the flagstones beneath Sorcha's feet felt slick with it as she walked. But she did not mind the damp. Nor was she chilled, because as usual when Hugo was beside her, she could feel warmth radiating from his body.

It occurred to her that such a mist could hide many things, even men. "Does this mist not make it difficult to guard the castle?" she asked.

"The safest way onto the promontory is over that treacherously narrow land bridge to the gate," he said. "Few men are brave enough to risk it without being able to see exactly where they are. Even if they make it to the gates, only a few can stand there. They could not position a ramming party, for example, nor could anyone easily breach our walls. Not only is Henry extending them considerably, as you know, but the new curtain wall stands outside the old one."

"But the new wall is not finished. What about an approach from the north?"

"The castle sits on the highest part of the promontory, and the hills to the north are rugged and heavily forested, as is the glen. So even in a much thicker mist, we're safe enough here. Today, I have lads in the forest and along the rim of the glen, watching and listening for trouble. The mist conceals them, too."

"You're leaving today," she said and was surprised to hear in her voice the sadness she had felt since waking.

He reached for her hand and tucked it into the crook of his arm, drawing her closer as he said, "Michael and I, and my father, will ride to Edinburgh this afternoon to meet Ranald and the cavalcade. Henry has a house there, as I may have told you, so we'll spend the night with him. I'll return tomorrow evening."

"Just you? Will not Michael and Sir Edward return as well?" She looked up as she asked and saw a muscle twitch in his jaw before his gaze met hers.

The searching look in his eyes told her that he still suspected she had been at the laird's peek, and she felt a tremor of guilt. Hoping the damp chill would keep her too-easy blushes in check, she continued to gaze innocently at him until she realized that his own cheeks had reddened.

"You are thinking what to say to me," she said indignantly, no longer caring what he had seen in her face. "You said you would always answer me honestly."

"Aye, and I will," he replied, his gaze meeting hers easily. "But you will recall that I also said I would tell you when I cannot give you all the answers you seek, because they are someone else's to give or because I do not know. I was but trying to decide which category this new question of yours fits. Michael and my father may return to the castle tomorrow, but I do not know exactly when, so I would ask you not to raise Isobel's hopes about Michael, as he is likely to sleep elsewhere rather than risk disturbing her."

She held his gaze a moment longer, but then his searching look returned, and not wanting to invite questions, she looked away first. That he had every right to demand equal honesty from her was one thing, but being obliged to answer honestly and then face his anger afterward was quite another.

"Your father may come with them, you know," he said in a gentler tone than she had expected to hear just then.

"I expect he will stay in town with his grace," she said. "He will not want to have to deal with me or with Adela's situation yet. Moreover," she added, forcing a more cheerful note, "Adela may be free by then, so if he does come, he will see that she is safe and will know that we did the right thing by coming after her. And then, if you still mean to do the honorable—"

"There is something else you should know," Hugo interjected.

Surprised but hoping his interruption meant only that he did not want to talk about his honor, that instead he might actually satisfy her curiosity about whatever was going to happen the next night, she waited hopefully.

He said bluntly, "Lord Ardelve rides with his grace's cavalcade."

"What?" She was surprised, but then she realized he was making too much of a small thing. "There can be nothing in that," she said. "The only reason he did not join them in the first place was that he'd expected to be a new bridegroom and did not want to leave Adela alone so soon after their wedding. But as they did not marry, he will have decided to support his grace. That's all it means."

"If that were the case, do you not think he would have attended his grace's installation, then come south to Lochbuie with us, rather than making what must have amounted to quite a scramble to join the flotilla before it departed?"

She shrugged. "The man has his pompous pride. It must have suffered a heavy blow when he saw his bride carried off, and worse if he believed as everyone else did that she was leaving with the man she loved. Doubtless, he wanted time to lick his wounds and did not want to face everyone so soon at the installation."

She felt him tense midway through her comments, and when she finished, he stopped her in her steps and turned her to face him. As her arm unlinked from his, she felt the misty chill again.

"Where do you come by such notions?" he demanded.

"No man likes his pride wounded," she said, surprised and defensive. "Nor does any man like to air his injuries in public."

"I don't mean that," he retorted gruffly. "I want to know where the devil you came by this fool's notion of yours that Adela ever loved me."

"I just know she does." She stared up at him. The mist had thickened silently around them as if Roslin Castle had vanished and left them in a world of their own.

He was glowering at her, not touching her, daring her to answer him. He looked about as angry as a man could look, yet she felt no fear. Instead, she felt warmed, as if a cozy fire burned within her.

She nearly smiled but fought against it, fearing he would think she laughed at him. That would not do at all, even if she could explain her feelings to him, and she doubted that she could because she did not understand them herself.

"Don't look at me like that," he commanded, his voice still gruff with that odd angry note as he caught her by the shoulders and held her firmly where she stood. "When you twitch that damned dimple at me, I want to kiss you, and since you have forbidden that, it is not fair to tempt me."

"It is hardly fair to blame me for looking at you," she said. "Nor can anyone control what a ridiculous dimple does."

"Aye, well, I think we should go back inside," he said, putting an arm around her shoulders. "You have not had much exercise, I know, but this mist is soaking us through, and before long we'll both be chilled to the bone."

He walked her across the courtyard as if he could actually see where he was going, and as she hurried to keep up with him, she could only hope the mist was thinner a foot higher than it was at her eye level.

Inside, they found the countess already at the high table, and Michael arrived minutes later, making Sorcha

glad that Hugo had decided to return. He took her cloak
from her and handed it to a gillie to dry by the fire. It had
kept her dry enough, but she was sure that Hugo, lacking
one, must be feeling damp.

If he was, he gave no sign of it, and when they adjourned to Isobel's bedchamber with Isabella's chaplain,
Hugo played his part in the naming ceremony to perfection. To be sure, all he had to do was to hold young
William Robert Sinclair, for that was the name Michael
had given the chaplain to speak for the first time as he
baptized him. Hugo then blessed the infant and vowed to
remain bound to him as godfather for life. The ritual not
only bound the infant to Hugo but tightened the bonds between the Robison and Sinclair families.

As she watched him tenderly smile at his godson, she
felt the same deep warmth inside her that she had felt
after the child's birth and so recently in the courtyard.
Since the circumstances were so different, she thought it
odd, but then the still-smiling Hugo looked at her, young
William Robert made chuckling sounds behind the tiny
clenched fist in his mouth, and she no longer thought it
odd at all.

After the brief ceremony, the men adjourned to their
chambers to tend to last-minute duties before their departure for Edinburgh. For a time, everyone worried that the
mist would linger all day, but by midday, sunbeams had
broken through here and there and the milk fog over the
river had dispersed. A breeze stirred, and an hour later,
when the men departed after their midday meal, all that
remained to remind anyone of the mist was a sky full of
billowing pale-gray clouds.

The rest of the day crept by at a snail's pace. No

message arrived from Edgelaw, a fact that by suppertime had put the countess in a black mood. And Sorcha's mood was no lighter.

She had wanted to look inside the chamber on the landing to see if Hugo had overlooked the helpful little stool or had removed it. She also wanted to see if she could adjust the cloth he had stuffed in the hole so she could peek past it without detection. She had not dared to try that the previous night, lest it prove impossible.

To her annoyance, she found a shiny new hasp and lock on the door.

Isobel kept to her chamber for the rest of the day and announced her intent to retire early. Not only had she enjoyed little sleep the previous night waiting for Michael, but she had talked long with him when he had finally come to her.

Consequently, Sorcha and Sidony spent a long, uneventful evening with the countess and found her singularly uncommunicative on any topic of interest.

At last, unable to stand her own boredom any longer, Sorcha said abruptly, "What will you do if he does not come, madam?"

"I will make him answer for his crimes," Isabella said grimly. "Abducting a noblewoman, particularly for nefarious purpose, is a hanging offense."

"And if he does come?"

"Although his ingratitude infuriates me, I will hear his side of it."

Sorcha had a strong notion that had the countess continued, she would have added, ". . . and then I will hang him."

Their conversation became desultory again, and it was

not long before Sidony was yawning. Sorcha excused them both for bed and found that she welcomed an early night, if only because the next day would come sooner.

The morning's gloom provided nothing to improve her mood. Rather than mist, however, she looked out on a heavy sky that threatened rain. The weather even clouded her thoughts, because all she could think was that it might prevent Hugo's return that night. And if it did, it might also prevent whatever mischief he and Michael had planned.

Not, she told herself, that they truly meant mischief, just to keep their secrets. And although she had not yet learned anything noteworthy about them, she certainly meant to find out exactly what those secrets were, one way or another.

Chapter 18

In the end, the day improved to a greater degree than Sorcha had expected, because the most threatening clouds moved on without spilling their contents. The sky remained cloudy, but she could not imagine that any mere promise of rain would delay Hugo's return. Only a deluge might do that.

By afternoon, with no message from Edgelaw, the countess could barely contain her frustration, and by evening frustration had grown to fury. In the solar after supper, as she pretended to busy herself with her tambour frame and needlework, Sorcha sorted threads for her and Sidony sat with a moss-green kirtle of Isobel's, ripping the hem to adjust it for her own height. In desperation, Sorcha persuaded the countess to tell them more about Roslin and its environs.

She had barely begun when the gillie Ivor came in to tend the fire. As he bent over it, Isabella was describing a nearby cave where Wallace had once hidden.

Ivor looked past her to catch Sorcha's eye. Then, fingering a bit of what looked like paper peeping from his sleeve, he finished feeding the fire without speaking and left the chamber.

Sorcha wrapped the sorted threads carefully into the white linen cloth on which she had laid them out. Then, waiting only until Isabella paused for breath, she said, "Forgive me, madam, but will you excuse me for a short while?"

"Certainly, my dear."

"Do you want me to go with you?" Sidony asked.

"Nay, you need not disarrange your work," Sorcha assured her with a smile, hoping her sister would not say that she also needed to visit the garderobe tower, which doubtless both of her companions assumed was her destination. She held her breath until Sidony nodded and returned to her ripping.

Emerging from the solar to the dais of the now-empty hall, Sorcha saw Ivor disappear through the archway to the northwest stair and hurried after him. She found him waiting in the corridor.

"Forgive me, me lady," he murmured, pulling the folded paper from his sleeve and handing it to her. "I didna ken how else to approach ye, and me cousin did say to give ye this gey quick so as no to get caught wi' it, ye ken."

"But how came your cousin by such a thing?" she asked, fearing from his twitchy manner that he would flee at any second.

Ivor looked over his shoulder before he murmured, "He serves the master o' Edgelaw. But he said to tell ye the lady did ask him to bring it to ye." Looking over his shoulder again, he fairly danced in his impatience to depart.

"You may go," she said, fighting to conceal her astonishment at receiving such a message in such a way. "But thank you, Ivor. I shan't forget this."

"Sakes, mistress, I hope ye will! Did me cousin no be a man o' fierce temper and a ready fist, I'd ha' refused him. I dinna want to think what Sir Hugo or the master will do an they find out I did give ye that without first showing it to one o' them. But Gil did say it be gey important ye get it tonight."

"I won't tell them," she promised.

With visible relief, Ivor darted back into the hall.

Hurrying upstairs lest Sidony change her mind and come after her, and hoping that Kenna was not already awaiting her, Sorcha went to her own chamber. Finding it blessedly unoccupied, she stood by the window and unfolded the paper. By the fast-fading daylight she saw, as she had hoped, a message from Adela:

Well-beloved sister,

I greet you well and have found a friend to aid my escape. If, God willing, you can come for me, he says we should meet near the abandoned peel tower a quarter mile northwest of this castle. You will see it as you come over the last hill. He says a private track leading south through your glen will bring you to this place.

If you can reach the tower by midday tomorrow, I will engage to meet you there, but pray, sister, do not fail me. I dare not wait

long. Nor can my savior escort me, for to do so
'twould be to risk his very life. And, for mercy's
sake, come alone!

I hope his lordship may be well occupied
then, but we dare not depend on that. He be-
lieves Countess Isabella will send men to force
him to submit to her summons, which arrived
here yesterday to his great fury. He has ranted
since and refuses to submit, swearing that his
service to his true Liege Lord supplants all else!

Pray, dearest, do not fail your loving,
most wretched sister,
A.

Sorcha read the missive twice through, then refolded it
and slipped it up the tight sleeve of her kirtle. Her first reaction was relief to know that Hugo had been wrong and
she had been right. Adela had not gone willingly with his
evil cousin.

Her next reaction, following immediately on the first,
was an impulse to call Ivor back and ask if he could describe how to get to Edgelaw from Roslin or, better yet,
if he would agree to accompany her there.

Then common sense intruded along with the memory of
her promise to Hugo to go nowhere from Roslin without
consulting him. Aggravating as that promise was, she knew
she would not be happy with herself if she broke it. Nor, she
had to admit, would she be wise to set out on her own or
even with Ivor, if she could persuade him to go with her.
That Hugo would doubtless forbid her to go, with or without an escort, only made the situation more aggravating.

Realizing that her strongest hope still lay in the countess's intention to call Waldron to account, and her legal control of Edgelaw, Sorcha returned thoughtfully downstairs. Perhaps Isabella might help her.

By the time she reached the solar, however, she had realized that although the countess clearly disapproved of abducting females in general, Isobel's abduction weighed more heavily with her than Adela's, if only because she believed Adela had gone willingly. To persuade her of anything else would take time, making it unlikely that Sorcha could do so before Hugo's now-imminent return.

As she lifted the latch of the solar door, she heard footsteps hurrying up the stone stairway from the main entrance a half-level below. Although tempted to wait and see if it was Hugo, she opted instead to rejoin Sidony and the countess.

She wanted at least a little time to think, to decide what to say to him and whether to show him Adela's message.

Sidony and Isabella looked up from their work and smiled as she entered and shut the door. Rather than take her seat, she crossed the room to one of the windows overlooking the courtyard, and looked out to see a gillie leading Black Thunder across the yard to the stable.

"Sir Hugo is back," she said quietly.

"Good," the countess said, setting aside her tambour frame. "I want to speak to him." As she moved to stand, the door opened and Hugo entered.

Isabella settled back in her chair, saying curtly, "I've had no reply from Waldron. If you will not confront him tomorrow, I'll go to Edgelaw myself."

His searching gaze had found Sorcha returning to her

seat, and she detected a look of relief before he shifted his attention to his aunt. He said matter-of-factly, "As always, madam, you have only to command me."

"Have you brought guests with you?" she asked.

"Nay, though several will arrive tomorrow with Michael and my father."

"Must you wait for them before you can attend to Waldron?"

Sorcha held her breath as she reached for the cloth of silk threads, not daring to look at him lest he detect how tensely she awaited his reply.

"I need not wait," he said. "I've not yet had time to consult with the men I sent to watch Edgelaw during my absence, however. Nor will I speak to them before morning. They should return soon after dawn, though, and may bring information that will help us determine our best course."

Isabella pressed her lips together, then said, "Very well, but I will not brook his insolence, Hugo. Choose your own good time tomorrow, but you will inform him that he must present himself here to explain his actions. Tell him also that if he cannot explain them satisfactorily, I shall end his tenancy at Edgelaw and try him for his crimes. You might also remind him of the penalty they carry."

Hugo nodded but said, "It might be wiser not to remind him of that until he does present himself, madam. I'd as lief not have to conduct a siege of Edgelaw."

"Very well, although he must know what the penalty is."

"Aye, but whether he accepts that it could apply to him is another matter. I would remind you that he believes God protects him in all he does."

"Aye, well, we'll see about that. But enough about Waldron," she added. "I warrant our guests want to hear about the opening of the royal court."

As Hugo described the pomp and ceremony of the occasion, and the official presentation of the second Lord of the Isles to his grandfather, the King of Scots, Sorcha listened politely, but she paid more heed to the speaker than to his account. Soon she detected signs of her own impatience in Hugo's demeanor.

It was not long after that when he excused himself, declaring that he had business to attend with his men. Then, he said, he would retire for the night.

Excusing herself again moments later, Sorcha looked for him in the hall, but he had already disappeared.

"Sorcha, wait!" Sidony exclaimed behind her. "Are you going to bed now?"

Practically growling in her impatience, Sorcha paused where she was until her younger sister reached her, then said quietly, "I want to talk with Hugo, dearling, so pray go upstairs without me tonight. And sleep well," she added belatedly.

Sidony shot her a curious look but, as usual, said nothing and obeyed.

When Ivor entered from the entrance stairs, doubtless to see if the hall fires required tending, Sorcha asked if he had seen Sir Hugo. Receiving a negative reply, she frowned. If Hugo had not met him, he had not gone to the courtyard, at least not by the usual way. Mayhap he visited his bedchamber first or the garderobe tower.

Turning to the archway that led to the northwest stairs, she went slowly in case he had gone up the main stairway instead of down it. But as she entered the short corridor, she heard steps coming down, and soon Hugo appeared.

"What is it, lass?" he asked, smiling warmly at her. He had paused on the last step and thus loomed even larger over her than usual. "Is aught amiss?"

"No," she said. "I . . . I was just going to bed."

"That's a good notion," he said, his eyes twinkling. "Sleep well."

Adela's message felt stiff in her sleeve, and guilt flooded through her as he passed her, heading for the archway. Then his footsteps faded in the distance as he crossed the hall. She had meant to tell him about Adela's message, but the moment had come and gone while the information stuck tight in her throat.

Knowing he would have no cause to delay once he heard what the men watching Edgelaw could tell him, and would likely depart soon after dawn, she knew she had to tell him before then. She could not hope to persuade Michael or Sir Edward—assuming they returned in time—to help her get to Adela if they learned that she had not dared to ask Hugo. She had seen enough of both men to realize that each would demand to know why she had not, nor could she imagine either one understanding that meeting Adela in this particular circumstance could not possibly be true defiance of Hugo's orders. He was the only one who might understand that.

Accordingly, she turned to follow him but had taken only a few steps toward the archway before she heard him returning.

She hesitated, meaning to wait for him, to avoid drawing an audience as she explained about the note. Then memory struck her of the tunnel he had mentioned to

Michael and his intention to use it for whatever secret purpose they had planned. In her concern about the message in her sleeve, she had forgotten that.

Without a thought, she turned and darted up the steps, grateful that Isobel's silk slippers made no sound on them. Just past the first turn, she stopped to listen.

Poised to fly if she heard him coming up, she felt a rush of excitement when he went down instead. Had he been going to the courtyard or kitchen, he would not have turned back, since he could reach both more easily from the main stairway. And where, she asked herself, would one be more likely to find a tunnel in Roslin Castle than at the lowest level on its landward side?

Quickly, she followed him, glad she could still hear his footsteps and certain he could not hear hers. She was so sure that he would go all the way down that she passed the kitchen-level landing before realizing that he had left the stairway there.

Returning, she heard footsteps echoing down the dark corridor, and when she saw that he had lifted a lit torch from one of the wall holders, her confidence in his destination increased. However, she had been on the kitchen level only to take her bath, and then she had followed Kenna down the main stairway to get there.

The area through which he led her was a warren of small dark chambers, some with doors and some with open archways. Peering into the dim interior of one of the latter, she decided they must all be storage chambers of one sort or another.

The entire area was dark except for the glow of Hugo's torch in the distance, so when he abruptly turned left and vanished, she picked up her skirts and moved as swiftly as she dared to follow him.

Her eyes adjusted so that she could see the faint glow of the kitchen fire ahead and judge approximately where Hugo had turned. She passed two arched alcoves before she came to the door. Sending a prayer to heaven that he would not be waiting for her on the other side, she lifted the latch and eased it open. That both latch and door moved silently reassured her. And when she saw that it was not pitch dark inside, she put her head in carefully and discerned, in the fading golden glow, just before it vanished, that the tiny chamber contained rows of stacked wine casks.

She had seen a narrow pathway between them and had noted, too, that the glow of torchlight had disappeared in a narrowing line, as of a closing door.

Shutting the chamber door silently behind her, she used the fingertips of her right hand lightly to guide her along the stacked casks, and her outstretched left hand warned her before she walked into the far wall. She touched wood and some sort of heavy cloth draped back to one side.

Finding the latch, she lifted it and eased the door open, rejoicing when it moved as silently as the other had. Again the glow of receding torchlight revealed the route before her, this time down another, narrower, winding stone stairway.

Moving as quickly as she dared on the wedge-shaped wheel steps, fearing she would be left in total blackness any moment, she tiptoed down until the flickering light ahead grew too bright to dare going farther. She heard him moving, then an odd sort of thud. A moment later, the light steadied.

Hoping he was not looking right at the stairway, she peeked around its curve. The stairs straightened from there to the bottom, where Hugo stood with his back to her looking at a solid stone wall. He had set his torch in a wall holder to his right.

Even as she tensed to run back upstairs, fearing he had made a mistake or had set a trap for her, he reached forward with both hands and pulled. Not until he turned toward the wall where he had set the torch did she see that he held a rectangular piece of stone facing about a foot long. As he bent to set it on the floor nearby, she saw that its removal had revealed a similarly shaped opening in the end wall.

Straightening, Hugo reached into the opening, then pushed against that wall. A narrow doorway opened away from him, and he stepped through it. After a pause, he stepped back, carrying a second torch that he lit from the first.

He hesitated then, glanced at the slab of stone facing on the floor, then shrugged slightly before passing through the opening again. The odd stone door shut behind him as silently as it had opened.

Fairly flying down the stairs, Sorcha put her hand into the opening and felt for the latch. Her fingers encountered a rounded iron bar about the thickness of her thumb and a bit longer than her palm's width. First she tried to lift it as one would a door latch. When that failed, she pressed down. The door began at once to move away from her, much lighter to the touch than she had expected it to be.

Then, abruptly, she stopped its movement, recalling the torch behind her.

With no notion of where she was going, the idea of extinguishing that torch was disquieting to say the least, but she dared not take it with her. Nor did she dare leave it burning while she opened the door lest Hugo see its light. Hurrying, growing frantic with impatience when the torch resisted her efforts to put it out, she finally had the satisfaction of being plunged into demonic blackness.

Hoping she was not walking toward yet another pitfall, she discovered that the door had shut. Finding the opening again, she pressed the bar, and pushed.

More blackness greeted her when the door opened. As she stepped through, she recalled that the wine chamber was on the kitchen level and that the stairway from it had been no longer than any other from landing to landing. Since even the dungeon level of the castle was well above the river, she moved forward with the greatest care, feeling in all directions, trying to suppress the awful dread that one hand or the other would strike Hugo, lurking in the darkness to catch her.

Instead, her seeking right hand touched hard, dry stone, and her silk-slippered right foot told her it had reached the edge of a step. As she eased her way down, she noticed that she could make out a very faint glow ahead.

The steps proved both dry and surprisingly level, and her right hand found a taut, oiled-rope railing on the outer wall of the stair that made the going easier. Holding her skirts up with her left hand, she moved with greater assurance until the light ahead began to increase, telling her that she was catching up with Hugo.

Relief nearly made her dizzy, but she drew a steadying breath, exhaled completely, and went on. The stairway seemed to go on forever, and she began to fear that it was taking her all the way down to hell, when suddenly it ended.

Far ahead, she saw the outline of Hugo's now-wildly-flickering torch. He was moving faster than before, and she hoped she could keep him in sight without having to go so fast that she tripped on what was bound to be uneven ground.

To her surprise, the pathway they followed proved surprisingly even, too. She could feel the occasional rock through the thin evening slippers, but their silence on the hard surface made up for the lack of more protective soles.

Hugo wished the nagging sense of pursuit would ease. As certain as he was that it stemmed from nothing more than having left the latch covering on the floor, he still could not seem to shake it off.

He had glanced back more than once but had seen and heard nothing. His hearing was excellent, as was his instinct for danger, so he was as sure as a man could be that none lurked behind other than a small chance that a Sinclair servant might enter the wine chamber, notice the tapestry covering for the stair door thrust back, and have the temerity to investigate. Since that likelihood was so remote as to near the impossible, he decided he was simply on edge because of the full moon and the eerie, unending darkness of the new tunnel.

He would have liked to have had someone with him to replace the facing on the latch opening, but only Henry, Michael, and he knew of that tunnel entrance. And to ask someone to watch the cask room would only draw attention to it.

He realized then that Isobel might know of the tunnel. She knew a great deal, but even if she did know about it, he would not have asked her to leave her bairn and her bed so soon after giving birth, just to stand guard for him.

He could have snuffed the torch, of course, but it would snuff itself long before he returned and might well have done so before he reached his destination had he brought it along. It had, after all, been burning in its sconce for half an hour or so already. That was why they had put extra, well-oiled torches inside the tunnel entrance and at the cavern end, as well. In any event, having left the stone facing in plain sight of anyone coming down the stairs, who doubtless would have a torch of his own, he had seen no reason to take the time required to extinguish it properly.

One change he could and would make would be to set a bucket of water at the foot of the cask-room stair, so one could quickly put out a torch if necessary.

Having passed beyond the strongest portion of the tunnel, he knew he was now south of the river. The tunnel began to slope upward, and not long afterward he discerned the entrance to the cavern ahead.

Sorcha's feet hurt. Silent or not, ladies' silk slippers were not intended for walking any distance, and she thought she must have walked for miles. Clearly the tunnel did not lie under the castle or even close by, and since she had not the least idea what direction she had been walking after going down and down the winding stairway, she could not even guess with any accuracy where she was now.

As the thought crossed her mind, Hugo disappeared and blackness engulfed her so dense that she could not see her hand before her face. She stopped, telling herself that her eyes would adjust as they had before, that she would soon discern light ahead to guide her. Instead, as she strained to see, tiny white stars danced in the air ahead of her.

Hugo is there somewhere, mayhap just around a curve.

She nearly spoke the words aloud, but knowing he might hear her in the confines of the wretched tunnel, she held her tongue and ruthlessly stifled her fear.

But try as she would, knowing the tunnel was straight as far as the last place she had seen him, she could not walk straight without touching the wall on one side or the other. So although the thought of touching a spider or other insect—or worse—made her skin crawl, she let the fingers of her right hand skim the wall of the tunnel and held her left hand out in front of her as she had in the wine chamber. Then, taking care to keep silent, she moved forward as fast as she dared.

She slowed some distance before her outstretched left hand touched stone. But at nearly the same time, her right hand lost touch with the wall beside her. Feeling carefully, she found that the tunnel jogged briefly to the right before it ended. Since the walls felt as smooth as the one at the foot of the wine room stairs, she felt for a similar opening and latch, and was relieved to find one.

She had to pull the door toward her, but it came easily and silently, and to her enormous relief, torchlight gleamed ahead of her in an immense cavern. The area just beyond the doorway provided reassuringly deep shadows, however, cast by what appeared to be oddly shaped rock formations and immense boulders.

She could not see Hugo but believed she could enter the cavern undetected. Putting a hand to the other side of the door to hold it, she slipped through the opening, noting that the door wanted to follow her. But so intent was she on moving quietly that she was all the way through before it registered that the near side of it felt like rough, damp rock rather than the finished stonework on the tunnel side.

The light ahead flared brighter as if someone were lighting more torches.

Fearing that the increased light would reveal her to a watcher, she swiftly stepped into deeper shadow, and as she did, the door shut with a dull, barely audible sound. Immediately afterward, the reverberating sound of a trumpet startled her nearly out of her skin.

Under cover of its multiple reverberations, she moved to one of the tallest rock formations, peered around it, saw torchlight reflected on water, and realized that the cavern contained a large pond or lake. As the trumpet's last echoes faded, sounds of tramping feet replaced them.

She crouched low. Other odd, shadowy formations blocked portions of her view, but she saw a line of a dozen men or more dressed all in black entering a flat space on the far shore of the lake. They divided into a triangular formation of three lines, facing the mirrorlike water and the front edge of what looked like a dais.

Through the cavern then echoed an unfamiliar voice raised in stentorian tones: "Sir Knight Warder, have you informed the captain of the guards that we are about to open a council for the dispatch of business, and directed him to station his sentinels at their posts to guard this council?"

"Aye, sure, I have, sir," a voice that sounded like Einar Logan responded. "The guards do be at their posts."

Wanting a wider view, Sorcha had decided to shift position when movement to her right drew her attention, and she froze at the sight of a male figure coming toward her from that end of the lake. To her relief, he stopped yards away and turned in a sharp, military way to face the men across the water, clearly on guard.

The first voice said, "Are all present true Knights Templar?"

The second replied, "All present be true Knights Templar, sir."

"Most eminent grand commander," declared the first, "the council awaits your pleasure."

The nearby guard stood stiffly still, his gaze fixed on the activity across the lake, giving Sorcha confidence enough to shift position so she could see the dais.

A chair sat upon it, and a fair-haired man with a gold circlet on his head sat in it with his back to her. Two other men flanked him, also with their backs to Sorcha, but she easily recognized Hugo as the nearer of the two. He wore black clothing like all the others, clothing that he had not been wearing when she followed him to the cave. Two banners flanked the dais.

The man in the chair stood, revealing himself to be as tall as Hugo before he stepped to the ground and moved to face the assembled knights. He, too, wore black with lace trimming, and he had a medallion around his neck that she saw when he turned to walk in front of the assembly. The circlet on his head, his shoulder-length hair, and the medallion with its chain all glinted golden in the torchlight. He looked enough like Michael and Hugo to make her suspect he was Prince Henry of Orkney.

The third man on the dais turned, and she recognized Sir Edward.

Having walked two sides of the triangle, the fair-haired commander turned back to stand at the triangle's center point, facing the men who formed it. Although he did not speak loudly, his voice carried easily to Sorcha's ears.

"Sir Knights, you will now give the signs."

So fascinated had she been by the ceremonial gathering, the dais, its occupant, and Hugo that she had paid scant heed to the other men except as a group. But the first one to step forward in obedience to the command was Ranald of the Isles.

Ranald went through a series of unintelligible movements, then turned sharply and returned to his place, whereupon the next man stepped forward. One after another, they followed.

Rapidly growing bored with the ritual, Sorcha was repressing a fatal impulse to shout at them to get on with it, when a man from the depths of the triangle strode forward and torchlight fell clearly on his features for the first time. Recognizing her father, she clapped a hand over her mouth to stifle any audible sound of her dismay.

Macleod of Glenelg went rapidly through the same movements that the others had. The man who followed him was one she had seen at his grace's installation, but she did not know any of the others until the last, who was Michael.

Only then did she notice that Hugo was no longer standing beside the chair on the dais. With prickling unease, she wondered where he had gone.

The council proceeded with more ritual, including prayers and an odd recitation of numbers from each man in response to a question from the commander about encampments, which made no sense to her.

Her unease increased until she knew she would be wise to leave before the men did and Hugo returned to the tunnel. As quietly as she could, she eased back the way she had come until she reached the rough stone wall. Feeling for the door and finding what she was certain was one edge of it, she moved her hands gently over the nearby area, concentrating, searching for the latch opening.

By then the prickling had increased until it was unbearable, but she sensed no noise or motion until a hand tightly covered her mouth, a head bent near enough for lips to touch her right ear, and a menacing whisper she could identify only too easily murmured, "Not one sound, Skelpie, or I swear I'll throttle you right here."

Chapter 19

⁓

With no more than the hand over her mouth, Hugo held her hard against him, but Sorcha knew it would be both foolish and useless to struggle. When the door opened, she heard nothing but sensed only a change in the air. He shifted her a bit as he turned, so she could see the guard, still standing stiffly, still looking the other way, obviously unaware that anyone else was near.

Hugo lifted her and carried her through the opening, letting the door shut silently behind them before he set her down. Then he caught her hard by the shoulders and turned her to face him, his grip bruisingly tight.

"What the devil do you think you're doing here?" he demanded, his voice clearly under tight control, as if he feared it might otherwise somehow reach ears on the other side of the thick door. "You promised not to leave the castle."

"I said I would not leave without you," she said. "And

I followed you, but why is my father here? And Ranald? And what was all that about encampments?"

His fingers tightened until she winced, but he abruptly released her, saying, "I cannot talk now, because I must get back before the others miss me. Doubtless they think I'm checking on the guards, and I'll certainly have something to say to that one standing like a stone out there. I have much to say to you, too, so you will remain here until I return. And if you cannot look me in the eye then and swear you did not so much as touch that door again, I'll put you straight over my knee. That's a promise this time, and you should know by now that I keep my promises."

He did not await her reply but turned away. Then she heard the almost silent click and knew she was alone. The darkness closed heavily around her, but she was glad he had gone and glad, too, that she had not been able to see his face. Not that she had needed to see it. His fury had radiated from him, and he'd frightened her.

She could still feel her heart pounding, could almost hear it. For anything else she could hear, though, she might have been the last person left in the world. She had never known such total lack of human voice or footstep. Not even a shadowy rustle of a small creature going about its ordinary business disturbed the unnatural silence.

In truth, she decided, the last thing she wanted to hear in that clinging darkness was the sound of a rat or mouse or even another human—not until Hugo returned—because anyone else would have less right to be there than she did.

While her attention had been fixed on the rituals, she had forgotten her sore feet, but she felt them now, and although the idea of sitting on the tunnel floor did nothing to cheer her, imagining the walk all the way back to Roslin decided the matter. Feeling her way, she sat down and leaned against the wall to wait. As she rested her hands in her lap, she felt the stiff message from Adela in her sleeve.

As angry as Hugo was, the thought of telling him about the message was daunting, but she had no choice. That she had promised to consult him was reason enough. That neither she nor Adela dared trust Waldron was even greater reason.

She would tell him about the message at once. In his present mood, she doubted he would be reasonable about it. But he would listen, and if she could not persuade him, perhaps she could distract him from scolding or punishing her.

But when he returned, torch in hand this time, he did not come alone. The fair-haired man came, too. Although he no longer wore the circlet, Sorcha scrambled hastily to her feet and swept him a low curtsy.

"The lady Sorcha Macleod," Hugo said grimly. "Little though her behavior recommends her, my lord, I thought you should first meet her privately rather than before the family. This gentleman, as I see you already suspect, lass, is my cousin Henry of Orkney. As I told you, sir, she saw and heard far too much tonight for our safety or her own. The fault is mine. She followed me through the tunnel."

Still in full curtsy, head bent, Sorcha tensed as an icy

chill swept through her. She had not spared a thought for what her actions might mean for Hugo.

Gravely, Prince Henry of Orkney said, "'Tis a serious matter, cousin. But as you assume responsibility, I'll expect you to deal with it. I'd suggest some degree of severity, but I don't doubt you can persuade her to hold her tongue. She is Isobel's sister, after all. You may rise, Lady Sorcha," he added sternly.

"Thank you, my lord," she said, looking at him as she rose. When she stood before him, she added sincerely, "You need have no fear, sir. I'll not betray you."

He held her gaze for a moment, nodded curtly, then said to Hugo, "See to it then. You have my leave to do whatever you deem necessary."

Then he was gone, and she was alone again with Hugo and the fervent hope that Henry had not been suggesting that he murder her.

"Did you touch that door?"

She looked him in the eye. "You know I did not."

"And you know what you deserve for this," he retorted.

"I know what you think I deserve," she said, taking a wary step backward but resisting the impulse to place protective hands on her backside. "I do deserve your reproaches for putting you at fault with Prince Henry, but whatever you mean to do, I wish you will just get on with it. I've something I must tell you."

"It is true that if I skelp you here, no one else will hear your cries," he said thoughtfully. "Mayhap that would be best."

Tensing, she glanced at the torch he held, wondering what he'd do with it.

"If you look at the walls, you'll see holders along the way," he said, reading her thoughts easily. "Shall I use one now, or would you prefer to tell me your news first? I should perhaps warn you," he added gently, "that it had better be important."

"Adela wants to escape," she said. "I got a message. I was going to tell you when you came home tonight, but . . ." She swallowed. "I should have, of course."

"But you decided instead to see if you could discover where I was going. So you *did* spy on us last night from the laird's peek."

She licked suddenly dry lips. The conversation was not going as she had hoped, and she had just given him another excuse to punish her. Even so . . . She squared her shoulders, reached into her sleeve, and extracted the message.

"You'd better read this," she said, unfolding it before she handed it to him since he could not do so while he held the torch.

He shot a frowning look at her, then quickly read the message. Looking at her again, he said, "How did you get this?"

"I cannot tell you," she said. "I promised I would not."

"Aye, well, I can guess," he said. "Ivor Ross has a brute of a cousin who serves Waldron. Doubtless Gil brought it to you."

She met his gaze. "Whoever brought it is not the one at fault here, nor will I say who it was. We must rescue Adela, sir. I know Countess Isabella expects you to confront him tomorrow and demand his presence at Roslin to answer for his crimes. But by all you have told me, I doubt he will obey her."

"He will resist to the end," Hugo agreed. "I just hope he does not barricade himself inside Edgelaw. A siege can be long and expensive."

"Well, I don't want Adela stuck there even one more day," Sorcha said bluntly. "I mean to help her. I told you I would consult you first, and I have—"

"Just what do you imagine you might attempt that I could not prevent?"

"I don't know," she said honestly. "I just know I'll keep trying, because I *won't* abandon her. I had hoped for your help, though, because the very fact that she has sent for me proves she is not with him willingly."

"Do you know how much this cost?" he asked, holding the message out.

"That paper, you mean?"

"Aye, 'tis made from linen cloth. It is very expensive and must be imported from France or Italy, so how do you think your sister came by it at Edgelaw?"

She hesitated. She had not thought about how Adela had acquired the paper, but she recognized the course of his thoughts because her own had taken a similar path. "Your cousin must have got some from his French kinsmen."

"Do you think he just leaves it lying about where anyone can use it?"

"I think he gave it to her and helped her write that," Sorcha said. "Adela makes her letters better than I do, but she always asks for help spelling out her recipes. I doubt she has written a message to anyone before. And she would never feel obliged to explain so much. I think he told her exactly what to say."

His gaze sharpened. "To what purpose?"

"I don't know," she admitted. "Mayhap he has grown tired of her."

"More likely, he is still using her as bait."

She nodded. "The way he intended to use her and Isobel at Ratho."

"And the way you used yourself to draw me to Ratho," he said gently.

"Then you think his purpose is to lure me to Edgelaw, to hold me as well."

"I'll say this much for you, Skelpie, you are not slow-witted. But you see why I cannot let you go, even if I had the smallest inclination to do so."

"But I don't see that," she said. "If we prepare against such an outcome, you can keep me safe. And we cannot ignore this, because we could be wrong about it."

"What if he wrote the thing himself and has no intention of letting her go?"

"Adela made those letters," she said. "And he will certainly let her go as far as that tower if one can see it from the hilltop, in case anyone is watching."

He frowned, but he was no longer frowning at her.

She held her breath.

He said, "Waldron will set his own watchers if he has not done so already."

"You told Sir Michael that you'd set extra guards," she reminded him.

His eyes narrowed, and recalling how she happened to be aware of that particular fact, she snapped, "Don't look at me like that! I *was* at the laird's peek, and you can say or do whatever you like to me for that later, but for now—"

"For now," he interjected, "I need to think more about this. Also, there is still something we must do here before we return to the castle."

She tensed again, but to her surprise, his lips twitched and a twinkle lit his eyes. "I'm glad to see you show some respect for my right hand, Skelpie, but that is not my intent now. You gave Henry your word that you would keep silent, and he said that I must deal with you, so—"

"So, if you are not going to beat me, what *are* you going to do?"

"What you heard was Henry giving permission for me to tell you enough to convince you of how important it is that you keep your word."

"Mercy, I thought he was giving you permission to murder me."

"I may yet do that," he said dryly. "But first I want to explain what you saw in the cavern, so you'll want to sit again. I'm going to put up this torch."

She stared as he turned. He had surprised her before but never like this.

⁓

Hugo set the torch in a holder and leaned against the wall opposite her. He would have liked to sit beside her, but he knew he'd be wiser to maintain some distance, lest she say something that stirred him to beat her or kiss her. God knew that in the past half hour he had yet again been sorely tempted to do both.

Hands clasped around bent knees, she gazed solemnly up at him.

"Have you heard aught before about the Knights Templar?" he asked her.

She frowned. "I'm not sure. They were characters in stories Aunt Euphemia told us about Crusaders when I was a child. But I don't know much about them."

"The Order started during the Crusades," he said. "If you like, I can relate more of its history another time, but near the beginning of this century, the Pope declared all its members heretics. When King Philip IV of France tried to arrest the Templars in his country, many of them fled here to Scotland, to the Isles."

"What has that to do with the ceremony tonight?"

"The men who came here dispersed," he said. "Some helped the Bruce win at Bannockburn. Others went to ground, seeking safety in new lives. But they did not forget the Order. Originally, all Knights Templar swore a vow of chastity, but those who came here realized that to continue serving the Order and those it served, they had to set that vow aside. Otherwise, in a land most of them did not know, recruiting new members they could trust as implicitly as they trusted each other would be impossible. Then, when the living ones all died, the Order would die with them."

She nodded. "But family is family. So if they could father and train children, and educate them from birth, the Order might survive."

"Aye," he said. "Those early Templars made that decision before they scattered, and each swore an oath to keep the Order secret and pass on its signs only to their sons. But the Kirk still sought to find and kill them. Years passed before they felt safe enough to meet, and by then most had lost track of one another."

"But you found them."

"Some of them," he said. "Some months ago, we learned who most of those early ones were, and we managed to identify some of their descendants. The men you saw here tonight are leaders amongst those active descendants."

"My father?"

"Aye, your great-grandfather was a Knight of the Temple."

"But the Crusades are long over," she said. "What service do Templars perform now that they must still act in such secrecy?"

Hugo had not been able to decide how much to tell her, but as he met her steady, intelligent gaze, the decision made itself. He trusted her as he trusted himself, because she made decisions the way he did. She would do what she believed right and defy the consequences, but her sense of honor was as strong as his own. So the only secrets he could not tell her were the very few he had sworn unequivocally to take to his grave. It was as plain and as simple as that.

"The Templars were the world's bankers," he said. "Their Paris treasury was immense, containing gold, silver, jewelry, sacred relics, and other valuable items of every description. King Philip IV manipulated the Order's downfall with the aid of Pope Clement. On Friday the thirteenth of October, 1307, Philip ordered his men to arrest the Templars and seize their treasury."

"Friday the thirteenth?" Her eyes widened. "Is that why Father believes that day is unlucky?"

"Aye," he said. " 'Twas a dreadful day, because the

men Philip captured—and there were many—suffered the worst the Inquisition offered. Many died or committed suicide as a result. But those whom Philip failed to capture vanished, and the Templars' enormous Paris treasury vanished with them."

"So it came here, too, with them?"

"Aye, first to the Isles," he said.

"Where is it now?"

"That I cannot tell you," Hugo said. "At least a portion of it was hidden here at one time. I also know that the hills hereabouts contain other caves, including one the great Wallace hid in at one time, and another where the Bruce supposedly hid. But, thankfully, I am not burdened with knowledge of the treasure's present location."

He waited for her to ask the obvious: Who did know? But instead, she said, "That treasure is what Waldron seeks then, but why does he believe it should belong to the Vatican?"

"Because, according to the Kirk, the Templars served as the Pope's army. But Templars serve God, not His Holiness."

"*Were* they heretics, those early ones?"

"Nay, they just controlled too much money to suit Philip. He owed them a vast sum, you see, and he did not want to pay it. He was not the only such debtor, either. By then, the Order's wealth had grown for nearly two centuries. The Knights lent huge sums of money to many heads of state."

"But if they lent most of it out—"

"They still had plenty left," he said. "Moreover, the

services they provided continually added to their wealth. Their treasury must have been enormous."

"Do you mean to say you don't know how enormous?"

"I do not," he said. "I don't even know that all of it came to Scotland. Portions of it may well have gone elsewhere."

"But why come here at all? Were there not other havens closer to Paris?"

"The Templars were safe here because the previous year the Pope had excommunicated Robert the Bruce. So Bruce paid no attention to the order to arrest them if, as an excommunicate, he even received it. He valued Templar military skills and let it be known that any Templar seeking sanctuary could find it in Scotland."

"Mayhap the men who came here divided the treasury amongst themselves."

He shook his head. "Their leaders hid it, and I think it stayed in the Isles for a long time because Edward of England controlled all Scotland south of Edinburgh then. Eventually someone did move it, but by then most of those who knew of its existence had died. And apparently the men who moved it died without passing on their knowledge, so it lay hidden again for years."

"Hidden here."

"Aye, some of it, at least. And now Henry looks to use the cavern for our council meetings if it remains safe for him to do so."

"But the men I saw tonight did not enter it through the castle."

"There are other entrances," he said. As he spoke, a thought struck him and then the glimmering of an idea. He said, "There was only one entrance at first, but it resembled a well rather than anything more useful. Only heaven knows how the man who found the place did so, so we decided to create something more practical."

"Where is the original entrance?"

"Buried," Hugo said. "Too many folks knew of it. All are loyal to the Sinclairs, but we decided to make a change. I am not going to try to describe for you where the others are, either," he added with a smile. "Perhaps one day I'll show you, although the less attention they receive, the better."

"How many people know about the one from the castle?"

"To my knowledge, only Michael, Henry, you, and I do, but it is possible that Isobel does. You must not speak of this with her, though. Not only do I not know how much she knows, but to discuss the Order with anyone other than me, or in any place less private than this tunnel, would be to invite trouble for all of us."

"I won't," she said.

"I believe you mean that," he said. "You need to understand what such a promise means, though, because not only am I trusting you but Henry is, too, and revealing the smallest detail of what you've learned tonight to the wrong person could lead to disaster. Therefore you must learn to avoid certain topics altogether."

"Not speak of the treasure at all, you mean. But that is easy, since no one knows even to ask about it." She frowned. "But you mean things like the cavern and the council, as well."

"Aye," he said. "But secrets connect to things that seem not to be secret at all, so you must train yourself to avoid topics that may lead to the dangerous ones."

"I'm not sure what you mean."

"Even to let slip that you saw your father tonight could stir trouble," he said. "If someone should mention the cask room, you'd be wise not to show that you know what he is talking about. Keeping secrets is difficult, lass. That is why I told Henry what you had done. He is my liege lord, and if you let something slip, I will have to bear the responsibility just as I do for your being here tonight."

"But you could not have known I would follow you!"

"I brought you to Roslin," he said simply. "I stirred your curiosity."

"Sakes, if they fear discovery so much, I'm surprised Henry did not just order you to murder me and then hang you for it," she said.

"They trust me, lass, and I trust you. I know you won't fail me."

Sorcha's breath caught in her throat, and for a moment she thought she would cry. He had been so angry with her, and yet he believed he could trust her. And he could; he certainly could, because she would die rather than betray him. But there was one detail she feared he might not have considered.

"I cannot fail Adela either," she said, forcing the words out. "How can you be sure I would not reveal your secrets to Waldron to save her?"

His expression did not change. He said simply, "Because you are wise enough to know that if you did tell him, he'd have no further use for either of you. He would kill you both. However, since you mention that possibility and since I'm not particularly keen on marrying her, I may have to think again about allowing you to meet her at the peel tower tomorrow."

"Sakes, you've already said you won't do it."

"Aye, well, I've been reconsidering that. But whether I allow it or not, it is past time to go back to the castle."

She narrowed her eyes, trying to tell if he was just teasing her, not wanting to reveal her eagerness if he was. On the other hand, Hugo rarely made statements he did not mean, even when he did tease her.

He reached out a hand to her. When she took it, it wrapped warmly around hers as he helped her to her feet, and he retained his grip as he looked into her eyes.

She gazed solemnly back at him, willing him to say that he would let her meet Adela and bring her back to Roslin.

"If I do allow it," he said, reading her thoughts again, "I cannot go with you. They expect to see me at Edgelaw, and Waldron will expect to do any negotiating he does there with me. Nor can I provide you with a large escort. Not only do they command you to go alone but nearly every man I have will go with me or remain at his post to guard the glen and Roslin. But I do have one I can send with you. No watcher will see him, and we must assume that Waldron will send watchers."

"But if you fear that they mean to capture me—"

"We'll see that they don't."

There was more. She knew it. "You have a plan."

"Aye, I do. Waldron is too dangerous to leave there. He threatens all of us."

She grimaced. "So to you, as to him, I shall be just the bait."

"You know better than that."

"Do I? I know you wish you had not promised to marry Adela. I know the countess says you flirt with every woman you meet. What more should I know?"

He looked at her, and suddenly she was far more aware of the energy crackling from him than she had been just a moment before. She was aware, too, that she trod on dangerous ground.

"W-we had better go now," she said.

"Aye," he agreed. Taking the torch from its holder, he turned back to the door into the cavern and took an unlit one from the holder there. Lighting it from the one he held, he extinguished the latter.

As they walked, she said quietly, "I'm sorry."

She thought he chuckled, but clearly her mind was addled.

He said, "I'm curious to know just why you are apologizing."

She sighed. "I'm sure you must be, because I've done so many things to vex you. I was apologizing for starting all of this."

"Do you wish you hadn't?"

She started to say that of course she did, but the words stopped on her tongue. If she hadn't sent the messages, she might never have met him. She certainly would not be walking now with his arm so comfortably around her.

Still, her conscience pricked her. "I cannot say I wish that, but poor Adela! I hope she never learns that only your sense of honor compels you to offer for her."

"I am not feeling at all honorable right now," he said.

"Why not? You've done naught that is *dis*honorable."

"Perhaps not, but I'm about to," he said gruffly. The

arm around her shoulders tightened, turning her toward him as he reached to set the torch in a holder. His free hand caught her chin, and his mouth came down hard on hers.

He was angry again. She could feel it in every line of his body. His arm held her tight, and the hand at her chin shifted to cup the back of her head as if he feared she would try to pull away. She melted against him instead, pressing her body against his, and parting her lips willingly when his tongue moved across them. He thrust it inside, moaning softly when she moved her own tongue to taste it, then to tease it. It felt natural to do that, as if she had done such things with him always.

The hand that held her so tightly moved down her back, pressing her against his hips. She could feel his lust.

Every movement, his or her own, stirred her blood and sent it racing through her body. Her nipples hardened and her breasts swelled until they strained against her bodice. When his stroking hand moved to cup the left breast and his thumb brushed its nipple, she was the one who moaned.

As abruptly as he had kissed her, he released her. He did not speak. He just stood, looking at her, and his eyes seemed dark, his thoughts impenetrable.

"Let's go," he said then, and she nodded silently.

He did not put his arm around her again. Her lips felt swollen. Her body sang.

When they reached the entrance to the castle, he stopped before working the latch to say, "Take care once we are inside, lass. We cannot return together, because it is too late. My aunt may still be up, even so, and it would not do for her to see us together. Nor would it be wise to let your father or mine see us just now."

"My father is staying at Roslin?"

"Aye, he will arrive with Michael tonight."

"But what about all the others?"

"Returning to Edinburgh with Henry. No one will know they went any farther than to supper at his house near Holyrood Abbey. Hush now, not another word until you are safe in your own chamber," he added, opening the door.

Near the foot of the secret stairs, he picked up the torch she had left on the floor there and set it in the holder. The one he had carried through the tunnel still burned steadily enough to light their way upstairs.

At the doorway to the cask chamber, Sorcha had a sickening thought.

"Wait! I forgot about Kenna. What if she has raised an alarm?"

"She won't, lass, not tonight when we have guests arriving. She'll have been busy all day and will have expected you to send for her if you needed her."

Hoping he was right, she stood impatiently while he eased the door open. It was too late to expect any servant to come to the cask chamber, if any ever did come there, but she had expected him to put out the torch. Only as he stepped boldly into the chamber did she realize that no one would question his being there.

"I'll go first," he murmured as they crossed the room. "I can delay anyone heading to the stairs from the hall whilst you go up. Then you need worry only if you meet someone coming down who demands to know where you've been."

"The only ones who might do that are my father or Isobel, or mayhap the countess," she replied in the same tone. "But, pray, sir, do not leave before you tell me what you have decided about tomorrow."

"I'll send you with Einar," he said, his hand on the latch. "But do exactly as he tells you, Skelpie, and take no risk but that of meeting Adela and returning with her to him. The most dangerous time will be whilst you are alone in sight of the peel tower. We'll have no way to know how many may be inside. Which reminds me," he added. "If Adela is there, no matter what she says, do *not* go into that tower."

"I won't. But you know, sir, I doubt it would ever occur to your cousin that Adela may have wanted to save Isobel and me, and the baby, so he must believe she warned him as she did only to save him. What if he has simply decided to free her?"

"His intent does not matter, nor should you think about that. You need only meet her. If anything bad happens when you do, or beforehand, run back to Einar. If you can't do that, try to be civil and avoid more trouble until I can get to you."

"I will," she said.

"I'll send Kenna to you when it is time to go," he said. "You won't want to arrive before midday, and I must arrange a few things before you leave. As for my dishonorable behavior tonight, I was going to apologize, but I don't think I will."

He let go of the latch then, put his hand at the back of her head, and kissed her gently on the lips. Then he opened the door, looked out, and left the cask room.

She followed quietly as he returned to the hall level

and put the torch in its still-empty holder. Then he strode to the archway and waved her on up the stairs.

~

Hearing men's voices in the hall, Hugo glanced back to see her disappear around the first curve of the stairway before he went in. His aunt was not there, but his father, Michael, Macleod, and several others sat at the high table with goblets, jugs, and platters of food in front of them.

Michael grinned, "We have arrived, cousin. Come, greet my guests."

Hugo obeyed, but at the first opportunity, he approached Macleod and said he'd like a private word with him.

~

Sorcha reached her bedchamber without incident. Two cressets burned softly there, her bed was turned down, and the night shift she had borrowed from Isobel lay neatly across the coverlet.

She took off her clothes, washed her face, blew out the cressets, and got into bed. She had meant to think about the ceremony she had seen, to try to fix in her memory such details as she could remember, but try as she might, she could think only of Hugo's "dishonorable" behavior and her own mad betrayal of Adela.

Hugo insisted Adela was not in love with him, and to Sorcha's own knowledge, according to her father's notions, love was no reason for marriage. But she did wish Hugo had not been so frank about his feelings. Her guilt was powerful enough without living the rest of her life knowing she had forced him into a loveless marriage. When men said sacrifice was noble, she did not think they meant sacrificing someone else's happiness. The tears came then, and her face was still sticky with them when Kenna came in to waken her the next morning.

Chapter 20

⁓

"Ye're to dress gey quick, m'lady," Kenna said as Sorcha tried to wipe sleep from her eyes and tearstains from her cheeks without revealing the latter to her impatient hand-maiden. "I let ye sleep late, but Sir Hugo did say ye mean to ride outside this morning. He would choose a horse for ye afore he goes to Edgelaw."

"Well, I cannot ride in what I wore yesterday or the day before," Sorcha said. "Mayhap if you can find the clothing I was wearing when I arrived . . ."

"Och, nay, m'lady. Lady Isobel has a lovely green rid-ing dress ye can wear, and she'll no mind a bit. I'll just run fetch it whilst ye're washing your face."

Sorcha had not thought about riding, because if Edgelaw lay only three miles south of Roslin as Hugo had told her it did, it would take less than an hour to walk there. Moreover, if Einar expected to accompany her without showing himself to any watchers, he could scarcely be going to ride a horse.

In any event, her feet were still sore from the previous night's walk in Isobel's thin slippers, so she would not object if Hugo insisted. Moreover, if she and Adela had to make speed once they were away from the peel tower, they could do so much better on horseback than afoot, even if Adela had to ride pillion.

Twenty minutes later, wearing Isobel's forest-green riding dress, a pair of her soft leather boots, and a lace net beneath a flat green cap to cover her hair, she was ready. Hurrying downstairs, she went straight out to the stable, tearing chunks of bread from a manchet loaf Kenna had given her to break her fast.

As she chewed, she indulged in a brief vision of herself atop Black Thunder. He could certainly travel fast enough, even with two women atop him.

However, the horse Hugo led out for her was a gentle-looking gray palfrey that did not look as if it had galloped a step in its life.

She looked at Hugo, and suddenly it was as if he had just kissed her, for her body warmed at the sight of him, and her lips felt swollen again. When he touched her to lift her to the saddle, she wanted to put her arms around him and hug him.

Then he handed her a wooden whistle, saying with a grin, "If you need it, blow hard, lass. It makes a lovely, loud screech, and it will let Einar or anyone else who hears it know you need help."

She grinned back at him, excited to be doing something again. Then she said, "Won't your men think it odd that you are letting me ride out alone?"

"If they do, they won't say so," he said. "Now, heed me closely. You want to cross the river over the arched stone bridge. You'll bear left on the other side and follow the narrow cart track you'll see there, up the glen until you come to the top of a rise and see a gray stone castle in a big clearing a little less than a mile ahead."

"That will be Edgelaw."

"Aye. You'll see the tower, too, for it lies between the rise and the castle. My men and I will take the main road along the east rim of the glen. We should be in place well before you arrive at the tower. Einar will be nearby and may give you news if he has gleaned any. He may even tell you to return to Roslin."

When she stiffened, he put his hand on her knee, looked into her eyes, and said quietly, "I must know that you will obey him."

Sighing, she said, "I won't like it, sir, but I will do as he bids me. Just remember, though, that I am trusting you just as you are trusting me."

"I know that, and I'll not let you down. We'll have Adela out of there, and I'll do my best to make Waldron face the countess for what he has done. I cannot promise about either one, but my best usually serves the purpose. And if you do as I bid you, and as Einar bids you, you should all three get back here safely."

He reached out then and caught her arm, giving it a gentle squeeze as his gaze met hers. "Go warily now, and stay wise."

"I will, sir, and thank you for understanding that I had to go."

"Aye, well, I understand you well enough, Skelpie," he said with a wry smile. "It should please you to know that

I spoke with your father last night and told him that I'd be honored to marry the lady Adela if she will have me."

A tremor swept over her, but she rallied quickly. "Sakes, what did he say?"

"He agreed that it should answer the purpose admirably," he said. "Now, off with you, and may all go well."

Sorcha kicked the palfrey a trifle harder than she had intended.

⟶

Hugo watched her go, hoping he had not made a tragic decision. She was intrepid, quick of thought, and intelligent. And, too, she seemed to have a knack for coming through the most outrageous actions unscathed. But hitherto her success had depended as much on luck as on anything else, and as any soldier knew, luck was a two-edged sword. One had to expect the bad with the good.

He had no idea what Waldron had planned. So, although he had done all he could to ensure her safety, and had received no word yet to indicate that a trap awaited her, he could not be sure he had done enough.

At least he had talked with Macleod. And, although he had accurately reported what that gentleman had said, they had talked of much more. And, if what Macleod had said proved true, he had a chance to regain control of his own affairs again. If so, it would be worth whatever it took, but only if his lass could come through it all safely.

⟶

Finding the cart track easily, Sorcha resigned herself to the palfrey's pace, telling herself that Hugo and his men needed time to get to Edgelaw. Einar Logan had to be able to keep up with her, too, although she had seen no sign of him. Only once did she think she caught movement in the shrubbery, but try as she did, she saw no other indication that any watchers of Hugo's, or of Waldron's, lurked nearby.

The woodland through which she passed was dense and green. The day was clear, and sunbeams spilled through the canopy, glinting off diamondlike drops of dew on ferns and shrubbery. Birds chirped and squirrels chattered, but her ride was otherwise silent and not much faster than if she had walked.

She came to the rise at last, and saw the peel tower, looking like a tall standing stone in a clear space a short distance from the bottom of the hill. The castle loomed large beyond it in a great, grassy clearing with a frothy river flowing through it that she knew was not the river North Esk. Not only had she followed the Esk through the glen until the cart track turned uphill away from it, but in the moonlight with Hugo on Roslin's ramparts she had seen clearly that the Esk approached the castle from hills in the west, then looped around it to flow northward toward the Firth of Forth.

Coming from nearby shrubbery on her right, Einar Logan's voice startled her. "Dinna look this way, me lady," he warned. "Ride on down the track to yon tower now. But dinna get off the horse, nae matter what the lady Adela says to ye. She can climb on ahind ye gey easily from the tower steps or from some rock, but dinna get down—nae for any reason. And when she climbs on, turn the beast about and kick it hard. It'll bring ye back here at a good pace an ye do that."

When he said no more, she urged the palfrey on, watching the peel tower warily for signs of life. She saw none, nor any sign of Adela, even when she neared the clearing where the tower stood. She had a direct view of the arched, iron-banded door at its base. But not until she drew rein at the clearing's edge did the door open.

Adela stepped outside. Still wearing her bedraggled blue wedding dress with some sort of dark cloak flung over it, she silently motioned Sorcha nearer.

Increasingly wary, Sorcha glanced about her, knowing that Waldron could have set men in trees all around them. But she sensed no other presence, only Adela's. Wondering if she was being wise to trust her own senses, she gathered her courage and urged the palfrey to the shallow steps.

Adela stood there, unmoving, watching her wide-eyed. "You came," she said when Sorcha and the palfrey were right in front of her. "I did not think you would."

"Aye, sure, I came," Sorcha said as she turned the palfrey, which seemed to know exactly what she wanted of it. "Climb on. We'll soon be away from here."

Adela looked around as if she expected someone to stop them, but no one appeared. "This seems so strange," she said. "I have been captive such a long time that I don't feel like myself at all. Your being here with me simply does not seem possible. His letting me go seems even less so."

"Don't stand chattering," Sorcha said impatiently. "If you cannot climb on from there, we need to find something else for you to stand on."

"You are smaller and lighter than I am," Adela said. "Get down and help me up. Then I can pull you up."

"You must mount by yourself, Adela. I'll help you all I can, but I will not get off this horse. Not here. Where is Waldron?"

"He said he'd be in the castle. Sir Hugo is coming to try to make him appear before the countess. She is angry with him. Did I not tell you that in my message?"

"We can talk as we ride, so hurry! What if he comes after us?"

"He won't. He said he was letting me go. He had a sign from God telling him to set me free, he said, because he had punished me enough. But I do not think we can trust him. Indeed, I still do not know what I did to deserve such punishment."

Sorcha did not want to imagine how he might have punished her. She said more curtly than before, "Get on the horse, Adela. Now."

At last, Adela moved to mount the palfrey, and it proved easier than Sorcha had expected, for the animal stood as steadily as if it were made of wood. As she kicked its sides she felt a prickling sensation, as if someone were watching them.

She told herself it was no more than her own nerves reacting, but she eased the whistle from her bodice lacing, where she had tucked it after Hugo had given it to her. And she kept it in her hand as she kicked the palfrey harder. It began to move faster than she had expected, back along the track and up the hill.

The prickling sense of being watched did not desist.

Hugo and his men had arrived at the barred gates of Edgelaw thirty minutes before. But although he had shouted, demanding entrance, the response so far had been no more than a voice from behind the hoarding at the top of the left-hand gate tower, shouting back, "Aye, sir. I'll send a man t' tell the master!"

Knowing Waldron would like nothing better than to stir his impatience, Hugo steeled himself to reveal none. But his ears were on the prick for the slightest sound of a whistle from the west, where Sorcha should be meeting Adela at any moment, if Adela showed up.

After the first ten minutes, he had signed to two men to circle the castle. He also kept a wary eye out for archers above, but all seemed quiet enough.

Like most of his men, he wore a leather jack-of-plate, thick leather breeks and boots, and a helmet. The only thing to distinguish him from the others was the lad beside him bearing the Sinclair banner, and the fact that his own helmet was black and bore the white lion device of Dunclathy.

His father and Michael had donned similar leather garments and carried similar black helmets. Having ridden with the men, they waited with them now. And from a distance both looked enough like Hugo to be indistinguishable from him.

The voice from the hoarding shouted, "The master does say he be presently occupied wi' important business. He'll see ye in half an hour."

"Tell your master that, by the countess Isabella's command, if the gates of Edgelaw do not open to me forthwith, or if the lord Waldron fails to appear before her today, his tenancy here will end," Hugo shouted. "All within its walls will face charges of trespass and a hanging just as soon as she finds it convenient."

"I hear ye, sir! I'll take his lordship that message for ye."

Hugo prepared himself for another struggle with his patience.

Another horse moved up to a position just behind his, and Michael said quietly, "Do we know absolutely that he is here?"

Hugo grimaced. Without turning his head or moving his lips more than necessary, he muttered, "None of our lads saw him leave. That's all I know."

Michael was silent, but he and Hugo had no need of words to communicate. When the two men Hugo had sent round the castle returned to report no sign of siege preparations or any more activity than usual on the ramparts, Hugo did not need Michael's audible grunt of irritation to tell him that Waldron had most likely slipped away. The question foremost in his mind then was how many men he had managed to take with him and to what exact purpose.

His thoughts raced. He'd had men watching the castle and the area around it from the ridge above Roslin Glen since shortly after the countess had made her decision. But his cousin was as adept at concealing himself in darkness as Michael was, which was to say the man moved like a ghost. No army could have slipped out unnoticed, however, nor had Hugo's men seen any sign of a large force at Edgelaw. At most only two or three of Waldron's most skilled followers were with him.

Making his decision, he said quietly to Michael, "I

think he's gone. But if he has any of his army left, they are inside those walls, waiting for us. It's time."

"Aye," Michael said. "Let's move."

~

Sorcha's skin prickled now almost as if she had a fever.

Clinging tightly to her, Adela said, "Where are we going?"

"To Roslin. Isobel is there with her babe."

"Faith, I don't want to see her! How can I face any of them?"

"You will be fine," Sorcha said, forcing herself to add, "Sir Hugo means to make it all right, Adela. I know you love him, and he has told Father that he wants to marry you. No one can say anything then but that you are his honored wife."

"Hugo would do that? After all this?" She sounded stunned.

"Aye," Sorcha said. "He is sorry he neglected to tell us he could not set aside his vow to Ranald to support Donald's claim to the Lordship. Had he told us, no one would have thought it was he who rode off with you."

"Is that why he did not come?"

"It is, and had we known, Father and Ardelve, and all the other men, would have ridden after you and rescued you straightaway."

"I am not so sure they could have," Adela said. "But 'tis kind of Sir Hugo."

Sorcha wanted to say that it was not kind of him at all, that it was no more than a matter of his duty. But she could not bring herself to say that, because Adela loved him and she would not spoil that. Sacrificing her own happiness to restore Adela's reputation was but a . . .

The thought failed her, and she wondered abruptly where Einar was.

"I don't like this place," Adela said. "These woods feel haunted."

"Hush," Sorcha said, slowing the palfrey to its customary pace. She did not want to call Einar's name, because Adela was right. It felt as if watchers lurked everywhere, although she still saw no one.

Surely, unless Einar were dead, he would soon give them some direction.

The thought of him dead made her shiver, but she forced herself to keep her eyes moving, searching the trees ahead, watching for the slightest sign of trouble.

She wished the palfrey would go faster, but she did not want it to outrun Einar. She was also afraid that after pushing it up the hill, to push it farther might result in its refusing to go at all. The thought struck then that Hugo must have had good reason, beyond simply wanting time for himself and his men to reach Edgelaw, for choosing the beast for her. She tried to relax.

Adela gave a muffled shriek. "There's a man in those bushes!"

"Ride on, mistress," Einar muttered just loudly enough for Sorcha to hear him. " 'Tis only me. I'm following ahind ye, but ha' a care, and if aught happens, stay on the palfrey and cling tight unless I tell ye to dismount."

Relief flooded through her at the sound of his voice, and she nodded. She felt safe enough doing so, believing any watcher would think Adela had spoken to her.

They had ridden but twenty yards farther when a man darted from the bushes ahead and snatched at the palfrey's reins. To Sorcha's astonishment, the horse reared, viciously slashing the air with both front hooves. And when the man darted sideways away from it, it dropped its front hooves, whipped around, and kicked with both hind feet together, knocking the villain flat on his back.

Urging the palfrey on, Sorcha kicked hard again, and it broke into a lope as Adela cried, "Mercy, he's getting up! He's following us. Oh, Sorcha, he's going to catch us." Then, with a gasp, "Oh! He's fallen. He's . . . he's got a knife in his back, and he hasn't stirred. I . . . I recognize him, Sorcha. He's one of his lordship's men."

"Who's his lordship?"

"Waldron, of course. I don't know why I called him that again."

"Too bad it wasn't Waldron himself," Sorcha said, sure the knife was Einar's.

"You should not say such a thing! You don't know him as I do."

"I'd think you would be glad you needn't know him any longer," Sorcha said tartly. "He is an evil man, and the countess means to evict him from Edgelaw."

"He said he feared she might," Adela said. "But, truly, although he can be cruel, he is only a man doing what he believes is right."

Sorcha wanted to insist that Waldron was pure evil, a lunatic. But increased tension in Adela's voice stopped her, and she held her peace.

"Another man is following us!" Adela cried.

Sorcha looked back, saw Einar pull his knife from the

fallen man's back and drag him off the track. She reined the palfrey to an even slower pace.

"Mercy, what are you doing?"

"That is Sir Hugo's man, the one who spoke to us earlier from the bushes," Sorcha said. "We're well into the glen now. I expect he'll soon tell us we're safe."

She glanced back again just as, to her horror, Einar fell flat on his face with an arrow in his back.

Jerking the reins, she flung her right leg over the palfrey's neck and snapped, "Hold these, Adela," as she jumped to the ground. "If aught happens to me, kick hard and ride for the castle. It can't be more than fifteen or twenty minutes ahead now. Just don't let the palfrey slacken its pace, and you will make it safely."

"But Sorcha—"

Sorcha paid no heed but snatched up her skirts and ran as fast as she could run the short distance back to Einar.

"Please don't be dead," she said, flinging herself down beside him.

"I'm no dead yet, but he'll be on us in a trice," he muttered. "D'ye see yon great beech tree ahead o' us, where the track curves?"

"Aye, but I cannot leave you here."

"Ye can, and ye must, or the master will flay me an he finds out. So, heed me well. Ride on to that beech. Then dismount, the pair o' ye, and smack that beast gey hard three times on its rump. It'll head for its stable then. When it does, dive into the bushes beyond that great tree and push your way through as best ye can. Dinna let yourselves be seen from the track, though! Soon ye'll come to yon cliffside."

"Einar, if he's coming . . ."

"He's well back o' us in a tree, and he's got nae horse. It'll take him five minutes to reach us, mayhap a bit less," he added, wincing. "Enough to give ye a head start, so he'll follow the horse's tracks. D'ye recall the cave, lass?"

Shocked that he would mention it, but recalling the voice she had thought might be his, she nodded, realized his eyes had closed again, and said, "I do."

"When ye come to the cliff, ye'll see a scrub tree sticking out from its face. Just north o' that tree, ahind some thick myrtle bushes, be an entrance to the cave. Ye'll find it easily. But go now, and dinna make a sound once you're away from the track. If ye canna trust the lady Adela, send her on wi' the horse."

"Einar, I've got to get you hidden before we can leave."

"Ye're no to fret about me. I'll do for myself when I ken fine that ye're well away. It'll do me nae good to survive this day if ye do not. Now, away wi' ye!"

Sorcha went, but tears streamed down her face, because she was sure he had just sacrificed his life for her and for Adela. Even so, she could not heed his advice to send Adela with the palfrey. She did not believe Adela could betray her, and she was nearly as certain as she could be that if Adela tried to ride on to Roslin without her, she would not get there alive.

Accordingly, Sorcha ran back to the palfrey, and without trying to mount it, grabbed the reins from Adela, told her to kick hard, and then ran ahead to the curve in the track, past the beech tree. Once she could no longer see Einar, she ordered Adela to jump down, smacked the palfrey, and grabbing Adela by the hand, pulled her into the bushes, saying, "Not a word, for we must be as quiet as we can. But we must also move as quickly as we can to that cliff ahead of us."

"But why? I thought we were going to Roslin."

"Sakes, Adela, someone just shot Hugo's man who was guarding us with an arrow from a tree that he says is nigh onto five minutes behind us as a man runs. That man, to make that bowshot, has to be an extraordinary archer."

Adela gasped. "Waldron! It must be he. We cannot escape him, Sorcha. It is no use trying. Oh, I knew it!"

"If you cannot say anything sensible, hold your tongue," Sorcha snapped. "I won't leave you, so if he captures you, he will also get me."

"Oh, no!"

"Then come on! And try not to break any branches that he can see from the track. We want him to follow the palfrey."

Adela shook her head as if at a foolish child, but she made no more objections and moved as Sorcha told her to move until they were well away from the track. Had the cliff before them not been so high, they would not have been able to see where they were going any more than they could now see the track behind them.

When Sorcha spied the shrub Einar had described growing out of the cliff, they increased their pace.

"Look for tall, thick myrtle bushes near the cliff face," she whispered.

"I don't know myrtle, and all this shrubbery is thick," Adela said in a normal tone. When Sorcha gave her an angry look, she lowered it to add, "But why must we whisper? We're too far away now for anyone to hear."

"You don't know that," Sorcha muttered. "Now hush."

She had to feel through several bushes for an opening before she found one. Then she had to pull Adela with her to get near it. Up close, it seemed no more than a tall slab of rock with a narrow crevice behind, and for a moment, she feared she had mistaken some other oddity in the rock face for the entrance they sought. She was sure no adult male could slip through such a space—not Hugo, Michael, or Sir Edward, and certainly not her father, who enjoyed robust proportions.

But when she grabbed hold of the slab to try to squeeze into the space, the slab moved, and she saw that it was similar to the doors of the other tunnel entrances she had seen. Inside, the passage was wide enough for two to stand side by side, but when she tried to pull the door shut, it would go no farther than before.

"We cannot stay here," she said. "Any noise we made would easily reach anyone nearby. We must move farther inside."

"But what is this place?" Adela hissed.

"'Tis naught but a cave," Sorcha said, knowing Adela would ask more questions and trying to think what she could say. She did not want to lie but neither could she answer honestly without betraying her promise to Hugo. Then a memory provided her the words she needed. "Wallace once hid here. Or mayhap 'twas the Bruce. I forget which, but it is well known in these parts and should keep us safe."

"But if it is well known—"

"Just that it exists, Adela, not where it is. It is on Sinclair property, after all."

"But it's dreadfully dark. How long must we stay?"

"Until someone comes for us," Sorcha said, feeling more at risk with every word. Recalling the many hiding places in the cavern, she weighed the chance of Adela's later remembering where they were against the probability of Waldron's finding them if they stayed near the entrance. Even if she could persuade Adela to be silent, she was not sure she could trust her to remain so if he called to her.

But if she could not hear him . . .

"I've heard they leave torches not far inside," she said. "If we can find one, mayhap I can light it if they also thought to provide a tinderbox and flint."

Adela was clearly unhappy about the cave, but she was just as clearly more afraid of staying behind in the dark than of going with Sorcha. So they felt their way until Sorcha found the torches, flint, and tinderbox that she had felt certain would be there. Giving an unlit torch to Adela, and keeping one for herself, she made her sister keep walking until they could no longer see even a glimmer of light from the tunnel opening before she lit her own torch.

"Now, hurry," she said. "We don't want anyone seeing torchlight from outside." The more she thought about it, the odder it seemed that the slab had refused to shut behind them and lock the way the two tunnel doors had. Perhaps it had caught on something. She ought to have looked more carefully.

The great cavern loomed head of them, and although its size swallowed most of the light, Adela gasped. "Merciful heaven, is that water ahead?"

"Aye, there is a l-lake," Sorcha said, her voice stumbling when she held the torch higher and its light fell upon two good-sized brassbound chests, one at the water's edge not far away and the other sitting some yards from it, next to the dais.

"Faith, it's the treasure!" Adela exclaimed. "He'll come now. I know he will!"

⁓

Hugo urged Black Thunder to his fastest pace, fearing with every stride the great horse took that they would be too late. No whistle had sounded, or if it had, the lass had been too far away for him to hear it. He had known it would not carry beyond the walls of the glen, but the greatest danger had existed when she was near the peel tower, and he had wanted her to have it then.

Michael had taken command of the men after a neat maneuver in which Hugo had turned the horse he was riding through the men behind him, where he and Michael had easily traded mounts in fair certainty that the exchange would not be noted from the castle.

Not only did Waldron not know Black Thunder, because the horse was Hector's, but even if his men had seen Hugo riding the black on the road, there had been more than one black in their string, and Hugo had changed horses regularly on the way. Furthermore, he knew that anyone who watched the Roslin men from the castle now would be more concerned about the several who had ridden forward to make another circuit of it than about anyone riding away.

When three had ridden away, one on a black horse, the other two on bays, all looking like ordinary soldiers, he was sure word had gone round inside that he was sending to Roslin for reinforcements.

He and Michael had not exchanged helmets, but Michael now wore a black one with a white Sinclair cock on it. From the castle, it would look like Hugo's lion.

He had easily outdistanced the other two, who knew only that he was heading into the glen. Every instinct told him that Waldron was ahead of him.

Hugo believed his cousin would not kill Sorcha, because Waldron wanted her as a hostage to trade for information about the treasure. However, he feared that if Waldron decided he had no more use for Adela, he might kill her.

Hugo knew he could not let that happen, because Sorcha would never forgive him or herself if Adela died. That she still insisted he marry Adela was another matter. He could only hope Adela did not want the marriage any more than he did. But, whether she did or not, her life was in his hands now, and he could not fail her.

～

Sorcha stared at Adela. "What makes you think those chests hold treasure?"

"You said this is Sinclair land, so it must be the treasure they took from the Holy Kirk, the one Waldron seeks. What else could it be in a place such as this?"

"Sakes, I don't know," Sorcha said. "But you cannot go around talking of treasure. Men will think you are mad or else abduct you again in hopes of finding such a thing. Hold out your torch, for I mean to light it and put them in those two holders on the wall. We will be a deal more comfortable if we need not carry them."

"Aye, lass, give her the torch," a voice said, startling

both of them. "We want to light this place up, so we can see what is in those chests."

Sorcha whirled as Adela exclaimed, "I knew you would come!"

Waldron stood at the opening of the tunnel they had just come through, his hand on his sword.

His gaze shifted to Adela as he said, "Is anyone else here?"

Chapter 21

Wondering if the torch she held could possibly serve as a weapon, Sorcha stood still, trying to calm herself as Waldron approached them. She had slipped the whistle back under her bodice lacing, but it would be of little use to her with no one to hear if she blew it. And to do so would almost certainly infuriate him.

"Light Adela's torch, Lady Sorcha, and put yours in that holder beside you," he said. "And do it at once, lass. Don't think you can defy me."

Adela moved to Sorcha's side, holding out the unlit torch she carried. "Here, be quick," she said. "We must not anger him."

"Aye, sure," he said. "You learned that straightaway, did you not, lass?"

Keeping her thoughts to herself, Sorcha lit Adela's torch but hesitated to relinquish her own, knowing she would feel more vulnerable without it.

In a heartbeat, before she knew he had stirred a muscle, he whipped it from her grasp and raised his free hand to strike.

"Look, sir," Adela said swiftly, moving toward the glassy lake with her torch. "Do you not agree that these kists must hold the treasure you seek?"

"Stay away from them!" Lowering his hand, he turned toward her.

But Adela seemed not to hear him, for she went straight to the nearer chest, holding her torch so its light fell on the chest.

Waldron was nearly upon her, still carrying Sorcha's torch.

As Sorcha watched in astonishment, Adela put her free hand to the lid of the chest and tried to raise it. The lid did not move, but to Sorcha's shock, the chest did.

It slid away from Adela down toward the water.

Adela cried out, and Waldron leaped forward to try to stop its progress. As he did, it slid into the water.

"My apologies, cousin," Hugo said from the entryway, his sword in hand. "I know you covet all things Sinclair, but that chest does not belong to you."

Waldron spun, hurling the lit torch at Hugo as he did. Then whipping his sword from the scabbard on his back, he held it in both hands at the ready.

"By heaven, I welcome this day," he said as he leaped toward Hugo.

To Sorcha's amazement, although the torch had flown end over end, casting a shower of sparks, Hugo caught it by the handle with his left hand and shoved it into her hands as he passed her to position himself as quickly as Waldron did.

As their swords clashed together, Sorcha moved quickly to put the torch in one of the holders. Her hands were shaking, and she knew that steadier light would be safer for Hugo than light that danced about the cavern.

Adela still held her torch but stood stupefied, apparently frozen in place. Sorcha moved cautiously toward her, keeping her eyes on the men lest they leap her way. When she could reach the blazing torch, she gently took it from Adela. She could not have said why she thought that necessary, only that she did.

Adela did not resist. She seemed scarcely able to breathe, and her eyes did not shift from the combatants. Sorcha dared not speak to her lest one of them distract Hugo, but when she put her free hand on Adela's arm to draw her farther from the swordsmen, Adela jerked her arm away.

Then Waldron lunged at Hugo, his sword aimed at the center of Hugo's chest, and Sorcha's heart threatened to stop beating.

Hugo slashed upward with his sword, catching Waldron's and deflecting it.

So hard had he struck that Sorcha expected Waldron's weapon to go flying, but the battle raged on—fearsome, interminable—until Hugo stumbled.

Waldron rushed at him, but Hugo's sword flashed up again. This time, moving like a cat, he changed direction in midair. Thrusting hard, he leaped forward as Waldron leaped back a pace, forcing him back farther yet.

Then Hugo caught his cousin's sword yet again with a resounding clang. Knocking it upward as he twisted aside and away, he slashed hard at Waldron as Waldron, recovering, lunged forward again.

Sorcha thought Hugo's stroke must end the fight, but in a flash, before anyone was aware of her intent, Adela flung herself between the two men.

Waldron grabbed her arm and shoved her away, but he was not quick enough. Hugo's sword struck them both with his full strength behind it.

Waldron and Adela collapsed to the rocky floor.

Hugo moved swiftly to them, and in stunned horror, Sorcha raced to his side.

"Take care, lass," he said quietly. "There's blood everywhere."

"They are *not* dead," she said, ignoring his warning to kneel beside Adela. Thrusting the torch at him, she said, "Hold this!" Then, feeling for Adela's wound, trying to stanch the blood with her bare hands, she muttered, "She cannot die!"

Waldron groaned, but Adela lay terrifyingly still. A sickening amount of blood soaked through her gown and cloak from what appeared to be a deep cut.

Hugo knew that both victims of his slash were in dire straits. He did not much care about his cousin, bleeding heavily from the wound across his chest. He had meant to kill him, so fretting over his injury would be plain hypocrisy.

But it did create a dilemma for him.

He could send Sorcha back alone through the tunnel to the castle, or he could take her with him and Adela. In either case, he'd have to leave Waldron, because he did not know where his own men were. And, even if he had known, only one of the three in the glen was privy to the cavern's secrets.

"Where is Einar?" he asked Sorcha.

"Waldron shot him in the back with an arrow," she said, tears spilling down her cheeks. She had found Adela's wound and was pressing a wad of her dark cloak against it. As she smoothed strands of hair off Adela's brow, she added, "I . . . I had to leave him in the middle of the track. He told me to come here."

"He's a good man," Hugo said, adding gently, "We'll find him, lass. He was nowhere in sight when I came, and Waldron would not have buried him yet. So he must have gone to ground. I can take only one of them out by myself, though."

"You'll take Adela, of course."

"Aye, but although Waldron may look defenseless and near death, I dare not leave him here alone. And I cannot simply spit the man whilst he's unconscious."

"I'll watch him," she said impatiently. "Just help Adela."

"I don't like leaving you alone with him," he said. "But if you'll tear a strip off your shift, then hold this damned torch for me, I'll bind her up to slow her bleeding. We've people at Roslin who can help her, but I can do little for her here."

"How did you get here?"

"I left the men with Michael and my father at Edgelaw when we realized Waldron had got away. I feared what he'd do if he caught you, but once he found this place, I doubt he thought of anything but those chests."

"Adela pointed them out to him," Sorcha said as she ripped away as much of her cambric shift as she could and handed it to him, taking back the torch. "But you knew they were here," she added as she went to set it in a holder.

"Aye," he said, ripping Adela's clothing from the wound near her shoulder. He quickly did what he could for her, then moved to examine Waldron.

His cousin was still alive, but the wound in his chest was dreadful, his breathing rough, irregular, and congested. Hugo knew he would not last long.

Waldron's eyes flickered open and seemed to focus on Hugo, but he did not try to speak and they shut again.

Hugo glanced at Sorcha, trying to judge the limits of her strength.

"What is it?" she demanded. "Do you think I'll be afraid? I won't be."

"I know that," he said gently. "You have the heart of a lion, Skelpie, but for mercy's sake, don't try to aid him."

"I won't." She had come close again and stood watching Adela.

"You keep well away from him," he said. "He's got little strength left, but he's already proven himself well nigh indestructible, so don't go near enough to let him catch hold of you. I see you still have your whistle," he added. "Blow it if you need me. I'll not be far. I'll just shout up my lads and send Adela on her way."

She nodded, but he knew she barely heeded him, her thoughts now solely for her sister's welfare.

"We'll devise a way to get her to Roslin as quickly and comfortably as we can," he said. "My aunt and her people will do the rest. They are very skilled."

"Could you not just carry her through the tunnel?" Sorcha asked.

He glanced at Waldron to see if he was paying heed, hoping that if he was, his mind would be too addled from loss of blood to realize she did not speak of the passageway through which they had just come.

Satisfied that he was too weak to do much at all, Hugo said, "I won't be long. If one of those torches starts to sputter, there are more in that chest by the dais."

He picked up Adela as gently as he could and strode toward the passageway.

～

Sorcha watched as Hugo disappeared into the passage with Adela. Then, hearing a sound behind her, she turned back toward Waldron.

To her astonishment, he was struggling to sit up.

"What are you doing?" she demanded.

He was sitting now. He tried to stand.

"I want to look into the water," he said weakly but as if it were a natural thing to want to do at such a time. "Come, lass, help me up."

"You're daft if you think I'm getting anywhere near you," she said. "You're an evil man, Waldron of Edgelaw, but you are *not* an immortal one. Lie down, save your strength, and you may yet survive this day. I'll help Sir Hugo tend your wound when he returns, but that is all I'll do for you, and I'll do it only because I believe you sacrificed yourself to save Adela."

"You're the daft one if you think that," he growled. "I did what I had to do when your fool of a sister tried to interfere, but I'll live yet to finish God's work."

"She saved your life, and you know it," Sorcha said.

"She rushed between you because she feared Sir Hugo would kill you. She was watching him, not you. Still, if she lives, 'tis because of you."

"You're mad, or she is," he muttered, but his tone was sulky, like a boy talking of something that discomfited or embarrassed him.

"Neither of us is mad," she said. "Still, I don't know why she tried to save you. You probably raped her. You've certainly done all you could to ruin her. Did you know she loved Hugo? Is that why you did it?"

"Faugh, she does not love him," he said. "Anyone can see that you're the one who does, except perhaps our doltish Hugo."

"My feelings are of no concern to you or anyone else," she snapped. "And Adela does love him. But, doubtless, she fears he will not want her now."

"I did not rape her," he said. "She is as chaste as she was when I took her, not that you or others will believe that unless she submits to examination."

"She would enter a nunnery first," Sorcha said. Oddly, though, she believed him. "Why didn't you rape her?"

He snapped, "She is too old to tempt me." But he looked away as he said it.

"You're lying," she retorted. "As evil as you are, you'd ravish a hag to hear her screams or if you thought hearing them would distress others. You are no servant of God, sir! The devil is more likely to seize you when you die."

"You have a sordid imagination for one so young," he said. His voice had grown weaker, and he seemed to realize what that meant, because he stopped speaking and struggled harder to get to his feet.

"Where do you imagine you can go?" she asked, watching him. "The only way out of here is the way you came, and you cannot possibly walk so far as . . ."

On his feet now, holding himself upright with obvious difficulty, he staggered toward the water.

"If you mean to drown yourself," she said, "perhaps you should wait until Hugo returns and ask him if that lake is deep enough."

"The water is clear," he said. "I can see how shallow it is."

He stepped in and began wading away from the shore.

"Where *are* you going?"

She had forgotten the chest in the water, but she saw it then. Brassbound and the size of a sumpter basket, it had slipped some ten feet away from the lakeshore in the water. It certainly looked as if it could be a treasure chest, so although Hugo had said the treasure was not there, she watched Waldron tensely.

His attention riveted to the chest, he moved more effortlessly and with purpose. It was, she thought, as if he were not even hurt.

Hurrying after him, she barely paused as she waded into the water. It was chilly, and it soaked the boots she wore and her skirts halfway to her knees, but she did not take her eyes off him. As powerful as he was, and as immortal as he had proven himself, she could easily imagine him picking up the chest and striding off with it to disappear forever into the blackness of the huge cavern.

If that happened, Hugo would have failed to protect the treasure. The honor of the Sinclairs and the secrets of the Scottish Knights Templar would be gone.

She could not let that happen. The Templars had suffered too much to protect their Order. She would not be the one who allowed them to lose everything.

"Stop," she cried, reaching to grab his arm. "You mustn't take that!"

He jerked away with ease, kicked the chest farther from shore, then followed it. It moved with astonishing ease, and as Sorcha waded toward him and reached for his arm again, she realized why when her feet skidded on smooth, suddenly steep, sloping rock and slipped right out from under her.

Fighting for balance, she grabbed Waldron's arm again to steady herself, but he twisted with a snarl and shoved her back. Her feet continued down the smooth slope, and she fell, landing with a heavy splash.

Realizing she was in imminent danger of sliding all the way under, and that in boots and her heavy skirt, she might not be able to pull herself out, she scrabbled for any sort of handhold. Managing at last to curl her fingers around what seemed no more than a nubbin of rock, she dug in her heels.

It was enough to stop her momentum. Returning to the shore then required only care and patience. The slope was slick, but a tense few moments later, she crawled onto the dry part at the edge of the lake. She had lost Isobel's cap and the net to which it was pinned. And she was soaked from head to toe.

Waldron had disappeared. When she stood, other than a few ripples, she saw no sign of him or the brassbound chest.

The damned chest had kept sliding after he'd kicked it, and fury had engulfed him at the thought that even this small bit of the treasure might continue to elude him. So he had lunged for it and caught the nearest brass handle.

Agony from his wound seared through him as he did, and it was all he could do to wrap his fingers around that handle and hold on. His feet could gain no purchase. They shot behind him, plunging him into the water face-first.

He had no strength left to fight for anything but the chest. Full of the stolen gold and jewels, as it surely was, it was incredibly heavy.

It continued to pull him deep below the surface, but he held on. God knew how weak he was, and God would help him. He would float both the chest and His faithful servant to the surface again.

Then he need only stand, and God would grant him the strength to carry it to shore. He would return it to the Holy Kirk as proof that he had found the long-lost Templar treasure, and as proof, too, that the damned Sinclairs had hidden it all these years. Then His Holiness would send the papal army to . . .

He *was* floating . . . no, sinking, now diving. Something pulled him straight down, a powerful force that held his hand with a grip of iron.

His thoughts shifted abruptly when light glimmered in the distance, but it was not the shimmering golden light of saintly haloes and the cities of Paradise that he had heard men describe. This light was fiery red. He could almost feel its heat. Perhaps the devil had caught him, just as the lass had prophesied.

When he gasped at the dreadful thought, water flooded his lungs and his wet, chilly grave returned to blackness.

~

Sorcha was still standing on the lakeshore, staring into the water and shivering, when Hugo returned. She was aware of his footsteps, knew it was he, but took a moment to collect her wits. Then fear for Adela flooded back and she turned.

As she did, he caught her roughly by the shoulders. "I told you to stay away from him!" he exclaimed. "What happened? Are you all right?"

"Aye, he's dead, I think. How is Adela?"

"We stopped her bleeding and Wat MacComas has taken her to Roslin. Tam Swanson is searching for Einar. Now, tell me why you think Waldron is dead."

"Because he went after the chest Adela pushed in the water when you came. It's gone, too." She frowned. "I thought you said the treasure was not in here."

"It isn't," he said. "Like the chest beside the dais, that one contained supplies and ceremonial gear like the circlet you saw Henry wearing last night."

"Well, Waldron wanted it, and he managed to get to his feet again to go after it. I thought the lake was shallow. I was afraid he would carry it into the inner chambers and disappear again."

"He could never have done that. I'd have sworn he was too weak to stand!"

"I, too," she said. "But he did stand, and I thought your honor was at stake, so I tried to stop him."

He made a sound like a growl, but she ignored it. "The

chest kept sliding, and when he lunged for it, he just disappeared. He's been down there for a very long time, too, because I counted to a thousand before I heard you come in."

"Then what, exactly, accounts for your being soaked to the skin?" he asked.

"Don't use that tone to me," she retorted. "I'm already shivering from falling in, and when you speak to me like that, it puts icicles right up my spine."

"It should. I know I ought to be grateful that you showed such concern for my honor, but I told you to keep away from him. So, if my tone of voice gives you that sensation, my lamb, consider what the image in my mind of Waldron grabbing you and carrying you with him down into that watery grave does to me."

"Sakes, sir," she said, looking up at him, "you've wanted to murder me more times than I can count since we met. Would it really have upset you so to—?"

Her words ended in a shriek as he grabbed her and pulled her close enough to kiss her thoroughly, apparently not put off by the fact that she was soaking wet.

She threw her arms around him and hugged him tight.

～

Hugo held her close, savoring the taste of her, thinking of how easily he might have lost her. Wet as she was, he did not want to let her go. He told himself it was because she was so wet and cold. He just wanted to warm her a little.

She did not resist his kiss. Indeed, she responded admirably, but after a moment she pulled back. Her face still tilted up to his, she said solemnly, "I'm sure it is most uncharitable of me, but I am glad he's gone."

"Aye," he said.

"You meant him to come here," she said. "The entrance was open."

He nodded. "I did not mean it to happen as it did, though. Einar was going to bring you, knowing Waldron's skill at tracking, and we left the entrance ajar for him. But we thought Einar would have time to hide you, and I thought I'd be right behind Waldron."

"But Waldron was already in the woods," she said. "Another man was with him, too, because he jumped out of the bushes and tried to catch the palfrey's reins."

He smiled. "You need not tell me what happened next. That palfrey is Isabella's. My father taught it not to let men grab it like that."

"It's a fine beast," she said. "But then someone shot Einar from a tree."

"Waldron was a fine archer."

"What if he had captured me at the peel tower?"

"We knew he wasn't there," Hugo said. "A man took Adela there and returned to Edgelaw just as anyone might have expected from her letter. But Waldron must have hidden in that tree long before anyone realized he had left Edgelaw. We should go now," he added, kissing her again.

When he moved a hand down her side, thinking to rub some warmth into her, she snuggled closer, pressing against him. His body stirred then, apparently not realizing that she just sought warmth.

"Let's get you out of here," he murmured, kissing her damp curls. "I'll do my best to keep you warm, but it is likely to be a cold ride for you."

She tensed then, and he knew she had remembered Adela again.

"Look at me," he said, cupping her chin. "We have done nothing wrong, lass. Everything will work out as it should."

"How?"

"I don't know yet, but have faith. It will."

Even in her guilt at having briefly forgotten Adela's very existence, Sorcha wanted with all her heart to believe him. But Adela had not denied her love for him, and he had told Macleod he would offer for her. So Hugo could not back away now, nor, she decided sadly, could she in good conscience allow him to.

Outside, the fact that the sun still shone startled her. So much had happened that she had expected dusk if not darkness. But her mood lightened when they reached the cart track and found two men sitting against the huge beech tree, awaiting them. One leaped to his feet at their approach. The other did not, but he did raise a hand in greeting and grin at Sorcha.

"As ye see, m'lady," Einar said, "I'm still no dead yet."

"He's wounded, sir, but his jack-o'-plate saved his life," Wat MacComas said to Hugo. "He says he can ride, and I'll gladly take him up with me."

"Aye, Wat, if he says he's fit, he'll do," Hugo said cheerfully. "I'll take my lass with me."

"You should not call me your lass," Sorcha muttered to him as he settled her before him on Black Thunder.

"Have faith," he said again, adding, "and put this on."

He slipped off his jack-of-plate and wrapped it around her. "It was too heavy to put on you before, but it may help keep you warm now."

Just being so close to him was warming her as always, but she did not disdain the heavy leather garment still warm with his body heat.

The ride back to Roslin seemed to take no time at all, but by the time they arrived, despite his warmth and the jack, she was shivering and her teeth chattered.

The courtyard teemed with men and horses. Michael and Sir Edward had returned, and came to meet them. Looking at Hugo, Michael raised his eyebrows.

"He's dead," Hugo said.

Michael nodded, saying, "His men surrendered not long after you left. They told us he'd gone, taking only Fin Wylie with him, but we searched Edgelaw from hoardings to dungeon to make sure he wasn't there." Eyeing Sorcha's wet clothing, he added, "You can tell us your tale later."

Nodding, Hugo dismounted and lifted her down. "I'll carry you in," he said as a lad ran up to take Black Thunder.

She did not argue. The last thing she wanted to do was walk across the courtyard in Isobel's wet kirtle and his jack-of-plate. But when he carried her past the great hall, she said, "I want to see Adela, sir. I must know she is safe."

"We'll find out soon enough," he said. "You are not going anywhere until you are warm and dry again."

On the next level, he carried her to her bedchamber, having sent a passing gillie running to find Kenna. Inside the chilly room, he put Sorcha down and said, "Turn around, and I'll undo your lacing. Have you a cloak here that you can wrap around you till Kenna gets here, or do you want to get into the bed?"

"Sakes," she exclaimed, looking over her shoulder at him. "Are you going to stay here whilst I undress?"

"I am not letting you out of my sight again until we settle things, Skelpie."

"So you're going to watch me?"

He grinned. "I'll turn my back, but that is all. Now, cloak or bed?"

"Cloak," she said, unwilling to get naked into bed with him in the room. "You will find it in yon kist by the door."

He finished unlacing her, found the cloak, and handed it to her.

"Turn around," she said firmly.

Chuckling, he obeyed her. But when Kenna came in moments later, Sorcha was not surprised that he still refused to leave.

"Rub her dry with towels," he said. "Then put her in the warmest dress you can find. And when you leave, take her cloak and dry it by the kitchen fire."

"Aye, sir," Kenna said, eyeing him warily.

Sorcha was soon warm again, and in a silk kirtle and wool surcoat, with her still-damp hair bound into a net and covered with a silk veil, she felt ready to face whatever lay ahead.

Kenna told them they would find Adela in a chamber near Isobel's, and they went together to see how she did. When they entered, Sorcha's gaze fell instantly on her sister in the high bed against the opposite wall. To her relief, Adela was awake and clearly much improved.

"Thank heaven," Sorcha exclaimed, rushing to her. "I was so afraid for you!"

"And I for you," Adela said, reaching out to grasp her hand. "He is a dangerous man, dearest, and you are too quick to stir anger."

"He will not harm anyone again," Sorcha said. "But why did you leap between them as you did?"

"Faith, I don't know," Adela replied. "I never seem to know anymore *what* I may say or do, or even what I may think! But I could not let Hugo kill him."

."As you see, I've brought him," Sorcha said before she could lose her resolve.

Adela smiled at Hugo, but then she looked back at Sorcha and shook her head. "I know you believe I fell in love with him, dearest, but—"

"You didn't deny it earlier," Sorcha reminded her.

"Oh, but I did, many times," Adela said.

"Not today."

"No, not today. But until I arrived here at Roslin, I did not feel safe. Indeed, I had not felt safe for . . ." A shadow crossed her face, and she drew a long breath before she said, "But I do not want to talk about that. All I really heard when you said that was that Hugo would stand by me. But then I learned that Ar—"

"But how can you *not* want to marry him?" Sorcha demanded.

Adela smiled. "Because I do not love him, or he me. Indeed, dearest, I think you must know who Hugo loves. Would you truly sacrifice that love for me?"

Sorcha's throat suddenly ached, and she turned to Hugo. He stood right behind her, his expression watchful and wary as if he were uncertain of what she might say. She bit her lip, and a tear trickled down her cheek.

When he opened his arms, she walked into them. But

even as he held her, she turned to Adela. "I would have done it, you know. But what will *you* do? You cannot happily stay at Chalamine if Father weds Lady Clendenen."

"Ardelve is here," Adela said simply, and her smile widened.

"Do you mean he still wants you?" Sorcha asked bluntly.

"Aye, and I want him more than ever after this nightmare. Don't you see, dearest? He is all that is kind, and he dotes on me whilst requiring naught in return but my affection and my ability to run a household. He is not too old to father children, either. But more than that, he is the kindest man I have ever known."

"Sakes, I believe you really care for him!"

"I do, and I have Hugo to thank for bringing him to me."

"Nay, lass, 'twas your father who summoned him," Hugo said. "He sent a messenger last night. But 'twas Ardelve himself who came to Edinburgh, and I believe he came because he heard that your abductors had brought you here."

"He came with his grace's flotilla," Sorcha reminded him.

"Aye, but he was never strong for Donald. Rather, he was one who wanted Ranald to seize the Lordship. When I put it to Macleod, he agreed to send to Edinburgh for him. So you'll take him, my lady?" he asked Adela.

"Aye, sir, and happily," she said. "I wish you happy, too."

"I mean to be," he said, smiling tenderly at Sorcha. Then, briskly, he said, "But first, I wager, there will be all manner of fuss and ado. Michael wants to discuss all that has happened, as does my father. And likely Isabella will be planning weddings for each of us, or one for all. There is also your father, with all his superstitions to satisfy. I fear we may see no end to the business!"

Sorcha winced. Much as she wanted to marry him, the way he described the likely consequences of telling everyone else sounded daunting to say the least.

He was watching her, his mood apparently resigned. "I suppose we had better go downstairs right now and tell them to get on with it," he said.

She nodded, going with him, uncertain about facing them all but unwilling to discuss her feelings in Adela's presence or on the stairway.

At the entrance to the hall, he stopped and turned to her. "I'm hoping you do want to marry me, sweetheart, but it's occurred to me that I've not yet asked you."

"You know I do," she said, smiling.

"Then will you trust me?" His eyes twinkled. "You delight in contradicting me, but if you do so this time, we're sped."

When she nodded, he kissed her quickly, and they went to find the others.

They were in the solar, all of them. Sir Edward and the countess were playing chess. Michael and Isobel sat together near the window with tiny William Robert Sinclair in his cradle beside her, while Sidony sat on a pillow next to the cradle tickling the baby's chin. Ardelve and Macleod cast dice on a nearby table.

Hugo left the door open and stopped just inside with an arm around Sorcha.

When everyone looked up, he said, "I've come to tell you that, the lady Sorcha having agreed, we hereby declare ourselves married."

Clamor broke out but stilled at once when he raised a hand to silence it.

Then he said, "We are leaving now for Hawthornden, and we ask you to grant us three days alone there before you begin your bride visits."

Isobel said, "But you'll need clothes, Sorcha. Tell Kenna to—"

"Sakes, she won't need any for at least three days," Hugo said. "Someone can bring them then." And with that, he whisked the astonished, laughing Sorcha out of the solar and shut the door on the uproar.

"How could you do that?" she demanded. "Marriage by declaration is for times when no priest or chaplain is at hand, for emergencies!"

"Aye," Hugo said, pulling her into his arms. "And if ever there was an emergency, Skelpie, this is it."

Chapter 22

~

Hawthornden Castle, Lothian

They reached Hawthornden as darkness was falling, so Sorcha gained no real view of the landscape thereabouts, or of the castle itself for that matter, except as a hulking mass of stone atop its high crag. But she did not care. Her only thoughts were for Hugo.

When they entered the hall, Hugo ordered supper for them and told the gillie to bring claret at once. "I would toast my bride," he said.

As the lad ran to do his bidding, Sorcha said, laughing, "Sakes, sir, you've dismayed him. Indeed, you've dismayed me. Are we truly married?"

"Aye, sweetheart, so you will have to obey me now," he said as he guided her to a chair at the high table.

Sitting, she said, "I do not recall pronouncing any such vow, sir."

He chuckled. "Then I shall have to persuade you."

"How?" she asked.

His expression sobered, and he sat down beside her.

"What do you know about the duties and pleasures of marriage?" he asked.

"Only that I shall be your wife and have duties to look after servants and such," she admitted. "But I know that Isobel loves being married to Michael, and I certainly expect to enjoy being married to you. I want to bear your children, sir. You will teach me what I need to know, won't you?"

"Aye, lass, I'll teach you; I'll teach you all I know," he said, smiling again.

"Do you know so much, then?"

His eyes twinkled, but he said only, "Ah, here's our wine now." Taking the jug from the gillie, he poured wine into her goblet and handed it to her.

She sipped, watching him pour his own and thinking that Adela was crazy to prefer Ardelve. That thought stirred another, and putting down her goblet, she exclaimed, "We never told Adela that Waldron is dead! We should have, Hugo. She would feel much safer, knowing."

"Nay, lass, we'll let Ardelve do that," he said. "She will need him when she learns that Waldron is gone. It was not to save me that she flung herself between us. Nor was he thinking of me when he lowered his guard to push her away."

"But she cannot have loved him!"

"I don't know what she felt for him," Hugo said. "But it was strong enough to fling her into the path of a sword that would have sped him to hell. Passion like that does not just vanish. It will take time for her to get over what happened to her. Drink your wine now. I'm not sure I want to wait for supper."

They did but hurried through it. He kept looking at her,

and whenever he did, it was as if he kissed her. Heat surged through her.

His voice was husky when he said, "Come upstairs now, sweetheart."

She felt suddenly shy. "Do you know, sir, had anyone told me I'd marry a man I had known only six days, I'd never have believed it."

He shook his head, "Women often marry men they have never seen before, men they know nothing about, just because their fathers arrange it for them."

"Aye, well, I knew I did not want that," Sorcha said. "My sister Cristina married at Father's command, and Hector did not even want her. I would have run away had Father tried to do that to me."

"You did run away," he reminded her, adding as he opened a door, "This is my bedchamber."

Inside, someone had lit cressets and a fire on the hearth, and a ewer of hot water waited on the washstand. But it was the bed that drew Sorcha's attention. It was an ordinary bed, but it was Hugo's, and he meant to share it with her.

She trembled, wondering if she would know what to do, wondering if she would please him, if she would like marriage as much as she hoped to like it.

He stood before her, his hands lightly on her shoulders. "Art willing, sweetheart? I want you to enjoy coupling with me."

"Aye, sir," she said. But her palms felt damp. "Are you really going to take away my clothes for three whole days?"

"Not if you don't want me to," he said, pulling her closer to kiss her. "I did not tell Isobel, but my sister Kate left dresses here that I'm sure will fit you. You'll like Kate, I think, and Meg, come to that. I don't know about Eliza. She is as temperamental as you are, and she is older than I am."

"Aged and decrepit then," she said.

"Ah, lassie, I cannot wait any longer," he said, pulling her to him.

His hands moved over her body as his lips captured hers, and she responded to him with an abandon that astonished her. She had no more qualms and no inhibitions. She wanted to learn how to please him, and he clearly was willing to take his time to please her and show her how to enjoy this intriguing new pastime.

He had the wool surcoat off her and on the floor in a trice, and the kirtle followed swiftly, falling in a pool of silk at her feet. But when she stood before him in her shift, he said suddenly, "You'll grow cold again, lass. Let's get you into bed."

Without waiting for a response, he picked her up and carried her there. As he tucked the coverlet up to her chin and turned to add fuel to the fire, she watched him with a loving smile but thinking that she would have to teach him not to make all her decisions for her. Heaven knew, that would never do.

When he returned to the bed, stripped off his clothes, and climbed in beside her, she forgot everything except what he could teach her.

She still trembled at his touch, but as his hands moved lightly over her body, caressing her, she began to calm and then to stir in new and delightful ways.

His body was so warm against hers that it was like having a fire right there in the bed. His touch ignited her senses, and the joy she felt at being alone with him so was unspeakable.

His lips possessed hers and his tongue quickly penetrated her mouth. She welcomed it and teased it with her own, playing lightly with him, wondering what he would do next.

—✦—

Hugo could not believe the soft silkiness of her skin. His hands moved all over her, delighting in its smooth texture as he kissed her. As one hand moved to cup and stroke one soft breast and then the other, he shifted his position slightly to watch his thumb tease a nipple. Then with a last, lingering kiss for her lips and another for her neck, he shifted lower to capture that nipple with his mouth.

She arched her back in response to his continuing caresses, and as she did, his right hand moved lower to the joining of her thighs. Heat seemed to radiate from every place he touched her, but especially there. With a finger, he gently parted the lips there and although she gasped again and tensed, she did not object.

She was breathing heavily, and with his right ear so near her chest, he could hear her heart thumping. She made a little sound in her throat when his finger penetrated, but she was moist and nearly ready for him.

He had no illusions that she would enjoy every step of their first coupling, but he wanted her to know something of the pleasures before she felt the pain, and he knew that the more he prepared her for him, the less pain she would feel.

Even so, her caresses, tentative at first but more

passionate now, had stirred his body until it was clamoring for release. He knew he had better begin before his exploding lust overcame his good intentions.

Accordingly, he shifted to recapture her mouth, pressing his finger farther into her hot, moist depths as he did. She gasped beneath his lips and arched against him. When she reached lower to touch his belly and below, he caught her hand and moved it to hold him, groaning as her slim fingers grasped his penis.

She turned her head a little, and he raised his. "Am I hurting you?"

"Nay," she said, "but will you fit there?"

He chuckled. "Aye, I'll fit, but it may not all be pleasant for you the first time. After that, it will get easier. Ah, lassie, you are so smooth and warm."

"You are warm, too," she said. "I have noticed that before now, but this . . . this, I never imagined."

He moved over her then, easing first one knee between her soft thighs to spread them, then the other. His whole both thrummed like a tautly strung bow, ready for release.

She was tense now, her lips parted in anticipation, her expression wary but curious, too. Her beautiful breasts, golden in the light of the cressets and firelight, rose and fell quickly with her breathing.

He kissed her, then carefully eased himself atop her, spreading her gently to accommodate him. He hesitated briefly, then eased into her. Hearing her breath catch, he knew she felt pain, but he pressed forward more before easing back. In this manner, he continued until the way felt lest constricted, and then at last, thrust firmly into her. Exerting stern control over himself even at her faint cry, he continued smoothly and steadily until he could no longer deny his lust free rein. With quick, furious movements, he reached his climax, gasping.

Rolling off her, he saw that she lay wide-eyed, lips parted again, breathing almost as hard as he was.

"Are you all right?"

"Aye," she said. "I didn't know."

"Know what?"

"That a woman could feel like that."

"Didn't I hurt you?"

"Aye, but you said it won't hurt again. And the rest . . ." She grinned at him.

"I love you," he said, moving to get up. "I'll get something to clean us."

"You say that now, but I'm guessing that the first time I defy you, you'll say something else, sir."

"I was going to show you more pleasuring," he said, returning with a cloth he had dipped into the still-warm water in the ewer. "But if you are going to talk of defiance . . ." He let the thought hover between them as he began to cleanse the blood from her thighs. "Are you going to defy me again?" he asked.

"Oh, I expect so," she said, then gasped as he parted her thighs again to clean her there. "It . . . it seems to be a part of me. I expect it comes of having a father who issues orders and then forgets he's issued them. Oh, my, don't stop!"

He chuckled again as he moved away to pour water into the basin to clean himself. "Macleod should have beaten you soundly when you disobeyed," he said over his shoulder.

"Well, he did sometimes," she said, relaxing against the pillows again. "But his furies were quickly over, and then there would always be something else I wanted to do. So, you see, even if I try not to, I'll probably make you angry again."

"I see," Hugo said. Then, grinning as he climbed back into bed with her, he said, "I should confess to you, Skelpie, I once had a vision of a perfect wife."

"I'm afraid she was not like me," Sorcha said with an exaggerated sigh.

"She bore not the least resemblance to you," he agreed.

"What was she like then?"

"Just a boring woman of pleasing looks and figure who could manage my household and bear children who would all be as well behaved as their mother."

"Are my looks not pleasing?"

"You are beautiful in every way imaginable. But, sithee, I anticipated a married life of perfect peace and amity. No strife, no fuss or ado."

"And what was your contribution going to be to this perfection?"

"This," he said with another chuckle as he held her and began kissing his way slowly down her body until his lips met her nether ones.

"Oh," Sorcha said with a gasp as his tongue began to tease her. "If you do that as often as you scold and correct me, I vow, sir, you may scold me all you like."

Dear Reader,

I hope you enjoyed *Lady's Choice*. Before discussing historical points in the book that might interest you, I am obliged to correct a slight error that Sir Michael St. Clair (certainly not the author) made in *Prince of Danger* with regard to what his title would be after his brother became Earl of Orkney.

Had Henry been acknowledged as Prince of Orkney in Scotland, Michael might have held a courtesy title as Lord Michael. But as *Prince of Danger* made clear, Henry was "only" Earl of Orkney in Scotland. His son later took the title of the barony (of Roslin) and would have been Lord Sinclair, but even as Henry's heir, Michael would still have been Sir Michael, not Lord Michael. I don't know what he could have been thinking, but I can assure you, he's sorry!

I should perhaps also clarify a point for those of you who believe first births always take much longer than Isobel's did. Not so. The author endured only an hour and twenty-seven minutes of labor, from first contraction to squalling child, when her son was born in Omaha. Only made it to the hospital because a huge blizzard was fast approaching and four babies had been delivered by their own fathers, who had received instructions over the phone, during a previous one just a few weeks before.

As to the paper on which Isobel wrote her letters and Adela her message to Sorcha, some may question its availability. It is true that paper was rare in Britain before the mid fifteenth century, but it was available in Italy, France, and other places to which the Sinclairs and people of the Isles and western Highlands had access. The

Chinese invented it in the second century A.D. (105), and it came west by way of Baghdad in the eighth century. It was available in Italy nearly a hundred years before this story takes place.

With regard to Adela's behavior as Waldron's hostage, many of you may recognize symptoms of the Stockholm Syndrome. Although not defined until the twentieth century, the effects of this syndrome have affected people since the dawn of time—not just hostages of criminals and other terrorists but also battered and abused children and spouses.

For those of you who, like the author, collect trivia, according to the *Collins Encyclopedia of Scotland*, Glenelg is "said to be" the only seven-letter palindrome in Highland topography. Glenelg village is wonderfully remote and scenic. Of particular interest to the author was a tombstone in the village kirkyard that exactly fits the description of Templar tombstones with skull and crossbones. That discovery and her love for Glenelg did much to determine the location of fictional Chalamine Castle.

Waldron of Edgelaw's beliefs derive from those of the Assassins' cult during the Crusades, as well as beliefs held by the Knights Templar and other Crusaders. The Templars and the Assassins had numerous known connections to each other, and the Crusaders' belief in divine protection for any deed performed by a soldier of Christ was echoed (perhaps even inspired) by the Assassins' belief that a soldier serving the Almighty would be forgiven anything he did, including torture and murder, as long as the man believed he had done it in holy service.

The notion of numerous virgins as heavenly rewards for such men derives solely from ancient Assassin beliefs and survives to this day in some extreme religious factions. Waldron's notion that God sent a message of celibacy to him through Isobel's victory on the ramparts of Roslin Castle (*Prince of Danger*) is, however, Waldron's personal interpretation of what happened to him.

Details for the installation of Donald as second Lord of the Isles are from *House of Islay* by Donald Grumach (Argyll, 1967) and from *The Clan Donald* by the Reverend A. MacDonald (Inverness, 1896).

Details for the ceremony Sorcha observed in the cavern are derived from "Knights Templars," *Richardson's Monitor of Free-Masonry*, by Jabez Richardson (New York, 1993, pp. 109–23).

As mentioned in *Prince of Danger*, questions exist about exactly when all the tunnels at Roslin were dug. Many were created when William Sinclair, fourth Earl of Orkney, built his famous Rosslyn Chapel in the sixteenth century. However, Prince Henry is known to have initiated a good deal of construction at Roslin Castle.

The nearby Wallace's Cave, named for William Wallace, who may have taken refuge there, was also known long before the fourth earl.

For more about the Templar treasure, I suggest once again the following sources: *Holy Blood, Holy Grail*, by Michael Baigent and Richard Leigh (New York, 1982); *The Temple and the Lodge*, by Michael Baigent and Richard Leigh (New York, 1989); *Pirates & the Lost Templar Fleet*, by David H. Childress (Illinois, 2003); *The Stone Puzzle of Rosslyn Chapel*, by Philip Coppens (Netherlands, 2004); *The Da Vinci Code Decoded*, by Martin Lunn (New York, 2004); and *The Lost Treasure of the Knights Templar*, by Steven Sora (Vermont, 1999).

DEAR READER

For more about the Assassins, see *The Assassins*, by Bernard Lewis (London, 1967).

Thanks again to Donal Sean MacRae and Alasdair White for their continued willingness to share their extraordinary expertise.

As always, I'd also like to thank my terrific agents, Lucy Childs and Aaron Priest, as well as Beth de Guzman, vice president and editor in chief of Warner Books, and the world's most exciting editor, Devi Pillai.

I could not do what I do without every one of them!

Nor could I do it without all of you who read my books and provide me with constant commentary on them. Thank you all, once again, for your continued, faithful support. Your letters, comments, and observations continue to inspire me, not just in my writing, but in all that I do.

If you enjoyed *Lady's Choice*, please look for *Knight's Treasure*, the story of what fate has in store when Adela Macleod marries Lord Ardelve. It will be at your favorite bookstore in February 2007. In the meantime, *Suas Alba*!

Sincerely,

Amanda Scott

http://home.att.net/~amandascott

About the Author

AMANDA SCOTT, best-selling author and winner of the Romance Writers of America's RITA/Golden Medallion and the Romantic Times' Awards for Best Regency Author and Best Sensual Regency, began writing on a dare from her husband. She has sold every manuscript she has written. She sold her first novel, *The Fugitive Heiress*—written on a battered Smith-Corona—in 1980. Since then, she has sold many more, but since the second one, she has used a word processor. More than twenty-five of her books are set in the English Regency period (1810–1820), others are set in fifteenth-century England and sixteenth- and eighteenth-century Scotland. Three are contemporary romances.

Amanda is a fourth-generation Californian who was born and raised in Salinas and graduated with a bachelor's degree in history from Mills College in Oakland. She did graduate work at the University of North Carolina at Chapel Hill, specializing in British history, before obtaining her master's in history from California State University at San Jose. After graduate school, she taught for the Salinas City School District for three years before marrying her husband, who was then a captain in the Air Force. They lived in Honolulu for a year, then in Nebraska for seven years, where their son was born. Amanda now lives with her husband and son in northern California.

GET A SNEAK PEAK AT

AMANDA SCOTT'S

NEXT NOVEL.

Turn the page to read
a preview of

Knight's Treasure

〜

AVAILABLE FEBRUARY 2007.

Chapter 1

~

Roslin Castle, Midlothian, May 1380

Smile, Adela. A bride should look happy on her wedding day!"

Lady Adela Macleod turned slightly to face her younger sister, Sorcha, who was certainly beaming brightly enough for both of them. But although she tried to obey the command, she knew the attempt was feeble at best.

She had hoped that her second wedding, unlike her first, might proceed without undue fuss or drama. But although she could still hope to avoid the sort of drama that had attended her first one, there had already been far more fuss and ado than she liked, and she knew that before the day was over, there would be more.

Not only were there now two brides and bridegrooms instead of a single couple but when one's hostess was a powerful countess in her own right, one had to expect such an occasion to merit extraordinary pomp and circumstance. And when one's younger sister had married the countess's favorite nephew by declaration little more than a sennight ago, one could scarcely cavil when the fond aunt and one's own fond parent insisted on a double wedding to sanctify both marriages properly.

But even her father, Macleod of Glenelg, whose word was law back home in the Highlands, had had little if any say in today's wedding plans—not that he had tried to interfere, for he had not. Nor had Adela expected him to, because the royal court was in residence less than ten miles away in Edinburgh, and he was himself planning soon to wed a widow in comfortable circumstances, which included a fine house in that royal burgh.

Adela had therefore understood from the outset that she must expect a larger, grander wedding than that first attempt, which had taken place in the Highlands just weeks after the death of the first Lord of the Isles. Nonetheless, the result exceeded anything she might have anticipated, because Isabella, Countess of Strathearn and Caithness, and the rest of the powerful Sinclair family had spared no expense to arrange a truly splendid affair. Adela had not mourned the lack of splendor on that first occasion, but after all her hosts' effort and expense, she thought it a great pity that she could not seem to stir up more enthusiasm for this one.

As she waited near the elegant little chapel's entrance with Macleod and the other members of the wedding party for the select, noble audience crammed into the chamber to quiet down, she wondered why she did not care more. After all, other than the much larger group of friends, kinsmen, and others unable to squeeze into the chapel but assembling now in the castle's great hall for the wedding feast to come, nothing but the setting had changed—except for Sorcha's role, of course, and Sir Hugo Robison's presence today at Sorcha's side.

Adela's bridegroom remained the same, and a generous, kind man Ardelve was, too. He was fond of her and would make few demands with which she would not willingly comply. So far, he had asked only that she run his large household in Kintail, near her own home, a responsibility with duties familiar enough that she expected to manage them easily and to enjoy them far more than she had the years of running her father's much less manageable household and family.

Although Sorcha frequently said that Ardelve was too old and too pompous to make a good husband, Adela liked him. To be sure, he was nearly as old as her father, had been twice married and widowed, and had a grown son older than she was. But his children had raised no objection to the marriage, and his cousin, Lady Clendenen, the wealthy widow whom Macleod intended to marry, waited now in the front row, with an approving smile, for the ceremony to begin. As a result, Adela believed her marriage to Ardelve would be as happy as anyone could wish. So what, she asked herself, was wrong with her? Why did she not feel *something*?

So lost in her thoughts was she that when Sorcha touched her arm, she started, noting at once that her sister's beaming smile had faded to a worried frown.

"Do pinch your cheeks," Sorcha said. "You look as pale as chalk. Is aught amiss? Are you feeling sick?"

"Nay, all is well," Adela said.

"You don't look it," Sorcha replied with her usual candor.

"Easy, lass," Sir Hugo said, laying a gently restraining hand on her shoulder.

Not, Adela mused, that anyone—even Hugo—could restrain her sister unless Sorcha chose to allow it.

Hugo smiled as he said to her, "Doubtless you are recalling the last occasion, my lady. But no raiders will interrupt today's festivities. That I promise you."

Politely if automatically returning his smile, Adela said, "I have no such fear, sir." She could hardly tell him she felt nothing at all, that it was as if she were in a dream, disembodied, watching someone else about to walk to the altar.

The look that crossed Sir Hugo's handsome face then nearly matched the deepening frown on Sorcha's. Adela saw his hand increase its pressure on her sister's shoulder, as if he sensed without looking at her that she was about to speak.

For a wonder, Sorcha kept silent.

Hugo said quietly, "You should not wonder if you do not feel the usual bride's excitement, Lady Adela. After the experience you suffered last time, it must be only natural to feel reservations now. Sithee, I have seen similar reactions in men after a battle, and I warrant it must be much the same way for you now as for them."

"Pray, sir, do not concern yourself," she said mildly. "I cannot imagine how what happened last time could possibly match aught that occurs in battle. I suffered no injury, after all. Indeed, I do not believe he would ever have harmed me."

Hugo grimaced but did not contradict her aloud, saying only, "I think the piper is about to begin playing."

Macleod, who had stood quietly, taking no part in the conversation, said, "Aye, he is, lass, so take my arm. We're to go first, ye ken, after your maidens."

She and Sorcha had four bride-maidens for this wedding, although they barely knew three of them. The one they did know was their youngest sister, Sidony, blue-eyed and fair, looking beautifully serene as she waited for the piper to begin. Two of the other bride-maidens were Sir Hugo's younger sisters, Katharine and Margaret Robison. The remaining one was another niece of Countess Isabella's.

Since Sorcha and Sir Hugo were already legally married, having taken advantage of the ancient Scottish tradition of simply declaring themselves husband and wife, they would walk together to the altar. Sorcha had said she couldn't imagine why they need marry again, but Countess Isabella had declared that she intended to see them properly wedded by her own priest, and that had been that.

When the piping began, the four bride-maidens went single file up the narrow aisle between the flanking rows of standing guests. When the maidens had taken their places, two on each side of the steps leading to the altar, where Ardelve and Isabella's chaplain waited, Adela put her hand on the arm her father extended to her. To the accompaniment of the piper's tune, they proceeded slowly up the aisle to meet her bridegroom.

Though only a few years younger than her father, Ardelve was a handsomer, more dignified-looking man with a neatly trimmed beard and grizzled dark hair. For the occasion, he wore a high-crowned, white-plumed hat, a cut-black-velvet, sable-trimmed robe belted over parti-colored hose, and fashionable pointed-toe shoes. Standing straight and proud beside Isabella's chaplain, he watched his bride walk toward him, and when his gaze met Adela's, he smiled.

She replied with the same fixed smile she had summoned up for Sir Hugo but kept her gaze fixed on Ardelve, wanting to avoid meeting the eye of any onlooker. She had small inclination just then for polite gestures and wanted only to have the ceremony and the subsequent feasting well behind her.

She reached the halfway point aware only of her hand on Macleod's arm and of Ardelve's face before her. Then, an abrupt movement to her right and the clink-clink of something falling to the chapel's flagstone floor caught her attention.

Turning her head, she looked straight into the jade-green eyes of one of the handsomest men she had ever beheld.

He had finely chiseled features, smooth chestnut hair that curled slightly at the ends, broad shoulders, a tapered waist, and muscular, well-turned legs, the three latter features displayed to advantage in an expertly cut forest-green velvet doublet and smooth golden-yellow silk hose.

He had begun to bend down, so he had certainly dropped something. But whatever it was lay where it had fallen, because as Adela's gaze collided with his, he froze where he was. Then, slowly he straightened, his gaze still locked with hers.

His remarkable green eyes began to twinkle. Then, impudently, he winked.

Startled, she wrenched her gaze away and sought Ardelve again, relaxing when she saw him still smiling calmly. She did not look away again.

The piping stopped when she reached the shallow steps near the front of the chapel, leading up to four kneeling stools awaiting the two bridal couples.

"Who gives this woman to be wed to this man?" the chaplain inquired.

"I, Macleod o' Glenelg, the lassie's father," Macleod said clearly.

The priest beckoned to Adela, and releasing her father's forearm, she went up the steps to stand beside Ardelve. Sorcha and Hugo followed, taking their places to her left. All four faced the altar and Isabella's chaplain.

The audience was silent for a long moment before the chaplain said, "I be bound to ask first if there be any amongst ye here today who kens any just cause or impediment to a marriage betwixt Baron Ardelve and the lady Adela Macleod. If anyone does, pray speak now or forever hold your peace."

Adela shut her eyes, for it had been at this very point in her first attempt to marry Ardelve that the interruption had occurred.

Today, aside from some brief shuffling, silence reigned.

The priest did not ask the same question with regard to Sorcha and Sir Hugo, as the two of them were merely sanctifying an already existing union.

Adela was glad to note that they seemed blissfully happy. She had seen them only once since their declaration, because they had removed to Hawthornden Castle, a mile up Roslin Glen, immediately after Hugo had declared them married. Three days afterward, she had accompanied Isobel, Sidony, and the countess to pay them a bridal visit, but she had not seen either since then until that very morning.

Isobel, who was now Sir Michael Sinclair's wife and thus daughter-by-marriage to the countess, stood in the audience with her husband. But with time so short, their other three sisters Cristina, Maura, and Kate were at home with their families, Cristina on the Isle of Mull and the other two in the Highlands.

When the chaplain spoke Adela's name, she wrenched her attention back to the ceremony, responding as he bade her, and doing so calmly and clearly. The double ceremony was mercifully brief, and if the nuptial mass that followed was longer, at least she could recite her responses by rote and would not have to think.

When the priest declared them husbands and wives in the sight of God, Ardelve took Adela's hand warmly in his and did not let go until they were offered the bread and wine for communion. After that, the Mass soon came to an end and Adela found herself hoping no one would ask what she had been thinking about or if she had enjoyed it, because the entire service had registered no more than a blank passage of time in her mind.

Isabella did not allow the bridal couples to linger but whisked them off to the great hall to receive their guests and begin the wedding feast.

Music and laughter greeted them long before they entered, for the festivities had already begun. Musicians in the minstrels' gallery played lively music until the bridal party appeared in the doorway, at which time Isabella's chamberlain stepped forward and in stentorian accents announced both couples:

"My lords, my ladies, and all others in the chamber, pray stand to make welcome Lord and Lady Ardelve, Sir Hugo Robison, and Lady Robison!"

Amid the cheering and resumption of music, Adela noted that a clear space in the center of the hall stood

ready for the jugglers, acrobats, dancers, and other enter-
tainers Isabella had hired to perform during the feast.

As she and the others skirted that clearing, Ardelve bent
his head close to her ear and murmured, "I would speak privately with you, my lady wife, afore we feast. Isabella has
kindly offered us her solar, if you will oblige me."

"Aye, sure, my lord, as you wish," she said, hoping she
had not already done something to vex him. She remembered the man with green eyes but quickly dismissed that
possibility. Ardelve had displayed no indication that he
might be either a possessive husband or a jealous one.

They crossed the crowded dais, moving around the
long high table that would soon groan under the weight
of many gold and silver platters and trays of food, and
jugs of whisky and wine—not to mention the guests' goblets and trenchers that were already in place—to a door in
the center of the wall beyond it.

With a deep bow, a Sinclair gillie opened the door for
them.

Nodding to the lad to shut it behind them, Ardelve
guided Adela a little away from it before he said gently
and without preamble, "One hesitates to speak to a lady
about her looks, my dear, but all this splendor appears to
have worn you to the bone. If you wish to retire, I would
willingly make our adieux and depart at once."

"'Tis kind of you to offer, sir, but it would be most un-
kind of us, not to mention ungrateful, to cut short the cel-
ebration after Countess Isabella has put so much effort
into all these preparations to honor us."

"Faugh," he said. "Isabella does what she does for Isabella or for Roslin. In truth, I am a trifle weary myself,
but if you are sure you are feeling quite well . . ."

"I am, sir," she said. "I am a little tired, perhaps, but no more than that."

He looked searchingly at her for a long moment, then said quietly, "If it is any relief to your mind, I will tell you that you have naught to fear from me tonight or any other. If you prefer to have time to adjust to our marriage before taking up all your wifely duties, I will certainly understand. I am in no great hurry, myself, and would understand your preference for a more peaceful place to get to know your husband. Do you understand my meaning, Adela?"

"Aye, sir, I do," she said, aware that she was blushing. "My sister Isobel explained what my duties will be. You are very kind, sir, to be sure, but I do want children, and I have no objection to taking up my wifely duties whenever it shall please you. Indeed, if you do not *want* to stay now, that is quite another matter."

He patted her hand. "I am content," he said. "You are quite right to think of everyone who has worked so hard to provide our wedding feast."

"I do look forward to returning very soon to the peace of the Highlands, sir."

He smiled then. She thought his smile a particularly charming one and responded to it with her own first entirely natural smile of the day. No matter that Sorcha thought she was making a great mistake. Sorcha, after all, had married Hugo, a man who always wanted his own way and made no secret of that fact.

Since Sorcha's nature was much the same in that respect, Adela could not doubt that sparks often flew between them. With Ardelve, she was certain that she would enjoy a far more peaceful, and thus a more comfortable, life.

He rested a hand on her shoulder. Then, as she turned back toward the door, he lowered his hand to the small of her back, and she was astonished at how reassuring it felt as they moved to rejoin the boisterous company. When she took her place at the high table next to Sorcha, in one of the four central places of honor on the long side facing the lower hall, Adela was still quietly congratulating herself on her wise decision to marry Ardelve.

Members of the Sinclair family comprised much of the company on the dais: Countess Isabella stood to Ardelve's right with her eldest son, Prince Henry Sinclair, the owner of Roslin Castle, on her right. Lady Clendenen and Macleod stood beyond Henry, with an empty space at Macleod's right. Sorcha stood to Adela's left with Sir Hugo beyond. Isobel stood on Sir Hugo's left, Sir Michael on hers, and then came Hugo's father, Sir Edward Robison, flanked by a daughter on one side and an empty space on the other. They faced the rest of the wedding guests who had gathered around trestle tables set lengthwise in rows around the lower hall clearing.

After the countess's chaplain had spoken the grace before meat, the company noisily took their seats, the carvers entered, and Adela sat quietly, speaking only when someone spoke to her. At one point, she caught sight of the handsome young man she had noticed in the chapel, speaking to one of Sir Hugo's sisters. She thought it was the older one, Katharine, but their gowns and veils were much the same, and the two girls were nearly the same height, so she could not be sure.

Glancing past Sorcha at Sir Hugo, she was not surprised to see his frowning, intent gaze fixed on the couple. She was certain he must be a most protective brother and had little doubt that he would have stern words for his sister. She sighed. To think that her own sisters had once expected *her* to marry Hugo!

Turning to Ardelve, she smiled, then shifted slightly to allow a gillie to pour wine into her goblet. She reached for it but pulled her hand back in almost the same movement when she remembered that there would be toasting.

Beside her, Ardelve said, "Go ahead and take a sip or two, lass. No one will mind. The carver is flashing his knives, but the ceremonial nonsense has only just begun. They'll be parading platters of food from one end of this hall to the other for some time yet, so I'd advise you to take a few bites of bread with your wine, too."

Another gillie, overhearing, instantly offered rolls from a basket, and Adela took one gratefully, breaking a bite-size piece off and eating it before she tasted her wine. It was fine claret, she was sure, but her sense of taste seemed to have deserted her along with the rest of her senses.

Ardelve, too, sipped wine, and when the ceremonial presentation of dishes had ended at last, buffered on one side by her sister and the other by her husband, Adela was able to eat her meal in peace. Gillies kept food and wine flowing, and the company was an appropriately merry one. She began to relax and soon realized the claret was a bit heady for one who rarely drank more than half a goblet of any wine.

At her left, Sorcha chatted merrily with Hugo, doubtless most improperly, too. Adela had noted that the two of them seemed to talk about any subject that entered their heads, and she could not approve. People—ladies, at least—should display more decorum. But she had long since stopped trying to persuade Sorcha of that.

"Where is Sidony?" she asked when Sorcha turned to her. "I saw her earlier in the chapel, of course, but I've not seen her since we came into the hall."

"I'll wager she went upstairs to look in on our new nephew," Sorcha said with a grin. "She spends more time with him than with anyone else, and you can see for yourself that Isobel is quite calm and relaxed. Had wee William Robert been lying alone upstairs all this time, you can be sure she would be fidgeting by now." She turned to a passing gillie and asked him to pour her some more wine.

"Dearling, you should have let Hugo give him the order," Adela said gently.

"He is busy talking to his sister Kate," Sorcha said.

Adela realized that Hugo must have somehow summoned Katharine, because Isobel had shifted to a seat beside Sir Edward, and Katharine was taking the seat beside Hugo. Adela saw, too, that Katharine was indeed the one who had been flirting with the handsome stranger. Trust Hugo, a notorious flirt himself, to call his sister to order for engaging in a similar practice. Kate looked annoyed, too, as well she might, Adela mused, recalling that she herself had once emptied a basin of holy water over Hugo's head when she had heard more than enough of his lecturing.

Recalling again that many folks had expected her to marry him, and that she had once sincerely contemplated the possibility, she wondered at herself. She liked him very much, to be sure. He was handsome, charming, and a famous swordsman, but he had an annoying tendency to order people about, and she preferred not to have orders flung at her. Sorcha dealt with him better than she ever would have.

Ardelve would suit her much better, Adela told herself yet again. She would live close to her own home and would be able to see old friends and family whenever she liked, and Ardelve was wealthy enough to provide every comfort.

She turned to smile at him again.

He was staring at his goblet as if he considered refilling it, but he seemed to sense her gaze, for he turned his head and smiled at her. "You are so beautiful," he said. "I believe I am quite the most fortunate of—"

To her shock, his face seemed to freeze, except for his lips, which opened once or twice as if he gasped for words to finish his sentence. Then, just as she realized that he was gasping for air, he slumped awkwardly against Isabella, and as the countess exclaimed and tried to hold him, Ardelve collapsed to the floor.

Adela stared at him in shock.

"Sakes, I didn't think he was even in his cups," Sorcha exclaimed.

"He isn't," Hugo said, leaping quickly to his feet.

"Adela," the countess said in a quiet but firm voice, "turn away, my dear, and attempt to compose yourself. It will not do to cause any great stir. Indeed, I am sure this is naught that should distress you."

"His eyes are open, but I do not think he sees me," Adela said without looking away.

Hugo was kneeling beside Ardelve. After only a cursory examination, he looked up at her and said gently, "I'm sorry, lass. I'm afraid he's dead."

Adela gasped, and tears sprang to her eyes.

Isabella signed at once to the minstrels in the gallery, and the music grew louder. Startled, Adela turned her head in time to see jugglers running to the clearing in the center of the lower hall.

As she began to turn back to Ardelve, she saw that although nearly everyone below had turned to watch the jugglers, one person at least had not.

The man with the jade green eyes was looking straight at her.

THE DISH

Where authors give you the inside scoop!

From the desk of Amanda Scott

I've always loved Sir Walter Scott's poem "Lochinvar," the tale of a young Scottish hero who rode off with his lady-love from her wedding to another man:

> *While her mother did fret, and her father did fume,*
> *And her bridegroom stood dangling his bonnet and*
>   *plume;*
> *And the bride-maidens whisper'd, " 'Twere better by far*
> *To have matched our fair cousin with young*
>   *Lochinvar."*

While constructing the plot for **Lady's Choice**, I was hiking in the High Sierras one day when that poem popped into my mind and every writer's favorite phrase began to twitch: What if I were to begin **Lady's Choice** with a fourteenth-century Highland version of that wedding? What if the "Lochinvar" everyone cheers turns out not to be the young gallant, "so daring in love and so dauntless in war," but someone truly dangerous?

To stir more trouble, *what if* my Macleod bride believes at first, just as everyone else does, that the abductor is her Lochinvar? And *what if* her own sister, firmly believing the bride loves someone else, set the whole thing in motion and then has to deal with the consequences when she learns someone has usurped her plan to suit his own evil purpose?

Best of all, *what if* Sir Hugo Robison, the hero meant to benefit from that plan, knows nothing about it because he did not bother to reply to the urgent messages sent him by the bride's loving, caring sister, or to attend the wedding? And *what if* all of the above somehow impacts the fate of the legendary, long-lost Knights Templar treasure found by Lady Isobel Macleod and Sir Michael Sinclair in my previous book, **Prince of Danger**?

To say that **Lady's Choice** was fun to write is an understatement. I hope you enjoyed it.

Sincerely yours,

Amanda Scott

http://home.att.net/~amandascott/

♥ ♥ ♥ ♥ ♥ ♥ ♥ ♥ ♥ ♥ ♥ ♥ ♥ ♥ ♥ ♥

From the desk of Candy Halliday

When my editor mentioned she'd like a switch in my next book from single-in-the-city to married-in-the-suburbs, I jumped at the chance. *Finally*, I thought. Domestic divas are going to get their due. Any wife will tell you that as hard as it is to find Mr. Right, the real quest begins after the wedding. Making the marriage a success—now that's the challenge of a lifetime. Or a hopeless cause, to some desperate housewife.

Like Zada Clark, my *she*ro in **YOUR BED OR MINE?** (on sale now). Poor Zada thought she'd found Mr.

Right—until she realized his name was Mr. *Always Right*. Divorce has to be the only solution, but the old-school judge won't grant it unless she and Rick reach a compromise over who's keeping the dog and the house.

What does Rick do? Move back in and challenge Zada to a real-life game of *Survivor*. The first one to outwit, outplay, and outlast the other wins. Never one to back down from a challenge, Zada says, "Game on!" Of course, Rick doesn't know she's got a secret weapon: the three other members of her Housewives' Fantasy Club. Together, they'll help Zada create a fantasy that will *out-tease, out-tempt, and out-tantalize* Rick into losing the game with four little words: Your bed or mine?

The battle of the sexes has always been fascinating to me, and boy did I have fun forcing Zada and Rick to live together again. The icing on the cake for me, however, was creating a group of women best friends who stick together (yes, I'm a *9 to 5*, *First Wives Club*, and *Thelma and Louise* junkie) but in YOUR BED OR MINE? I've added a slightly naughty but incredibly delicious twist—these women are sensuously secure enough to get together once a week to share their most secret desires.

Need a little spice to jump-start your sex life? Want to be entertained with thoughts of guilty pleasures you'd never allow yourself to pursue? Welcome to the Housewives' Fantasy Club series. Viva Domestic Divas, ladies! Enjoy the fun and start a Housewives' Fantasy Club of your own.

Cheers!

Candy Halliday

http://www.candyhalliday.com/

*Want to know more about romances at
Warner Books and Warner Forever?
Get the scoop online!*

WARNER'S ROMANCE HOMEPAGE

Visit us at www.warnerforever.com for all the
latest news, reviews, and chapter excerpts!

NEW AND UPCOMING TITLES

Each month we feature our new titles
and reader favorites.

CONTESTS AND GIVEAWAYS

We give away galleys, autographed copies,
and all kinds of fun stuff.

AUTHOR INFO

You'll find bios, articles, and links to personal
Web sites for all your favorite authors—and
so much more!

THE BUZZ

Sign up for our monthly romance newsletter,
and be the first to read all about it!